Except the Queen

"A magical tale.... Unconventional narrative techniques and a full dose of magic and folklore give this urban fantasy a lyrical, mythic feel." —*Publishers Weekly*

"A wonderful romp of a book, full of unlikely heroes and heroines, thoroughly nasty villains, and natural magic seen through a kaleidoscope's eye in vivid, ever-changing detail.... The writing is fast-paced and powerful.... *Except the Queen* is indeed a treat for the fantasy lover." —Patricia A. McKillip, author of *The Bell at Sealey Head*

"This is a great urban fantasy with an atypical feel to the story line that enhances the otherworldly tale. Fast-paced from the onset, fans will welcome the siblings as each struggles with adjusting to the world of the mortals." —Alternative Worlds

"Reminiscent of the urban fantasy of Charles de Lint in their ability to blend human characterizations with the world just beyond the borders of human perception, the authors succeed in crafting a modern fairy tale." —*Library Journal*

"Jane Yolen really can't be beat when it comes to traditional fantasy. This is a beautifully written novel." —So Many Books, So Little Time

continued ...

EXCEPT
the
QUEEN

Jane Yolen
and
Midori Snyder

A ROC BOOK

ROC

Published by New American Library, a division of
Penguin Group (USA) Inc., 375 Hudson Street,
New York, New York 10014, USA
Penguin Group (Canada), 90 Eglinton Avenue East, Suite 700, Toronto,
Ontario M4P 2Y3, Canada (a division of Pearson Penguin Canada Inc.)
Penguin Books Ltd., 80 Strand, London WC2R 0RL, England
Penguin Ireland, 25 St. Stephen's Green, Dublin 2,
Ireland (a division of Penguin Books Ltd.)
Penguin Group (Australia), 250 Camberwell Road, Camberwell, Victoria 3124,
Australia (a division of Pearson Australia Group Pty. Ltd.)
Penguin Books India Pvt. Ltd., 11 Community Centre, Panchsheel Park,
New Delhi - 110 017, India
Penguin Group (NZ), 67 Apollo Drive, Rosedale, Auckland 0632,
New Zealand (a division of Pearson New Zealand Ltd.)
Penguin Books (South Africa) (Pty.) Ltd., 24 Sturdee Avenue,
Rosebank, Johannesburg 2196, South Africa

Penguin Books Ltd., Registered Offices:
80 Strand, London WC2R 0RL, England

Published by Roc, an imprint of New American Library, a division of Penguin
Group (USA) Inc. Previously published in Roc hardcover and trade paperback
edition.

First Roc Mass Market Printing, April 2012
10 9 8 7 6 5 4 3 2 1

For Terri Windling, Ellen Datlow, Isak Dinesen, Angela Carter, Alice Hoffman, Ellen Kushner, Delia Sherman, Pamela Dean, Patricia Wrede, Holly Black, Emma Bull, Patricia McKillip, Ellen Klages, Kelly Link, Diana Wynne Jones, Robin McKinley, Shannon Hale, and all the other sisters of fantasy.
—JY

For my mother, Jeanette Snyder, who made sure I knew how to swim in the river of myth and fairy tale.
—MS

1

The Queen Remembers

You are in the forest that is not your own. You squint at its brightness; the sunlight bleaching the familiar green, the scent of the trees dusty as pressed flowers. You have come out of curiosity, and shivering beneath the glamour you are wearing, you roam through the quiet pines and birch. You have left behind your armor, your rank, your power, your great age. Here you are young, beautiful and fragile as the lily, your throat white and perfumed. Birds trill a warning and fall quiet. And then you hear it, a man singing softly under his breath, something tuneless, without true shape to change the world.

You stop and wait, frozen as the deer, for this is what you have come to see, to learn, to experience. For an eternity you have existed in another time, but now you are in this moment, and desire burns away the practiced control.

You see him weaving in and out of the sunlight, his chestnut hair stippled like a fawn's hide. Yet he moves purposefully, hunting for you. You can smell the oil of his rifle, cradled in the crook of his arm. Alarm prickles your skin, crying *run*. But you will not. You want to see what happens. You want to know what it feels like, that pain that is human love, that weakness that binds stronger than spells. You, who have never given so much as a mustard seed of power for free, you have come to give yourself away.

The man moves into the clearing and hesitates as if he knows you are there. And why should he not feel you? Have you not come here the last three days to spy on him? He is well made, with a comely face that pleases you. He is dressed like an oriole, the dark wool of his coat partially covered by a shrill orange that makes it easy to spot him even in the brush.

You study his face, wondering if you can allow yourself this indulgence. All the others have had their dalliances, their madcap affairs—everyone except the Queen. But you are here now and strangely calm as he turns toward you. You raise your arm and the dun-colored sleeve covers your face as you bend from your supple waist. You hold your breath for you hear the soft snick of the gun, feel its eye upon you, and you brace yourself for the stinging touch of iron.

The shot cracks the air open like a nut and it is too late to change your mind. You cry out as the bullet passes beneath your ribs and out your back. How could you have known it would hurt so much? Blood spills, staining your white shift crimson and you fall into a nest of autumn-bitten bushes. You can hear him now, *running* toward you, the gun dropped behind him when you screamed. Already he bleeds too; despair, hope, and love spilling out for you as he runs to where you wait, wounded in the bloodstained green.

2

Meteora Spills a Secret

In the Greenwood, the fey do not write accounts of their own doing. Yes, we have bards whose entire lives are spent composing heroic verses to praise those we claim as heroes or those great and terrible loves that have nearly destroyed whole clans. Yes, we have history. But we do not care much for personal memory. When you live each day as we do, nearly immortal, there is no day that is unlike the other, there are no rites of passage but those of the seasons, there is no memory of consequence. Each day is the same tale, so there is no need to remember it at all.

But the Queen has requested that my sister Serana and I chronicle our time in the world and so it must be. And in this body unexpectedly aged by exile, it is indeed comforting to record these events for myself and my sister. We can no longer return to what had been for us a blithe and pretty life among the green. We have been transformed by exile that made us strangers dependent on the generosity of other strangers quite unlike ourselves. Our fey lives have been deepened with the tincture of mortality.

How it began was simple enough. Serana and I had escaped to the edge of the Greenwood, looking for sport. Lovesick boys wandered in these margins, saplings with sad eyes and dirty nails. There were rough-hewn men sometimes, but then, we were strong enough in magic to tame those flat-footed satyrs into playmates. We were beautiful then; our bodies fleshed full and ripe, skin scented with honeysuckle, and shoulders dusted with amber pollen. Bees kissed our mouths and our lips as ruby as pomegranate seeds.

On that day we heard the moans and the soft slap of skin against skin before we saw the couple. Serana, her berry-black eyes wide with delight, placed a finger against her lips to remind me to be still. I suppressed the giggle, though it bubbled in my throat. We crept silently through the brush, following the sound, stopping only when we had reached the boundary between our world and theirs. The green shadows hid us in the leafy arms of a viburnum, its tiny fruit dangling like drops of blood.

On a field of cut grass, someone had spread out a blanket, and on the blanket was a golden-haired child in a pale blue dress sleeping soundly on her back. Pretty thing she was, with pouting lips, creamy round cheeks touched in the middle with a bright red blush. Serana and I exchanged looks and I knew what she was thinking—that we should steal her; bring her back to court as our precious pet, our wild strawberry.

We glanced around and realized that the couple had indeed slipped into the woods a little way so as not to disturb the napping child. Their moans were reaching a crescendo, something that of course amused us even more than the child. We crawled through the bushes and parting the branches, we saw them.

It was known that the Queen did not engage in carnal play as the rest of us did. She held herself aloft, as though her power and her crown made her untouchable to such passionate fires. Or so we had thought. Even as I write this now, I am struck remembering how vulnerable she looked in his arms—head thrown back, the pulse of her veins against the white skin, her shimmering hair falling on the ground like spilt honey from the comb.

And the man? Mortal, we knew by the gamey smell that prickled our noses. We were shocked into laughter.

Imagine our haughty, Highborn Queen rolling in the dirt with a common man. I recall very little of his looks, only that we could not fathom how this man had found favor enough in the eyes of the Queen that she should shield the brilliance of her power beneath a glamour intended to make her seem ordinary as a haymaker. And I know that even as we choked on the surprised laughter, the sound escaped in peals that rang clear as a wind chime disturbed by a breeze.

The child began to cry. The couple sat up, dazed for a moment. Wariness hardened the man's features as his eyes searched for us. We were not afraid of him, for we knew he could never see us in the Greenwood. But the Queen could and before she could rise from the ground, Serana grabbed my hand and we ran, scampering through the dense brush like squirrels back to our own nests.

The Queen was cold and merciless and we knew that punishment would be swift and unpleasant if we were found. So all that day and night we hid in the hollowed trunk of a knotted pine, our arms wrapped around each other, fearing the sound of her hunting horns. Serana whispered hiding spells softly over and over, and I—for once—was very quiet.

But except for the patter of rain that fell on the second day, the Greenwood remained silent of rumor. On the third day we came to the conclusion that perhaps we had escaped unseen. And perhaps, if we kept the secret to ourselves and told no one, the Queen might never know that it was us who had spied upon her in the woods.

"You must never tell," Serana warned. "The Queen will not forget this."

WE RETURNED TO COURT AS innocent as lambs. Seasons came and went, and though there were many times I wanted to spill our secret while frolicking with a new playmate, I did as my sister instructed and remained quiet about it. But my cheek twitched during the solemn court rituals to see the Queen standing at regal attention, so unlike that time in the woods. And then I would feel Serana's hot gaze, the stern set of her lips beneath her flashing eyes, reminding me to forget that old secret once and for all.

But an arrow loosed in the world must eventually find its mark, and there are few secrets that do not eventually fly into the shell of an ear.

I was napping in a field, when through my dreaming I overheard a pack of boogans talking as they set traps on a farmer's field.

"Do ya think he's the one? You know, the one that giped the old girl. Aww . . . can you imagine that, then? Her on her back, legs to the sky. What a sight, eh?"

"Nah," chaffed another voice. "She said it were a different man. Not a farmer."

"What then?"

"The mason, you know, a man who lays the bricks."

The boogans were guffawing now. "He laid her, 'tis true. Trowel in hand, he stuffed her, he did, working that yellow hair of hers into the dirt, while the babe wailed in its cradle."

From the depths of sleep I blurted out, "What did Serana tell you about the Queen and her man?" I sat up and rubbed my eyes, confused. Then turned in horror to see the boogans, stunned into silence.

They stared at me slack-jawed, their bottom tusks more in evidence than usual. They were surprised as much by my question as by my sudden resurrection in the field. But their expressions quickly turned sly, then nasty, the leers splitting their faces till they looked like frogs.

"Oy, then, so the Queen herself is a-laying with the mason. Busy man he is. And she got with a wailing baby too. Now that is news!"

"No, you misunderstood me. Not the Queen." I tried to call the words back into my mouth.

"You said the Queen. Your sister was it told you?" The boogans snickered. "We all heard you and anyway who cares if it's true or not? It's a good lark. And we'll just blame the pair of you if we get caught." Their heads goggled excitedly. "Let's away then, boogans, there's more tricks afoot to be played with this thread of news than watching a farmer's old nag turn lame in one of our holes."

They dashed away into the green and I knew that within a heartbeat, the story would grow and I would be the root of it no matter how far the branches spread, or how bright the leaves of the tale unfurled. I spoke from a dream and there it was, the secret nocked to the quickest arrow in the quiver. There was nothing I could do to stop the rumor. I had to find my sister to warn her. We needed to hide, somewhere safe from the Queen's wrath. The Highborn clans were gathering at the Great Hall, Under the Hill, and I prayed that we might have the chance to scamper while they were so engaged.

3

Red Cap's Dark Lord

Listen! She knows winter comes, knows *we* come. When shadows be longest, we UnSeelie rise. So She gathers light into Herself to hold Her weakling people through the cold.

Ha! How I love it then: gnashing of teeth, trembling of limbs, tooth red in the gum, stone in the eye, heart beating in the hand. How I love to hear the weak puling of those milklings, whose blood be like whey. The struggle, dark/light, death/life. Ho!

Already, we prepare the way. Listen! The scream of an old woman brought down by a Ravener. Smell! A man in Founder's park strangled with twine and mistletoe. Taste! A village well poisoned, a crop blighted, dung in the porridge. Touch! A child stolen from his cradle, a wooden log sprinkled with blood left in his stead.

This be my duty.

This be my delight.

I write sonnets in my enemy's blood. I dip my red cap in a thousand years of war. Ho!

Strength be needed now: fist, spear, blood. Now I cry vengeance, argue it in our own court, the *Un*Seelie. I stand here, cap newly red with blood. The old woman's blood. The man in the park's blood. The boy child's blood. My muscled legs spread apart. Let them see my maleness. Let them desire me. Let their jealous natures feed me. All help me reach my ends.

"We be under threat," I tell them. I speak first in that hushed voice that draws all ears. Even my dark lord listens.

Then loudly I say: "Humans and their iron destroy our world. Let us hunt them as once we did. Not one by one by one. But all of them. Let us make tithes of blood sacrifice. Let the winter be long. Let the dark be king."

Jackdaws caw my name. Wolves howl. Jackal-headed men caper on the red carpet. Overexcited, one squats and lets loose a series of black pebbles. The King blows him into ashes, along with his shit.

My voice rises even louder. "Now be the time to cull their weakest. Pull down their strongest. Take back their power. No more this easy pax. We must war on the Seelie court. Take the Highborn and we take the Game."

And then the hall bursts into flames of laughter, shouts of my name. Only my King sits silent on his throne. No smile creases that dark face. But I know he agrees with me.

After all, he has not blown *me* into ashes. Hah!

4

Queen's Plaint

Beneath the blazing torch light, you hold your head high, your slender hands resting at your sides. Betray nothing, you counsel yourself. Let them see only the glamour regardless of what it costs you. There will be time later to rest. But not now. The clans of the Seelie and UnSeelie court have gathered Under the Hill to celebrate the Solstice, the slow turning of day into night, green fields into the black muck of winter. They come to consume the light and unleash the darkness. As it has always been.

The predatory eyes of the UnSeelie devour your flesh. They pace the hall and their claws strike sparks from the flagons. Hobs and sprites scurry in terror behind your dress, while the Highborn study your movements, your face, looking for signs of weakness. You must reassure them. You walk to the bright center of the hall, then cross into the shadows, until you are mingling among the UnSeelie, who growl and hiss in flecked tongues that threaten but do not touch your pure white skin.

The Highborn follow in your wake, forced by convention to stand beside you, but you can feel their reluctance. They do not know if they can trust their lives to you, though you have given them no reason—other than that you are female—to doubt your power. You tremble with the effort of maintaining the glamour of youth. But none must know the truth.

Heat licks the nape of your neck and you turn to see Red Cap standing close, his nostrils fanned to catch your scent. In spite of your resolve, you shiver and he smiles smugly, the row of sharpened teeth like a rusted saw. You inhale the metallic reek of human blood on him and notice that his cap, vest, hands are freshly stained mulberry. And while once you might not have noticed or cared, now you care very much.

Standing this close you must push back the brutal hand that culls the sweetness from life. You must show there is another way. You draw your hands together, palm to palm before the pale skin of your breasts. You float your pressed hands to your forehead and rest the tips of fingers on your brow. You bow to him, offering the unexpected: a gesture of peace.

He snarls in answer and shifts his body away from you. You smile, triumphant.

And then you hear the undertow of whispered words you have long anticipated. And for the first time you learn the names of those who have betrayed you. Fear takes you. But you know the words cannot be stopped. They drift around the room, and you see the startled looks as the story scatters like feathers from a torn pillow. Red Cap's ears have twitched forward, a leer spreading slowly across his brutal face.

You see it, but all you can think of is *will they believe it*? You struggle to banish the heat of shame from your face.

Red Cap grabs his groin and laughs, and a furious color stains your cheeks. Even now he has caught your true scent and has guessed what lies beneath your glamour. He will have no trouble believing the tale. No trouble twisting it like a knife against you, against your court. You turn away, so that he cannot see your expression for too much has already been given away. You must act quickly now.

When you turn to your own clans, there is contempt on the faces of the few Highborn Lords you once took to a barren bed. Their dams regard you with envy and bitterness. If they believe the boogans' tale, they must accept that what was denied to them has been given to you. Lips pressed with scorn, your court draws back to let you pass.

Only quickness now can serve your plan. Only rage can save you. And this time it will not be hard to find the meddling pair on whom to pour out your fire.

5

Serana's Expulsion

Green. So many shades of it filtering through the canopy of trees. The gray-green fingers of late summer maple. The stubby dark green lobes of oak. Heart-shaped silver-green of the birch trees. The matched light green droplets of the rowan, dark green rounds of alder and beech, the lighter green spray of ash, the hazel's double-toothed hairy green leaf.

And me, lying on my back, in my nest, under the trees, the green light covering my legs and belly and the areoles of my nipples, all green.

I was dallying with a favorite lover, a hob with soft hands and a slow manner. We sought one another out once a decade or so when neither of us wanted hard sport or a fleeting wild plundering. His love-name was Will Under the Feather and he had just gotten under my feathers indeed. And with a will.

We were speaking together of the green light, of the night's party to come, and laughing. I remember most the laughing. It made little motes of light spark around the nest. Not enough to set the nest on fire, of course, but enough to remind us of the danger. We were hazy in the afterglow of lovemaking, and hazy with the glowworm evening. His fur-covered foot touched mine, and his hand trailed down my throat.

"Berry-eyes," he murmured. "So delicious. I could eat you up forever."

I responded with a kind of throaty purr that made him laugh, but in that satisfying way that turned me warm all over. My left hand played with Will, while my right stroked the bits of feathers and silk, colored yarns and shiny stones that were stuffed into the crooks and crevices of my nest. My precious things taken down from the branches of trees where humans had tied them, offerings to the fey.

Without warning, the Queen appeared, looming over me, her golden hair blazing around her shoulders. "Out! Out! Out!" she cried, her face a harridan's mask. "Gossip's cup and sneak thief, spreading lies and calumny. Out! Out! Out! I command."

I gaped at her, rising before me in a column of flame and I knew with a terrifying coldness that Meteora had spoken aloud the words that were meant to disappear. And she must have included my name, which the Queen now screeched into the boiling air.

I had no chance to be angry at Meteora. Putting my hands to my ears, I prepared for the worst. Blood rushed around inside my head, hot rivers of it threatening to overrun the sides. I could feel my right hand wet with something as the eardrum burst. But I was not dead.

Not yet.

Then courage and instinct took me by the left hand and threw me over the side of the nest. I heeded neither the scratching of the dried grasses on my legs nor the *thwack* I received from Will's heels as he bailed out the other side.

As I fell away from the nest, I glanced over my shoulder. The Queen was holding up a rosewood wand, the bumps that would one day be thorns as red and pulsing as pustules. Not her oaken staff. Not her silver mace. Not her rowan switch. So it was to be a punishment, and not death this day. *I can live with that*, I thought.

I ran full out with scarcely a strip of cloth covering

me, remembering only too late that one does not turn one's back to the Queen, whatever the hurry.

The rosewood wand hit me high up on the right shoulder, breaking the skin, and my arm was all at once red, looking more like a sleeve made of holly berries than a naked arm covered with blood.

There must have been a spell. The wand should not have extended that far. But if there had been a spell, I never heard it spoken; or if I did, it did not register. All that registered was pain. Pain, fear, and darkness. And then the Queen's voice calling after me:

> Should Sister meet Sister in Light again,
> Then falls the iron rain.

I tumbled in the air and was somehow transported over the hill and away from home. Away from the body I knew, away from the world I was fond of, away from the sister I loved. I did not know if Meteora, too, had run, leaping over the side of her nest, leaving her lover as fast as I had left mine. And to be truthful—which is not always a mark of fairy—I did not at that moment care. All I cared about was my own pain, my own fear, and the darkness around me that was every color intermixed but green.

As I fell through the cold, unknown air, I fell out of magic, too, felt it being stripped away from me as if I'd been skinned. As if a hunter had taken a piece of cold iron and slipped it around me with such precision that I was now naked to the elements. And so I entered the new world raw, unprotected, veins open to the earth, sky, and all about, and *that* was the worst pain of all.

I AWOKE ON A GRAY table in a gray hall, covered by a gray sheet. There were low lights and a buzz of voices.

And the smell. Oh, sweet Mab, the smell.

It was as if all the meat of the world had spoiled, and I along with it.

I turned over on my side and did something I had never done before in my long life. I let what was in my stomach empty out onto the gray floor.

"Oh for fuck's sake," I heard a voice say. "These street people. Look what the cat's thrown up now. Jenny—get the mop."

WHEN I WOKE AGAIN, I was starving. My stomach felt scraped and my throat was raw. My shoulder, where the Queen's wand had struck, ached down to the bone. I was wrapped in some sort of winding sheet that smelled ever so slightly of flaxseed. It was as gray as the room.

I tried to call out, but my voice sounded scratchy, and as ancient as the great holm oak that sits atop our green hill. But someone must have heard me, for an unhandsome woman ran in. She had a shock of black hair that had strange white roots, as if she had put a glamour on that had worn off raggedly.

She glanced at me, pulled a long silver needle from a pocket in her gray coverall, and then attempted to shove the needle into my upper arm.

I screamed and sat up—who wouldn't? Any fey knows that poison loves the needle. In the same movement, I unwound the top part of the sheet and tore my arm from her grasp. Then I slapped her. My fingerprints blossomed on her cheek. I stood, despite the best attempt of the bottom part of the sheet to keep me down, spoke a curse, and waved my hand to turn her into a toad. She looked at me with a mouth slightly awry, not at all toadlike. I stood there like a gob, staring at her unchanged shape as she grabbed up my arm again and this time shoved the needle straight in.

It stung, but far less than I had expected. There was a sudden sweet flavor in my mouth, not quite nectar, but not far off from it, which was odd because I had had no drink at all.

As I fell back hazily onto the bed, I noticed my arm and hand for the first time. Or at least what should have been my arm and hand. Where was my alabaster skin, the agile wrist, the tapering pink nails? What was this long, plump protuberance covered with fine, dark, curling hairs? These fingers as thick as cow dugs? What lines were these across the back of my hand, like folds? And why was the fat, horrible hand clutching a piece of silk the color of a summer rose?

Whose arm is this, I thought, for surely it was not mine, no matter that it seemed firmly attached to my shoulder.

A dream, I thought.

A nightmare, I corrected.

And then I thought: *The Queen's spell.*

Knowing I was right at last, I let the nectar take me into sleep where I stayed through day and night and into the following morning.

6

Meteora Runs Away

Word was spreading fast from court as I searched the Greenwood for Serana. But there was no sign of her. All I found was Will the hob, shaking with fear, tucked in between two rocks.

"Where is she?" I whispered.

"Gone," he answered, his eyes rimmed white.

"Gone where?" I demanded.

"Wherever the Queen has sent her. Quick-like in a shout." He squeezed out from between the rocks and bolted into the dense bracken.

Those words, how they stabbed me to the heart. *Serana gone!* I knew she had no time, no chance to reason with the Queen. With naught on her back, she had disappeared and only the Queen knew where.

And I was next. I was sure of it. Fleeing to our quarters, I arrived at my room unseen through the mouse holes we had built as a secret passageway to the little springs where we liked to bathe. Frantically, I gathered up beloved things: a silver dove, milky crystals, a lozenge of copper, a pouch of amber beads. I hid these treasures in a band hastily made from my dam's torn silk petticoat and tied it around my waist. I thought in all foolishness that these things might be of use when I found Serana wherever the Queen had sent her. I held that thought hard and close to my guilty heart.

Just as I was tying a blue cape around my shoulders, I heard someone enter. Heart pounding, I turned. Of course it was the Queen. Who else dared enter without permission? Perhaps if I begged she might let me share my sister's place of punishment. At least we would be together. But I quaked before her, my resolve unraveling in fear. She stared at me with an odd mixture of fury and desperation. But there was no mistaking the danger that smoldered in her narrowed eyes.

I threw myself on the floor, reaching out a tentative hand to touch the doe-white skin of her foot.

"Oh Gracious Queen, our Queen, your worthless servant begs you—"

It was useless of course. Even as I had begun pleading, the Queen spit forth a banishing spell that pierced my flesh the way summer hail shreds the tender leaves. Groveling in pain, I wept quicksilver tears, unable to speak further.

A murderous clap of thunder hurled me from light into dark, from mist into mire. I groaned, my cape soaked through, my face pressed into the soggy earth. I turned on my back, and gasped as rain pelted my cheeks, and pooled in my eyes. I reached out a hand for protection from its stinging cold, seeing only the thrashing branches of storm-tossed trees.

"C'mon, Grandma!" a shrill voice shouted. "Get up, damn it! I can't carry you." A small hand tugged at mine, now grown swollen and useless.

Dazed, I struggled to my feet, only distantly wondering where the Queen had exiled me.

"C'mon!" the voice insisted and I looked down through the sheeting rain barely able to make out a girl-child, feral from the look of her matted hair and ragged clothing. "Hey, somebody give me a hand with this one!" she whined.

From the rain-soaked bushes came an explosion of small bodies, some human children by their clothes, some spriggets and hobs, their naked pelts slick with rain. I balked like a nag refusing to plow but they shoved, cursed, and finally kicked me into motion.

I lumbered down a steep embankment, the girl-child tugging frantically at my hand as though we were being chased by unseen demons. Infected by her fear, I stumbled over root and mud to catch up to her.

"Get down," the girl ordered.

Aided by other hands tugging on my cape, I was pulled to my knees and then forced to lie prostrate in the drenched grass. Twin ribbons of light swooped over us and when the night returned to darkness and rain, the children helped me to my feet again.

"Who are you?" I asked, finding the sound of my voice strange—thick and husky, as if I had caught a human chill.

"Later, when there's time. We have to get you over first."

"Let's go! Or we'll miss the train!" shouted a lanky boy, his hair shaved into spiral patterns over his skull.

"You gotta run," commanded the girl who was still holding my hand.

I started to trot with a clumsy gait, when I saw again the twin lights approaching. "Wait! Wait!" I shouted, trying to drag my companions to a halt.

"Aw, shit. We got no time for this," the boy yelled and slapped me on my flanks. "Run, now! Or we're all dead!"

I ran nearly insensate with terror, as the children dragged me by the hand over a gravel path and across a hard road to the other side. Midway, blazing lights captured us in a net of silver rain, a horn blared an alarm, and the monster screeched and swerved, but still we ran, our bare feet pounding the unyielding roadway, until we had crossed over.

Crossed over . . .

I was panting, the breath knocked from my chest, my feet burning from the hard slab of the road. But the children continued to push and pull, curse and cajole, dragging me farther into the woods on that other side until again we were on the crest of a hill. Below us on the edge of an open field, I could just make out the rails of iron

gouging the earth. Even on the hill, I tasted the bitterness of rust.

Looking around wildly, I realized that I was now
alone with the children, for the spriggets and hobs had
not ventured onto the road. They had been there only to
see me off into my exile, no doubt to report back to the
Queen that I was now fully lost to the Greenwood.

"Let's go," said the lanky boy, grabbing my arm at the
elbow.

I resisted his grasp and stumbled back onto the
ground. "I pray do not kill me thusly. Do not tie me to
the iron that her hands may be clean of such a shameful
death. For though I have wronged the Queen, I do not
deserve this. Give me a dagger of silver and let me end
my disgrace with some honor."

Another girl, this one with hair rolled into a hundred
braids like the mane of a fairy horse, clasped my face in
her small hands. She leaned in close so that I could see
her simple, heart-shaped face in the dark. "We're supposed ta help you. Not kill you. You gotta trust us. There
will be wood over the rails and you'll sit on that and the
iron won't burn you. I promise."

"You're changelings, aren't you?"

"Once, but not anymore." She shrugged, releasing me.

"Tossed out like the trash," retorted a third girl in a
dress of pieced furs.

"Shut it," snapped the boy. "Didn't she promise to
bring us back if we helped?"

"Who promised?" I asked.

"No time for talk. The red-eye's almost here," the boy
said. He grabbed at my cloak, roughly bringing me to my
feet again.

A shrill whistle screamed over our heads. The children were moving at once, dragging me in their tow to
where the path of rails curved away into the forest again.
An iron dragon screeched as it rumbled over the rails,
steam exploding around the long segmented body snak-
ing across the field.

Now we were running toward it, and though I gagged at the stench of its bellowing breath, I let the children pull me alongside its slow-moving flanks. The boy was searching as each armored segment passed, until at last a long wooden tail appeared. A door slid open in its side and a stout pair of arms reached out with expectant hands.

"Take a hold and jump in," the children shouted.

Before I could protest, those broad-fingered hands grabbed my wrists, and I was forced to run faster alongside the open door or fall beneath the dragon's churning belly and onto the iron rails.

"Jump! Jump!" came shouts from all sides.

I pulled in a gasping, painful breath and jumped ... landing hard on the threshold of the door. My legs dangled uselessly over the edge behind me, my arms nearly wrung from their sockets, my stomach roiling against the poisonous iron. I flailed like a reluctant mermaid. But the grip on my wrists remained tight, nails digging in and cutting the flesh.

The iron dragon picked up speed, and I was relieved when at last I felt the planks of dried oak beneath my cheek and thighs. Effortlessly, the huge hands hoisted me up until my back rested against a wooden wall that rattled and bucked as the iron dragon galloped over the rails.

"Good. You have come," said a gruff voice, chuckling. Actually it was more of a growl and the sound of it lifted the hair on my beck.

I stared up at my rescuer, visible in the flashes of distant lightning. Long hair billowed in the wind, sweeping across the rough-hewn features of a hag. In the middle of her broad forehead, thick brows met over a bulbous nose. The mouth was a wide grin filled with glimmering teeth above a knobbed chin. Between the black strands of drifting hair, the eyes flared red like embers ignited by a gust of wind.

"Who are—?"

"Shut the door!" a man's voice barked and two others

rose from the shadowed recess of our hold to push their shoulders into the heavy wooden door, so that sky, the rain, and even the faintest hint of light were obliterated.

Only the eyes of my rescuer, still holding my gaze, continued to burn.

7

Serana Finds Herself

The sun rose and as I lay in the nest of covers, I heard the dawn chorus struggling through what I would later come to know as glass. It was not spring of course, where birdsong pulses with life and invitation. Now they sing more quietly, in anticipation of autumn, bidding one another safe passage to the summer lands far away.

But for the moment, they were so muffled, I believed that this strange enchantment had somehow stifled the very birds.

And then I saw again those hands that I had concluded were my own. Rough. Plump. Squared fingers. Aching joints. With not a bit of the old, familiar magic in them, the magic that used to rush along the blue rivers down the back of my hands and the front of my wrists.

I turned my palms up and then down, as if by moving my hands, I could make them change back to the way they had been in the Greenwood. But they remained horrid, gross, inert troll hands. To look at them made me shudder.

Now, we fey understand glamour. We live our lives surrounded by it. We wear our young faces, our lithe bodies without consciously thinking about how we got them or why. They are as they are. We are so painted with the stuff of glamour that every movement elicits desire, every cough a laugh, every tear an ocean. We know we are glamoured, but we forget it as well. It is simply a cloak against the cold, a mask to hide the ugly. We do not think of the stink of a cave full of bones, or how dim it is. It is to us as well as any viewer a palace of diamond-sharp lights and the overwhelming scent of roses, for glamour makes it so. We do not feel how coarse leaves are against the skin, or how prickly the nest we lie in. Silk and down is what we see. We fool ourselves that we gain succor from dew, the taste sometimes sweet, sometimes tart when there is no taste at all.

Magic disguises. Magic contrives. Magic convinces.

And I had no magic now. My rigid, aching fingers told the truth. When a carer—young and pretty in a red striped overgown—gave me a mirror, the fat, old lady looking back at me told the truth.

At first I'd thought she was some visitor come to beg a potion from me, like the old ones wanting surcease from wanting. I thought her a stranger until I watched her speak the very words that were in my mouth. Over and over and over again until even I *had* to understand.

She said/I said, "Where is this place?"

She said/I said, "Who are you?"

She answered/I answered, "I do not know."

But I knew.

The woman was me. I shook my fist at her and she shook hers back.

And then I cried.

Yet even as I wept, I watched her in the mirror and it was not pretty oceans that fell from my dark eyes, just a drizzle of snot from my nose, and tears like globules of fat running down my large cheeks. And hers.

I lay back down heavily on the bed. Looked down at the flaxseed cloth on my body, this body, this sunken, fallen, flabby body. And knew that for me, for some reason, there was no glamour anymore.

And while I was engrossed in my misery, all alone, the young carer long gone to others needing her, a knock sounded on the door, like a knell. A voice spoke so cheerily, like tinkling bells, I wondered briefly if I were wrong. Perhaps there *was* still some glamour in the human world.

"Hello! I'm here to help you. May I come in?"

Of course with magic, entrance must always be asked for, before it can be offered. I have known this since ... well, since forever. No one except the Queen can enter unbidden. Though the carers had—the girl with the mirror, the mean woman with the needle of sleep.

I looked up and saw Miss Jamie Oldcourse for the first time. Plain-faced, plainspoken Jamie Oldcourse, with a body like a twisted oak and a face like a peach left too long in the sun and sunken in upon itself. Still, her voice belied her ugliness, her lameness, and she had a name like a glade, or a lea. For the first time in my life, I had nothing to say.

Miss Jamie Oldcourse did not seem to notice that I was suddenly tongue-tied, or at least she did not let that stop her. Even without my offering, she walked in as if she were the Queen, and sat down next to me on the bed. She took my hand in hers. Her skin was peachlike, too, soft and slightly fuzzed. I let her keep my hand. Indeed, without magic I had no will to take it away.

"Now, dear," she said, and I heard for the first time behind the sweetness, that hint of sour. Or maybe it was a hint of strength. Hard to tell. "Now, dear," she said, "no one seems to know your name."

"One does not give away a name just for the asking," I replied, firmly. It is the first thing a fey learns. "Or one gives away power."

"Power," she said and smiled. Then nodding wisely added, "People of the street must find power in small things."

"I am not of the street," I answered back. "I am of the hill and the trees, the moonlight and ..."

Still smiling, she interrupted, "Then give me something I may call you," she said with a smile. "*Hey you* seems so awkward."

It did not seem awkward to me, but I looked over at the mirror again and this time saw just my face and neck and a bit of my shoulder. I gave her the name of *that* thing, with the fat cheeks and the wattle.

"Maybelle," I said, thinking of a farmer's cow not far from our grove. A brown-and-white cow with enormous dugs and big dark eyes. In this body, I looked remarkably like her. "The farmer's Maybelle."

"Mabel Farmers," she said, trying out the name. "A name not much used these days. But I think it suits you."

Oh what a coil, what a curse is naming. But suddenly I was stuck with Mabel. I thought: *Next I shall have to eat grass and moo.*

"And I am Jamie Oldcourse," she said, freely handing over her name without fear I might use it or abuse it. "*Ms.* Oldcourse. Your social worker."

I spat out her name, at the same time thinking of her as a toad, a tadpole, something silly and insignificant. Waiting for the change . . . which did not come. I shook my finger at her. I made a puff-mouth at her. And still she did not change. I said a word of transformation in the Old Tongue, then in the Middle Tongue. And *still* she did not change. She was right not to fear me. I had no magic anymore. Not an inch of it, not an ounce. I said her name again, this time with a kind of resignation. "Miss Jamie Oldcourse."

She smiled. "That's right. Like the golf at Saint Andrews." Clearly something she said often. If it was an explanation, it meant nothing to me.

And so we met, my spirit guide to this new and awful Eden, and Miss Jamie Oldcourse became the first of my Helpers. For in this new world, one cannot navigate without them; the rules are so particular, so peculiar, and so dissimilar to the fey's.

First there is the *Law of Papers*. One cannot move, buy food, nest, heal, or otherwise live without papers. And of course I had none.

Second there is the *Law of Restraint*. Humans believe in it, the fey do not. Why consider restraint when you have magic that can overcome all restraints at will?

Third, is the *Law of Friendship*, which seems to supersede family, sept, clan, or court. It would be a long and hard while before I was to truly understand and trust this.

Three rules. Three unbelievable rules. But I quickly realized that as I was to live in this place for the unforeseeable future—and that time would be of the Queen's choosing, not mine—I would have to learn these rules. Even if I did not believe them. This did not make me happy and I told the Glade so.

She laughed. Again that tinkling, bell-like sound. I have never liked bells. I told her that, too. Which made her laugh anew.

It was not a good beginning. But at least it was a start.

8

Meteora Meets Her Guide

In the utter darkness of my rumbling prison I passed the longest night I have ever known, one without the comfort of stars or moon. A suffocating heat gathered in damp waves, infused with the sour stench of unwashed humans. I wept noisily until an unseen hand touched mine, sharp nails scratching the inside of my palm. Briefly her eyes flared into reddened coals, the dim light illuminating the hag's grotesque face.

"Quiet," she rasped, her breath pungent with wild garlic and leeks. Her callused hand cupped my cheek, holding it steady before gently raking her gnarled fingers through my sopping hair. "Show your courage, little one, and I will not harm you."

In the dark, I obeyed, stifling my sobs. Instinctively, I opened my senses to the aura of the power beside me, but there was only a deep well of nothing. Beneath my breath, I whispered the spell of shielding to hide me from the bold touch of this stranger. The hands continued to comb my hair, the splayed fingers snagging on the knotted tangles. I tried the spell of stabbing pain, followed by a spell of bursting sight. Desperate when none of those worked, I spoke in a loud voice the spell of endless shitting.

> *"In the gut, a long, sharp sliver;*
> *Down and out, the soft brown river,*
> *Till I cry 'Hold!'"*

This provoked a loud guffaw that ended in a snarl.

I froze as the hollowed eyes flared brighter. In the light of those terrifying eyes, I studied her more closely. Her misshapen skull was framed by matted gray hair. The bulbous nose cast a shadow over purple lips that parted to display two yellowed tusks, one broken and jagged. A thick tongue uncurled between rows of tarnished metal teeth and licked my cheek. I sat still, my stomach lurching at the overly familiar gesture. She sat back again, clucking her tongue against the roof of her mouth.

"Ah, *bednjaga.* It wasn't enough to cast you out. They stole from you too."

"Stole what?" I asked, forcing myself not to reach up and wipe away the damp trail of her tongue.

"Everything," she answered. "Now you must rely on good manners. Something your folk have conveniently forgotten."

"Who *are* you?" I demanded, my pride pricked by her insult. "Get away from me, you hearth-hag."

Grinning wolfishly, the light of her coal-fire eyes glancing off the metal teeth, she held me fast by the wrist. "Manners!"

"Help me, help me, good folk," I cried to the others who were hidden in the shadows. "Help me, I am being attacked!"

There was no answer. No rustle or movement, not even enough sound to indicate they'd heard but didn't want to get involved.

"They sleep," she said. "Maybe I eat later, maybe not."

"I pray thee, Black Annis, daughter of Giants, do not eat me," I burbled, suddenly very cold. "I am but small and insignificant."

She threw back her head and howled with crackling laughter. Beneath the hard knob of her uplifted chin I saw a necklace of delicate finger bones threaded with knuckles small as pearls. My heart leaped in my chest.

"Not small anymore." She poked me hard in the ribs.

"But I would not eat you. You are not the sweet flesh and wine-blood of man, which is what I crave."

I lowered my head in a hasty bow of obeisance and real fear. Of course. I knew her now. "My abject apologies, oh most Glorious Mother of the Woods, Slayer of Wayward Children, and Undefeated Rival of Koschey the Deathless. I apologize. I did not recognize you before, not in this place of iron and wood. I am your humble servant," I squeaked like a cornered mouse, and then dared her name. "Baba Yaga."

"That is better," she croaked, releasing me with a pat of her hand. She leaned back, all the while sucking on her lower lip, scraping her tusks against the purple flesh. She was wearing odd clothes—odd in the sense that she was wearing any at all—for the little I knew of her, Baba Yaga was not beholden to the fashions of the Seelie court or of man himself. She was old enough to have roamed pristine forests in gleaming nakedness when the first man and first woman still wore their skins in innocence. She could not forgive their betrayal, the death of those perfect forests, and now wore the skin of old age, of mortal corruption, to remind those who encountered her that she had not forgotten.

Serana and I had seen her once Under the Hill. Accustomed to the cloth of beauty and youth, we were goggle-eyed at her withered hide, her long sagging breasts hanging low over the bony chest. Her hips had jutted like the pelvis of a starved cow, the loose skin of her belly had lapped in folds over the tangled fur of her sex. But her spindled arms were wound with taut ropes of muscles, her hands broad as spades with thick fingers that ended in black nails, sharpened to razor points. At that time she had refused all gifts of clothing the Queen had offered her: the finely woven cloaks with silver clasps, the silken green gowns, the lace chemises and pretty petticoats.

Serana and I had talked about nothing else for days. How from a leather pouch slung low on her bony hips, Baba Yaga had withdrawn a necklace of little bones and knuckles and placed it around her neck. The court had flinched at the sight of it. Even Red Cap, there as an emissary from the UnSeelie court, bowed his head before the mocking challenge in her flaming eyes. All fell back from her, all except the Queen who bloodied her fine garments carrying the carcass of a new-slaughtered fawn and placing it as an offering in Baba Yaga's hands.

"Sleep," Baba Yaga commanded as we rocked in the swaying box, riding over the iron rails. "Sleep, little one, no harm tonight."

I willed my eyes shut, the red flare of her gaze still visible beneath the skin of my lids. Despite her saying I was not her type of meat, I waited in stillness for those taloned hands to tear me to tiny pieces as she had done the slaughtered fawn. We had stood speechless, watching her eat her fill, watching as she rolled the bones into the bloody hide, tying it with the sinews, tossing it into her mortar. She'd climbed in after it. Then, snatching up the heavy pestle, waved it in the air until the mortar hovered a few feet above the ground. The ancient doors that protected our court Under the Hill shattered with a huge blast of splintered wood. She steered her mortar through the ravaged entry, poling the air with the pestle until she found the open sky again.

Serana had said to me then, "Do not meddle in the affairs of *that* one, little sister. She will eat you whole and not even spit out the pips."

I SLEPT AS BABA YAGA commanded, but it was a sleep plagued by fitful dreams, most of them about Serana.

Since first I awoke in the Greenwood, I have known my sister; known her in the shared heartbeat and the quickness of minds that needs no words. If I touched a web of hoarfrost on stilled water, she shivered. If she ate wild strawberries, I tasted the sweetness. We were joined by unbreakable bonds. Until now.

Why had the Queen separated us? Where had Serana gone? In my restless sleep I searched for her, but there was not even a phantom echo of her presence. I was without her for the first time in my long life.

The dragon-train screeched and hissed and I felt the wheels grind as it came to a shuddering stop. I woke confused, blinded by a narrow band of dawn's light that fell into our dark hold. My unknown companions slipped out quietly, only the dull thud of their footfalls on the ground below to mark their passage.

"We go now," Baba Yaga said, roughly pulling me by the hand.

"Go where?" I stumbled as she dragged me to the open door.

"Other world."

In the pale dawn, I was startled to see that Baba Yaga had transformed her harsh crone's face into that of a smooth-cheeked elderly woman. The blazing eyes were now a faded blue, and her once unruly hair hung in a braid down her back. But she had not disguised those iron teeth. Perhaps she could not. She glanced both ways quickly before jumping down, and as she still held my hand, I was obliged to follow, though my landing was far less successful. I fell heavily and rolled, my free hand brushing against the iron rails. I screamed as it seared my skin, hot as a brand.

"Be quiet," Baba Yaga snarled, and hauled me back up to my feet. "Don't wake the dogs."

It was too late. A door slammed open, a voice called out an angry warning, and dogs began barking wildly. We heard the sound of their paws scrabbling over the gravel.

"Go!" Baba Yaga shouted.

But I couldn't. All around me the land was crisscrossed with bands of iron on which rested the hulking bodies of other dragon-trains. Steam hissed from beneath their bellies and the iron glistened.

"I cannot," I answered. Iron screeched into my blood, drove pins into my joints, nails into my stomach. I swayed on my feet, gripped by waves of nausea.

Cursing, Baba Yaga lifted me easily and tossed me like a sack over her shoulder, my head dangling down her back. She moved quickly across the iron grid, but not fast enough, for the dogs found her and as I lifted my throbbing head, I saw them bounding toward us, a man following close behind.

"The dogs . . ." I said weakly and groaned as she turned abruptly to face them.

Then I saw nothing, but I heard it: the squeal of the dogs as they rushed us, only to be tossed aside by the killing sweep of her hand, the razor claws gutting them as they leapt.

"Stop or I'll shoot," the man cried. Baba Yaga reached into the pocket of her trousers, pulled up a carved comb and tossed it on the ground before turning to run. Clutching her shirt to steady myself, I glanced up from her bouncing gait and watched the ground churn into a wave of gravel that rose and then crashed down on our pursuer. As the earth tumbled over him, the man flailed his arms, struggling without success to stay above the wave of rumbling rock. I closed my eyes, unable to watch as the dirt enclosed him in its fist, silencing his screams for help.

BABA YAGA RAN OUT OF the field of iron rails, down toward a gleaming lake where rocks and boulders littered its shore. As soon as we reached a grassy beach by the water's edge, she brusquely set me down on the ground and waited impatiently for me to stand. I was dizzy, a roar echoing in my ears that did not quite drown out the last cries of the doomed man. I rose again to my feet, swallowing hard at the taste of rust in my throat. Straightening my shoulders, I tried to look braver than I felt.

Grinning, Baba Yaga nodded approval. "Good. Tell me," she asked, head tilting to one side, "do you know yourself now?"

"What do you mean?"

She reached out and pulled my cape from off my shoulders. "Look."

I glanced down and gasped, seeing for the first time what

had become of me. Gone was my slender torso, the small hard breasts, the flat belly. Now I was stolid and thick-waisted, my breasts pendulous. My thighs had spread like yeasted bread, and creased over my knobbed knees. I lifted my hands, cried out at the web of blue veins, and the little gold rings embedded in the swollen flesh of my fingers.

Walking to the water's edge, I leaned down to see my reflection in the calm surface of the lake. My face was wider, with cheeks and chin padded and softly wrinkled. My eyelids drooped sleepily, the lids darker and more deep-set. My hair once the color of acorns and burnished leaves was graying at the temples and crown.

I stumbled back from the water, shocked and then angry. "That miserable bitch. Wasn't it enough to banish me? Why did she have to leave me . . . so . . ."

"Old?" finished Baba Yaga with a snort. "Foolish thing. You have been old a long time and still you know nothing. So, your Queen has done this to you? For what reason?"

"We spied her rutting with a mortal."

"And you told?" she asked, one eyebrow lifted in amazement.

"I didn't mean to," I protested and then hung my head. It was my fault. *My* fault. Under the witch's unrelenting gaze, I accepted that terrible truth. My fault, yet both—Serana and I—were paying for it.

Baba Yaga waited with bemused curiosity. Small flames flickered in the pale blue eyes. "So now you need help."

My pulse quickened with reckless hope. "Yes, help," I answered, forgetting my fear of the old witch in my desperation to change my fate and that of my sister.

Baba Yaga was silent, as though waiting for something else.

Manners, I thought, frightened. And then: *A gift*. But how could I hope to parley for help with nothing to offer in return? My heart sank. I had nothing that might have interested her.

Baba Yaga yawned noisily to show her growing impatience, and I saw the broken tusk protruding through the mortal mask she wore. I murmured thanks to magpie habits and promptly dug around in the folds of my waistband while Baba Yaga watched me with renewed interest.

"I have a gift for you," I said, and retrieved the pinkish lozenge of copper. I showed it to Baba Yaga, who frowned.

"What do I do with this?"

"It's copper and will mold to your—your broken tooth. It will make it whole."

"Let me taste." She snatched it from my hand and placed it on her tongue. She rolled it in her mouth, from side to side as though it were a sweet. Rumbling with pleasure, she nodded her head. "I like it." She spit the copper lozenge into her palm and began kneading it until it was soft. Then she folded it around the broken shaft of her tusk, shaping it to match its twin.

She continued to run her long tongue over the thin seam between copper and tusk until it appeared bonded and whole. Smacking her lips, she grinned. "Yes, I like this gift. I *will* help. And you, if you are wise, will survive. If not," she shrugged . . . "*someone* will eat you." She guffawed and slapped her thigh.

Then she looked me up and down. "Okay . . . first we dress you. No longer a little wood poppet. Now you are babushka—old lady, like me." She reached into the leather bag slung over her shoulder and began to pull out garment after garment—far more than should have been able to be stored in such a small satchel. There were things I had never seen before, much less knew how to put on. Something to bind my breasts, to cover my sex, to swaddle my legs and arms; in short to hide the body that was once my pride and was now my shame.

9

Serana Moves In

Jamie Oldcourse tidied the papers—Law number one. She had me sign on this line and that. Though it took me some while to remember to put the name Mabel instead of Serana there, she seemed not to notice.

"Take your time," she said. "I'm unfazed by your slowness."

Unfazed. What a fine word. It had a fey quality that I liked, a sense of magic and unmagic, Seelie and Un-Seelie.

After all was signed, Jamie Oldcourse said, "Now to get you out of that hospital gown."

Gown! As if this short, thin, open-backed, gray, flimsy excuse for a covering had even a nodding acquaintance with a gown. I remembered gowns that were silk, the colors of sunrise, with rose-petal softness, and bedecked with water jewels. I reached for the little piece of silk on the bedside table, all I had of my old life. Picking it up, I rubbed it against my cheek.

"Now, now," Jamie Oldcourse said, taking the silken patch from me, "let's get you dressed in real clothes."

Then she pushed and prodded me into human dressing. I suppose there was a kind of reality to them. They were scratchy, heavy, sogged with old perspiration and the breath of whatever human had worn them before me.

Unfazed, I tried to pull the neckline down, kirtle the

skirt, roll the long sleeves up. Jamie Oldcourse laughed that tinkling bell laugh and warned me about tearing anything off when in public. *Law number two: Restraint.* I doubted I would ever learn that one.

And as Jamie Oldcourse was all the people I knew in the human world, I had to trust her. *Law number three.* My sister, my clan and sept—all the fey that I had known—were dead to me; my court locked and barred behind me. The green world gone. So I would, all *unfazed*, be Jamie Oldcourse's friendly cow till I could get myself home again, however long that might take.

"Now," she announced, as I stood in my uncomforting clothes, "we need a place for you. You aren't sick any longer so the hospital can't keep you. And I'm damned if I'll let you back on the street. So we are off to get you somewhere to stay."

I noticed she did not say *home.* I knew—*she* knew— that whatever *place* she found for me could not be called that, and I was grateful for her restraint. I grabbed up my piece of silk and stuffed it into the pocket of my human dress, hiding away the last of my feyness from prying eyes.

"What we want," Jamie Oldcourse went on, ignoring what I had done with the silk as if I had actually been able to disguise my action with magic. "What we want," she repeated as if the two of us were going to be living there together, "is some place high enough above the road that you can breathe. Close to the shops. And some trees."

I nodded. I understood breath and trees, but what *shops* were I was still to find out.

"Yes," I said.

She smiled. I had not used that word with her before. "Yes," she repeated, "and I think I know just the place."

IT WAS A STREET THAT had no name, but a number. Now we fey call things by names that make and unmake: Under the Hill, Sun's Crossing, The Waters of Regret,

Way of the Deer. But give a lane or a lea or a place only a number? Unthinkable! Yet it turns out it is a very human thing to do. A kind of counting I do not yet fathom.

Jamie Oldcourse and I walked from the hospital, not more than a quarter mile, but my lumpy, bumpy, aching body protested every step. Her twisted, limping body made its passage with more ease and grace than mine. Was it only because she was long accommodated to it and I was not? Or was it some subtler magic than that? I squared my shoulders and looked straight ahead. If I had to be forced to live in this shape, I would take my lessons from her, and not from the Queen's punishing hand.

The noise around us was appalling: squawks and squeals, honkings and squonkings, and a series of loud wails. More than once I put my hands to my ears.

Let the rivers run through me, I whispered. *Let them stop the sounds*.

"Here we are," Jamie Oldcourse said in her soft chime that yet muted the terror-noise of the street. Almost like a spell, I thought.

She stopped before a narrow brick house fairly shoved in between two stark buildings made of glass and metal. There were three or four thin trees planted on the walk outside. I reached out to touch the trunk of one of them, just to feel the green marrow within. A slight coolness ran through my fingers, nothing more, where once power would have leaped greenly into my hand.

On a branch above my head, a dove sat cooing to itself. Like most birds—all excepting owls, jays, rooks, ravens, and crows—it had little to say. Little, that is, beyond *food*, *sleep*, *fly*! But it did open an eye when I touched the tree. I am certain the dove recognized me for what I am, or at least what I had been, for it nodded its head and fluffed out its feathers.

I looked back, *unfazed*. "Should I go in?" I asked the bird.

It cooed an answer. "Eat, sleep, fly well, Old One."

Old one! I shivered palpably.

"At least there are trees," I said.

"There are indeed." She took out a small golden key and put it in a hole in the door. I heard something click.

"Now, lift the latch," she said, "and go in. I will follow."

Using the long sleeve to cover my left hand to keep it safe from the iron latch, I lifted the handle, pushed the door, and walked in, with Jamie Oldcourse in my wake.

We climbed three sets of stairs—me breathing rather too heavily for such a small climb—and there, at the top of the building, was a green door, always a good sign. Jamie opened it with another key, this one gray as stone. Gold and silver. Another good sign. Breathing heavily herself, she pushed the door open and ushered me through. "I hope you like it. It's one of the nicer places."

There were but four small rooms, colored improbable shades of pink, like old, blown roses. The walls felt too close, and crowded in like the sides of a cave. The Un-Seelie folk may live in caves, but we of the Seelie court prefer the open spaces under the hill and over it. Still, there were windows in the front room looking down onto the trees, and water running from strange taps in a cooking corridor. The water tasted a bit off, not like the springs I was used to, but with a metallic burn. At least it was plentiful. Jamie Oldcourse showed me the cooker and the cooler. I could only guess at their functions, but I knew I would have time to explore once she left.

There was a nestlike bed in the small back room, but the window in that room looked out onto another building. Anyone might spy in while I slept. Anyone could fly from their nest into mine. With no magic, I could not make myself safe. I knew I could not sleep in there. But Jamie Oldcourse said nothing about my having to leave the bed where it was, so I determined to move it to the front room before I passed a night in my place.

My place. I had already agreed, of course. The green door. The gold and silver keys. That was enough to convince my senses that I could at least make a nest of it.

Still, it was not *home*. Never home. Just a place of my own.

"Yes," I said to Jamie Oldcourse. "Yes."

It is a word that evidently means much to humans. And to be honest, at that very moment, it meant much to me as well.

SO SHE LEFT ME THERE, with the two keys that must have had iron at the core, so I had to pop them immediately into the pocket of my skirt. She gave me as well a handful of paper that she called money, telling me to spend it carefully on what I needed; me who has always spent my magic freely and with great ease, and who rarely needed anything at all.

"There will be more later, but this will tide you over now," she said.

I clutched them tightly, which seemed to be the proper thing to do, for she smiled.

Then I listened as her footsteps went down the steps, and I heard the snick of the door open and then close. I thought about going to the window in the front room to watch her go along the numbered street, but instead I sat on a soft nesty chair and looked over the money in my hands. They were a strange green covered with writing and human likenesses and numbers I did not understand. I worried that they might be like fairy gold that one has to use quickly or it is gone.

What did I *need*? I already had a nest and water. I had clothing I did not like, but at least it disguised this sagging body. I was warm enough, high enough. And I was alone at last, to think, to feel, to plan. *And to mourn.* I missed the Greenwood, the meadows, the dances, the joy. I even missed Will of the Feather. But most of all I missed Meteora, my other self. I wanted to be angry with her, for it was her loose tongue that had brought me to this miserable fate. But I could not hold such anger against her. She was breath and blood to me, and I knew that in all likelihood, she too had not escaped the

Queen's rage. My silly, little sister, out in the wilds of the world. What would become of her?

Suddenly I recalled the last words the Queen had shouted:

Should Sister meet Sister in Light again,
Then falls the iron rain.

Was it meant as a spell? Or a curse designed to keep us forever apart? Tears welled in my eyes.

And as I was deep in these mournful maunderings, my stomach made a horrible sound. Of course, I did not recognize it at first. Under the Hill there is no hunger. When we want honey or mead or a sip of dew, a taste of berries, mushrooms—they are simply there. Wish and get. And in the hospital, regularly at times even I could recognize, I had been brought platters of things to eat. Of course in the hospital, it was not food I liked. Still, it was edible, and some of it had an almost pleasing sweetness, like the brown drink they called hot chocolate, though why it was called "hot" I do not know. It was tepid at best.

Nevertheless, here in my new place, my body kept protesting. I placed my hand atop my belly—a belly so pouchy and distended that I did not want to look at it without clothes on. Still, as I felt the sound under my hand, I suddenly knew it for what it was. I had heard animals and humans make that sound. No—not the angry sound, but that other one. A growl. It made me laugh.

Then another growl.

I must go out before the sun sets, I thought. *I must chance the steps, go down the noisy street, and find some human market. Use my money quickly before it disappears.*

I counted what I had. There were five pieces of the paper. The numbers on them were 20, 20, 20, 5, 5.

Glancing through the window, I saw that the leaves of the trees were barely trembling. The sky shone a brilliant blue. If there ever was a day that signaled success, this was it.

Wrapping the keys in some bone-white paper I found hanging in the smallest room—for I understood that without them I could not get back into my place again—I stuck the small packet of keys and the money papers into my pocket, nestled against my patch of silk. Then I kirtled my skirt above my knees, and went down the stairs.

The door snicked shut behind me. I turned to memorize it, a solid oak door painted green with a carving of vines. It had no name, but a number. Thirteen. Yes, full of magic. I would know it again.

Turning, I walked first to the tree. There was another dove sitting on a low branch: a male, quite fit. He cooed when he saw me.

"Keep watch, my man," I cooed back, "and there will be something for you."

He fluttered his wings, then stretched his neck, and turned his beady little black eyes toward the steps of my place.

"Fly well," he said.

I nodded, then walked down the street, turned a corner, and ran right into chaos.

10

Juan Flores Observes

The first time I see her, she comes down the street just as the police car blocks the avenue and the fire trucks drag out hoses like great gray anacondas. I note she is frightened.

She has a lovely face, like a Madonna, with sharp black eyes, though who has dressed her in those awful clothes I cannot guess. Perhaps she is one of the *locas* who stroll around here mumbling and stealing my apples.

This one, though, she walks as if she remembers being young and beautiful and cannot quite understand how she has gotten to the age she is, shoulders back but with her hands tight at her sides. However, there is wisdom in her eyes and I smile at her. Wisdom is so seldom found here in Nueva York, we must prize it when we can.

"*Buenos dias*," I say to her, because it truly is a good day, if one discounts the swirling light of the police car, and the shouts of the firemen as they set their ladders against the wall of the tenement across the street. With the sun out and shining down in the canyons of this great city one can believe, if only for a moment, that things are clean and bright here, which is a kind of *magico*.

She leans down and smells the *fruta* displayed on the front shelves. Not touching, not like the others, the *locas*, who just look around quickly to be sure no one is watching before grabbing. Or the bad boys who do it openly and lift the finger to me. But I watch her and think: *maravilloso!* How else to tell the age and the ripeness if one does not smell the *fruta*. Also I think, for a moment, that she must be from the old country, so I address her in Spanish. I say, *"Claro, Dona, ustedes conocer las frutas."* The minute she looks up, those blackberry eyes not quite in focus, I see she is no Latina but someone more exotic. I do not know exactly what. But I say quickly in English, "My pardon, lady, I have mistaken you. Call me Juan Flores. It means Flowers in the English tongue."

The smile she gives me is gracious and full. "Your fruit is fresh, sir, and I wish to have some."

Her accent is strange, and I cannot place it. "Have or buy?" I ask. I have lived here in this country long enough to be forward.

She puts a hand into some hidden pocket of her voluminous skirt and pulls out five bills and a set of keys wrapped in toilet paper. I am careful not to laugh.

"Buy, of course," she says. "One does not take without compensation. I would not be beholden to thee."

Her way of speaking is, somehow, *arcaico* and I like that, wherever she is from. I nod.

She chooses five Galas, ripe and beautiful, plus four Bosc—though these are still hard and not ready for eating.

"For later," she says.

"Keep them in the paper sack," I tell her, "and they will ripen more quickly." I wrap them for her and she smiles broadly. Her teeth are even and very white.

She takes also wheat bread—the new-baked kind I get fresh daily from the bakery, not what comes in plastic wrap—three kinds of cheese, a handful of dark green spinach, and pots of marjoram, rosemary, and thyme.

"I cannot live without these," she says. "Can you get others?"

I nod again. "What would you have?"

She closes her eyes, thinks for a bit, then says, "Lady Bug Bean, agrimony, bitter aloes, angelica ..." She smiles. "Especially the angelica."

"Wait, wait," I tell her, for none of those do I know. I take a pad of paper from my breast pocket and a nub of a pencil and have her say those things over again so I can write them down.

"And asafetida, barberry, bay leaf."

I hold up my hand. "Dona, I *have* bay leaf."

That smile again. It is so much younger than she.

"And basil."

"That, too." I go back inside the *bodega* and get both, and she hands me all her money as if she does not know its worth. The keys she replaces in her pocket. Carefully, I count out the change. When I touch her hand, it is soft as if she has never done a day's work. "The rest I shall find for you if I can."

She touches my hand back. "Blessings." And smiles once more, as if consciously trying to charm me. Which she does.

I start to pack everything in a brown paper bag, but she takes the bag from me and places everything carefully in it herself, speaking to each fruit and vegetable, each herb in some language I do not think I have ever heard, but it is sweet and full of watery sounds. I am thoroughly confused by her, but it is a pleasant confusion. I take the paper bag for a moment and fiddle with the top, hoping to keep her here longer.

"I need paper and something to write with," she says, "such as the little things in your hand. Do you have those, too? I do not see them in your . . ." She waves a hand.

"My *bodega*," I say. "My shop."

"Yes, shop, that is what Jamie Oldcourse calls it." She runs her tongue over her top lip. "But I like your word, *bodega*. It has the sound of water over stone. I *appreciate* it and will use it, Man of Flowers."

"Juan," I say. And then I tell her about the stationers, which is well away from the firemen and the police car; how she is to go straight back the way she came and then to the left at the light to find it. And without a word more she walks off.

I smile at her back, having made her a present of a star fruit that she will find when she opens the bag. Not to be *beholden* to me—what a lovely way to say it—but to remind her that there are friends here whatever terrible passage she has recently made, for I can tell she has not been here long.

As she heads off, I realize I am moved as I have not been since my Marianna died. It is a long time since I have been with a woman. Five years, twelve days.

I wonder if this dona lives in the neighborhood. I wonder if I could ever tell her that she is dressed like a bag woman who should have been wearing the clothes of a queen. With women in this country, I am never certain how they will take such words.

Perhaps my nephew will know. He knows more about *Americana* women than I will ever learn, though he knows nothing about *fruta* and nothing at all about putting customers at ease, or selling except to take the money and give the change.

11

Meteora Arrives in Town

The sun rose out of the lake's blue horizon and spilled its golden light across the humped rocks and sand. As we left the beach, I was wearing a voluminous garment, printed with a bright pattern of crimson roses and green fronds that Baba Yaga called a "house dress." I also wore white leather "walking shoes," and was most disappointed that they had nothing in common with seven-league boots, which magically transport the wearer long distances. It appeared I had to do the walking on my own.

Baba Yaga also gave me a large purse in which to carry my belongings that now amounted to several pairs of "panties" that gripped my loins in all manner of uncomfortable ways; two "bras" that dug into my padded flesh; three dresses of various patterns; and a huge maroon scarf, also printed with flowers in riotous colors and tied with a fringe. I learned about zippers—Baba Yaga's favorite convenience as they involved rows of miniature silver teeth that clenched tightly together. I hid my treasures wrapped in fairy silk in one such zippered pouch inside the purse.

Baba Yaga slung her leather bag over one shoulder. "Ready?"

"Yes, I think so," I answered, hoisting my large purse onto my shoulder.

"Good. Follow me then and pay attention. I will teach you some useful things about this world." Baba Yaga walked toward a road that followed the shore of the lake, her bowed legs moving with surprising rapidity. I had to hurry to catch up, tripping every now and then in the unaccustomed shoes.

We reached a tree-lined street that at that early hour was quiet. Arched branches of maple and elm swayed gently over the path providing a green shade. Set back from the path were rows of tightly packed houses, three stories high and most with steps that led up to broad porches. There was grass, though it was sparse and down-trodden, littered with cups, paper, and empty bottles. Occasionally, a few flowering shrubs festooned with torn paper huddled miserably against the flank of a house.

As Baba Yaga instructed me, the city around us gradually awoke. Shutters opened with a clatter, horns sounded, and workmen in orange-and-yellow vests shouted at each other across the road. Two men clung to the back of a huge green wagon reeking of spoiled food. It rumbled down the street, stopping every few paces where the men scrambled down to pick up another barrel of rotten goods to toss into the wagon's waiting maw.

"Cars, trucks, buses," Baba Yaga said, pointing out all manner of conveyances that had begun to crowd the streets. "No horses here. These go fast; they do not stop unless told by that red light. Don't get involved with them or you'll get hurt," she warned. "Stay always on the sidewalk," she added pointing to the paths we now walked. "Cross only when others do, that way you won't make mistake and get splattered."

"Splattered?"

"Tenderized." She grinned. It did not suit her. "Like tough meat."

I began to see why she liked it here.

AFTER A MORNING OF WANDERING through the city, I wondered if I could ever make sense of it, much less call it home. There was too much noise, too many people, and all of them so young they seemed to mock my new identity.

I asked Baba Yaga about it and she shrugged. "We are near a university—a place where these children pretend to learn. But really, they do very little that does not involve too much drink and too much sex."

"So why do you come here?" I asked.

She turned to me and I saw the fiery glint in her milk-blue eyes. "They no longer come into the woods. I must seek them out and give them a chance to *really* learn."

"And if they don't?"

She shrugged and waved her hand in the air. For a brief moment the blue-black nails gleamed. I thought of those nails in soft flesh and shuddered.

In the sunlight, I became keenly aware of all the youths now strolling in the streets. Some were seated at tables drinking and talking, while others lounged on benches or the grass, harmless as mayflies. Serana and I might have meddled, tricked, and addled our human playmates, but never had we ...

I shuddered again—*eaten* them.

"Bah!" Baba Yaga puffed, glancing down at me and reading the horror on my face. "I don't do *that* ... anymore. But I do like to fuck up their lives for a while," she sniffed. "At least until they learn a thing or two."

"*Fuck* ... up?"

"Yes," she answered. "A useful word in this place. Of course you already know it, but here, everyone says it for everything. It can even be a greeting. Watch this," she said and shoved her elbow hard into the shoulder of a slender young man walking toward us, books nestled in the crook of his arm.

"What the fuck!" he shouted as the books tumbled to the ground.

"Yes, fuck you," Baba Yaga said gaily.

"Fuck *you*, lady," he snapped. "What the fuck's your problem?"

"No fucking problem, really."

"Yeah, well fuck off then."

"See? Many uses," Baba Yaga said, pulling me away from the angry boy who was muttering *Stupid bitch* as he gathered up his books. "Shit is another useful word. Also very common. For example, pleasantly surprised? You say 'No shit?' You think someone tells you tales, you scoff, 'You're shitting me.' You find something you like very much, you exclaim, 'That's good shit!'" She looked down at me to see if I was following the language lesson, when in truth I was appalled. Not that we didn't have our own bawdy language, but it seemed somehow richer and more expressive. Here there was only *shit* and *fuck*. What had happened to *prick-louse* and *pig's spawn*? Or *clay-brained apple-john*? Or *canker-blossomed coxcomb*?

"Don't worry, you'll get it," Baba Yaga encouraged. "You will hear it often enough."

As if to demonstrate the truth of her words a girl in front of us stepped off the curb and into the street. A careening conveyance, horn blaring, would have struck her had she not jumped back in time. "Fucker!" she shouted at the open window. "Shithead."

Baba Yaga gave me a knowing nod as if to say, *I told you.*

On one street we passed a number of small shops selling trinkets and clothing all clustered around a much larger shop called "The Co-op." The cheery blue-and-orange-painted entrance was washed in morning sunlight. On either side of the front door were little wooden benches interspersed with huge pots of flowers, some spilling their blossoms gracefully over the sides.

"In here," Baba Yaga said, motioning with her head. "I need tobacco and papers."

Inside, the shop was cool and scented with lavender, sandalwood, and the tart fragrance of mustard leaves, kale, and spinach. Shopkeepers busied themselves, stacking and sorting fruit, straightening rows of bottles and jars, or just sweeping debris into dustpans near huge bins of rice, wheat, and oats. But despite its name, I saw no signs of fowl anywhere being offered for sale.

"Buy your food here," Baba Yaga said. "It's cheap."

"I have no human money," I replied.

"Shit," she grumbled. "You will need to work for paper money. What can you do?"

It was a difficult question, because I knew that no matter what I answered, it would be insufficient. I could dance, I could sing passably, I could weave spider's silk into shawls, and I was good at pranks. All these skills might have meant more here had I been youthful and beautiful. But I noticed as we walked through the city, that as elderly women we had become almost invisible. No one met our eyes, nor nodded in greeting, though more than once I entertained a glance at a handsome face.

"Think about it, while I get a few things," Baba Yaga advised. "Stay here, don't move." She hustled down an aisle, leaving me alone in the shop.

Glumly, I looked around, feeling foolish and gawky in my aged body. These children moved with purpose, slim and fresh as the produce they were arranging. I brightened, however, when I noticed a little counter lined with a collection of small potted herbs, all of which were familiar to me. Rising up behind the counter were shelves containing glass jars of dried and powdered herbs. A girl with fat rolls of fuzzy blond hair was dispensing bad advice on how to use pennyroyal tea to another pale young woman with short black hair and red lips.

"My pardon, goodwife," I interrupted, "but if she drinks that pennyroyal as you suggest, she will spend her days shitting and pissing blood." I was pleased that I had managed to work one of the new potent words in the conversation. She wouldn't really have had trouble with her bowels, but she would have bled dangerously from her loins, for even without magic, I could smell the yeast of pregnancy on her skin.

The blond girl gaped at me, pushing the wheat-colored rolls of hair back from her forehead. "For real?"

"Yes, for true." Turning to the pale girl who was now eyeing me coldly, I inquired for what condition was she seeking a cure?

"Cramps," she said, and pursed her ruby mouth in annoyance.

"Of course," I nodded, hearing the lie in her voice. "Try the peppermint or chamomile teas. Add a tincture of anise to calm the nerves. And maybe . . ." I looked at the shelves and began to pull down glass jars, mixing a brew for her right there in a little clear bag. Glancing again at the shelf of herbs I added "mother's ease," and "bone-strong" to the mix for her unborn child too in the hopes that she might reconsider her first option. "Maybe this will help."

The girl glared at me, but took the bag of tea and abruptly left without a word of thanks.

The guileless goodwife touched my arm and smiled. She was pretty in a simple way, a dusting of freckles across her creamy skin, and wide hazel eyes.

"Hey, thanks a lot," she said breathlessly. "I don't really know what the hell I'm doing. I just give them what they ask for most of the time. You know, they read about it on the Internet and then come here to try it out."

Internet, a word I squirreled away for later. "She asked for the pennyroyal?"

"Yeah, to regulate her periods, she said."

"It is to abort her child. But it would have made her deathly sick and done nothing to shift the child in her womb."

"Jeez," she said, grimacing. "I'm glad I didn't give it to her. That's nothing I would've wanted on me."

Baba Yaga reappeared at my side and tugged my sleeve. "We go now," she ordered.

"Bye," the girl called with a little wave of her hand. "Come back sometime okay? I could really use the help. My name's Julia. I work on Mondays, Tuesdays, and Wednesdays."

"As you wish," I replied with a quick nod of my head as I hurried to catch up with the Great Witch.

Once outside on the sidewalk again, Baba Yaga reached into her bag and handed me a peach. It was ripe and juicy, and I ate it slowly as we walked, savoring the velvety skin and the slick, sweet flesh. I thought about the Coop-without-chickens, and wondered if Julia might offer paper money in exchange for my knowledge of herbs. It was such simple lore to me, so simple I had not thought it a skill, but rather like breathing, which is effortless. Or *was* before I had been turned into this fat, old thing. I imagined I could do as well as any mortal goodwife, providing relief from grippes and nausea, headaches and healing bones, menses that came too often or too rare, maybe even to help the lovesick and forlorn. That little hen Julia was sweet and well intentioned, but she had no knowledge of plants. Perhaps I *could* be of use . . . and find a way to fill my empty pocket as well. I licked the juice from my fingers and felt a spark of encouragement.

It was short-lived, however, drowned in the deluge of Baba Yaga's instructions. "Do this," she would say, "don't do that." "Go here. Stay away from there." My head throbbed with so many rules, so many obligations and prohibitions, so many new expectations. How was I to remember all of this? Tears burned behind my eyes, but I blinked them away, not wanting to show any weakness that might cause Baba Yaga to withdraw her help.

12

——

Meteora's Home

It was dusk when Baba Yaga finally stopped in the middle of a block of houses. I was exhausted, my feet throbbing in the new shoes, blisters bubbling at my heels and toes. We had eaten a noon repast, an entire cooked chicken for Baba Yaga and a wedge of soft cheese and brown bread for me, purchased at a different grocery shop—this one brightly lit and humming with music from its walls. But now my stomach rumbled and gurgled.

"There is my home," Baba Yaga said, pointing a gnarled finger across the street to a squat, three-story house half hidden behind a pair of tall pines. Partway down the walkway, the flickering leaves of a silver birch shimmered, luminescent in the dimming light. The house walls were a deep red brick with gray shutters bordering every window. I shivered for it reminded me of a baker's oven.

"Where are the chicken legs?" I asked. I had heard enough tales about her traveling house to be curious.

"They are there, at the bottom of the stairs, though most would not think to look for them."

A light turned on in a small dormer window jutting out below the eaves of the roof. It was then I noticed the gutters; they ended in downspouts shaped like chicken heads, the open beaks ready to disgorge excess rain.

"Good." Baba Yaga nodded. "They are waiting," she said to the lit windows. Then she grinned at me and I drew back, uncertain as firelight bloomed in her eyes. "Listen," she commanded, "I am not done traveling, but you may stay here and mind my house while I am gone. You will live up there, on the top floor, where there is light in the window. Below you, children—students— rent the rooms."

"You are too generous, Mother of the Forest," I murmured, relieved that I might have shelter, even if for a little while.

"Nonsense," she scoffed. "You will work. Keep the children from breaking things. And see to my garden."

"Of course," I answered, wondering how difficult could that be?

Baba Yaga guffawed. "I read your thoughts, you know. Not so hard with a poppet like you. I tell you, these children are your trial. They do things that bring police— nosy, snoopy people who ask too many questions and want to see your papers—"

"Papers?"

"You don't have any. So you must be sharp as the axe and not let them succeed in throwing you in the oven."

"Agreed," I said, thinking how much easier it would be if only I could spell them into toads or dogs, anything small and manageable.

"And one thing more ..."

I waited, worry and hunger gnawing at my rumbling stomach.

"You will have help. There is a girl on the second floor. She collects the rents. And my personal servants will assist you, but only when they wish to, so remember your manners."

"Yes, Gracious Mother," I said humbly.

"Here is the key to the top floor. It is silver, so you may safely hold it. But do not lose."

"Gracious Mother, I am forever in your debt," I said meekly.

She clapped a heavy hand on my shoulder, her nails

digging a warning into my flesh. "Yes, you are. Remember—take care of my house and don't fuck up."

I CROSSED THE STREET ALONE, but only after Baba Yaga snapped at me to remember to look both ways, or else "be splattered." Although I was grateful for her help, I was still very afraid of her, and even more afraid of her house. It loomed dark and forbidding in the early twilight. Walking down the little stone path to the stairs, I tensed at the sight of a skull's head embedded in the dirt near the steps. *A cannibal's home*, I reminded myself. The bottom step rested on a pair of carved chicken feet and I could imagine that the back of the house had another door and steps resting on chicken feet just like it.

At the top of the stairs I paused, surveying the huge porch that had been hidden by the pines. Light from a first-floor bay window illuminated a collection of lumpy, stained furniture along with a few spindled chairs. Empty bottles, cups, and soiled paper plates cluttered the porch wall. A small brazier held the remains of charred meat and burned corncobs. I wrinkled my nose at the pungent odor of stale beer and rotting food.

Moving toward the main door, I was searching for the lock when the door was thrown open from inside, revealing a tall scantily clad girl, all arms and legs, standing in a dimly lit hallway. She was looking over her shoulder, shrieking at someone in the house. I stepped quickly out of her way and saw her tearstained face, red and white with rage. Music howled behind her in the hallway and I covered my ears at the sound.

"Fuck you, I'm leaving. I'm tired of cleaning up your shit, you stupid prick!" She turned, and bolted from the door without a look in my direction.

"Babe, wait, don't be like that." A young man followed, trying unsuccessfully to grab her by the arm.

She twisted away and continued down the porch steps, her long white legs scissoring into the night.

"Fuck," the man said despondently, and I added a new shade of meaning to the word.

"Aw, let her go, dude. She's a bitch," called another male voice from a doorway down the hall. "Fergit her. Come on, Nick, it's party time, man."

Nick leaned hard against the doorway, seeing me now for the first time. His boyish features hardened as he frowned. Barefooted, wearing only short pants, his soft pudgy body was like a little child's. His hair was clipped close to his head, and he ran his hand through the bristles until they stood up, slick and damp. He swayed unsteadily, his sweat reeking of hard spirits. He looked me up and down and sneered as the harsh music railed around us.

"Suppose you gonna call the police," he snapped at me.

I took my hands from my ears. "Not if you remember your manners," I said, wondering if I sounded anything like Baba Yaga, and then guessing I didn't because he kept on sneering.

"So—what are you doing here?" he challenged.

"I live here."

"No you don't. All the apartments in this house are rented already, so I know you don't live here."

The other man had come out to join Nick, and I was well aware that both men towered over me. The friend was broad in the chest and broader still across his belly. He was wearing a torn black shirt with the words How About a Nice Cup of Shut the Fuck Up? in white letters across the chest. Like Nick, he was drunk, and from the dull look in his eyes, stupid too.

"Third floor," I said, pointing a finger upward.

They both stepped back, chastened and studied their feet.

"Sorry, I thought you were, you know, gone for a year. That's what the rental agent told us," Nick mumbled.

"I'm back," I announced emboldened. If they didn't know who Baba Yaga was, then I could play the role of the Mistress. "And furthermore, clean up your *shit* out here immediately or *you* will not live here anymore." I stood as tall as I could manage and glared at them.

Their response was immediate. Deflated, they lumbered across the porch, one holding open a bag while the other dumped in garbage, bottles, and the rotten remains of their earlier meal. Watching them work, I reflected on how useful it was to be able to speak the local dialect.

I entered the hallway and walked up the stairs. A door cracked open on the second floor and I got a glimpse of improbable caterpillar green hair and the ghost of a face. *A girl,* I thought, *not wanting to get into a mix with the young men.* Before I could say anything, the door closed.

Just beyond the second floor, I cursed my aged body for its trembling muscles and the breath that would not come easily into my laboring lungs. But I kept going up and on the third-floor landing, I stood in front of an oak door, a brass skeletal hand as a knocker and a heavy lock shaped like a mouth with teeth beneath the doorknob. I inserted the key, my pulse fluttering. What would I find on the other side? *Chairs of bones, lamps of skulls, pillows stuffed with the hair of the dead?*

Standing on the threshold of Baba Yaga's home, I was suddenly relieved enough to break into the tears that I had denied myself during the long day.

Then the door creaked open and I peered in.

No bones, no scent of decay or rot. Instead, the rooms were very neat and cozy if a bit small. The whitewashed walls had been painted with scrolls and flowers over the windows and along the edge of the ceiling. The oak floors gave off the sweet scent of beeswax polish. In the sitting room was a rug of finely knotted wool in a beautiful pattern of imaginary flowers. Two embroidered chairs waited by a little potbellied fireplace. On a side table, covered in a linen cloth finely cross-stitched with red silk borders, a candle flickered in its silver holder.

What I took to be the cooking place was small, but functional. A maroon oven rubbed shoulders with wooden cupboards whose doors were carved with acorns and oak leaves. Scrubbed plates and cups sat waiting in a rack above a basin. A table and two chairs occupied a narrow space by another window. I peered out, but could see nothing in back of the house except a large expanse of land and other buildings huddled around it.

The bedroom was almost entirely filled with a sturdy wooden bed, piled high with feather quilts. The pillows were covered in fine linen cloth made of the same stuff as the sheets and decorated with cutwork embroidery. At the foot of the bed, I opened the lid on a fragrant chest smelling of cedar and found more clothes, shoes, woolens, and scarves. A window opened to a small wrought iron ledge and I could just make out narrow stairs leading down to the ground below.

Off of the bedroom was an even smaller room containing a white tub perched on clawed feet. There was also a basin like a chair filled with water, and a taller basin with brass handles and a spout. I may have lived my immortal life Under the Hill and in the Greenwood, but even I had heard about these little rooms from brownies who often visited human houses. I turned the brass handles of the tub and basin, delighted as water spurted out, some hot, some cold. As for the chair-basin, I toggled the handle, until it too whooshed, drained and then refilled. I guessed at its purpose, confirming my suspicions when I checked under the bed and found no *pot de chambre.*

I returned to the sitting room, kicked off the painful shoes and sat heavily in one of the generous chairs. Closing my eyes, I drifted into a light sleep, my body gratefully releasing the memories of my terrifying flight through the storming forest, the rattle of the dragon-train, and the terrible weight of all I had to learn in order to survive here.

A tap on my shoulder startled me and I lunged forward like a breached trout. A pair of hands—just hands and not matching either though they *were* right and left—floated in front of my astonished face, waiting for me to fully wake.

"Are you . . . are you Baba Yaga's servants?" I asked. Gracefully, the hands turned themselves over, palms up in a gesture of supplication. One hand raised a finger to signal "*Wait,*" and then both hands winked out of sight, only to reappear a moment later with a tray, on which were a steaming pot of Russian caravan tea, a mug, milk, sugar, and a plate of thick slices of buttered black rye bread. The hands settled the gift on the side table next to the candle and then beckoned me forth.

Remembering my manners, I whispered, "Thank you," and bowed my head before them. The left hand crossed over the right hand and they disappeared, leaving me to my evening meal. When I had finished eating, I dragged myself to the bedroom. But before I lay down, I tore a thin strip of my Dam's white silk and tied it to the railing outside the window for protection. It fluttered in the dark, soft as a feather.

LATER THAT NIGHT, LYING NAKED between Baba Yaga's linen sheets, I woke from an exhausted slumber to hear the boys of the first floor thumping like trolls, perhaps dancing to their loud raucous music. From the second floor, someone ran down the stairs, and pounded on the door, while a dog barked, agitated by the uproar. A girl shouted, "Shut the fuck up or I'll call the cops!" The noise subsided and the door must have been opened because I heard the angry voices of the boys protesting. But the girl was adamant in her threat, repeating it over and over, while the dog continued to bark. Finally, the door slammed, the music was silenced and I heard the girl's footsteps on the stairs. She shushed the dog, who obeyed at once, and the house grew still.

I was almost asleep again, when the plaintive cries of a cat outside the bedroom window woke me once more. Slipping from bed, I opened the window and a scrawny black cat with a white throat darted inside. After a quick glance my way with yellow eyes, it promptly made itself at home at the bottom of the bed.

Finally, all the chicks were tucked in, and the house settled like a hen at roost.

13

Sparrow's Tattoo

Sparrow groaned, folding the pillow around her aching head as sunlight poured into the window through the torn shade. Her temples throbbed and she could feel a wave of nausea in her complaining stomach. What had she tried this time? Tequila? It tasted like acid on her thick tongue. It hadn't worked of course. The old nightmares always found her no matter how deeply she tried to bury them in different spirits.

Angry with herself for having spent another useless night alone with a bottle, Sparrow threw back her covers and willed her body upright, swinging her feet over the side of the bed. For a brief—though vertiginous—moment she thought she was all right. And then her head exploded in pain and her stomach clenched. Bolting from the bed, a hand cupped over her mouth, she fled to the bathroom. She vomited as she threw her body toward the toilet, grasping the rim in both hands to steady herself against the involuntary heaving. She had eaten very little along with the tequila, and now it tasted like brewed poison searing her throat as she retched. She flushed the vomit away, washed her mouth with tap water, and waited for the next wave. It hit soon after, leaving her gasping for air and groaning.

"Wow, did you get fucked up," her roommate Marti announced, leaning against the bathroom door and holding a steaming cup of tea. She was tall and willowy, dressed in a faded cotton kimono with a pattern of blue maple leaves. A long braid of fine brown hair hung over her shoulder, while stray tendrils framed the sleepy face. "Even the dog decided to give you some room. She slept out on the couch." At Marti's feet sat Lily, a white and liver-spotted pit bull, panting through a wide, tooth-filled smile.

"I feel like death," Sparrow moaned, knowing it was close enough to be true. She reached out and gave Lily's velvety ears a quick rub.

"I can't imagine why," Marti said dryly. "You know, that was my expensive bottle of Patrón you dusted last night? Just tell me you didn't accomplish that all by yourself." She blew cooling air across the surface of her teacup before taking a small sip.

"I'm sorry," Sparrow said, suppressing a wave of nausea. "I'll replace it as soon as payday comes. I promise." She sat back, balancing her buttocks on her heels, one hand on the toilet while she wiped her mouth with the back of her other hand. "I guess I just didn't realize how much I was drinking."

Marti had put her teacup down on the rim of the bathtub and was running cold water over a washcloth. She squeezed out the extra water and handed it to Sparrow, who took it and laid it lightly over her face. The cool, damp cloth smelled fresh. "Thank you," she murmured from under the cloth.

"You want tea? Chamomile maybe? Settle your stomach," Marti said.

Sparrow smiled weakly. "Yeah, sounds good. Thanks." She lifted the washcloth to show Marti a grateful expression.

Alone again, Sparrow washed her face at the bathroom sink, swallowing mouthfuls of water and spitting it out to rid her tongue of the acrid taste. She ran the cold cloth across her neck and then straightened up to confront herself in the mirror.

Pretty bad. Sparrow took in the hollowed eyes, the

bright green irises flecked with dots of blood. The purple bruises under her eyes from sleepless nights contrasted sharply with her dyed neon-green hair. She thought she looked like a battered doll with plastic hair and a paint-smeared face. Her head throbbed with a headache and she closed her eyes over the welling tears. When was the last time she had truly slept free of nightmares? *Long ago,* she thought, *when I was lost among the deer in the forests.* But that world was gone. And she was here.

Sparrow opened her eyes, washed her face vigorously, and combed wet fingers through the short spikes of her green hair. Not for the first time she wondered what had possessed her to dye it such a garish color. Or why she had pierced her eyebrow, her nose, and ears.

Maybe to fit in, to find solace in a tribe of other like-marked men and women. Maybe to hide in a crowd.

Returning to her bedroom, she pulled off her nightshirt. She was thin, her clavicles rising sharply beneath the taut skin. Her small breasts bloomed above the corset of rib bones, while her waist arrowed into the soft curve of her hips. An old ragged scar marred the inside of one slender thigh. She searched quickly in a pile of mostly clean clothes and pulled out a red T-shirt she had picked up from a thrift store. Wriggling into a pair of tight, low-slung jeans, she grabbed a half-smoked pack of cigarettes and a lighter off her nightstand and padded to the kitchen in bare feet, hoping the tea was ready.

Sitting at the table, Marti was fussing over a teapot. Dry toast waited on a blue plate, next to a jar of dark honey. Lily slept in her usual spot under the table near Sparrow's chair.

"Just in time," Marti said, grabbing a mug from the counter behind her and placing it before Sparrow.

Sparrow filled her cup, squeezed out a liberal spoonful of honey, and started stirring it.

"Take," Marti ordered, handing Sparrow a couple of aspirin.

Sparrow obeyed, even though she knew it wasn't necessary. In an hour her body would be restored, healed of whatever damage she had inflicted on it the night before. She had learned that about herself when she was twelve. In one of his drunken rages, her father had stabbed a knife into her thigh, as though he thought he could pin her to the motel bed. She'd screamed and he'd reared back, horrified at the sudden rush of bright blood that spilled over her thigh and the cheap bedspread. Panicked, she'd pulled the knife free and—ignoring his hoarse cries—fled into the woods behind the motel. She'd wandered for hours through dense pines, until collapsing at last in a bank of ferns. Curling into a knot of pain, she'd pressed one hand against the pulsing wound in her thigh.

In her fitful sleep she'd heard them come, stepping quietly through the ferns: three deer—a buck and two doe. They lay down around her, the sheltering warmth of their bodies lulling her into a deep, irenic sleep. In the morning, only the tear in the fabric of her jeans and the pucker of a new scar remained.

"So are you doing all right?" Marti asked.

Sparrow blinked, aware that she had been silently stirring her tea much too long. Taking a sip, she smiled. "Yeah. I'm okay, really. Just got caught up in Saturday-night blues, I guess." She broke off a piece of the toast and handed it to Lily, who had awoken and was now sitting with her head on Sparrow's knee.

"You know a bunch of us are going to a late lunch at The Twisted Fork, around two. Why don't you join us?" Marti offered. "It's good to get out once in a while, you know. You've been living like a nun in this house."

Sparrow ducked her head and freed a cigarette from her pack. She put it between her lips and pulled a small tin ashtray closer to her. She was going to light it until she noticed the frown of disapproval on Marti's face. She put it down with a sigh and saw the clock, telling her she was late.

"Yeah, maybe I have, lately," Sparrow admitted. "I'll try and make it. And thanks for the tea too," she said in a rush. "I better hurry and get going." Sparrow reached under the table for her sneakers and put them on with a rough jerk. Lily stood up, her tail thumping in expectation of a walk. Sparrow grabbed the leash and clicked it onto Lily's collar. "I promise, I'll stop by after work," she added as Marti, teacup in hand, headed for her bedroom.

"Later, then," Marti called, with a wave of her hand.

Sparrow and Lily bounded down the stairs to the front door, Lily growling in the back of her throat when she passed the door to the downstairs apartment. "Assholes," Sparrow muttered. Had she threatened to call the cops on them last night? *At least they were as drunk as I was*, she thought. And maybe they wouldn't remember who had spoiled their fun. Their payback was always nasty.

Outside, smoking a cigarette and waiting for Lily to hurry up and pee, Sparrow kicked the plastic skull half buried in the dirt and made a note to herself to finally dig the creepy thing out when she had the time. But right now if she and the dog didn't hurry, Sparrow was going to be late for work.

"Come on Lily, yer done!" she shouted and jerked the dog back up the stairs. Pausing on the landing, Sparrow remembered seeing a woman standing outside her door late in the night. Had she imagined it? The face looked lost, childlike and old at the same time. Sparrow shook her head. It was a face out of her dreams, one from a lineup of foster parents perhaps, laced with half a bottle of tequila. Forget it, she told herself.

AN HOUR LATER SPARROW UNLOCKED the door to The Constant Reader Bookshop, and was greeted by the jangle of tattle bells hanging on the door. She inhaled the musty aroma of book dust, and turned the sign on the door from CLOSED to OPEN. It was Sunday, and she knew there would be few customers in the small shop, which suited her just fine. Throughout the morning she worked alone, straightening shelves, and boxing up books for return on Monday. The first customer, an elderly gentleman named Frank who came every Sunday to read the papers, didn't show up until midmorning, just as Sparrow was opening the new boxes of books and entering them into the computer. Sparrow smiled at the old man and left the counter to make sure the tea urns were filled with water. Frank liked his tea good and hot.

Sparrow worked through lunch and then, catching sight of the time on the store clock, made the decision to join Marti and her friends. *Why not*, she thought. *Just this once.* It had been a long time since she'd gone out. Sparrow called gently to the old man who was half dozing behind his paper in one of the store's big overstuffed chairs.

"Hey, Frank, I'm closing up early today."

"Yeah? Got something special to do?" Frank asked, carefully folding his paper and tucking it under his arm. He patted down a wayward strand of white hair over his pink scalp.

"Late lunch with some folks." Sparrow decided that maybe Marti was right. It was time to go out for once.

"Good. Pretty girl like you shouldn't hang around with old geezers like me." Frank touched his hair again as if flirting with her.

"Hey, I'm all yours next Sunday," Sparrow said, and laughed.

WHEN SPARROW ARRIVED, MARTI AND her friends were already sitting down at a table outside in the small patio. Sparrow recognized the square-chinned, dark-haired man next to Marti as her boyfriend Mitch, who was working on his degree in art. They made an attractive couple, she thought, fair and dark together. Three other women crowded together on one side of the table, dressed like parakeets in bright blues, yellows and greens. They were chatting loudly, breaking out in spontaneous laughter and hitting each other on the shoulders.

They were Marti's friends, that was clear from the way she leaned her body into the semicircle of laughing women. Opposite Marti was another woman. *A friend of Mitch's?* She was dressed in dark clothing, a book bag stuffed with sketch books, and wearing a bored expression as she observed Marti's chattering girlfriends. Her hair was shades of black and purple, her heavy lipstick startling on her pale face.

"You made it," Marti called out as Sparrow approached shyly. "Take a seat," and she gestured to a free chair next to the dark-haired woman.

Sparrow sat down, nodding to the woman as she glanced at Sparrow. Black-lined eyes followed the contours of Sparrow's face and then her body. Sparrow waited, uneasy under the silent scrutiny. Unexpectedly, the woman smiled at her, and reached out a hand to grab Sparrow by the wrist.

"You've got great skin," she said, stroking Sparrow's forearm. "It's so translucent. And pale. A perfect canvas."

"Thanks . . . I think," Sparrow said with a laugh. Unused to strangers touching her, she pulled her arm free of the woman's grasp to reach for a glass of water the waiter had brought her.

"Don't mind Jenna. She's got a thing for skin. Go on," Mitch urged, "show Sparrow."

Jenna took off her black sweater, revealing not only the sleeveless T-shirt underneath, but her arms covered in sleeves of finely drawn tattoos. "I met this guy, Hawk, and he's an amazing ink artist. The best I've ever seen. I couldn't resist getting the work done. He said I had perfect skin. Just like yours," she added with a smile.

"It's beautiful." Sparrow was transfixed by the intensity of the vivid artwork. Fanciful creatures, some with horns and fangs, wings and claws, furred and scaled, were entwined among scrolls of etched vines and leaves of fox grapes, mistletoe, nightshade. The vibrant colors pulsed, and when Jenna flexed her arm reaching for her glass,

Sparrow gasped, for it seemed as if a wolfish-looking creature opened wide his mouth to attack her.

"I am having more work done," Jenna said and Sparrow thought her eyes glittered feverishly, like lust or hunger. "You could come and watch if you like? Really it's very cool. And the place has a good vibe, almost like a temple."

"That's ridiculous," Marti said and Mitch frowned at her. Sparrow wondered if the couple was as matched as she thought they were. Clearly their friends had nothing in common.

"No, it's not," Jenna said archly. "Tattoo can be very sacred, you know. Not like bullshit you see frat boys getting. Hawk's tattoos have a way of making you feel reborn. It's a very spiritual experience."

Marti rolled her eyes and her parakeet girlfriends turned their heads, trying to hide their obvious amusement.

Leaning back in her chair, Sparrow listened as they argued the merits of tattooing, spiritual rebirth, and—later—who owed what on the bill. She was glad enough to be out in the sun, eating a salad, and sitting on the edge of someone else's conversations. It was enough to keep her engaged, but not involved. Just the way she liked it. Sooner or later, when people got to know her, they always asked about her past, her family—two subjects Sparrow didn't want to share.

As they stood to leave, Jenna turned to Sparrow and took her by the wrist again. "Come with me to Hawk's place," she urged. "You can check it out for yourself. And I'll bet you anything you wind up getting one of his tattoos."

Thinking of Lily waiting at home, Sparrow wanted to say no, but hesitated, feeling the heat of Jenna's hand on her wrist.

"Really," Jenna said. "It's awesome."

Something tugged at Sparrow, pulled her into Jenna's voice, into the intensity of Jenna's dark eyes. She found herself changing her mind, suddenly wanting to please Jenna. She would go, meet this Hawk, and see his work.

"Okay," she said. "Just for a little while. Then I got to get back."

"Cool." Jenna smiled warmly and linked her arm with Sparrow's. Sparrow felt the subtle tug again in her chest, and when Jenna began walking swiftly up the block, Sparrow didn't hesitate to follow.

14

Hawk

The girl beneath my needle moans and I brush my lips over her mouth, my perfumed exhalation returning her to a deep and empty sleep from which she will find no rest, only pain and sorrow. She has returned to me for a second time . . . as I knew she must. For each tattoo marks her as my chattel, my offering of blood, and binds her to me as a willing servant. Her head rolls to one side, sweat-slick hair drifting like a shadow over her cheeks. From lips red and curved as Puck's bow, she sighs. Smiling, I stroke her flesh, tease the nipples to hardness and when she sighs in pleasure, I clutch her breast, squeeze it hard.

"I shall prick you," I hum softly. "I shall stab you with a pin." And the girl groans, tries in her sleep to avoid the stinging tap, tap, tap of the needle but I hold her firm and she must take it, and give to me what I want. "I shall hold the basin, to let the blood flow in," I sing to her as I sing to all of them. When the little rivers of blood have collected into a crimson pool in the hollow of her throat, I apply a small glass pipe and draw the blood, releasing it to a silver reliquary I wear around my neck. Blood to pay the tithes. Blood to make the clans strong again.

I hear someone behind the curtain and my jaw tightens. None may disturb me at my work.

"Excuse me, Hawk, there's someone here to see you,"

whispers the woman I let run my shop. She is huge and ugly, unafraid of anything, except me.

"Who disturbs me?" I ask.

"A girl named Jenna. Says she has something for you."

Jenna, I think, recalling the arabesques of leaves that hide the snares I have laid over her body. She serves me, hungry for more, which I will gift her if she brings me others like herself with pure skin, smooth as canvas.

I kiss the girl on my table and she falls into a deeper sleep, unaware that she is weeping. Standing at the doorway to the waiting room, I glance over Jenna's head and see the girl sitting, palms pressed together, shoved between her knees. She looks awkward, as though she might bolt at any minute.

But her skin gleams, white like a sliver of moonlight in the softly lit room. Her chins lifts, her head turning slightly to the side to gaze at a painting on the wall and I can see the arch of her neck. It is slender, graceful like the swan, though the girl is unaware of its beauty. And I can feel the design twitch at my fingertips, the mark that I will leave on that perfect neck.

15

Sparrow's Tattoo

"Let me make you beautiful," he said and Sparrow blushed. Hawk was handsome, smooth pale skin and white blond hair pulled back in a ponytail that was bound with a silver clasp. His voice was low, melodious, and seductive. "A small one here on that gorgeous neck of yours." He placed his fingers against her skin, and her pulse had quickened.

"Will it hurt?"

"I won't let it," he answered smoothly, helping her lie down on the table.

Sparrow was surprised at how quickly she'd arrived at this moment: alone in Hawk's studio, stretched out on his table. She'd merely meant to visit, or just watch as Jenna had a new piece to her own tattoo touched up with more color. But Hawk had come into the room, and a short time later, he was kissing Jenna good-bye and leading Sparrow into his studio.

"Something pretty," Jenna had called out to her before closing the door.

She and Hawk had talked about her skin, Hawk had stroked her arm, and Sparrow found herself agreeing to a small tattoo. She wasn't sure she was the "pretty" tattoo kind but she didn't tell him that. There had to be trust. He'd said that. She trusted him.

He sat next to her and leaned down close to her face.

"Don't be afraid," he said and as she inhaled the sweetness of his breath, she felt herself become relaxed and sleepy. Almost like being hypnotized. Or drugged. She felt his hand warm on her throat, stretching the skin where he would begin the design. She stared up at the smooth arch of his brows, the almond-shaped eyes of malachite green, and waited for him to begin.

He was beautiful, but he lied.

It had hurt a lot, stinging like hundreds of wasps injecting fiery venom into her neck. Yet, each time Sparrow gasped, clenching her fists against the pain, his eyes met hers, and the pain subsided in his cool forest gaze. Had she slept? She wasn't sure, but something dark skittered like an insect across her vision. She felt it enter her blood, felt her veins contract. Her heart pounded violently and she groaned, trying to waken. But each time she surfaced, Hawk was there, murmuring into her face, stroking her cheek. When he was finished, he oiled the tattoo with a thin layer of Vaseline and taped a bandage over it. As he sat her up on the table, she felt the fear subside.

"Can I see it?"

"Later," he said. "When the swelling goes down and it's not so raw. I promise you it's just what you wanted."

His green eyes sparkled beneath the cool lights. He touched her shoulder, slid his hand down her arm and held her wrist for a moment.

By the time Sparrow was on the street walking home, she could hardly recall the pain of the needle, only the longing sensation of wanting to return to Hawk's side. She clasped her hand over the bandage to keep it secret, needing to hold on to the intimacy of the event.

MARTI WAS OUT WHEN SPARROW arrived home and she was grateful that she didn't have to explain just yet about the tattoo. She took Lily on an urgently needed walk around the block and then fed her.

Sparrow thought about eating something herself, but

nothing in the fridge seemed appetizing. Instead, she grabbed a handful of crackers, washing them down with a glass of milk that hinted of turning sour. She poured the remains of the milk down the sink, suddenly tired, as if she'd been awake for a month.

Twilight had settled into darkness, and though it was still early in the evening, Sparrow undressed, climbing into bed with a book. Though she was exhausted, she couldn't sleep, but instead read feverishly and without pleasure, turning the pages of her book rapidly. She thought she could still taste the sour milk, her mouth flooded with a bitter gall despite smoking cigarette after cigarette to rid it of the unpleasant taste. As she turned a page, she burned her leg with a careless flick of hot ash. Rushing to the bathroom for water to cool her skin, she banged her head along the bedroom doorjamb. In the bathroom she administered cold compresses to her leg, then checked her temple in the mirror and saw the reddish bruise welling up. She tossed back two aspirins in hopes they would soothe the headache that was sure to follow and returned to her bed.

Late that night, the moon a dagger in her window, Sparrow sat up on the edge of her bed and shivered violently, her arms clutched tightly around her shoulders. She was weeping uncontrollably, stifling her sobs so as not to disturb Marti and Mitch who had come home late and were sleeping in the next room. She had awoken from a string of nightmares, each one more brutal than the last. They'd never been this bad before—the searing flashes of beasts chasing her, fangs tearing at her throat, her breasts, while she ran and fell and ran again with infinite slowness, blood everywhere, slick and stinking. She moaned, and clamped a hand over her neck where pain, real pain, throbbed and itched like a burn.

Her legs trembled as she walked to her dresser and fished out a small mirror from the top drawer. Standing in a rectangle of blue moonlight shining in her window, she held the mirror up and removed the bandage taped to her neck. She burst into fresh tears seeing the circular knot of a gnarled sprig inked into the skin, still glistening with oil.

She lay back down on the bed, trembling, dazed. And a new string of howling nightmares began, one following another on its heels, giving her scarcely a moment to wake between them. She managed to rouse herself finally, and sitting up in the bed, her eyes full of the vision of blood and terror, she was plunged by memory into the life she had left behind with her father: the constant beatings, the rages, the verbal abuse, and then finally, the attempted rape in the motel.

You are shit. You are worthless. You'll never be like her. It's your fault she left. Please baby, I need you. Be her for me . . .

In the dark, Sparrow gagged on the tormenting weight of the past. There had to be a way out of its powerful grip, but she couldn't think what. There was only the abyss and the lashing sting of the tattoo on her neck.

16

Serana's Doves

On my return to Number 13, I was careful to avoid the chaos of before, walking round and about widdershins till I found the right number and the green door. I crossed and recrossed the streets many times for fear of someone stepping on my shadow or speaking my name aloud. I did not know if the humans in this great village had any magic—and none actually knew my name—but better to be safe than buried. This was not the Greenwood where I could touch elderflower if my nose began to drizzle or chew on a rosemary sprig if I feared my new lover might smell my morning breath and leave me for another. This was a new world of strange stone-and-iron buildings where folk spoke casual curses and did not honor the old gods. Who knew what they might do given the chance, or the push. I do not want to die here, so far from the green that nourishes me.

Yet, for all the peril of these strange streets, I did delight in finding the place the Man of Flowers sent me to, with its windows filled with pretty papers and writing tools. I stepped inside and smiled, relieved for a moment of my fears. Oh, the colors there, like a pied meadow. I finally chose papers that had names of growing things: lavender, marigold, madder, apricot, violet, straw, and a blue the shade of a robin's egg. I also purchased a pen with no iron in it that wrote with ink the color of an otter's wet coat.

WHEN I GOT BACK TO my nest, safe at last, the rooms seemed airier than before, and then I noticed I'd left the windows wide open. Probably not a good idea, with chaos about and me without the protection of my magic, but there was a serenity here that made me think no UnSeelie thing had gotten in.

I put the papers and pen on the table next to the bed. However, it took me longer to decide where to keep the food. The cold locker seemed right for some of the fruit and the green leaves. But as for the herbs, I spread them about the windowsills, some to find the sun, and some the shade, where their homey magicks could do the most good. Across the windowsill, closest to the dove's tree, I spread crumbles of bread as well.

Then I moved the downy mattress into the front room and lay down on it to rest, my rosy silk patch clutched in my hand. Walking so much on the hard human roads in this aging, aching body had left me more tired than I realized.

WAKING, I FOUND THAT MY old feathered friend from the tree was the first to find my offering of bread crumbs. I got up carefully, tiptoeing to the window where I watched him eat his fill. Afterward, I put my hands around his stout body, pinning his wings, but gently. I did not want to fright him, only get his attention. Most bird brains are not made for long thinking, though some have deep, almost fey thoughts.

"I need you to find my sister," I said to him. "I do not know if she is in the Greenwood or out in the world, if she is in this village or another. She is a fey of uncommon beauty, with eyes that are berry black and a nose that uptilts. I will tell you her secret name." I whispered it to him; not Meteora's true name of course, but her Name of Finding.

He cooed his acceptance, and gave me his name in return, Coo-coo-rico, which means Old Man of the Small Tree.

"Well, Coo-coo-rico, you will have many miles to go before you can rest again in your small tree." Then I opened my hands, and he was gone.

I tried this with three more doves, two female and another male, who was smaller than the first, being no more than a yearling. They were called Fly By, Leaf By Linden, and Puff Boy. By the time I was done, the bread was all gone.

I had no idea how long the search would take them. If Meteora was safe and in the Greenwood, they would find her with ease. But what if she had to hide, having seen what the Queen had done to me? Or worse, what if she had been stripped of her own magicks and banished somewhere, too? This last did not bear thinking of. I forced myself to shut the thought away.

Doves, I told myself, *think upon the doves*. I knew they were strong fliers. They can always find their way home. I had their names. And they were entirely loyal. More I could not do. The only problem was that they were often prey of greater birds, and if Meteora was far from here, there might be hawks or merlins or shrikes to contend with. That's why I sent out four of them. I did not like putting them into danger, but they were all that I had, now that magic had been taken from me. And having fed at my hands, they and their small natures were mine to command. I could only hope that at least one of them was stalwart enough to find my sister.

To ease my mind, I sat down and made packets of thyme to carry in the seams of my clothes to keep me healthy and to help me make money. Though I was healthy enough for this new age, no more money had come to me while I was out, and I had only copper coins left, change from the scrip that Jamie Oldcourse had given me. I did not know when I would see her again. Or indeed, if I wanted to.

I left the other herbs in their pots or in pieces on the windowsill: basil for the peaceful home, bay leaf against jinxes, marjoram to drive off those who would harm me and mine, rosemary for protection against evil and to give me dominance in my home.

I thought about speaking again to the Man of Flowers. I would do it because of the Law of Friendship and because he had given me a gift of a strange fruit with a star at its center. I knew not how he managed to sneak it into my paper sack. But now I was beholden to him.

Also, I wanted to say to him, "If I tell fortunes, and make predictions, can I be given money for this?" I knew that the Rom, the traveling folk who have small magicks, often do such a thing. They are the nearest of human folk to the fey. Telling fortunes and making predictions was a magic that did not depend on what had been stripped from me. I could still read tea leaves, palms, the pattern in a swirl of hair, the lines of a face. All such readings are accurate to a degree as long as the reader has some small part of fey blood.

Suddenly, I remembered how Meteora and I had teased the locals who came with gifts to our faerie market, telling them outrageous lies, the exact opposite of what we read on their hands, on their faces. But if I told fortunes properly here, perhaps I could make enough until Meteora and I could figure out how to get home again without suffering the iron rain.

If the Queen would let us back in.

Always, it came down to the Queen. I knew that. Meteora did, too. But oh, how I wished it were not true.

17

Meteora and the Dove

When I woke the following morning, I was confused by the greening light spilling across the tousled sheets. It wasn't until I rose, lips parted expectantly, that I realized I was not at home in the forest. An ancient ash tree sheltered the bedroom window and the morning sun was filtering through its lush canopy. Though comforted by its presence, I rose weary at heart to be so reminded of my loss.

Opening the window, I had my first glimpse of the back of Baba Yaga's house. There were few signs of a garden, which should have been in full bloom at the height of summer. Instead, there was only a patch of choked wildflowers, their small blossoms almost color-less in the dry, rough soil. There was more garbage here, too: broken chairs and rain-soaked boxes that must have lain out for most of the summer. The only bright color came from winking shards of broken glass—brown and green bottles from the looks of them.

I shut the window and began to worry about my debt to Baba Yaga. Had she known the state of her garden? I had certainly never labored before, and the task now seemed daunting. Yet, I wanted to be brave. I wanted to learn how to survive here. I wanted to find my sister again. I wanted to flourish in spite of the Queen's punish-ment. I wanted . . . *to eat*, I realized as my stomach rumbled its own wants.

Throwing on the housedress, I went into the kitchen, sat at the table, and waited. And waited. And waited.

"Hands?" I asked. "Are you there? Please," I said in my most polite voice, "if you may, could I have some victuals? Tea would be nice. Bread too."

There was no answer. And only then did I recall that Baba Yaga had said her servants could choose to help me or not. It was becoming clear that I had not yet earned the right to that help. Last night, I was a traveler, a guest of the great witch, come in from the night. But today, I was a servant like them, here at Baba Yaga's discretion. By their silence, I understood that I was expected to perform my own tasks.

Determined, I went to the stove, noting the small rings of iron, and beneath a tiny blue flame. Fortunately, the handles were white porcelain, so I experimented, turning them this way and that. At first they hissed, and then popped into a brilliant fire. I quickly learned that turning them one way brought the flame higher, the other way dampened it to almost nothing.

At the sink, I marveled that water could travel so far from its source to arrive in my little basin. I filled the kettle, set it on its ring, and turned up the flame.

The cupboards were easier. I found the tea, a brown teapot and a little silver tea strainer. There were also jars of beans, sugar, bay leaves, honey, a tin of paprika, and kernels of polished rice. When the kettle sang, I spooned tea into the pot, followed by the boiling water. A second search of the cold cupboard offered up a little milk, most of a loaf of bread, a stick of butter wrapped in white paper, a few wizened carrots, half a cabbage, and two beets. Another drawer revealed sharp knives, cutlery with antler bone handles, a butter knife carved from olive wood, and serving spoons of black-and-gold lacquer. It was a treasure trove and I marveled at how cunningly everything was put away and memorized it.

I cut the bread, buttered it thickly, and poured steaming tea into a cup into which I had also poured the last of the milk and a generous amount of honey. My preparations finished, I brought my meal to the table and sat down again.

For a moment, I was pleased. This indeed was the first meal I had ever made for myself, except for picking berries or finding mushrooms in a hidden dell. But unexpectedly, as I sat in the silence of the little kitchen, steam from my cup gently drifting away, I started to cry. It was also the first time I had ever eaten a meal alone. No longer hungry, I pushed the plate away, cradled my head in my arms on the table, and wept inconsolably. What did it matter if I had survived my crossing over? What did it matter that I had found shelter and food? What did any of it matter without my sister?

"Serana, Serana, where are you?" I cried into my hands.

A tap at my shoulder made me sit up, shuddering with the effort of my sobs. A hand—the male one I am sure from the few dark hairs on the knuckles—handed me a linen hanky. The second hand—female from its pearl-colored fingernails—stroked my hair. The storm in my breast subsided, and in between hiccups, I wiped my eyes with the proffered hanky and finally, stood and washed my face at the little sink. Then I sat again and took sips of the fortifying tea. When I was done, I looked at the hands that were now waiting, palms downturned on the table.

"Thank you for your consolation," I said and the female hand turned her palm up to accept my gratitude. "I need to go out," I continued, "and I need your help." An idea had come to me as I was splashing cold water over my face. "I need to work and to be in this world among people—even those not of my kind. So I must return to a shop Baba Yaga took me to. The Co-op. Do you know it?"

The hands waved excitedly—which I took to mean "yes." It is difficult to tell with hands.

"Can you show me the way? I believe I can find work there . . . as a goodwife dispensing simples, salves, and tinctures."

The male hand opened a drawer and produced a

piece of heavy cream-colored paper, while its feminine partner found a pen. She wrote the name: "Co-op" and drew a map for me, naming the streets and placing a little star over Baba Yaga's house.

"Thank you," I said, folding the paper and placing it in my bag. I retired to the bedroom to wrestle myself into my matron's attire. Exploring the chest at the end of the bed, I found a pretty blue silk scarf that I tied around my throat. I combed my graying hair and twisted it into a knot at the nape of my neck. Surprisingly, Baba Yaga had a silver comb set with seed pearls and I borrowed it to keep my hair from tumbling free.

I returned to the sitting room and snatched up the key from its hook by the kitchen door. The hands were still waiting on the table and I stopped, hearing something in their stillness.

"Is there something I can bring you?" I asked, wondering what hands could possibly need.

The female hand flew to the drawer and retrieved another piece of paper. She wrote a single word and then handed the pen to her partner and he wrote something as well. Then almost shyly, they handed it to me and I read "flowers" and "cigarettes."

"Of course. I shall bring them back for you," I said, grateful to have found a way to honor my debt. Though I wondered what "cigarettes" might mean. I hoped it wasn't too large to carry.

Standing at the edge of the walkway to the house, I studied the map and tried to orient myself in the correct direction. I turned the paper around and around until I was sure I knew which way it was leading me. As I began walking, I heard a sniggering, then a shushing sound. I looked about, and then down when I heard another burst of giggles near my feet. There was only a stray clump of spindled grass rising between the cracks of the path. I bent over and patted the grass, wondering if I had found a patch of stray-away-sod on this city street.

"Did you lose something?" someone behind me asked.

I glanced up and saw two stripling girls, hair pulled up on the top of their head into swinging tails like ponies. From their pink cheeks, I was certain they were biting their lips in an effort not to laugh. It only then occurred to me, that in bending over, perhaps I displayed too much of what was underneath my dress. Apparently, there was no shrift for aged flesh here at all.

"Ah no, not really, I thought I saw something . . ." I let my words fade away as the pair was anxious to get past me before breaking out into more stifled laughter.

And this is what I learned that first day: that unless one makes a spectacle of oneself—such as muttering aloud useless spells of finding when one has gone astray despite a map—women of a certain age do not exist. No one saluted me, and I quickly learned not to offer such a gesture, for it was met with a stony stare, or even worse a subtle movement away from me as though I were no more than a moonstruck fool. Much later, when my feet had grown tired from wandering in circles on streets named for trees that were no longer there, I finally saw the blue and orange walls of the Co-op. Only then did I wonder: *What can I say to make them "see" me first, in order for them to then want me?*

Before crossing the street, I kneeled down in a patch of clover-rich grass growing by the road and plucked a small handful of the bright leaves and shaggy-headed purple blossoms. This too was another one of those spectacle moments. I heard as I gathered my posy the snide comments of youngsters on their way to their own follies. I no longer cared. I chose to cling to any hint of magic, any hope of charms still available to me that might secure my fortunes here. Tucking the little posy in the folds between my breasts, I hurried to the door of the Co-op.

"HEY, HI! HEY HERB-LADY, REMEMBER me?" a voice called out.

Turning to the benches, I saw Julia, the sweet, gormless

maid from the day before. She had gathered the thick rolls of her wheaten hair into a bright turquoise scarf that intensified the blue of her eyes.

"Good day, Miss Julia," I answered, nodding to show that I had remembered her. In fact, I had been hoping to find her here. "I have come to offer my help, if you will have it."

"Cool," she said, folding up a book and tucking it into her purse. "Come on back and I'll introduce you to the boss, Raul. We might have to talk him into it a little, but I think he'll dig it. Oh, and what's your name?" she said with a little laugh. "Might help when I introduce you."

I winced remembering how easily these children gave away their power with their names. I stuttered for a moment, to hide my unease with such a request and then thought of one.

"Sophia," I answered, invoking one of the goddesses of wisdom to help me now. What other questions had I not thought about?

"I love that name," she smiled. "So . . . um, where are you from?"

"Russia," I answered, thinking of Baba Yaga.

"Oh, that explains your accent. I was wondering about that yesterday."

Accent? How was I to know my speech was anything but common enough?

"Have you been here long?"

Questions, more questions . . . must these children know everything about one? "I have arrived recently," I added, for that was true enough.

"Wow, your English is like really good!" she said, impressed at what appeared to be yet another skill of mine. Of course I didn't tell her my Russian was terrible. I knew the word babushka and that was all.

I followed Julia into the store, noting the way her freckles splashed across her narrow shoulders, like a fawn. She was slim as a reed, the thin fabric of her shirt clinging to her body. *I was like that once*, I thought with a stab of envy. *Once! I was like that only days ago.*

Despite my situation, I will say that I was born beneath the luck star, for it didn't take Julia long to convince Raul that I was a worthy addition to the Co-op. Julia explained how I had been helpful the day before. She invented a few tales about me, embellishing the extent of my skills. I did not interrupt her because mostly what she said about me and herbs was true. Every sprite and fey, every Seelie and UnSeelie, knows these things. We learned them in the same moment we learned to walk, to fly, to swim, to speak spells. Not one day of my long life had passed without reaching for succor from Nature's prodigious larder. Yet, I was touched that Julia had such blind confidence in a stranger that she was willing to stand up for me.

Perhaps it was Julia's buttermilk face that made the bargain so sweet, for Raul seemed to study her intently as she spoke. And at the end of her urging, I was allowed a post behind the herb counter as Julia's assistant, and I was to be paid, as Julia said softly, "under the table," which seemed a rather mysterious process.

"Thank you," I answered, bowing my head, relieved. I was quite humbled by their decision and wondered if in the past I had ever extended such generosity to a mortal.

I SPENT THE REMAINDER OF the day following Julia around the store. Together we inventoried most of the herbs, correcting the names where necessary and throwing out those that had lain too long in jars to hold any healing worth. A few interested customers came to our counter and I made simple cures for coughs and running noses—which seem abundant among these children—and one tincture for a woman plagued with screaming megrims, though she called it "stress."

When Julia was ready to leave, she opened her money box and handed me a fistful of paper bills. There was no table to pass these things under, and I was relieved. After she explained that my labor entitled me to a lower price for goods in the shop, she went with me to help pick out cheese, bread, a few eggs, fruit from the cooler that was fresh, and a glass jar of milk. At the last moment I remembered the requests from the hands.

"Flowers and cigarettes," I said, "for friends. And something for a cat."

Julia helped me select a pretty bunch of flowers and after, I was surprised when she handed me a small colorful box. I sniffed it curiously, and recognized the pungent odor of tobacco from my time with Baba Yaga. Then Julia handed me little "cans" of meat for the cat. All I had to do was pull the magic ring on top to open it.

IT WAS WELL THAT I remembered Baba Yaga's servants. For no sooner had I arrived home than I heard a wild commotion on the balcony outside my bedroom window. The cat was there, a dove in its jaws, while the poor creature flailed its wings, crying out my Name of Finding.

Only one person besides me knows that name. I dropped my bag and ran to the window, opening it as quickly as I could. The little strip of white silk on the handle fluttered like the dove in the cat's mouth.

"Do not harm it," I commanded, but the cat regarded me with baleful eyes and snarled a warning from the back of its mouth. "I will feed you something else, but you must give me the bird," I tried again, hearing the dove call my name over and over.

Slowly, the cat released the quaking dove from its jaws, but held it down under one paw, the talons digging beneath the ruffled feathers.

I reached into the bag and grabbed one of the little cans with the magical opening rings. I pulled it and the scent of meat made the cat lift its scrawny black head. I set the opened can down on the balcony and the cat released its grip on the dove. Scooping up the terrified creature, I noticed with satisfaction that Baba Yaga's cat had buried her head in the can and was eating like a panther.

"Poor thing, poor thing," I cooed, wrapping the dove

in my blue silk scarf. I mixed some water and honey together in a glass, and then drizzled it into his opened beak from the end of a tiny silver salt spoon. There were spots of blood on his wing, and two of his tail feathers had been torn out. But though he panted, I thought his injuries not serious. Only fear could kill him now. So I sat in one of the big chairs, and held him on my lap while I sang a lulling song to infuse his body with a sense of peace and security.

Serana is alive, Serana is alive, I thought as I continued to pour out my healing song. And I willed the dove to live that he might return to her with a message from me.

IT WAS ONLY AFTER THE quarter moon had risen that I felt the dove stirring in my hands. I fed him once more, and he called me again by my Finding Name.

Sister, I cried from the sheer joy of knowing that you are in the world somewhere with me and that this, our messenger, will return to you from me.

Opening the window, I plucked a new green frond from the ancient ash, thanking it for the gift. After stripping the leaves from the stem, I tied the supple stalk into a secret knot and tucked it high on the dove's leg as a message. I offered the dove a chance to sleep safely under my eaves, but now roused, he seemed in a hurry to complete his journey as much as to be away from the devil cat. I opened the window and watched him lift high into the sky on white wings, until he became a speck of moonlight.

It was then I remembered the other goods in my bag. I quickly opened it, fearing the state of the flowers, but was delighted to discover that Julia had thoughtfully wrapped them in wet paper and they were as fresh now as when I had left the store. I filled a glass and placed in it the small bouquet of stately blue iris for friendship and sunbursts of zinnias for goodness. I set the box of cigarettes down beside the flowers.

As I put the milk, the eggs, cheese and fruit into the cold storage, I noticed a bottle of clear spirits in the back. Thinking Baba Yaga would not mind, I pulled it out and poured out a small dram in a little crystal glass from one of the cupboards. I swallowed it quickly, in one gulp. My lips burned as I inhaled the pungent flavor, and the soothing finish warmed my throat so parched from singing to the dove.

Only then did I stumble to bed, feeling relief at knowing my sister's messenger had searched and found me, thanks to the little flag of silk on my window.

I dreamed that night that I was flying over fields of ripening wheat and corn, across sparkling rivers and softly pleated mountain ranges, returning to Serana to tell her the news, "I am here, Sister, I am here."

18

Serana Receives a Message

When the doves left, I went down to the Man of Flowers' shop and bought milk. Imagine! It comes in a cold package, not still steaming from the cow. And I bought as well honey, and two loaves of bread with the last of my coins. Once I was home, I did not go outside again for fear of missing the doves. Keeping the front window open for them, I sat by the window in the single soft chair and watched the sky.

The sky. How different it looked from the window of a house than that which peeks through the green woods. Different from the great swath of sky that hangs over the meadows. This sky seemed squeezed between tall buildings, fitted and cut down and seamed together like one of the Queen's formal dresses. It was neither a comfortable nor comforting sky, being an unhappy human color as gray as the buildings.

By the third day, I had eaten through the green leaves and the fruit and had but one cheese left, plus a full container of cold milk that I sweetened with the honey. I kept the loaves untouched, in case the birds returned.

The two females came back that night but with no news, the young male—Puff Boy—on the fifth day. He was severely dehydrated and I gave him water from my mouth, spitting it into his beak in little drips until he was able to drink on his own. At least the water from the taps was inexhaustible, though my food was not. But this dove likewise had nothing to report. I fed the three of them one of the loaves, crumbling it on the sill and they were grateful for my offering.

Old Man of the Tree had not returned in seven days, and I was at a loss. With no more money, I could buy nothing. I had maybe a single day of cheese and honey left, plus a tiny bit of milk only slightly soured. And water, of course. But seven days—I was in despair.

The local birds came and went in those seven days, hoping for bread. A small gray mouseling played around my feet. None of them had much conversation. If only Jamie Oldcourse had appeared, she would have been company of a sort, though wishing did not make it so. I had no more power with wishes than I had with the greater magicks. I even hoped that the wheat-colored flower man might come. But then, he did not know where I was staying. And besides those two, what humans did I really know in this great village?

I was about to lie down on my bed and weep, cursing this place, my condition, the Queen, when there was a fluttering at the sill. My heart fluttered in answer. Turning, I saw the old dove, and ran to help him in. He had lost some tail feathers and it was this that had made him so late in returning.

"Tell me. Coo-coo-rico," I said, in a soft voice, "have you found my sister?"

"She lives far away," he cooed back.

Could I believe him? Seven days away from here? Well, three-and-a-half there and three-and-a-half back. Crows are notorious liars, but doves have not the imagination for it. Still . . .

"She sends you this token." His voice was low and throbbing and he lifted his right leg.

How had I not seen it at once! On his foot, shoved up onto the leg, was a twisted stem from an ash leaf, in the knot that Meteora and I used for a code, meaning *It is I; all is well.*

"Oh, you lovely, lovely bird," I whispered and held him tight.

"Can't . . . breathe," he said, and I let him go.

"When you have taken a day to rest, and a day to fatten up on my crumbs, I will have a note for thee to take back to her."

He nodded in that way that doves have, bobbing his head so vigorously that his breast moved up and down. It is often amusing, and many times Meteora and I had imitated the movement, laughing. But now my laughter was pure joy. He had found her! He had found Meteora!

"Is she well? Is she safe? Is she happy?"

He shook himself all over. "She is fat," he cooed.

For a moment, I thought he meant she was beautiful. Doves like their females plump. But even before my head told me that was not what he meant, my heart knew. Meteora had been changed even as I had.

"And old?" I whispered.

His head went up and down.

I did not weep in front of him. That would come later.

"Pray tell your sisters and brothers, too, where she lives, so that if aught happens to thee . . ."

He nodded again. Doves have little fear of death for it is always their close companion.

Then I brought him the first of the second loaf, crumbling it into tiny pieces, and soaking half in milk and honey. All the while I was thinking: *Oh Meteora, dear sister, only friend, soon enough we shall be together again* before I remembered the curse of the iron rain. But I would chance that, truly I would, to be with her again.

COO-COO-RICO CAME BACK TO ME refreshed the next day, and I wrapped a tiny letter to Meteora in half of the rosy silk patch, tying it to his leg with a basil knot. If I had had any magic left, I would have used a word of binding. As it was, I had to trust my fingers, no longer as agile as they once were but surely as competent as Meteora's had been with the ash leaf. She would know the silk at once. And then she would come to me if she could. I had not told her of the iron rain. I could not think why. And then I knew: I did not have the courage to go to her, nor could I without the help of Jamie Oldcourse. Or—perhaps the Man of Flowers would give me aid if I asked. It was such a potheration. I would leave it up to Meteora. Because curses work only on those who hear them. She would be safe. I would not. But I did not care what would happen to me, only that I see my sister again.

My dearest Meteora,
    The view from my city window is but of a few spindly trees sending out fervent prayers for a bountiful summer that never quite comes. The pigeons crowd my windowsill hoping for a blessing of crumbs.
    My messenger tells me that you—as I—have been stripped of youth, thrown into a middle passage with its attendant agonies. Do you have any glamour or magic left? I have none. Yet in my head I'm more powerful than ever, understanding life as never before. Were we always old but living as if young? Did others laugh at us behind their hands? Magic and image have the same parent, you know. Were we fools in our own Eden? Is no one in the Greenwood still lovely and full of gaiety? Except perhaps for the Queen?
    Always except for the Queen.
    Who knew that bitch would go on forever?
    My fondest wishes (oh, that I could really grant them still).

        Your old and fat but still loving sister,
        Serana

*PostScript: Where are you? I am at Number 13 in a
large village called New York. How large, I do not
yet know. I will not go back to the Greenwood
without you. Write soon. Write soon. Write soon.*

I PATTED THE DOVE'S HEAD and gave what blessings I
could still manage. Small comfort where once I could
have covered him with fairy armor against beak and talons. And claws—for he had cooed to me of his near
death from Meteora's cat. She has a house among flour-
ishing trees and a cat! How astonishing that my little
sister, who has never fended for herself in any way, has
managed such a thing! *Perhaps*, I thought, *she is more in
tune with this world than I will ever be.*

And then the dove was off, flying past the spindly tree,
past the line of gray buildings, past the corner light now
green, before banking upward into the blue sky. I
watched as long as I could, but even after he had flown
out of sight, I kept watching as if there were actually
something to see but a trick of the light that looked—
now here, now there—like the beating of wings.

19

The Queen Scratches a Name

You are in the forest that is not your own, and you know from the rough, ridged bark of the ash trees that once were smooth saplings that much time has passed here in your absence. You had not wanted to come, it is too painful to recall. But they watch you all the time, beneath the Hill and in the Greenwood, pairs of eyes gleaming with hatred and mistrust. Highborn fey whisper in angry knots at court. Even your waiting women strip the gossamer sheets of your bedchambers as though to find hidden secrets. Once you discovered a bananach's feather teeming with lice left behind in your wardrobe. You ignore these signs, your solitary coldness mistaken for arrogance. It is all you have to make them cautious of challenging you.

You have come here on this dying day of summer to be alone, at least for a little while before they sense your absence beneath the Hill. They will not follow you here for they think it a place of no consequence, of too much sun, too close to the stink of mortal kind. They hear the sounds of the builder's hammer and they shudder, knowing it will mean the loss of more faerie land.

You have come out of an unexpected tenderness and shame. You stand in the greening shadow of the ash trees and see the lawn of wildflowers and choking grass leading up to the wall that was not there before. You can hear the man, shouting, grunting like a gored animal, but you do not need words to understand the anguish and rage that feeds such madness. This was your doing, you remind yourself, but it could be no other way. You touch the old scar beneath your breast, the small circle of ruched skin reminding you that all three of you paid the price, though none was asked. Such is the call of power that it levels all to its demands.

The shouting has stopped and suddenly he is there, standing on the edge of the wild, forsaken lawn. He raises his head, shaggy with unkempt hair, his once fair skin mottled brown and black like old leather left to wither in the sun and rain. You are still, unmoving, though your eyes gaze keenly at the man, taking in every line of his face, the eyes black and bloodshot, the lips dry and cracked. He inhales deeply, his wolfish head swinging slowly from side to side as though scenting prey. For one moment his eyes seem to rest on you, and you see the moment of shocked surprise, before his eyes roll back into white spheres of madness again. He falls to his knees and with outstretched arms, lifts his head, howling.

And in the small triangle of skin at the base of his throat, that skin that once you warmed with your kiss, you throw your silver blade. Your aim is true as always and the point plunges deep, strangling his howls. He falls and you watch him, horror and misery mingled with the confidence of your action.

You step from the edge of the woods and enter the fallow field, wildflowers brushing your ankles as you let yourself turn back to that first moment. Blood weeps beneath your breast, the old wound torn open anew. Slowly, you approach him and he watches you, the fury in his black eyes dulling like river-washed stones abandoned on the shore. He gurgles, hiccups as the blood pools around the stem of silver. But he does not struggle, for he believes again. You lean down to him and your honey-colored hair brushes his face. He thinks you mean to kiss him farewell, and almost imperceptibly he lifts his chin amid the pain of dying to receive it.

But you will not kiss him, for you know too much about his madness. Instead you free your blade from his throat and watch him die, quickly now as the blood spurts furiously, washing his neck and shoulders crimson. You wipe your blade on his filthy shirt for not one drop of his blood must enter the Greenwood lest they should know of it.

Later, in a cool spring, you will purify yourself, pouring the cold, clean water over and over your flesh until all traces of his animal scent and the blood of your wound reopened and now sealed again have disappeared. But one last gesture you cannot resist. On a small bayberry leaf dangling close to the edge of the spring you have scratched your child's true name with your fingernail in lines so small, not even a spriggan could read it between the green veins. And you wonder as you do so whether you have made a mistake after all.

20

The Dog Boy Marks His Territory

My time comes each month when the moon is up and I can find my way into the Greenwood again. The healing green. Too many days, too many nights, I must live in the gray place. My father sends me into exile there. His magic keeps me there. Except for the full moon when I must return. To the Greenwood. To his hand.

My father. I piss on his name.

This last time in the Greenwood, I came upon a field by accident, only in the green there are no accidents. There was a smudge in the air that I could see but could not see through, as if someone worked hard to disguise being there. So I waited. I am good at waiting when the moon is high. Not so good other times.

When the smudge had gone—like a cloud drifting away from the moon's face—I walked the perimeter of the field carefully. Sniffing around, I found my way past the flowers that masked the smell. How long had he lain there, his death creeping out of his throat through the dark slit? The body was not yet disturbed, the blood still running. And my nose confirmed what my eyes told me. Not long. Not long at all.

This, too, was no accident. But not, I think, my father's doing. His smell—that dark, dangerous tang, like the death cap mushroom—was not here. Yet this man did not die alone. I smelled another blood, sharper, still living. I smelled a heady mix of perfumes too, compounded of crocus for foresight, heather for solitude, and the strong, sharp rhododendron that signifies "beware." I will know that scent should I ever meet it again. I followed it on the wind, and found more on a leaf of a nearby tree.

Something written. Something hidden. Who would — who *could* — do such a deed? It had the look, the smell of a fey thing. I trembled, on point, like a hound.

Taking the leaf in my hand, I shook it loose from its brown and bendy twig. For a moment I held it in my palm and then it started to die as if I had brought autumn with my touch. The tips turned inward, the color began to fade, the sides became brittle. What had been written was now scrawled into my skin. A name. Passerinia. I crumbled the dead leaf and dropped the bits at the tree's base. And then, I pissed on it, marking it as my own. No one, not even my father, would see what had been written there now.

But I did not howl. In the Greenwood I never howl lest *he* hear me.

21

Sparrow Under the Influence

Standing outside the tattoo parlor, Sparrow hesitated before she went in. She studied the artwork in the window, intricate Celtic knots and the sort of tangled designs of animals and nature one saw on the pages of illuminated manuscripts. There was nothing in those designs that suggested the maliciousness of the knotted sprig now inscribed on her neck. Self-consciously, Sparrow placed her hand over the tattoo and felt the dark lines throb beneath her palm.

She had healed in three days, which struck her as a long time, considering her nature. But at least the tenderness was gone, and the oily redness of the fresh tattoo had finally faded. Yet the last three nights she had been awoken by a stampede of continuous nightmares only to discover the tattoo oozing drops of blood on her sheets and pillows. Still, in the morning, the raw wound would heal as soon as sunlight crept through the windows.

What have I done to myself? she wondered. *What has he done to me?*

Angrily, she thrust her hand away from her neck and shouldered her way into the tattoo shop.

"Can I help you?" A red-haired woman at the counter looked up from her magazine. She was big and full figured, and her strapless top barely concealed the prominent tattoo across her chest—a black-horned Japanese *oni* with fierce red-rimmed eyes glaring above the edge of the fabric.

"Yeah," Sparrow said, shifting uneasily. "I need to talk to Hawk."

"Get in line." The woman shrugged toward a row of seats, most of which were occupied by women.

Sparrow glanced at them over her shoulder, noting they all had the same harried look, the same anxious pale face she saw when she stared at herself in the mirror.

"I'm not here for a tattoo," she said, turning back to the red-haired woman.

"I don't care why you're here. You'll have to wait." The woman returned to reading her magazine.

Anger drummed in Sparrow's veins and she resisted the urge to grab the magazine and strike her. But she knew the woman was only a gatekeeper demon designed to shuffle victims quietly into their seats. *You don't have to take this*, Sparrow told herself. She clenched her hands into fists and rested them on the pages of the woman's magazine.

The red-haired woman looked up, annoyed, and Sparrow knew by her appraising stare that such defiance didn't happen very often with Hawk's clients.

"Get him, or I swear I'll—"

"You'll what?" a low voice interrupted.

The red-haired woman straightened up, her expression apologetic as she gazed over Sparrow's shoulder. Behind her, Sparrow heard the soft, murmured sighs of the women waiting in their chairs.

Sparrow turned to face Hawk, grateful for the distance between them. It allowed her not to feel so intimidated . . . *Or seduced*, she thought, her resolve weakening in the sudden warmth of his gaze. That's it, she realized. That's how he does it. She set one hand on the desk, its firmness allowing her to resist the subtle pressure to move closer to him. From there she studied him, trying to discern his true nature beneath the handsome face.

He was wearing a tight, sleeveless black shirt tucked

into a pair of old jeans that showed off his muscular arms and lean waist. His sand-blond hair was pulled back into its ponytail, revealing the delicate shape of his jaw and high curve of his cheekbones.

It was hard to see past the glamour of beauty he wore, but from her distance, Sparrow understood two things about him: his own skin was pure of any tattoos, and, although he smiled at her, his eyes were cold, the obsidian pupils sharp as knives in the green iris. His smile faded beneath her appraising gaze and his fingers curled into fists at his side. But his voice was still inviting.

"Why don't you come back to my office," he said.

"No." Sparrow's instincts alerted her to an unnamed danger. It was the only thing she had to thank the nightmares for—the foreboding, the sense of being hunted. The tattoo on her neck prickled and burned, as though her body fought to reject it.

"Then what can I do for you?" The soothing voice was growing edged.

"The question is what did you do *to* me?"

He laughed, slowly stroking one hand up the length of his bare arm, and Sparrow's heart skipped at the memory of those agile fingers, stroking her neck.

"I only gave you what you asked for," he said. "Don't you like it?"

"No. It's . . . ugly," she said.

"Let me fix it for you," he offered. "No charge. What do you want, roses?"

Sparrow's heart was pounding now. The pull toward him was a commanding current. She struggled to resist, digging her heels into the ground, gripping the desk's edge more firmly, and biting her cheek. A burst of pain followed, then the taste of blood. She closed her eyes to clear away the vision of Hawk, opening them again quickly, as she felt him suddenly near.

"Who are you?" he whispered sharply and reached out a hand to grab her.

Sparrow twisted away, shouting, "Don't touch me, you freak."

The parlor erupted into a brawl as the red-haired woman lunged across the desk to strike at Sparrow. Sparrow ducked, grabbed a ceramic jar of pens and pencils, and threw it at her. Hawk stepped back, getting out of the way as the other women rose out of their chairs, and physically shoved Sparrow out of the shop's door and onto the sidewalk.

"Fuck you," Sparrow shouted back at them. "Fuck all of you. You deserve whatever he's doing to you, you stupid bitches."

The door to the tattoo parlor slammed in her face, leaving Sparrow panting with rage outside, surrounded by a group of curious onlookers.

"Get out of my way," she growled, elbowing her way through the crowd. She drove her body down the city streets, trying desperately to get as far from the tattoo shop as she could. The bright sunlight glancing off the shop windows and cars hurt her eyes and she had to squint against the piercing pain. After three blocks, she ducked into a delivery alley and vomited. She waited there, a hand braced against the wall until the spasms stopped and she could breathe again. *Why did I go to his shop?* she wondered. *What did I hope to gain?*

Wiping her mouth with the back of her hand, Sparrow stumbled out of the alley again, and slowly made her way home.

BY THE TIME SHE'D REACHED the house, she was shaking with fever. Tears poured down her face as she turned the key in her front door. The apartment was empty as Marti had gone to work. *Like I should,* Sparrow thought.

But she just needed to rest a while first. She'd call in sick before her shift at the bookstore. Lurching down the hallway to her bedroom, she threw herself down on the unmade bed, and piled the coverlets over her shivering body, clutching pillows tightly around her head to try to ease the pounding headache. Lily jumped onto the bed and tried to lick her face but Sparrow pushed her away.

Undaunted, Lily stationed herself at the bottom of the bed, her head lifting with a worried glance every time Sparrow turned over with a groan.

It's much worse than a hangover, she thought. It was like withdrawal from a powerful drug. There was nothing to do but ride it out. Ride it out and hope for the best.

LATE IN THE AFTERNOON, SPARROW woke to find herself coiled on the floor, mouth parched from the heat of the fever, eyes burning as though scrubbed with sand. She was shaking with chills, every muscle in her back and legs contracted and screaming with pain. She swallowed four aspirins but they did nothing to ease the agony.

"I can't take this anymore," she croaked, and wrestled her body to a sitting position. "Think girl, *think*." Closing her eyes, she tried to imagine what might offer relief that didn't involve killing herself. And then she remembered Marti's wisdom teeth surgery. Marti had prided herself on using plain aspirin, hoarding the Vicodin the doctor had handed her for a future "just in case" moment.

"Well, it's just-in-case time," Sparrow said aloud.

Staggering into Marti's bedroom, Sparrow ransacked the closet, pulled open drawers, but found only clothes. She peeked into the little baskets beside Marti's bed. There were condoms, hair ornaments, vials of body oil. But finally, in Marti's jewelry box, Sparrow found an envelope and when she opened it, almost cried seeing the long white pills. She quickly swallowed two without water, and stuffing the envelope into her jeans, returned to her own room.

As the opiate coursed through her veins, the pain in her muscles gradually subsided. She uncurled her legs and stretched out, relieved at last. For a quiet half an hour, she thought she was through the worst of it. Until she started to cry.

She couldn't stop herself; the sobs rose in her chest, issuing forth like the cries of a wounded animal. *What's happening to me?* she thought. She was very afraid, but she had no idea of what. Exhausted, she still forced herself to get up and start pacing with staggering footsteps around the room.

Lily whoofled her concern once, then just watched from the foot of the bed.

Sparrow didn't want misery and grief, she wanted the razor-sharp edge of rage. But the sorrow wouldn't leave her. *What to do? What to do?* As she paced for a third time around her room, she suddenly understood what her body had already known: she had to walk off the nameless sorrow that threatened to drown her. And she must cry it out until there was nothing left of it. Only then would she figure out what had been done to her. And only then could she make Hawk pay for poisoning her. Pay deeply. Pay endlessly. Pay well.

22

Meteora Learns About Mail

I watched in the mornings and then again in the evenings for signs of Serana's dove. I fretted knowing only too well how dangerous life on the wing for a simple dove can be. I fed Baba Yaga's cat whenever I could and now it was beholden to me not to harm the creature when it returned.

Before going out, I left a small scattering of seeds and dried berries on the bedroom balcony, hoping to glean more information from the pigeons and doves that gathered there to feed. I was aghast when returning from the Co-op to find bloodied feathers and a discarded pair of pigeon feet on the walkway. Looking up, I discovered a sharp-shinned hawk watching my balcony from a nearby roof. I could not in faith deny the beautiful creature her sustenance, but I didn't want to encourage her to find her victuals on my balcony either. So I stopped leaving seeds, and just watched.

I forced myself from the house in the late mornings, going to the Co-op to assist Julia in her little herbal shop. She turned out to be a good student. I had to show her only once how to combine herbs into a tea and she remembered. She had a good sense of smell, too, and with practice learned to recognize the potency of herbs from their scent. Small farmers who brought produce to the Co-op now brought us living plants and took away our lists of others we required: red root and yarrow, white sage and arnica, wild ginseng root and cinquefoil. In only a few days Julia gained confidence with her new knowledge and I was able to use the paper money to purchase fruit, cheese, bread, occasional packets of cigarettes for the hands—and food for the cat.

I, too, became a student, though Julia was unaware of how much I was learning from her. The Co-op was a sleepy place. Especially in the late afternoon. Then only a handful of ragtag children ever seemed to wander in to buy a few items, occasionally coming by the herb store to utter small exclamations of surprise before moving on.

"Wait 'til school starts up again, then this place will be insane," Julia warned, carefully drawing a spire of Hag's Taper on a card announcing one of our new remedies. "It's still summer so most of them are home. A couple of weeks from now, the neighborhood will be jumping. Hope you live on a quiet street," she said, looking up at me and smiling. "It can get pretty loud around here on Friday and Saturday nights."

"Oh, my place is very quiet," I assured her, though not with much confidence. The inhabitants of Baba Yaga's house continued to battle over the troll music the boys insisted on playing. I did nothing to stop it myself. Indeed, I could not turn them into puff balls and scatter their annoying dust to the wind. I could only hope that they would soon leave, migrating like noisy rooks to some other place. And recently one of the girls in the floor below me had cried at night with sobs that caused me to turn in my sleep.

"Lucky you! I'm surrounded by three houses filled with jackasses. Two nights ago a bunch of us called the cops because they kept setting off firecrackers in the middle of the night right into the frigging street! I thought they were going to set the trees on fire."

Of course! That's why Baba Yaga enjoyed her house, deep in a forest of badly behaving children. What punishing lessons had she already meted out? I wondered with a little shudder.

"Hey, can you hand me the envelopes and stamps

from that drawer?" Julia asked, looking up from her drawing. "I want to mail this out to my sister Annie. She works at a medical clinic, but I think she'll dig it, even though she's all about straight medicine."

I looked in the drawer and found the envelopes, though I could not find wax or stamp. "There is no stamp here," I said, rifling through the papers.

"Oh, here, they are," she said, pulling out a sheet with little squares, each holding a picture of a bell and the word "forever" inscribed on it. She peeled one off, put it on the envelope—and it stuck there! She placed her decorated card inside and carefully wrote on the front of the envelope.

"What are you writing?" I asked, curious. This seemed a useful way to send messages.

"Her address at the clinic, of course." Her blue eyes twinkled with amusement. "Sometimes I wonder about you . . ."

"Address?"

"Name, street number and name, city and zip."

"Ah," I answered as though I understood. *Best she not become suspicious.* I watched as she placed it in a basket where—it appeared—other envelopes were headed for their intended readers. All of them carried the little picture of the bell, which I suddenly realized was what Julia called a "stamp." And studying the writing, I realized that these "addresses" were the locations of the future readers.

Quickly, I memorized the requirements: a name, a number, a street, a city, two letters that indicated perhaps a province or a shire, and then a series of numbers for which I could find no explanation at all.

"Yeah, I know, it's old school," she said, and I realized she thought I had been teasing her with my questions. "I could have just e-mailed her, but you know, I still think it's fun to get letters in the mail, don't you?"

"Absolutely," I answered, thinking of Serana, and a letter somewhere perilously traveling on the wing. *E-mail, another word to learn.*

While I worked, I constantly checked the basket, waiting to see what would happen to its contents. I was watering a little pot of marjoram when a man in blue came to the counter, took the basket of envelopes and emptied it into a bag on his shoulder. I was startled and then pleased to see the design of an eagle on the bag and thought it a much stronger and more reliable carrier than a dove.

I WALKED HOME SLOWLY THAT night, realizing that there were more children beginning to gather on porches and in front gardens. They were burdened with boxes, mattresses, desks, and lumpy chairs. They were moving in, wearing down a path in the trampled grass as they lumbered from their huge vehicles to the houses. Around me the streets buzzed like a spilled hive, their excitement palpable in the rising noise of their arrival. From opened windows music poured forth, some which made my steps lighter, others which hurt my ears.

But I also noticed that joining the students in the activities were the glamoured forms of more sinister folk. *UnSeelie folk.* Fall was approaching and the crisp nights, the faint hint of decay in the leaves gave power to the Love-stalkers and Bloody-Bones who pretended to languish in the disguise of drunken young men engaged in seemingly harmless banter with clutches of doe-eyed girls. Beneath the hem of a long green dress I saw the goat hooves of a Glaistig, her beautiful human arms wrapped around an unsuspecting boy, demanding he dance with her there on the street. I averted my eyes from his adoring look, as he happily embraced his coming death. Though I saw them, my eyes still keen despite the loss of my own magic power, they saw in me only an old woman, stumbling, and weak. I could do nothing for those mortal souls ensnared by the darker clans. That was the way of it. Night and winter were coming, and only the Queen could protect mortals if she chose. *And she didn't choose*, I thought angrily, scandalized by the very public and flagrant hunting of the UnSeelie host, a full two moons before the change of seasons. They had no rights yet to these streets though they seemed to claim them without consequence.

And I, who had never even given much thought to humans before, much less worried about their being hunted either early or late, mused upon it all. Did being old change me? Or had I—by becoming old—become mortal as well, which changed my attitude toward the humans? I wanted to ask Serana. She understood these sorts of things as I did not. I would send her mail as soon as I heard from her again and could get an address. I hoped she would understand about addresses.

SHAKEN BY WHAT I HAD seen, I then discovered a party of boisterous louts spreading out over the steps and porch of Baba Yaga's house. Music was hammering the air, shaking the glass windows and driving every living creature from the trees. I confess, I immediately forgot my concern for human children and in my anger would have at that moment gladly sent them all to their ruin amid the UnSeelie host.

"Grow claws," I admonished myself. "Be Baba Yaga."

I approached them, frowning and squinting my eyes in what I hoped was a look of menacing disapproval. They stared back, bleary and stupid like stunned bulls. Clearly they considered me in the wrong place and any moment would disappear and leave them to their swill. A girl came out of the house, screeching in high-pitched laughter, saw me, and stopped instantly. She went inside the house again, which I took to be a sign I had won some battle until she returned with Nick and Alex, looking irritated, their faces flushed with spirits and bad humor.

"The music stops now," I said, going up the steps.

"It's not late," Alex complained. "We don't have to turn it down until after ten o'clock."

"The music stops now," I repeated, "or you will be removed."

"Yeah, fuck that," Nick said. "We signed a lease for a year and you can't just kick us out."

"Are you sure about that?" I said, raising my voice over a pounding drum and angry troll chant. I was bluffing of course. I had no idea what could or could not happen here.

"Hey, buddy," a man called from the shadows. "Turn it down or I'll call the cops and stand here while they ticket you for noise and underage drinking." He stepped forward into an oval of light cast from the porch light. He was gray-haired with a grizzled beard, but still straight and strong in limb. He held his arms ready at his sides, his legs planted as though he were prepared for trouble. He carried a small hammer in one fist, and a much used chisel in the other.

The boys on the stairs stood awkwardly, their legs as unsteady as those of newborn colts. "Shit, I'm outta here, dude," they muttered and sauntered down the path, edging away from the gray-haired man. He continued to watch Nick and Alex, whose angry sneers and furtive glances at each other betrayed their uncertainty.

"Fuck," Alex muttered as he turned abruptly and stomped into the house. In midhowl, the music stopped and a deep abiding silence filled the street.

I turned to thank my rescuer, but he had already returned to the shadows, though I could have sworn I caught the faintest whistle of a familiar tune, a reel to which my sister and I once danced until the tall grass of a moon-swept field was well and truly trampled. And then I heard the soft sounds of cooing above in the ancient ash and rushed inside as fast as my stump-muscled legs would allow.

LATER, SITTING BESIDE AN OPEN window, the dove resting in my lap, I read Serana's letter by candlelight over and over. Though it was short, the dove had labored to carry it over great distances. I touched the words, sensing in the thrum of each letter her hand on the quill. I held the paper to my nose and inhaled the scent of a foreign city, dusty and oily, mingled with Serana's distinctive musk of pressed roses and sweet rue. I cried to know that she shared my fate, stripped of magic and locked into a hag-bound body.

I realized that when first I saw the dove, I had hoped for better news. I wanted Serana to save me. I wanted my older sister, the farsighted one, to have saved herself and to come rescue me. But it was not to be.

I pondered our misery, our exile, our loss. I was not like Serana, a poet full of sharp words that pierced any veil. My words were long, rambling, fumbling ... the need to reveal themselves at greater length. No dove could carry all my words to her. It must be the eagle. So setting the dove down in a box of linen towels, along with a bit of bread crumbs and a bowl of water, I slipped from my rooms and headed down the stairs.

I walked down the street to where I knew a sign was planted beneath a burning light. "Farewell," it said. So— Baba Yaga's house resided on a street with a name that mocked my loneliness. So be it. I returned to the house, now settled in the thick dark shadows of the pines, and on the porch searched for numbers. On two black boxes I saw two sets of numbers. On a hunch, I reached into one of the boxes and pulled out an envelope. I smiled, seeing the same "forever" stamp, and the address of my own house, clearly printed beneath the name "Occu-pant." I decided that I was an occupant as much as any-one, so I put the letter in my pocket and went upstairs again.

On the second-floor landing I heard again the sound of a girl crying—mournful, heart-wrenching weeping; a despair so intense it held me like a spell. It was the voice I had been hearing the last few nights. I wanted to knock, to call out, to do anything to make that pitiful wailing cease. I raised my fist, then stopped. I had a letter to write. I had my sister to think of. Indeed, I had my own deep misery to deal with. So I merely continued up the stairs to my rooms.

On a tiny piece of paper and in the tiniest of letters, I wrote to Serana, trying desperately not to drown my poor messenger with the weight of my thoughts.

In the morning I fed the dove, tied the rolled message to one leg, and sent him on his way. And then the waiting began again. But this time I waited in hope, not despair.

23

Meteora Sends a Lesson

Dearest Sister,

I shall tell you of my living situation only if you promise not to feel any more sorry for me than I do for myself.

After She banished us—so close to the Solstice and the dark times—I found shelter in the attic rooms of an old building owned by Baba Yaga herself. How I met her is a tale for another letter. My first days here have been quiet but alas, the streets now erupt with students returned like rooks to a cliff and my head aches from the constant din. Were we ever that noisy? I mutter the old spells that no longer have meaning, thump around the house, and wonder how I could have become so powerless. At least Baba Yaga has her iron teeth.

As to the Queen, she has kept her power close and does not drizzle it away. And who knew that the threads of power that surrounded us, cradled us, held us firm, could become unknotted, leaving us as weakened as we are now? As pretty seedlings we squandered our power, giving it to any who pleased us, never thinking for a moment we might be emptied of it like an upturned basket of seed.

There is so much I want to tell you, but this little dove of yours has not the strength to carry away many pages. So let me tell you how they send long letters here. For a few coins you can purchase a little seal—called for some reason a "stamp"—with a picture of a bell with the word "forever" on it. Stick this seal on an envelope after putting your letter inside and write the following in three lines I shall include at the bottom of my letter. No doubt you see the humor in my new name, Sophia Underhill.

Now, you must write your Mortal Name, the number, street, city, state, and code of your abode on the back of the envelope. Find a letter that surely will be in a little box by your door. It will have all the information you need. There are big blue boxes on the street with eagles painted on them, put your letter to me there and a man dressed in blue with an eagle sigil on his breast will take it from the box and bring it to me. Better an eagle than a dove, don't you agree?

There's a girl that weeps every night in the rooms below. I have decided I shall go down there to see what has so ailed her. I may not be able to give her something to alleviate her sorrow, but I can still make tea and offer a comfortable shoulder. And perhaps find my own comfort in your absence.

> *She who cries every night for you,*
> *M now called Sophia*

24

Serana and Paperwork

The minute the dove took off, I thought to go exploring. It would be a few days before he could possibly return with a letter for me from Meteora. Besides, I had a new plan. If I had to remain stuck here in this place so sogged with humanity, I knew I had to learn its twists and turns. Also, the day was pearly and I was desperate to be outside. I missed being where there was grass underfoot. *Surely*, I thought, *in this village there has to be a green somewhere*. I just wanted to find a place where flowers pied the meadow and oaks whispered secrets into a soft wind, and I could lie down among the greens and golds.

But I needed to speak with the Man of Flowers in his bodega shop. About the village greenery first. And second—if I thought him true enough—to ask for help finding my sister. For though I could not go *to* her without bringing the iron rains, I thought I could perhaps tell her how to come to me.

But to my surprise as I opened the front door, a familiar person was walking slowly up the stairs, her old peach face wearing a serene expression.

"Jamie Oldcourse," I said. "I have been wondering where you were." Though of course I had not been thinking of her at that moment.

She grinned up at me. "I was just coming to see you, Mabel." The tinkling bells were still there in her voice.

For a moment, I forgot who Mabel was. I remembered only in time to wipe the confusion from my face with an answering grin.

"And why are you here now?" I asked.

"Paperwork," she said, as if that explained everything.

Ah, I thought, *the Law of Papers* and nodded my head.

"Come join me at a café," she urged. "This is easier done over tea and cake." She said it as though adding honey to a bitter brew.

No sooner had I set foot on the stairs when the smell assaulted me. "By the moon and stars. . . ." I gasped.

Jamie Oldcourse, unperturbed by the stench, continued chatting about paperwork.

I was afraid to say anything, for fear of exposing my innocence. But I looked hard around me and finally saw the huge black bags of some slick material up and down the walk. They even spilled over into the road. More black bags piled up against the spindly trees. Some of them had fallen open and from what I could see, they were full of the tag ends and rag ends of dinners. So *that* was the awful smell! But how long had they been sitting out here in the sun? Since I had not been out for days, waiting by the window for my messenger's return, I did not exactly have a count. But how they stank! I took out the silken patch and held it to my nose.

"Sure is ripe," Jamie Oldcourse said.

"Assuredly. Do you know what has happened here?"

"Strike." Then seeing the blankness of my face, she added, "The garbage men have gone on strike. They refuse to collect the garbage until they have been paid more."

"Then pay them," I said.

She laughed as if I had said something amusing, and we made our way toward the café.

Two young women dressed like men in blue striped pants and jackets stepped around me quickly as though I were unclean. A girl with hair an improbable shade of red, and with a strange small blue stick in one ear, brushed past me, talking to invisible spirits. A father carrying a child on his back nearly plowed into me. Through it all, Jamie Oldcourse gently steered me across the street toward the place of cakes.

I soon realized that I had become invisible to almost everyone we passed, the result of being old and fat in this world. No doubt seeing the shadows that crossed my face, Jamie Oldcourse patted me on the shoulder. "Not to worry, Mabel, I shall explain more fully once we've had a sit-down and something to eat. You look a bit pale, dear."

But even after an hour sitting in the café shop, though we both drank tea and ate the most delicious cakes with the odd name of *profiteroles*, I still did not tell her of my invisibility, nor did I understand the importance of those papers. Except that I was to receive an "allowance" of some money, and though it was not much, it might relieve me of the task of finding work. Thus, dutifully did I sign everything she handed me, using her pen and her ink and the name she knew me by. In exchange, she gave me an envelope with some of the green bills and a paper sack of foods that she bought right there: bread that smelled sharply of chives, a glass bottle full of something called olives, another larger bottle of sparkling juice of green grapes surprisingly called white, several cheeses, and three more of the profiteroles. "Because you like them so much."

I was now so beholden to her, I would never be free, but that I could not help. I had to live after all, and perhaps this was the human way. *But being beholden to Jamie Oldcourse is better than being beholden to someone else*, I thought, as I walked quickly back to Number 13.

I WAITED ONLY TWO DAYS for a reply from Meteora, for this time Coo-coo-rico knew the way, but—oh!—he was a bedraggled mite. I held him close, fed him honey water and bread. Even though I was desperate to read what my sister had written, I waited until he was safe and fed before I even took the note from his leg. Attention must be given to our minions, or the world falls into pieces. The Queen should remember that.

The letter was as tattered and torn as the dove. I unscrolled the fragment of my sister's love and read: *Dearest Sister* and immediately broke into a cascade of tears. I do not remember ever weeping this way in the Greenwood. Yet here, in the gray stone walls of a human city, I cannot seem to stop myself.

She said: *"Promise not to feel any more sorry for me than I do for myself."* And I realized my tears were for both of us, apart and desperately unhappy. I gawked at Baba Yaga's name. That my sweet sister had touched the Old Hag's heart. Who could believe it? And then I sighed when she said so pointedly, *"As pretty seedlings we squandered our power ... never thinking for a moment we might be emptied like an upturned basket of seed corn left to scatter."* Who could have guessed she would become the wiser of us? And so she further proved, having discovered the eagle mail.

I promised myself that once Coo-coo-rico was recovered, I would go down the street, to the Man of Flowers, and using some of the money given to me by Jamie Oldcourse to buy things at his store, ask him to show me the eagle mail. Surely, as he had been kind before, he would be so again.

As for my address, it seemed that Jamie Oldcourse had solved that for me already, for the paper sachet with my money in it had an address on the outside with my name and many numbers, and not all of them magical, but it would have to do.

LATER THAT NIGHT, I PUT the bird in a little nest made of toweling, and sat down by the light of the moon to write.

My dear Meteora:
How your letter, the script as perfect as new

*ferns uncurling, made me recall those wonderful
times. Wonderful except for the Queen, of course.
My smallest finger itches where once magic used to
reside. Your new place of residence sounds Edenic
compared to mine, but to be alone and apart can
make even a palace a dreary place.*

*As for me, I live on a side street in a city called
New York that could delight the senses if it just
learned to pick up its trash. Well, perhaps "delight" is
too strong a word. It would no longer so grossly
offend the senses if the trash were gone. For reasons
I do not understand, the collectors of the trash have
refused to cart it away these last three days. It piles
up on the streets in great black bags, as if the
UnSeelie themselves had brought the leavings of
their unholy banquets here. To think I used to love
turning over a farmer's midden heap if he forgot to
leave me milk. Well, multiply that midden by a
million and you have what assaults my nostrils daily.*

I stopped, thinking of how to end the letter. I remembered the women who crossed the street rather than be
near me and the man with the child giving me a grim
look. And the waiter at the coffee shop who refused to
look me in the eye, but spoke only to Jamie Oldcourse.
Had my sister suffered such slights too? And I wrote,
rather more strongly perhaps then I meant:

*Humans really are such dregs. Forget that girl
weeping downstairs, or turn her heart to stone if
you can. It is better that way.*

> *Ever thine,*
> *Serana, known here as Mabel. I will tell
> you the story of that name someday
> and we will laugh at it heartily, I
> promise.*

Though I said to forget the weeping girl, I wondered

if I would take my own advice and so easily forget Juan
Flores in his shop. I suspected Jamie Oldcourse would
tell me an emphatic no. She would say—all the bells in
her voice tinkling—that we need all the friends we can
get in this gray place. And after all, I *did* need him for
information. So I was determined that in the morrow I
would go to his shop again and with all the centuries of
faerie powers of seduction behind me, make friends.
After all, there was still much I had to learn.

25

Serana Finds the Post Office

I awoke to a morning so sharp and clear, I thought at first I must be back in the Greenwood till I tried to rise and everything ached.

"Oh!" I said aloud, remembering who I was and what I was now. I took a long waterfall in the white tub, the water first hot and then cold but at last just right.

There is nothing like this hot waterfall in the Greenwood, I told myself. *Or profiteroles*. I could still taste them and thought I might have one for breakfast. And so it was that I began to understand that not everything in the human world was bad.

Afterward, I dried myself, dressed in the same old dress, slipped into my shoes, grabbed my sachet of money and my letter, and went down the street to talk to the Man of Flowers. Flores was not there, but a nice lady the color of tree bark with surprised brows told me how to send an eagle letter.

"You can get a stamp and an envelope at the PO, dahlin.'"

"PO?"

She cocked her head to one side like a slightly demented dove. "Post Office."

When I still looked puzzled, she added, "The mail place, honey. You ain't from here now, are ya?"

I shook my head, and she explained in patient detail how to get there.

As it was some way to the place of mails, and I still had so much of the food Jamie Oldcourse had bought for me, I did not buy anything but two apples to eat along the way, with a promise to return. She smiled at me, her teeth white against the dark skin.

"You do that, dahlin'," she said. "I'll be here."

"And the Man of Flowers?" I ventured.

"Old Juan? He's home sick. So he says. But the Yankees are playing today, so you know ..." And she winked at me, which changed her face from a stranger's to someone so familiar and Puck-like, I almost hugged her even though I had no idea who the Yankees were or what they played.

"Now remember, dahlin', it's two times to the right, cross the street, and then left and ..."

So I DID THE TURNINGS she suggested, and found the place of mails with the big eagle sigil on the wall. I did not see any of my sister's men in blue, but there was a lady behind some bars—caged like a farmer's cows— who told me to put the letter into an envelope and seal it. I wrote Meteora's new name and address on the front, my cow name and address on the back, paid one of my pieces of paper money for the *envelope* (that was the name of it) and the stamp and was given coins "in change." The lady behind the bars promised me it would reach Meteora in two days.

"Two days?" Complaint edged into my voice. "But I thought this is eagle mail. The dove can do it in that time and for nothing more than some honey water and bread."

She looked at me as if I were crazy and I looked at her as if she were mad. Then she glanced over my shoulder and said, "Next!"

For a moment we stared at one another, and then the man behind me tapped me on the shoulder. "I'm next," he said, his face wreathed in anger.

"I am Mabel and I am here."

The people behind him mumbled. One put her hand in the air, her middle finger extended toward me, which carried some dark magic at the core, though not enough to hurt me.

The impatient man stepped around me. The people behind him elbowed me aside. And so I was dismissed.

I walked out confused but still trusting that what Meteora said about the eagle mail was true, and that she would get my letter. However, I kept its contents in my head just in case, saying the words over and over as I walked along the street, not caring which way I was going or who crossed the road to get away from me.

26

✦

The Dog Boy Seeks
But What Does He Find?

My father left blood spoor at my door in the hind end of the night. It was a child's blood, one not yet weaned. I had to follow; there was never any choice. Gods, how I hate him. And how he feeds on that hate.

The trail led me to the park as I knew it must. He does not like the gray buildings. They heap him. They leech him. They age him as they age all fey who settle here in the human towns. Green runs in our veins like sap. It keeps us young.

If I am ever to throw my father over, it will not be in the park but in the grayness or on the iron trail. Yet I went to the park. The blood called and I had to follow.

He waited beneath a linden tree, its heart-shaped leaves serrated like the teeth of little saws. I think he waited under the linden *because* of the leaves. He loves such metaphors. He is telling me by waiting there that I must do his bidding or he will put a saw to my heart. And I believed that. I am his child and his dog only so long as I am useful to him. After that, I am mere meat.

"Welcome, son," he said in his growl of a voice. Sometimes he laughs, but not this time. I was glad of that. His laugh is worse than his growl. I hate these visits, but I cannot stop them. *Small favors*, my mother said before she died, meaning that he did not visit her anymore, had already torn her up so much inside that there was nothing left but a hollow. I wish he would do such small favors for me.

He stood there, arms crossed. He did not open them to me. It was not that kind of a relationship. "Welcome once again."

I nodded at him and could not help but smell the blood on his cap. It was more of the child's blood. He always dips that awful cap in his kill. A woman will weep tonight, I thought. And then I thought—*many women will weep tonight. That is the human way. As my mother had wept. For herself. For me.*

"I need you to seek."

Of course he did. That is all I am to him. His hound. His Dog Boy. The one who seeks.

He told me no name. Names do not help me in the finding. But he gave me a taste of the scent he wanted me to follow. I was surprised. It was a strange combination of human and fey, a bit fetid as if the two had not combined well.

"Do not kill," he said, "but follow closely. There is another who may come too, attracted by the light of your prey. Younger, sweet-fleshed and fey. Bring that one to me. And if you are successful, I will unleash you at last."

I nodded and looked down at the ground, never into his eyes. Did he mean what he said? I doubted that. But I did not *fully* disbelieve. If I thought I would never be free of him, I would have to kill us both.

Instead I pissed on the roots of the linden as he watched. He laughed, thinking I did it to mark my territory, but I did it to dishonor him. He knew that as well, but would not let himself know.

Until it is too late, I told myself. It was my only hope.

27

Meteora Finds the Changelings

I had been in Baba Yaga's house for almost ten days. Three days addled and tripping over my once nimble feet, two days learning how to behave as a woman of my new age, four days waiting for mail that would not come, and seven nights awakening to the sounds of a young woman crying her heart out in the rooms below mine.

That night, I did what I had never done before and knocked on a mortal's door.

"Who is it?" she answered, her voice hardly more than a rough whisper. I could hear the dog snuffling beside her.

"Are you all right?" I asked her. "Can I be of help? Your tears have drawn me here . . ."

Whatever else I meant to add was interrupted by the door being violently flung open. The girl stood before me, her green hair like a patch of forest grass that had not been rained upon in days. She was wearing only a long shirt with nothing under it, and she smelled ever so slightly of mold. Along the side of her neck I saw the mark of trouble etched in her skin. Swaying, one hand clutching the door as though she might fall, she closed her eyes.

"Perhaps I could make you some tea . . ." I reached out a hand to steady her.

Her eyes snapped open and she backed away from

me in alarm. "Go away, get out of here. I told you before just leave me alone. All of you, get out of my life." She shut the door hard in my face and I heard her retching on the other side.

I stood there perplexed. I had never spoken to the girl, yet she spoke to me as if she knew me. I was ruffled, my pride insulted at being confused with someone else, someone clearly undesirable. But what could I do? My help had been refused so I returned upstairs. *She has the dog*, I thought, and put her out of my mind.

THE FOLLOWING DAY WAS FULL of sun so I went in the afternoon to a coffee shop where I knew I could purchase a meal "to go," then took myself to a nearby wooded park. I sighed as I sat down, not even minding the dampness of the grass beneath me. Reaching into a paper bag, I took out a little bundle wrapped in white paper and opened it with curiosity. All I could recall in the busy crush at the coffee shop counter was asking for something named "5," and that it contained cheese and no animal flesh.

I smiled down at the sight of two slabs of brown bread, thickly buttered, layered with green sprouts, tomatoes, ruby onions, and slices of golden cheese. In my pocket I had two peaches that I had purchased the day before at the Co-op, and in the other pocket, three buttery sugar cookies, also from the Co-op's bakery.

I felt elated basking in the late summer sunset, buoyed by an unexpected rush of happiness. Everything seemed more important, more precious, and more beautiful for its fleeting temporal nature. I watched young couples walking together on the little paths, suddenly aware of how many children and infants there were in this world. And how few had been in mine. Two towheaded girls, dressed in bright pink T-shirts proclaiming them "fairy princesses" skipped in front of their parents, stopping every now and then to pick the last of the dandelions, which they waved around as if they were wands capable of granting wishes.

Perhaps, it will not be so bad to live here, I thought. I inhaled deeply, smelling the fusty dampness of the earth, the sugary sweetness of the little girls, the dusty fur of a dog that stopped to sniff the uneaten sandwich on my lap. There was chatter and talk all around me; the scolding of a squirrel, the squeals of delight as children ran through the park, the insistent calls of their parents reining them back to their sides. Someone was singing—or perhaps it was the noise that seeped through those little white buds the students liked to wear in their ears.

And then abruptly, I heard a familiar voice, sharp and unhappy, pitched like a magpie defending its nest. It was coming from just behind me, back in the shelter of the trees. I turned my head to the side, not wanting to let on I knew they were there. I needed to see them first, believe with my eyes what my ears had revealed.

The three were sitting on the ground beneath the spreading branches of an old oak, its leaves already turning rusty brown. Though they were wearing more clothes—mostly dirty T-shirts and torn bluish trousers—I knew them at once. The boy had the same dark hair shaved close to his scalp in spiral patterns. The girls wore their hair in thick-snarled plaits, tied off with beads and bits of black feathers.

I turned back to watch the passersby on the sidewalk, but tuned my ear to the squabbles of the three behind me. *Why are they here?* I had left them far behind on the edge of the forest that rainy night they pushed me toward the iron dragon, fleeing as soon as Baba Yaga grabbed my wrists. How did they know where to find me?

I heard them quiet down as the tips of my ears flickered, catching the sound of their voices. *It is no good*, I thought, *they will leave if I don't stop them.* I bundled up my lovely sandwich back in its wrapping, grabbed my paper teacup, and stood up. Behind me there was silence.

I smiled broadly and walked briskly toward them. The grass was moist and springy beneath my feet. They looked startled and rose as a group, prepared to flee.

"Wait!" I called. "Don't go. I bring a gift."

They hesitated, the smaller girl pulling on the oldest boy's T-shirt. As changelings they had learned long ago in the Greenwood to live on almost nothing but air. But human children needed more to sustain them and I knew they would remember the taste and pleasure of food. I handed the boy my white bag and he snatched it from me as though I might change my mind. He put his face into the bag and sniffed. The others stared at him expectantly. He motioned them to sit down and took out the sandwich. As the girls watched, licking their lips and wiping their dirty fingers on their even dirtier clothing, the boy carefully tore the sandwich into three sections, leaving one for himself and handing out the other two pieces.

I sat down on the ground beside them and pulled out the two peaches from my pocket. I split them into halves and gave them to the children. The older girl squealed and snatched the sweet fruit from my hand. But the smallest child, the girl with the heart-shaped face, reached out a grimy hand and patted the hidden lump in my pocket.

I laughed and withdrew the cookies for them. Then I presented the children with the half-filled cup of now cold tea and they passed it around, swallowing quick sips in between bites of bread and cheese, fruit and cookies. I leaned back, quietly waiting for them to finish eating.

It did not take long, and looking almost abashed at the eagerness with which they had accepted the gift of food, the eldest boy lowered his head.

"We are in your debt," he said softly.

"Not at all," I replied. "You have already helped me once before, that night—"

"Shhh. Don't speak of that," he said, darting glances over his shoulder to be certain there was no one to hear our conversation.

"Why are you here?" I asked, lowering my own voice. "How did you find me? And why would the Queen wish to spy on me? Except to convince herself I am as miserable as she hoped?"

"Too many questions," the boy said.

"We are to watch . . . and wait . . ." said the older girl. Her long narrow face ended with a pointed chin but her golden eyes were large and round as an owl's.

"For what?"

"For what comes of it," she shrugged, and retucked a black feather into her braid.

"Comes of what?" I asked, growing more confused and alarmed.

"They are looking for it," the little girl said, licking the last of the cookie crumbs off of her palm.

"For what? And who's they?" I asked.

The boy gave a coarse laugh. "Riddles are not meant to be answered like tallying sums in a shopkeeper's ledger. Though you appear old and plump as a vintner's wife, you've not lost your true nature to seek beneath the signs. Use it instead. We'll give you no more, for it means danger for us."

They stood and I did too, albeit with more effort. The boy reached down a hand to help me. They may have been half wild, but they still remembered the rules of hospitality. I wished at that moment that I had more food, anything to keep them close and talking to me. But I knew I had nothing left to give them but one rare and private thing.

"I trust you," I said to the boy, who seemed to be the leader. His brown eyes widened with surprise. And it was true. I saw them—like me—as outcasts longing to return home. We were all pieces of a game, not certain of the hands that moved us. Mice hiding in the pantry of big cats. And mice need to stick together. I leaned forward to the boy, and spoke my true name into the shell of his ear.

His eyes glistened for a moment before he blinked it away. He turned to leave, and then as if thinking twice about it, he abruptly turned back and leaned in close. He closed his hand around my ear and whispered his own name, *Awxes*.

I touched his shoulder, grateful for the gift. Whatever

else they were doing here, I believed they meant me no harm.

I watched them depart, strolling through the shadows of the trees until they melted into the green leaves. And as I walked back toward the path, I heard the harsh cawing of crows and saw them break through the canopy of tree branches to streak above me, their black wings stark against the fading sunlight.

I walked home in the encroaching twilight, the newly lit streetlamps casting shadows across the sidewalks and streets. A chilly breeze rustled through the trees. I could smell rain approaching, only moments away, and hurried my steps. By the time I turned down Farewell, I was shivering in a brusque wind that rifled through leaves and caused the branches to moan and saw against one another. I dashed into the house as the first heavy spatters fell from the sky.

For once the house was quiet. No troll music, no barking dog, no crying girl. I walked up the steps and got halfway up the first floor, then stopped and turned around. It was a vain hope, but I wanted there to be a letter. I wanted to feel my sister close to me.

I looked at my black letterbox, and through the opening spotted the envelope. Trembling I fetched it out and saw the words written in delicate lines across the front. At first, I didn't know whether to laugh or cry to see the name I had chosen written there and in the corner, hers—"Mabel Farmer." I burst out laughing. We sounded like nothing more than a pair of milk cows. I pressed the letter to my breast and mounted the stairs, desperate for news.

LATER, SITTING IN THE KITCHEN, lit only by a single candle, I replied. Outside the rain lashed the windows, a dismal harbinger of the coming autumn. I was wrapped in one of Baba Yaga's woolen shawls, a pot of strong tea to hand. The cat slept on the chair curled into a knot, with her tail firmly pressed over her face. I was grateful when the hands suddenly appeared, the feminine hand in a lacy fingerless mitten, and showed me how to send heat into the little vents near the floor. The house slowly warmed, but I could not remove the chilled sorrow from my heart. I tried to put my muddled thoughts into words that might enlighten Serana but not reveal too much— for I thought of the changelings somewhere outside, huddled in this cold rain, and I didn't want to say anything that might bring them harm.

Folding the letter, I slipped it into an envelope and put a stamp on it. I wrote down Serana's address, feeling how odd it was that there was this place I had never seen, that held the body of my sister. I could not imagine how she might look standing in a room of such a place, staring out the windows and searching for my face.

Much later I got into bed, pulling the coverlet over my shoulders and up to my ears. I was almost asleep when I heard the girl below me crying again, her long sobs wrenched from deep within a wounded heart. And try as I might, I could not imagine what horror coiled so deeply in her breast.

28

Meteora's Melancholy

Dearest Serana,

You were right. I should never have gone downstairs to that weeping girl. What was I thinking? I offered solace and the surly child snapped at me, bid me leave at once, and shut the door in my face.

Dreadful-looking creature she is too. Woeful offspring of misery. Cropped hair, sticky as thistle and a poisonous green. Her eyes beneath all the black running tears might well have been pretty, but they were red and baleful with weeping. And no wonder she was crying and wretched. Some UnSeelie trickster has tattooed the front of her neck with the twisted sign for trouble and its aura swirls around her. Take care, my gentle sister, we are not alone in this world and we do not have the protection of our court. And certainly not that of the Queen.

I let her slam the door and left without so much as uttering a single word. I do not want to help her, or worse, call the UnSeelie trickster to my side by meddling in her life. But, dearest Serana, these mortal children aren't all dregs. Just hopelessly misguided and dangerously ignorant. And haven't we in our own past made much sport of their *innocence? We were scarcely older in our time than that girl and yet we squandered our power, thinking it eternal. If only we had known that age could invade our bodies like a canker, stripping the bud of beauty.*

I am tired tonight, sitting by my candle, writing these lines, while outside my window the rain weeps against the window. I am surprised by this foreign body, these veined hands that can write letters but can no longer shape the destiny of others. Oh this terrible exile from ourselves, from our lands, from all that was familiar.

Forgive me my melancholy. Earlier, I had been thinking myself lucky to be here and now am drowning in the rain's loneliness. So it goes. I wait for more eagle letters from you, Serana, your sharp tongue like a knife cleaving me from these dreary thoughts!

Always yours,
Meteora

29

Serana Among the Trees

Three days passed, dark and full of thunderstorms, and not a word from my sister. On the fourth day, the sky cleared and I ventured out, thinking to go to the store and buy food. I had finished all that Jamie Old-course had bought for me. The olives especially had been a new and delightful taste, being salty and tangy at the same time. When I drank the juice left behind in the bottle, it was so strong, I coughed until salt came out my nose, but it was wonderful nonetheless.

Surprisingly, Juan Flores' store was closed. Perhaps he was sicker than the bark-brown lady had suggested. Worried, but with no one to ask, I walked farther along the block, and then two more long blocks, seeking another store with fruta in it, till at last I came to one like Juan's, only larger, with huge signs on the windows promising sales. I bought two apples, the color of old gold, but they were dearer than I had expected, so I purchased nothing else, and went back out into the sunshine, preparing to return home. I would have the apples for my dinner, and on the morrow return to the Man of Flowers' store.

Just then I smelled something that I had not a whiff of since Faerie—a copse of trees. Not just the spindly things that lined my block. The scent was so faint, I wondered for a moment if I were mistaken. Standing on my tiptoes,

I glimpsed far ahead the green tops of a full grove of trees. So I shoved the apples into my skirt pocket and dove into the noise and the stink of the city. Dodging colorful bags swung by careless walkers and racing in between the cars, I walked as quickly as this body allowed toward the tempting green. As I went, I began humming a song Meteora and I had made up years ago.

> *Green in the morning, green in the gloaming,*
> *Under your branches, I come a-roaming.*

The next lines I sang out with gusto.

> *I come a-flying and light as a feather*
> *For this is the green time, the last of good weather.*

Suddenly the people ahead of me scooted to the far sides of the walk, leaving me a clear path. That made me laugh out loud, which further worried them. Clearly, I had a different kind of magic here and human folk were afraid of it. I tucked this knowledge away. Perhaps I could use it to get back to Faerie.

Booming the tree song and its chorus loudly along four more blocks to the green, I soon came to a pretty park that sat alongside a silvery river. The river was not like rivers in the Greenwood, which are narrow and wild, filled with riffles, rills, white water, and dark, peat-bottomed pools. This was a fat, domesticated river waddling between far-apart banks, singing sluggishly as it flowed. But at least there were trees.

And music!

Long before I crossed the wide street, before I went down a waterfall of stone steps, I heard drums and strings and a high wailing of some sort of pipe. The music was not quite fey, but it was fairylike. I almost danced down the stairs.

Ahead were many colored flowers—red and pink, scarlet and mallow. They were set in contained beds as if the gardener feared they might escape and run riot up the hillside. I went to the nearest patch of greensward, took off my shoes, and let my toes wriggle in the green, though the grass was shorn like stubble on a human man's face.

Easing down carefully, I turned over to lie with my face down in the grass. It did not smell like Greenwood grass, a scent compounded of dark earth, rain, and sun. Rather it smelled a bit like the black trash bags and a bit like the pickles I had eaten earlier, sharp and bitter. Still, it *was* green and after so many days without, I reveled in it.

All of a sudden, I heard the music again and realized that it had been silent for quite a while. Had I, all unknowing, silenced it? Perhaps it had already accomplished all it was meant to do—summoning me to this place.

Standing, I smoothed down my skirt, then began walking toward the sound, past the garden with its reds and pinks; past seats of wood and iron; past a woman lying on a stone, eyes downcast, gazing into a small pool. I might have thought her alive had not three children been bouncing on her side. The music grew louder, closer, insistent. I forgot the flowers, forgot the madewoman, and instead raced across the grass, shoes in hand.

Closer to the sluggish river, on a stand of stone, stood three musicians. Banging on a drum was a man as black as crow feathers, dressed in a long coat of many colors. Next to him, a slim girl with white-gold curls and an unnatural dark part in her hair sawed away on a fiddle. As she played, she danced, her striped skirts swirling about her. The third of the troupe was a young man with dark hair curly as a ram's horns. He blew through a small silvery pipe as well as any Pan. Occasionally he put the pipe down to pick up a different instrument that looked very like a lute, only with a straighter neck. As his fingers flew over the strings, he plucked fairy music from the air, looking at sky, ground, trees.

They played jigs and reels. A few I recognized like "Toss the Feathers," and "The Gay Gordons," but the rest were strange to me, almost noise. Still, as my Dam used to say before she went off to the West, "All one needs to dance is a fairy tune and two good feet." Even my extra flesh could not stop me from dancing. Flinging the shoes to one side, I began to spin around and around and around, till I could feel my heart double its beat and the sweat run down between my thighs.

Eventually, minutes later—perhaps hours later—the music ended, though it was certainly sooner than a faerie band would have stopped. The black crow-feather man stowed his drum in a bag, then slung it over his shoulder. The girl put the fiddle back in its hard case. And the piper packed away his long-necked lute in a larger hard bag and stuck the silver pipe in a pocket of his shirt. Then he picked up a well-washed red hat that I had failed to notice before. I shivered to see such a thing, but it looked nothing like the one that dreaded creature wears, having a broad brim and some writing across the crown. Something about a bong, which made no sense. He turned the hat upside down, catching the coins and the paper that fell out. Some he took for himself and some he shared with his band mates.

"Forgive me, good folk," I said, breathing hard, "I did not know you played for pay. I will give you all the gold I have. Even if it beggars me." Putting my hand into my pocket, I pulled out the sachet that Jamie Oldcourse had given me. "It is little enough for the joy I have had." I handed the sachet to the girl and sighed. Now I truly had nothing. Nor would I get more, according to Jamie Old-course, for another thirty days.

The piper looked at me sideways, from under leaden eyelids, as if they were too heavy for him to raise fully. He sniffed derisively, then with a stiff-legged bow, took the sachet from the girl, and thrust it back at me. "If that is all you own, lady, keep your gold. We want none of it." He turned and walked away.

Oh, no. I was already indebted to too many. How could I be beholden to this stranger? And a rude one at that. "Wait," I said. "Let me do something for you. Let me read your faces and palms. At least then we will be quits."

The black crow-feather man laughed, his voice all angles, as if laughter were not his native tongue. He started to turn away, but the fiddler girl said, "Face first?"

So I let my fingers run over her face like friendly breezes, and then stared deeply into her eyes. I shuddered with what I read there. "You have left a bad home," I said, adding, "and a wicked father."

Her eyes got wide and she drew back a bit.

"Who *are* you?" she asked. Then turning to the crow-feather man, added, "Chim, who *is* she?"

Chim shook his head. "Too old and too fat to be undercover. Bring her along till I can sort it out."

I suppose I should have run, but when I quickly read him where he stood, I could see no evil in him, only a long wound in his past that the music was healing. And something about busybody aunts.

I remembered again Jamie Oldcourse's third rule about friends and the need for them. The Man of Flowers was becoming one. But perhaps this trio would mean even more to me. After all, three is a number of enormous magical potential.

"I come gladly," I said. "No need to bring."

WE WANDERED AMONGST THE TREES, going far from the made-woman and the waterfall of steps. And then a persistent gnawing took my attention and I realized that I was starving. My stomach had begun the growl I now recognized as hunger. I was about to reach into my pocket and remove an apple, meaning to share it with my newfound companions, when the girl said, "Here!"

Here was a small square of grass between trees. A thrush of some kind was singing flutelike from a low branch.

"*Catharus guttatus*," said the piper. "Hermit thrush." He set down the lute bag and took the pipe from his pocket. Putting it to his lips, he began to blow, imitating the birdsong perfectly. Then he left us to go stand under the birch trees, playing to the bird.

"Robin taught himself the pennywhistle because of

the birds," the girl told me. "The guitar came after. He plays fiddle, too, though not as good as me."

"And he has a bird's name," I mused. "I am partial to birds. Though *he* looks little like a robin." *But cocky enough*, I thought.

"He named himself," the girl said. "Even I don't know his *real* name. And we've been friends on and off forever."

"She says forever and means a year. As for his friendship, more off than on," Chim said. "He's never around when we need him."

"I speak to birds, too," I admitted.

The two of them looked at me strangely.

"Mumbo jumbo." Chim reached into his drum bag and pulled out a large covering of some sort, spreading it on the ground. "I suppose you believe in magic, too."

"Of course. Doesn't everyone?"

He houghed like a horse, through his nostrils.

But the girl paid him no attention, sitting down on the covering, and delving into a rather large bag named Whole Foods Market. Pulling out cheeses, cakes, tiny squares of some sort of brown color with nuts in them, she said, "Don't mind Chim. He calls himself the ultimate rationalist though he is magic to his bones."

I turned to the black man. "Chim," I said, making a swift, small curtsy, "I am Mabel." It was a safe name to give. I doubted Chim was his true name anyway. It did not fit him.

He houghed again, dismissing me entirely.

The girl patted the covering beside her. "He was brought up with magic and has disavowed it. Went to Princeton instead. Sit here, and never mind the gruntings of the rational mind. He moans more as the moon wanes, weeping about his missing children, though they are not missing at all but live with his ex-wife. And Robin moans more as the moon grows. What a pair!"

An invitation is never to be refused. I sat and took out the two apples from my pocket. "Let me add these to the feast."

"See," the girl said to Chim, "domestic magic. Loaves and fishes."

"I see neither loaves nor fishes," I said. "But Jamie Oldcourse says that people of the street must find power in small things."

She nodded. "That's true enough."

Shrugging out of the strap of his drum bag, Chim set the bag down carefully. "The only magic I indulge in are these—magic brownies." He picked up one of the brown squares and ate it in two quick bites.

"Brownies?" I shivered. "One does not *eat* brownies. Or spriggans. Or fairies. Unless one is the Dark Lord." I gasped and put my hand over my mouth. Chim *was* dark-colored. He went to a Prince's town. He had missing children. What had I fallen into?

"Flour, butter, eggs, cocoa, sugar, vanilla, baking powder, salt, and a pinch of . . . magic," the girl said, popping a pair of the brownies in her mouth, one right after another, and still smiling. I could read only amusement there.

"Try one—if you dare." There was a strange undertone in Chim's challenge.

"Chim . . ." the girl began.

"She *did* ask," he told her. "And May, you were the one who made the brownies and brought them to the park. I'm just being . . . neighborly. You always say that I am an un-friend at heart. Give me credit for trying."

I glanced at the brownies. I could detect neither character nor magic in them. But perhaps I no longer had the ability to do so. "May I?"

They said together as if it were an old joke, "May you and May, too."

May added, "And Maybelle for three, ding-a-ling," which set Chim off into a series of unmanly giggles.

Just then Robin popped the pipe back in the pocket of his shirt, left the trees, and came over to sit down with us.

"Robin, what do *you* think?" May asked.

He looked at her quizzically but said nothing. Indeed,

he seemed a person of few words, as if fearing to give himself away.

"The brownies." She dimpled at him and I could smell her desire, though he seemed impervious to it. "Should we let our guest have one?"

He turned and looked at me for a long moment. I felt naked under his gaze. Did he see the young and beautiful girl as I once had been, or the aged woman I was now?

"Two," he said solemnly, as if his words were pennies and he a miser.

I savored the first brownie slowly. It tasted of sweetness and—oddly—of dried grass. The second brownie I ate even more slowly, trying to make it last. I had never eaten anything so wonderful, and wanted more, though I had been allowed only the two and would not beg another from the rude bird-boy.

"Here," said May, "wash them down with this." She handed me a clear bottle of water, though it turned out to have a sweet tang. Was this, too, an enchantment?

I drank several gulps and all of a sudden started laughing with delight.

"See," Chim said, "magic!" before May shushed him with a finger to her lips.

But when I began alternately weeping and then laughing uproariously for no reason at all—I had to admit that it felt that a spell had indeed been cast upon me. "Are you fey, that you can make such magic brownies?" I asked May.

She must have answered, but that was the last I recall of the afternoon.

30

The Dog Boy Finds

I knew her by her smell, but she was not what I expected. Father had said she was fey and beautiful as he handed me a bit of her nest.

"Seek!" he had ordered.

What I seek, I find.

But she was not a slip of a faerie girl, rather a lump of an old thing, asleep on a bench in the park, her hip humped up like a mountain. And snoring. I had not found her so much as she had found me. She smelled a bit like my old, dear, dead dam—and fairy—two souls in a single breast.

Like me.

What is it that makes us the same? I asked myself, kneeling and sniffing her carefully.

And then I knew that I could never give her—my new dam—to my father's teeth and claws. Not if I could keep her secret. But it is hard, so hard, to keep anything from him when he raises his hand, when he leashes me with a look, when he strikes me with his iron-tipped stick. Then, oh then, I will do anything he asks.

But not—I decide—this.

I found some newspapers in a wire basket nearby. I

placed them over her. From head to toe. To shield her. To hide her. To keep her warm. And safe.

I would guard her from afar, but I *would* guard her.

You may hit me with the rod, Father, I think, *and try to leash my mind, but this time I shall not yield.*

I hope I am right. Or that he is wrong.

31

Serana Is Rudely Awakened

I woke up hours later, something hard striking my shoulder.

"Get up, lady, you can't sleep in the park."

I sat up, blinking into the dawn. Papers fluttered off me like wings.

The man standing over me was dressed all in dark blue. He had a round face with a nose as flat as a squashed peach, and the same color.

I was not in my bed at the Number 13 house nor—even with the trees I could see around me—was I in my nest in the Greenwood. "Where am I?"

"Riverside Park," he grumbled.

River side. Then I remembered the sluggish river. And something else.

"Music," I said.

"Not a sound," he answered. "Did you lose your iPod?"

It was as if we were speaking two different tongues. Perhaps I had been transported to yet another world even as I slept.

"Is it still the New York?" I asked.

"It's not the New Jersey," he said.

Suddenly, I recalled the red cap belonging to the piper, though I could not bring up either his face or his name. He had returned me my money. I touched my skirt and could hear the coins rattle.

"Lady, if you have money, what the hell are you doing sleeping out here in the park?" he asked. "Of course your iPod got stolen."

"What is an iPod?" I looked around for the creature and saw nothing.

"What you been smoking, lady?"

"I do not smoke."

"Well, you're sure high on something. You still flying?"

I shook my head, trying to clear the cobwebs. "I have not been able to fly since the Greenwood." And then I remembered the brownies and how their magic had made me laugh and cry simultaneously. Sticking out my tongue, I tried to taste them again, as if their magic still lingered in my mouth. But it was only a sour morning breath.

"Oh—just get out of here, before the kids come and I won't take you in." He pulled me to my feet. "Oh yeah, and no littering. Stow those papers in the can."

I figured out he meant me to deposit the large flapping papers in a nearby bin. Then I walked in the opposite direction the blue man had taken. Nothing was familiar. Suddenly, I feared *where* I was, and *when* I was. Had I slept away the afternoon and the night? Or had the magic lost me more time than that? A year? A generation? All the tales of faerie time ran through me like a river. But the trees were still in their late summer sheen. I had to believe not *too* much time had passed.

Either I have lost a day or found one, I thought, but three things were certain. First, humans have magic here in their village of New York. Second, I was suddenly and overwhelmingly hungry. And third, I was lost.

My heart beat as loudly as black Chim's drum. Now the sour taste in my mouth was fear. I thought then to pray to the gods of the Greenwood, yet I doubted they could hear me here, even with the trees and flowers of the Riverside Park.

As I stood dithering on the walkway, turning this way and that, a stranger put a hand on my arm and said, "Are you lost, old dear?"

Old dear? The woman was surely twice as old as I, her

face a mask of wrinkles with two dark eyes peering out like currants in a doughy bun.

"Thank you, good dame," I said to her, "but I am looking for the Number 13 and the Man of Flowers whose store is filled with fruta. Do you know them? Or perhaps the place where the made-woman lies with her face near the water." *If I could get back there*, I thought, *I might be able to find my way to my rooms.*

"Goodness, where do you come from?" she asked. "Czechoslovakia or summat?"

Because she said *goodness*, I knew her for someone on the Seelie side, and answered back with the same good grace. "Summat." It seemed a safe response.

She laughed. "Summit, New Jersey?"

Does everyone here know of this New Jersey? And is it important? I was mulling this over when she pointed to the corner, crooking her finger to indicate the direction. "I bet you mean that large statue called Memory; if memory serves, it's that way. Hah!" She laughed at herself. "Sure, I can take you there. But I can't do more than that. I'm on my way to see my grandchildren."

The touch of her hand on mine led me to turn her hand over and touch the palm. There was a knot under the lifeline. "There will be one more grandchild," I said. "At last, a girl." She would not live to see it. But at least I could give her this.

"How do you . . . know . . ." her voice trailed off.

"I accept your help," I said. Now that I would not be beholden to her for it. Though I would not have been beholden for long. The hand never lies, though the mouth can.

"Oh, I hope you're right. After five grandsons, a girl would be . . ." Her wrinkles all seemed to turn up at the thought.

"I am always right," I said.

WE WALKED THE REST OF the way in silence along the winding walkways until at last I realized where I was.

"This is it!" I said aloud. We were right across from the made-woman, and I stood still for a moment contemplating her. There was something infinitely sad about her that I had not recognized before. Perhaps the children bouncing on her side had distracted me. Perhaps the sound of the music.

I saluted the grandmother, who walked swiftly away from me, and then I retraced my steps from the day—or days—before. I remembered the way, going steadily along the walk where the young people on wheels had run by me, up the stone waterfall, over the road.

As I hurried along, I nodded at other walkers on the street as if I knew them, and a few of them nodded back. *Small magicks*, I thought. *A smile elicits a smile.*

At the spindly tree not far from Number 13, nestling near one of the stinking bags, something caught my eye. I bent down, knowing that if one does not look, one can never find. It was a stone I had not seen before, blue and green. A cleansing stone. I picked it up and slipped it into my pocket. After all, one must never ignore a gift.

Then I headed toward the stairs up to my home. *Home!* I wondered that I could call it so, after only a day or two away, but home it had become.

32

Serana's Scare-bird

I meant to go back out and buy food, but after I washed my face and changed my clothes, I lay down for a moment, and woke at midnight. Turned over, and woke again into the brightness of day.

Raising the window, I leaned out to get fresh air. Below me, huddled on my doorstep was something large and dark. For a moment I thought it a bag of garbage that had broken apart. Angry that I would have to clean it up, I started to pull back inside, but the thing moved, shook itself all over, lifted its head up, and glared at me through befogged eyes.

Quickly, I made the sign against the Dark, the two fingers crossed before me—male over female, life over death—and hurried downstairs to shoo it away. When I came close, the creature said a single word in a rough voice, the sound a shoe might make over stone.

"Sanctuary." The voice was human, young. Then he bent over again, put his head down on his arms, and promptly began to snore.

What else could I do? He had asked for sanctuary, an old fey custom that the humans have taken over, honoring it more in the breach than in the doing.

I raced to the Man of Flowers' shop where I quickly gathered apples, nuts, goat's cheese, eggs, milk, tea for a tisane, and an assortment of herbs, all ones I had not bought before. I would think about what to do with them later. I gave all the money in the sachet into Juan Flores' hands, glad that the strange bird-boy had pressed them back on me. "I was told you were sick. I feared for your safety."

He nodded. "I had the flu."

"Flu." I rolled the word around in my mouth. "Is that like flying?"

"Only when the fever is at its height." He smiled, almost shyly.

Even though I did not understand, I smiled back. Then I took a deep breath. "I like the bark-colored lady who was here the other day. Tell her I found my way to the mails with her good help."

"The malls?" He shook his head. "We don't have any around here."

"The place of mails. Where one can send an eagle letter." I saw understanding light his face.

He laughed, head back, full-throated and easy. "The bark-colored lady is named Nita. And I will give her your thanks, dona." He handed me back money since the trade was not for all that was in my purse. Then he packed my purchases into two sacks and walked me to the door.

Hurriedly, I walked back to my home, juggling the packages.

The stairs were now in sight and I hoped I had purchased the ingredients to make something the scare-bird could keep down. Also I hoped to clean him up and make him safe. Sanctuary he had asked for and sanctuary he would get. I am still a good fey.

But when I got back to Number 13, the scare-bird was gone. The stairs were empty. He had left nothing behind but a stink.

It WAS ANOTHER TWO DAYS before he returned, the same day that the Collectors came in their clanking vehicle and took away the black bags at last. People on the streets celebrated, waving and laughing and cheering them on. The sun was out, making the streets suddenly sparkle.

I would have waved and danced with the others, but I had no time to spare. The scare-bird sat on my steps, went away and came back like a shadow, depending upon the height of the sun. He did not speak to me again in all that time, and I wondered if I had simply misheard the word *sanctuary*. I tried several times to coax him upstairs, but he was like a wild thing that would not be caged. He was much taller than I but thin, his dark hair tangled practically beyond redemption, with a shadowy beard on his chin. He shivered in his frequent sleeps on the steps, moaning and making sounds but no real sentences.

So I left him tisanes and little packets of cheese and sliced apples, the goodness of each leaching into the other. He must have eaten what I set down beside him, for there was nothing left, not even crumbs for the birds or the persistent gray squirrel that haunted my stoop whenever the scare-bird took off. Indeed, the birds and creatures seemed frightened of him. Any blanket or toweling I put around him, he shrugged off. I never left either blanket or towel outside, but took them back inside, washing each thoroughly before using them myself.

Once I touched the scare-bird as he dreamed, picking up his hand to read the palm. The tremors that ran through him would have made a mountain collapse. His blood was filled with bile, the lifeline kinked like a broken promise. I should have let him go, but stupidly I had already made him mine.

And then a man with the sigil of an eagle on his breast came to the step as I was sitting there next to the boy. He thrust three envelopes into my hand. Two were not for me, but one had Mabel's name. I tore it open and read it right there.

I wondered that Meteora had not turned that dreadful green-haired girl into a toadstool and then remembered that she could not. *Woeful offspring of misery* indeed. I put a hand up to my own neck as if tracing an

UnSeelie tattoo. I could not believe that all this was co-incidence. Chim the dark prince, May who cooked magical food that made two days and nights fly by. And perhaps even this scare-bird, though he seemed more lost than wicked. But what were the connections— besides evil being attracted to good, besides all of us being fairies thrust out of Faerie into a world of iron, stone, and dark?

Oh my sister, I thought, *you have the weeping girl, I have the dreaming boy. What are we to make of this? Everything—or nothing?*

When the scare-bird stood, looked about wildly, and left me this time, I went upstairs to write. Whether my letter went by eagle or dove, it could not go until I wrote it. Keeping Meteora's newest missive by my hand, I began.

It took me all day and half the night and I used up five pieces of my precious paper, crossing out words, phrases, entire sentences, then writing them all over again. But at last I was done and put the letter in the envelope. I fell into a deep and dreamless sleep. I would go to the place of mails and send it off in the morning.

My dear Meteora:

I sit here in the growing dark, which had once been such a friend. Not even a candle stub to pierce the gloom for new candles are expensive and so I husband them carefully. I am cold, cold Meteora, who was once so warm. Fire shot through my veins and I could dance till dawn. The partners we had then: the daft little fauns with their capering legs and high, trilling giggles. The village men, half drunk on our wine, half drunk on our beauty.

What I miss are not the glamours, nor the dances, nor the glowworms caught in the trees for lanterns. I miss not at all the politics of the court. What I miss most are the friendships, for you are but a piece of paper and ink to me now. Human friendships seem as gossamer as their lives.

And yet . . .

And yet I think we are missing something, sister.

Let me explain. Everything we Fey do has meaning. This we know from our acorn cots. And yet, sundering us from companionship, the friendships of touch and taste and the intertwine of limbs has forced me to think as I have never thought before. I have asked myself these past gloaming days what meaning have we not understood, so deep in the gloom of these new lives?

Here, I have lighted the candle stub. See how it pushes back the dark. Where it touches the edges of the room, there is a soft glow, like those living lanterns in our trees, so much better than the human lamp overhead that gives much light but little warmth. What if we are meant to be glow-worms in these last years? Shall we try to hang upon humanity's top limbs and give them light? Is that the meaning? In other words—that green-haired child of yours—can she be tamed? Can she be helped? Can she be transmuted without our magic into her deepest, best human self? There is the question.

I have a similar child sleeping on my doorstep upon occasion who once—or so I think—made claim on me for sanctuary. He is thin as a scare-bird, his hair a toss of darkened straw. He shivers and moans in his sleep. I touched him once and his dreams spoke of monsters that would fright even a Red Cap. His blood runs with something the color of bile. His anger is as bitter as vetch. He has been vomited into the world by something even he does not dare name. There is a will-o'-the-wisp quality to him, yet the burnished steel of an unsheathed sword beneath. He is a puzzle. But I have promised that he has sanctuary here.

Oh, I know what you will answer. A moment ago I would have said the same myself. We should be finding a way to return to Faerie, not trying to heal humanity's running sores. Well, our own threw us out, Meteora, and not just because of our misplaced laughter. All we have left are these children and our glowworm dreams. Even if we cannot help them, we shall at least be back in the game, whatever game it is.

Your old dear,
Serana

33

Sparrow Buys a Present

"Damn, Sparrow, have you looked at yourself in the mirror lately? I mean really looked at yourself?" Marti asked. She was leaning against the kitchen sink, a cup of steaming coffee in her hands.

Despite the dull ache behind her eyes that threatened to bloom into a headache, Sparrow looked up at Marti and tried to feign ignorance. "What's the matter?" She hated the way Marti was scrutinizing her, as if she were a plant in need of tending. Something to be pushed into the light and pruned to keep healthy.

"You need to see a shrink. You've been sobbing your heart out every night for the last two weeks. You hardly eat, you look like a total mess. When was the last time you did laundry? Are you even *going* to work?"

Sparrow rubbed a hand across her eyes. The headache was beginning to pound. "Yeah, I am going to work. It's hard. But I go because I have to eat. I'm just trying to work through something on my own, Marti. Something tough. But I think I've got it under control, now," Sparrow said softly. That much was true. The last two nights, she had succeeded in beating back the demons that invaded her dreams. The burning tattoo had stopped its nighttime bleeding, and the soul-wrenching sorrow and fear that had consumed her nights was abating.

"Are you sure?" Marti sat down next to her and laid a manicured hand over Sparrow's nail-bitten fingers.

Sparrow gave her a wan smile. Marti was dressed for her new job, a professional one in an office in town. Sparrow couldn't remember what it was Marti did now, but she had shed her street look of vintage clothes and long braids for something much more upscale. Her mouse-brown hair, now glimmering blond and smelling of expensive shampoo, was cut and styled to a few inches beneath her chin. Her eyes had a smear of amethyst powder on the lids, and the once pale gold lashes were thick and black with mascara.

"You look beautiful today," Sparrow said, and meant it. "That blue sweater suits you perfectly. Very classy."

Marti blushed, and tried to wave away the compliments with a perfect berry-colored-nailed hand. "I just think you should see a counselor, or a shrink, Sparrow. You're obviously suffering from depression. I know you've got your secrets, but sooner or later you've just got to face it once and for all."

Sparrow reached out for a cigarette from a pack on the table and stuck it in her mouth. She dug in her pockets for a lighter and steadied her trembling hand long enough to hold the flame to the cigarette's tip. Inhaling deeply, she held it for a moment, and then released a veil of pale smoke. "Sometimes howling at the moon *is* facing it," she said, replacing the cigarette in her mouth.

"Yeah, but it freaks out my boyfriend. In case you haven't noticed, and I know you haven't because you've been so preoccupied with howling. Mitch doesn't want to stay here. And I hate, hate staying at his place. His roommates are pigs."

Sparrow shrugged, meaning that she needed to fight her battles on her own terms.

Marti stood up and opened the kitchen window to let in some fresh air. "Okay, okay, I get it. You don't need to smoke me out. I was just trying to help. When I was younger, my parents got divorced, and I went to a counselor to deal with some anger issues. It really helped me a lot to talk to someone."

Sparrow felt instantly guilty. It wasn't Marti's fault that she didn't understand how weird—not just dysfunctional—Sparrow's life was. And a well-meaning counselor, like the ones she'd encountered in the halfway houses, wouldn't be able to understand either. If she told them the truth about how she'd survived in the woods, they'd have considered her delusional, and locked her up and stuffed her full of mind-numbing pills.

"I know you mean well. And I am sorry about freaking Mitch out. I promise, I'll keep it down. But you gotta let me do it my way."

"So long as you promise me that if your way doesn't help in a day or two, you'll consider dropping in at the Fourth Avenue clinic and find a professional to talk to about it. I don't want to come home and find you've done something horrible to yourself, you know?"

Sparrow crushed out her cigarette in an ashtray and waved away the smoke. "I'll be okay. It's just a thing us former street kids go through. Like the flu. It's almost over, I promise. "

"Okay," Marti nodded, and then glanced at her watch. "Shit, I'm late for work." She reached for her coat hanging on the back of a chair.

"Yeah, me too. I'd better get a move on, especially as this one needs her morning's constitutional," Sparrow said, nudging her foot affectionately against the sleeping dog's round belly. "Walk," she told Lily.

The dog scrambled to her feet and performed a little dog dance, shuffling back and forth, tail wagging. "Come on, girl, let's go and wake up the squirrels." She stood and got down the collar and leash. Snapping it briskly onto Lily's collar, she followed the eager dog out the front door, and down the stairs.

Outside, Sparrow paused on the bottom step and inhaled deeply, while Lily was off watering a spot beneath the bushes. The morning was crisp, and the slanting sun gilded the tops of the trees in a buttery light. For the last two weeks, this had been the only decent part of Sparrow's day. No matter how exhausted she was from her miserable nights, every morning she was surprised by the restorative power that came with walking around the block, the dog leading the way from tree to bush, and occasionally dragging Sparrow across a yard in pursuit of a sleepy squirrel.

As they went along down the street, Sparrow found herself thinking about the elderly woman with the graying auburn hair and soft hazel eyes living upstairs. Sparrow was the only one in the house who knew the woman wasn't Baba Yaga, the owner of the house. But she hadn't told anyone, not even Marti, because that would have meant revealing her agreement with the witch, something even Sparrow wasn't foolish enough to consider.

It had been late spring when Sparrow had first arrived in the city, searching for a place where she might stay just long enough to make a little money, and then maybe go north to the woods before winter. She'd been sleeping in the park for a few days when Baba Yaga awakened her with a tap on the shoulder.

"Who are you?" she'd demanded and Sparrow had bolted upright at the sight of the old woman's blazing eyes, her iron teeth, the sound of her rasping voice. "Who *are* you?" she asked again.

"Sparrow," Sparrow had answered, giving the most recent of many names she'd used over the years.

"Sparrows sleep in trees. You are more like a mouse. Trying hard not to be seen beneath the leaves."

"Nothing wrong with that." Sparrow was alarmed that the crone had guessed correctly.

"Depends on who is looking. Any night hunter will find you here soon enough among the trees."

Sparrow clutched her backpack, afraid of the twisted face and the fiery eyes that studied her so carefully. "Are *you* a hunter?"

"Yes. And these are my woods."

"Have you come for me?"

"Yes, but not in the way you think. Listen, child, I

have a proposition." Baba Yaga had squatted on her heels, dimmed the red flames of her eyes. Scratching at stiff hairs sprouting on her chin Baba Yaga then grinned. That smile was less comforting than her growl of a voice had been. "I have a house, nearby. You may live there. There is furniture, kitchen, everything to make you comfortable."

"What's the catch?" Sparrow was always wary of unexpected generosity. Such gifts always came with attachments, most of them dangerous.

"Hah!" the crone said, approvingly. "I need someone to gather rents and put them in the bank for me. I don't like anyone to know who I am. So I will send you, little girl, to do it."

"But *I* will know who you are."

"Yes. But you are different. Like me, you have deep secrets. I can taste them. I will let you keep yours, so long as you keep mine." She spit into her palm and extended her hand to Sparrow. "There is safety in *my* house, more than others."

Sparrow flinched at the sight of the long black fingernails. She glanced up again at the old woman who grinned even more broadly, one broken tooth protruding like a fang over her lower lip. *She certainly isn't someone's kindhearted grandmother,* Sparrow thought. Still, the offer was hard to beat. The spring had been cold that year, the ground damp and her jacket thin. And if this crone could find her hidden in the bushes, others not so agreeable could, too. Besides, she needed a place to rest.

Sparrow spit into her own palm and gripped the crone's hand as hard as she could, just to prove she wasn't afraid.

Throwing back her head, the old woman gave a thunderous laugh. "Save your strength for others more treacherous than me."

Without asking any more questions, Sparrow had followed her home. When she saw the stone chicken feet, Sparrow at last realized who had invited her to stay. A lifelong reader, Sparrow had sought out libraries as a refuge, hoping to find answers in books to her own peculiar nature. She'd searched medical books, self-help books, New Age spiritualism, travelogues to exotic-sounding places, and romance novels, hoping to find someone who shared her visions and vivid dreams. Who healed as quickly as she did. Who could hide in plain sight, make herself invisible. Who held communion with certain animals and birds. None of the adult books helped. It was in the children's section that she found an echo of her own life. The lush illustrations of fairy tales had more in common with the night terrors and fears that haunted her than anything else she'd ever seen. Hungering for more, she moved on to their adult counterparts in the myth and folklore sections of libraries and bookstores and found some of the peculiar contours of her life explained.

Standing in front of the chicken feet, Sparrow turned and started to ask, "Are you—?"

"—Shush," Baba Yaga put a finger to her lips. "Secrets, remember? I am not staying long. I live on the top floor. You will live on the second floor. It is empty now, except for Lily, my dog. But tomorrow there will come a young woman looking to share the rooms with you. You will say yes to her and you will have the key to empty the rent box in the front hall and take my money to the bank. You understand?"

"Yes," Sparrow had nodded. "But why me? Why did you really pick me? Everyone has secrets."

Baba Yaga shrugged. "I am returning a favor." And after handing Sparrow two keys, a silver one to the apartment on the second floor, and a slim gold key for the rent box, she'd turned and retreated into the shadows again.

"Come on, Lily, that's enough squirrel chasing," Sparrow said and gently jerked the dog back toward the sidewalk. Sparrow hurried her steps, suddenly wanting to get home.

Home. Was it her home or the old witch's? For the last three months, she'd dutifully collected the rents, depositing them into a *Bettina York*'s account at the bank. She'd followed written instructions that came in the mail about the two jerks living in the lower apartment. But Baba Yaga had said nothing about the old woman now living on the third floor. Sparrow cringed, faintly remembering the elderly face at the door. She had answered the knock while still caught in the grip of a nightmare, and yelled at the woman, mistaking her for the wraiths that were taunting her in her dreams. Sparrow had yelled, sent her away, and shut the door. *So, who is she?* Sparrow wondered. *Another one with secrets? And if so, why couldn't she keep to herself?*

UPSTAIRS, IN THE APARTMENT AGAIN, Sparrow removed Lily's leash and stroked the dog's ears, one white, the other a pale mahogany, smiling at the grateful creature, panting up at her. Everyone in the house complained that Lily barked too much, but Sparrow didn't mind. Lily barked at dark things that hovered outside her window, at the creak of unknown footsteps at the door, and most often at the dickheads who lived downstairs. Lily hated Nick and Alex almost as much as Sparrow did and never missed an opportunity to nip their hands or shoes when she passed them in the hall. Sometimes, Sparrow even let the leash slip out of her grasp just to watch the boys jump back into their own apartment and slam the door when Lily lunged forward.

Taking a fast shower, Sparrow dressed in the last few clean clothes she had, and went to comb her hair. She looked at the vivid green and decided it was time to change it. Maybe she could get it done at the discount salon around the corner from the bookstore. Magenta, or dark blue. *Yeah*, she told herself, *change is good*.

AS SHE LOCKED HER APARTMENT, Sparrow overheard the old woman scolding Alex down on the first floor. She was certainly acting tough, demanding he clean up the garbage, the garden, and most surprisingly, to quit harassing Sparrow.

Perhaps, she really is *tough*, Sparrow thought, listening to the edge in the woman's lilting voice. *But in a soft sort of way, like someone's pissed-off mother.* Again Sparrow felt guilty about being so rude when she was crazy with pain. She was also a little worried that she might have disrespected one of Baba Yaga's friends.

You better do something nice for her, Sparrow thought, waiting for the old woman to leave before she headed down the stairs. *And do it soon.*

In the alley behind the house, Sparrow peered into the backyard and saw the woman—arms full of shovels and rakes—heading toward the battered remains of the garden. Sparrow watched as she kneeled in the dirt, leaning forward to inspect the ruined plants. Pinching a few leaves between her fingers, the old woman held them to her nose, inhaling their fragrance. When she untied the scarf from her head, her gray-streaked russet hair tumbled down over her shoulders. She turned halfway, as if to look down the rows.

Sparrow thought how suddenly youthful, even beautiful, the down-swept hair made the aged face seem. For all of her years, this old woman was spry enough, stretching her body like a cat, wrenching weeds and clutter from the soil.

Yeah, Sparrow thought, *I owe her.*

THE STREET HAD BECOME CONGESTED by the time Sparrow arrived at the bookstore. She loved this block, each storefront decorated with big heavy concrete planters filled with marigolds and snapdragons. There were two coffee shops, and they still had tables outside for those hardy enough to enjoy the cooler temperatures of the morning. Across the street, the purple-and-orange face of the Co-op brightened the otherwise muted brick and concrete of most of the storefronts. Students lounged or studied outside at tables with huge paper cups of coffee.

A mother pushing a stroller with two small children stopped in front of the Co-op to let a third, older child walking beside her bend and stroke the ginger cat sleeping beneath a bench.

Approaching the bookstore, Sparrow reached into her pocket and fetched up a set of keys. In her mind she went through the ritual of opening up the store: counting the money in the cash register, turning on the lights, straightening books on the shelf, vacuuming the old rug, filling the tea and coffee urns with water, plugging them in, and last of all, turning the crank that released the green awnings over the front windows of the shop. Sparrow, whose life had bounced between chaos and abuse, had found this simple routine of opening the shop calming.

She stopped at the door, key in hand. Beneath the CLOSED sign was a second, smaller sign with a picture of Frank, her regular Sunday visitor and a newspaper article attached. The sign indicated that the shop was to be closed for the next two days in memory of Francis Murphy, the shop's original owner, who had died unexpectedly last night in his sleep. The police had been called in because a bedroom window had been smashed, but they had ruled out foul play, thinking the culprit had been the wind from a storm blowing a tree branch through the glass.

As Sparrow stood there reading the articles, tears welled in her eyes. *I hadn't realized. He'd never said.* No wonder the old man came every Sunday to the bookstore; in some ways, the shop was still his. She would miss him. Miss the sweet way he patted the silver comb-over on his head and stood a bit straighter when he saw her. Miss the gentle blue eyes rimmed with gray that twinkled impishly when he teased her. And she would miss his company, the two of them with their noses in a book, while the tea and coffee urns gurgled and steamed. The wake was to be tonight at a small bar about three blocks over, the funeral tomorrow.

Sparrow turned away from the door feeling hollow.

She replaced the keys in her pocket and stared numbly out at the street. The bright purple and orange of the Co-op caught her eye and she sauntered over to the shop. She knew what color to dye her hair: something black and funereal in Frank's honor.

Once in the Co-op, grim-faced and holding back the tears, Sparrow wandered aimlessly up and down the aisles until she came to the hair products, all which promised to make her hair glow with a healthy shine.

I don't want shine, she thought angrily, *I want it to be dull black.*

She found a box that promised to turn her hair "ebon" and decided that would do.

At the counter, she paid for the hair dye, handing her bills to a jaunty African-American man with dark freckles and long dreadlocks.

Taped to the side of the register was a poster asking for information about a missing woman. Sparrow often wondered how anyone could be recognized from these photos. In fact, after she'd run away from her father, she'd seen her own face on the back of a milk carton but not one person in the fast-food restaurant had identified her as the missing girl. *But this woman*—Sparrow leaned over and stared at the photo. She was sure she knew that one, not well, but enough to be jolted by the sight of her face.

Leaving the Co-op, Sparrow realized there were posters everywhere: stapled to public bulletin boards, taped in store windows, tied around streetlights, on the sides of mailboxes. Near the entrance to a tattoo shop, Sparrow stopped, suddenly remembering where she knew the woman from. It was Jenna. Sparrow looked closely at the photo in the shop window and realized she had not recognized Jenna at first because she was wearing a summer tank top and her arms, chest, and neck were all bare of ink.

Sparrow clapped a hand against the blue-black knot on her own neck. The woman in the photo was happy, relaxed, almost as if she were about to reach out a loving hand to the photographer. But when Sparrow had met her, Jenna's eyes had burned feverishly and she couldn't sit in her chair without stroking the tattoos on her arm as if to cool the skin.

If I had known her like this first, Sparrow thought, *and then met her again with the tattoos, I would have known something was wrong. Might never have followed her into Hawk's parlor and allowed myself to be marked by that monster.*

It reminded Sparrow of something she had learned as a child: of how easy it was to become prey—alone in the world. How hard it was to survive without a tribe, a pack, or friends. Marti wasn't really a friend. The witch, who'd given her some help, had left. Lily was loyal, but Lily was just a dog.

Sparrow felt a sense of urgency and, deciding quickly, headed toward the Farmer's Market close to her house. She'd buy something for the old woman upstairs and get back to the house's promise of safety. If Baba Yaga had trusted the old woman, perhaps Sparrow could as well.

But what can I give her? What gift might open the door to a friendship like the one she'd shared with Frank? It didn't have to be much; just enough to begin a conversation. Even if that conversation excluded things about her father and his hard hand, and all the rest.

Sparrow thought and thought—a scarf, something for the apartment, a small vial of perfume. And then she had a sudden revelation: plants for the garden, some bulbs, maybe tulips or iris. Something that would bloom with showy blossoms in the spring and they would both comment on how after a long, cold winter, such beauty was a welcome sight.

She smiled and her step quickened. The old woman would welcome a gift for the witch's garden and then they could be friends.

34

<hr/>

Meteora in the Garden,
Meets a Jack

One morning I realized that three mornings a week at the Co-op and waiting for mail were not enough to keep me occupied. And as soon as I acknowledged I was bored, I felt the wash of guilt that I had done nothing about Baba Yaga's garden.

It's time, I told myself. So I rose quickly, washed my face, selected a sturdy dress from the chest, and tied a scarf around my head. On the way downstairs, I stopped at the door of the crying girl. I hadn't heard her crying as much since our unfortunate encounter. But I still wondered about her. *Worried*, really, for her sorrow seemed too large for a child to handle alone.

I passed by the trolls' door, frowning. Alex and Nick had some noisy contraption playing, as if even in sleep, they could not bear the quiet. Music of a particularly unmusical kind always leaked beneath the door; sometimes loud talking; sometimes the sounds of fighting. But yesterday, I heard them haranguing the misery-girl. They called her all manner of brutish names, insulting her pleasure parts. I could imagine their words struck like bitter spells. I would have to do something about them, and standing before their door, I made the old signs that once might have forced painful transformations on those louts—especially on *their* pleasure parts.

Worthless, futile gestures. I steamed and kicked their door instead, which though it hurt, was remarkably satisfying. Then, squaring my shoulders, I prepared to greet the day with newfound defiance.

I marched over to the garden—but what a sight! The soil had not been turned in at least two seasons; coarse, hardscrabble plants had invaded the narrow borders. There was trash strewn around, all of which came from overflowing bins.

Furious, I returned to the boys' front door and banged on it with my fist.

"What the fu . . . ?" shouted Alex as he yanked the door open. He stopped when he saw me, his dull piggy eyes turning hard, but his mouth shutting on the words. He was barely clad in short pants and his naked pimply skin reeked of a sweetish smoke and stale beer.

I drew myself up as tall as I could manage, chanting "*Iron teeth, iron claws,*" in my head as I gave him an order. "Remove all your garbage from the back of the house to the street."

"Garbage day's not till tomorrow."

"Remove all the garbage *now*!" I commanded. "And when you are done with that, you and Nick may come in the backyard to clean all the rest of the garbage you trolls have tossed out your windows."

"I'm not a troll."

"You are right," I said, my voice still sharp. "Trolls have better sense than to defecate where they nest. Get out there and clean up the mess you have made. And put on some pants, you look like a whore's whelp in those things." I pointed to his short pants that were falling around his fleshy hips. The dingy fabric had yellow smiling faces on them, including one huge smiling face across the front where his pleasure parts no doubt were hiding from shame.

"Hey that's not nice, lady."

"And neither are those nasty insults you threw at the girl on the second floor. I heard you."

"*That* chick? Man, she's an ice queen. All she needs is to get laid."

"Not by you," I snapped. "And certainly not with that," I nodded toward a gap in the front of his short pants where his sorry sex was partially visible through the silly grin of the happy face. "I've seen better-looking worms on the end of an angler's rod. I warn you: not another unkind word to her or you two are gone. Now get on with it. I want the backyard cleaned up."

I stormed out the front door, leaving him cursing under his breath. Oh, he called me all sorts of names, but I could tell by the way he muttered them under his breath that I had given him a fright.

Good! There will be more of that anon, I promised myself.

IN A SHED NEAR THE GARDEN, I found a shovel, a rake, a trowel, and a pair of coarse leather gloves. The gloves were much too big but I put them on anyway as I knew my soft hands would soon be blistered and raw from garden work. Then I surveyed the damaged garden more closely, noting how rocks had been placed to shape the outlines of a simple maze. I worked methodically, clearing away dead plants, broken bottles, faded wrappings from foods I didn't recognize, an old shoe that was missing laces, a sweater the birds had partially unraveled to make a winter nest, a plate that still had the encrusted remains of a meal, and most distressing, the carcass of a maggot-infested crow.

Over my shoulder I heard Alex and Nick dragging the bins out to the street, their feet sloshing around in loose shoes that slapped sullenly on the ground. They made a poor effort at re-collecting the garbage that had escaped the overflowing bins, but at least things were now a bit better. I smiled. My imitation of Baba Yaga had worked its own magic.

Once tidied up, the garden appeared more promising. Though most of the plants had long since bolted and faded, I could find remnants of them—enough to be able to imagine how the place might look in the coming year—assuming I would still be exiled. Assuming Baba Yaga let me remain here that long. There was the trinity of snow trillium leaves, the last spikes of foamflowers, and a crumpled lady's slipper rising amid spears of brown spotted leaves. There was also shaggy-headed coltsfoot surrounding a stand of bristled goldenrod, Solomon's seal decorated with red berries, bladderworts, fairy spuds, and beechdrops. Plus parsley, tarragon, sage, and a brittle rosemary plant half buried in the dirt. Much I could use. Even more I could bring back to life.

I did not mind working in the garden—especially one filled with so many familiar reminders of my own forest. I am sure I did not make a pretty spectacle, kneeling forward, heavy as an auld ewe, to dig in the roots. But with the sun on my back and the scent of earth and sap in my face, I was—almost—happy. *Or at least content.*

I leaned back to take a brief rest and as I did, I noticed a man, bare feet the color of mud, wandering through the garden's labyrinth, whose low stone walls had become more noticeable as I cleared away the debris. He was gray-headed as the hare, bearded and unkempt, dressed in faded trousers and shirt, both covered in dust. *Where have I seen him before?* He bent to touch the blossoms of the fairy spuds, then straightened when he saw me. Brushing the dirt from his hands, he smiled. Those eyes were blue and smooth as robin's eggs, but the grin, crooked to one side, made me wary all the same.

"Name's Jack," he said and extended his hand.

Jack. Who could ever trust a mortal with such a name? All Jacks are tricksters, giant slayers.

The hand he held out to me was big and rough-callused. Fool that I am, I gave him my hand, and he received it with surprising gentleness.

"Sophia," I answered, and his smile widened, the eyes sparkling a little too brightly. I took my hand back.

"Pretty garden. Unusual too." He nodded. "Thought you might like a scarecrow," he said.

"Whatever for?" I scoffed, for there was no grain in this garden to attract them.

He pointed toward the oak and ash trees that lined the edges of the yard. There amid the green and brown leaves, I saw them, black and glossy, and too many to count. The crows were silent, except for the nervous rustle of their wings as they waited, cloaked together on the boughs. I thought of the changelings, and wondered if they were hidden amongst these birds in order to watch over me, or to spy for the Queen.

"Well?" Jack asked again.

"Yes," I replied, thinking a scarecrow might amuse them.

He shambled away, to a house on the other side of the yard, boldly whistling a stolen fairy tune I had not heard for many seasons. When he returned later, he was lugging something large and rattling.

"I saw this design in a dream," he said, struggling under the awkward weight of the thing. "Feels like it should go right here." He planted the figure just off center of the garden, balancing it, so that the small charms depending from the length of the outstretched arms jangled nicely in the wind.

Despite my apprehensions at having this Jack in my garden, I stared in wonderment. He had made it from the King's copper, bright and green. The charms clinked together and the crows craned their heads down to stare. Lifting from their branches, they took turns settling on the arms, which swayed up and down with the shifting weight, causing the charms to sing out even more. The crows cawed joyfully and I could imagine the changelings playing on the sculpture like true children once more.

Jack gave me his crooked smile. "Well, that's not much help, is it?" *Charming and charmed.* Even at my new age, I felt the blood rush to my cheeks.

"But I like the sound," I told him. "Much better than the troll music the boys in my house play."

He laughed at that and I laughed back. *Charming* I reminded myself, trying to be a bit wary even as I was being charmed.

I let him stay a while. He had a knack for the stones, lifting and turning them, finding the right face before he reset them in the soil. And from his broad hands caked in dusty soil, I recognized that Jack was the ghostly man who had come to my aid some nights back when the trolls had threatened the peace of the house.

Just as I was once again on my knees digging in the garden, thinking how inviting was the scent of turned soil and plant sap, I became aware of the prickling stench of smoke. The misery-girl appeared beside the garden path, a bag in one hand, cigarette in the other. She stared at the ground, pulling on the cigarette as if it were a breast. She looked weary, her hair no longer a vivid green but dull and black as coal.

"Sorry about the other night."

"Not to worry," I answered, still digging.

"I was just, you know, having a hard time with something and I thought for a moment you were someone else . . ." Her voice trailed off.

"It's quite all right." Suddenly I wanted very much to soothe her troubled heart.

"Here. I got you this. For the garden." She handed me a little brown bag.

I took the bag from her and felt the hard roots rattling in the bottom. Iris, I thought. Blue Flag perhaps. But when I looked inside, I paled. Two mandrake roots, male and female, withered and intertwined. I shut the bag, trying to hide my disgust and—I'll admit—my fear.

"How charming. Thank you."

The girl cocked her head, her gaze keen. She frowned. "The guy at the Market said I should plant them. Said I'd like them. But you don't like them, do you? So what's wrong with them?"

How could I tell her that these roots bled when cut? That they inflicted suffering; that they twisted a true lover's knot into a hangman's noose?

"They're wonderful," I lied. "I should like to meet this man and see what else he has."

"Every Wednesday and Saturday at the Farmer's Market over by River Park. Just the other side of the university," she answered. "I really thought they'd be, you know, something pretty."

"Thank you for the gift," I said, keeping the bag tightly closed. It pained me so to see the disappointment on her face but I could not say more without lying, which I cannot do. I would have to think of a way to help her. *But what is it human children need?* I wondered.

She tossed her cigarette down, stubbed it out, and left, her shoulders hunched like a rain-soaked thrush.

I watched her go, worried by the pall that was cast about her slender frame. *Strife and Woe.*

But the air brightened after she left, and a breeze washed away the last of her curling smoke. Sitting back on my heels, I inhaled the rich fragrance of newly turned soil, sensing the power emerging from the exhalations of the opened earth, and from the stones, resettled to create a boundary of safety. Silently, I thanked Baba Yaga for this unexpected gift and source of strength.

I rose then, brushed off the dirt, and said good-bye to Jack, praising him for his labor. I owed him now of course, but wasn't quite ready yet to repay him by inviting him in for tea and bread. He was still too uncertain a character for me to trust.

"Anytime," he answered, and flashed me his warm smile before rumbling off to his own house.

TWO NIGHTS LATER, I SAT in my small kitchen made bright by a bunch of yellow black-eyed daisies, blue Canterbury bells, and flaming salvia, which I had purchased at the Farmer's Market. I had gone there in search of the man wicked enough to sell a troubled girl mandrake roots. I had hoped he was merely ignorant, and unsuspecting. But I could not find him.

I did not stay long for a peculiar feeling stole over me, of being watched, or perhaps sought out among the throngs of people. It was like a sending, a brush against the back of my hands and neck, coaxing me to turn. And I did, if for no other reason than to rid myself of the sensation.

I looked through the crowd and spotted him at last: a Highborn Lord, dressed in mortal clothing standing beneath the dappled light of a huge ash tree. Despite his plain clothes, worn I suspected to dim the powerful allure of his nature, his long oval face was beautiful, fair-skinned, with almost delicate features. His wheaten hair was braided and tied with a leather thong. He was searching the crowd of people, his eyes lighting on the faces of young women, just long enough to catch their eyes. And they smiled back. Feeling the beckon as though it was their own idea, they strolled toward him.

I was relieved for it was clear from his choices, that it was not me he was calling forth. But I wondered what he was doing here? Dabbling with mortal women was frowned upon among the Highborn of the Seelie court. Was *I* not paying the price for having shamed our Queen by revealing her tryst with a human? For these Highborn lords, purity of the blood mattered more than one's name, more than one's status.

Did I know him? His face might have been familiar once, a long time ago. The edges of his profile shimmered and I realized that he wore a glamour, to hide his true face. I watched as he swung an arm around a young woman and smiled into her trusting eyes. He stroked her arms, and on her shoulder drew a pattern with his fingers. She laughed, and the bright flush on her cheeks revealed the touch had done its work well, arousing her with a spell.

Unsettled, I turned away and walked home where I was so preoccupied with my thoughts, I almost forgot to check the mail. Suddenly remembering, I returned to the box and cried out in joy seeing the golden envelope waiting for me. I devoured Serana's letter right there; the story of her scare-bird, her own farsight telling her—even as mine had done today—that something indeed was brewing. I took out a piece of paper and wrote my reply.

Dearest Serana,

So much has happened since last I wrote, and your letter has coincided with my news in wondrous ways. This is what comes of being sprouted from the same pod. The Queen worked at separating us, knowing that one alone was trouble enough, but two together was an invitation to chaos. That's why she cast us out here in this mortal place, to be weakened by age, robbed of our magic, and as far apart as possible. Indeed, she must fear us, and perhaps that is a consolation.

However, I think that the Queen wanted us gone for reasons other than my indiscretion, reasons I cannot yet put my weathered thumb upon. Except there was a child, an infant sweet as a rose there on the grass. What became of her? To whom did she belong? I never thought her the Queen's get, for it has been too long a time since a Highborn woman brought forth such a bouncing babe. Yet, my nose itches when I think on this child, for the Queen's rage now seems that of a lioness protecting a cub rather than merely about her sullied reputation.

The Queen might well have feared that we would spill too much about the jewel she wanted kept hidden. But out here, bereft of each other and weak with age, we present no threat. How little she understands our true gifts, those that have nothing to do with magic. We still feel danger in the lurking shadow because unlike the Queen who hoards the light for herself and thus blinds herself to the needs of others, it is our nature to push back the dark with the small flames of our beings.

There is danger here, dear sister. I can feel it brewing like a storm, threatening everyone in its path.

But what do I really know? Only a little, but it is a rough-coated seed. The changelings who tossed me into the iron-dragon have returned, shape-shifted into crows. That takes true power, which they do not possess. I have seen the UnSeelie sporting in the streets, plucking youths like unripe fruit well before their time. And I watched a Highborn lord wearing a face-hide glamour summon a woman in broad daylight for his own purpose. These are not good omens.

And then there is the Great Witch, Baba Yaga who happened along in good time and in whose house and garden I have found a refuge. Thinking myself safe here, I was surprised today by a Jack. He is charming, as are they all, and I swear to you, sister, I could not stop from giving him my hand.

And finally, my sorrow-filled girl appeared to me with an apology. She gave me a gift, which she knew nothing about, but thought would please me: mandrake roots. Mandrake roots, sister! She read my face and knew at once the roots were danger-ous, even as she knows the tattoo on her neck is the cause of her grief for I see her rubbing her palm against it as though to wear the ink away.

But who inflicts such deceitful spells on a woman's skin? And who sells mandrake roots to a woman so obviously in trouble? I have gone to the Market, but could not find the one responsible for such an odious gift nor the skin pricker.

And what of your unhappy young man? Who dreams such dark thoughts without first having been poisoned by a malicious power?

Glowworms, yes! We must be the light for these two who are all but lost in the shadows and we must do it because they have sought us out, drawn to our light. We are their sanctuary, but they may be ours as well. *There are no coincidences in this world or in the Greenwood. Someone is planning violence, someone is poisoning children for a reason. Keep your wits about you, my fierce sister.*

Always yours,
Meteora

—

35

The Dog Boy's Plaint

The moon having left the sky, my brain was soon turned to boiled oats, my stomach filled up with bile. Heat and cold ran alternately through my veins, making me shiver as if being shaken by some large beast. I could not wake yet could not sleep. Still, I managed to sniff out my new dam and sit on her stoop, talking to her of wishes and longings. Or else I spoke in my dreams to someone else. When the moon is away, I cannot tell what is dream and what is not.

I have not reported to my father nor will I. I have sworn to guard. And yet with oats for brains, I am a weak guard indeed.

Father waits out the moon in the Greenwood, kenneled in his Dark Lord's house, more dog than I. He licks the hand that beats him. He eats his own vomit. Neither bark nor bite belong to him yet still he thinks he is the alpha male.

Another day, two at the most, and the moon will begin its newest climb. And then I will howl. Oh, how I will howl. I will mark the street where my dam hides in her pretty house, talking to the doves whose little necks I can snap with one hand. If I want.

When I want.

But to sleep again. To dream of a soft hand on my

brow. To rise in man's form, not a dog's. To guard whom I want. To love whom I want. That will not happen as long as my father lives, with his Dark Lord holding the leash that binds us both. But I can dream.

And do.

36

Serana Sees Portents, Signs

I read my sister's latest letter with growing horror. A Jack? She invited a *Jack* into her life? Had her brain, now encased in old bone, turned to mush? All Jacks are tricksters and guisers; they are breakers not makers.

Sitting in my room, I worried over this bit of information. A Jack! Might as well have tea with Red Cap! If she thought her green-haired girl a problem . . .

I grabbed up a piece of paper, leaf green like the girl's hair had been, and began to write so quickly, it was almost impossible to decipher my scrawl.

Listen, my fern, I wrote, *you have begun something you cannot stop. It will be a story that devours you even as it unravels. It will . . .*

There was a noise outside. I put down the pen, as much to gain control of my roiling emotions as to see what was going on. I looked out of the window, and down onto the stoop. There was my scare-bird, back after a few days away. I had worried that the poor boy had died, been run over, run out, run off by who knew what kind of demons, his own or those I had dogging my footsteps. Or the ones, like the Jack, dogging Meteora.

Yet there he was, the stray, like a beaten dog, waiting for me on the stairs.

I flung open my front door and raced down the stairs. My cheeks flamed. My breath came in short gasps. I felt my stomach contract, both delightful and awful in one motion. It was as if I were young again, going to meet a new lover. But this was a young man, scarcely old enough for a beard, and I an old woman. What I felt was sorrow and anxiety and relief all intermixed. Like a mother with her mite. Poor little straw man. Poor lost waif.

When I got to him, he looked up at me with such adoration and poverty of soul, that I took him by the hand and he did not resist.

"Who are you . . ." I began

He was mute, but his eyes, the blue-black of a peaty lake, were voluminous in their conversation.

"*What* are you . . . ?" I wrinkled my nose. Rank as a badger, he smelled as if he had been rolling in a farmer's midden. Or the contents of the black bags. "*You* need a bath."

Taking him by the hand, I brought him up the stairs, stood him in the water room, and began to fill the big white tub. While the water ran, fast and hot and pure, I hastened back to where I kept the herbs. I pinched seven basil leaves from their stems, shook chamomile from the bottle, took a bit of sage and rubbed it between my hands till it warmed. Then I stirred in lavender, peppermint, and thyme all together widdershins with my left forefinger. I would have loved to have added clary and geranium to the mix, but did not have any to hand. I would need to visit the Man of Flowers again. But not now.

The scare-bird had not moved from where I had put him, but watched as I dropped the herbs into the tub that was now quite full of water.

"Now you," I said.

Perhaps he thought I meant to strip him, for he crossed his arms over his chest. His clothes were as rank as he and I did not want to touch them. Instead, using a shower cloth to cover my hands, I pushed him, fully clothed, into the bath.

He sank immediately under the water. I left him for one, two, three long shuddering breaths on my part, then thought the better of it and reached in to pull him up into a sitting position. I did not mean to drown the poor thing, only clean him and his clothes of their toxins.

But when I got him sitting, his eyes were closed and he hardly roused. I knew then that the poisons I had noted in his dreams must have run very deep in his veins.

While he soaked, I got out the stone I had found outside under the tree, the aquamarine for deeper cleansing.

"I give thee thanks," I whispered to whoever or whatever had dropped it there.

Then I went into the cook room and got out salt as well.

Once again back in the water room, I held the stone up to the light. Its very color seemed just right for soaking up hot, fevered blood. I wrapped it in three strands of my hair—that hair that was lately golden and fine and now is white and coarse—then stuck it beneath his knees. Then I sprinkled him with the salt.

Afterward, I said the words. I may be stuck here in a body like a moldering toadstool—but I did not forget the words. This I wrote later to my sister.

Much later.

Standing there looking down at the boy for a long time, I saw the water was now gray, heading toward black. There was too much iron in the bones of this building for magic to work as it does in Faerie.

If it works here at all.

FINALLY THE BOY WAS STRIPPED down and asleep under my covers, the stone carefully clasped in his hand.

But do I really want him here? Even cleaned up, there was a stink about him, like a wolf in a sheepfold or a dog in a farmer's manger.

Still, I thought, *he is here. And I have made him clean and made him mine though it has taken hours and all of my hot water to do so.*

At the last moment before he fell into sleep, the scarebird opened his eyes. I was stunned. Those were surely fey eyes. Not the peaty ones I had seen out on my steps, but a deep bronze shot through with haze, the lozenge-shape of a cat's eye. Or they were for a moment. And then one blink later, they were human again.

As I wrote to Meteora:

> I do not know what this means, darling M. I doubt anyone except the Queen knows the whole of it. Not even the Great Witch. But as you say, there is something else going on. You are right. I believe we have been dropped into this cesspit for a reason.
>
> Surely we are not meant to bring the girl and boy together. Surely not. For that would be too simple. And the Queen has never been simple, whatever else she may be. But what if it were so, and we too cunning to allow it to happen? What if we out-puzzled the prime puzzle maker? What then?
>
> The question that simply will not go out of mind: are we walking this maze of our own volition, or are we being walked through it by a greater player?
>
> I send a kiss for courage. I need one, too. Or something stronger. Magic, mayhem—or a drink of honey mead though I know not where such might be found.

> Your sister, loving always.
> Serana

37

Hawk and Aileen

I know well the sounds of my shop, even sequestered in
my room: the metallic hum of machines, the chime on
the door as it opens, the low conversation of the women
waiting their turn. But my ear is also tuned to a deeper
sound, the quiet crackle and decay of women's bodies as
charmed inks turn their spleens black as gall. I delight in
their febrile pulses as my spells invade the marrow. I
hum to the noise, shaping it into a death song so sweet
that even the hollow-eyed girl I am working on offers me
a hopeful smile. I stop tapping the needle into her skin
and stroke her cheek. She closes her eyes, grateful for
the soft touch of my hand, as tears escape from beneath
her pale lashes.

They will all die of course; some quickly of an unnamed illness, others by their own hand. And some I
help, like Jenna, whose skin was covered with my runes.
I refused her, angry that the girl she brought me did not
return. I went with Jenna down by the river, holding her
hand while she stumbled and wept. I promised her peace,
but did not tell her it would come in the grave. I sum-
moned the monstrous Jenny Greenteeth to the bank and
bid her feed. Hungry as always, Greenteeth made short
work of the woman, taking her by the ankles as she
waded into the river and dragging her beneath the dark
current. What harm was there in that? Let her death

offer nourishment to even the least of our kind who are still better than any mortal woman. The water churned as I watched from the bank, and only when I saw the thick, ruddy foam rise and float on the swirling eddies, did I turn and leave.

I look up from my work, suddenly aware of the silence. I hear nothing; not even the ordinary sounds of the street and the shop. I reach to draw back the curtains of my private room when they are drawn for me with the fierce jerk of a gloved hand. I curse that I have become so used to the mewling of weak women that I have not thought to keep my dagger close at hand.

A woman fills the doorway, wrapped in a full cloak of gray with a hood that hides her face. I step back, into the room, opening wide my arms and bowing my head just enough to acknowledge the power of the woman who has silenced even my own song. The girl on the table turns on her side, curling her knees up toward her wounded heart where I had placed a tattoo of a bell that she may know only the clang of calamity.

Flushing with anger, I am outraged at the impertinence of my visitor. I was once Hugh, son of Etar, clan leader of Inver Chechmaine, though now I am known as Long Lankin, the knight of blood and death. No one enters my rooms without permission. Not even here in this mortal realm.

But the silence holds me bound. I cannot speak or spell until the unknown woman releases me. My mind rushes like water spilling over a dam. *Can it be the Queen?* For the first time a prick of fear invades my blood.

The woman stands on the threshold of the narrow room, and I know that from beneath the hood, she is surveying it, seeking to know what I have kept hidden from the Greenwood and the courts Under the Hill.

Though frightened, I am defiant, my rage burning with the righteousness of a Highborn Lord. *Let her look,* I fume, fists curling around the poisoned needle still in my hand. *Let her feel* my *power in the branded girl on my table. Let her smell it in the caustic stench of my inks.* Suddenly, I do not care anymore that she knows. That any of them know.

She turns to me and pushes back the hood to reveal her face. It is in fact not the Queen, though the breath catches in my throat. It is Aileen, sister to Gwenth, my lost wife, and the only one who offered herself to me when I near drowned in sorrow. Despite my anger, I soften at the familiar sight of her face, the milk-cream skin framed by wings of black hair. I remember the feel of her breasts, and the comfort of her arms holding me while I grieved. But that was long ago and the bright gold eyes stare at me now with a mixture of pity and contempt.

"Is this how you honor the memory of my sister and your wife?" she asks, glancing at the girl coiled in pain. "How many have you marked, Hugh? How many have you doomed before their time?" She steps closer to me and I weaken at her scent—rosemary and betony—so like my wife's. "This is not our way."

"Aileen, why are you here? I did not send for you." I close my hand on the needle to feel its prick, thinking that the pain will destroy her glamour. I have no concern for the poison, for it is mine and it knows its master. Still, it leaps like fire in my veins.

"I heard rumors that Long Lankin was abroad again, come to the mortal realm to bleed a sacrifice for the tithe, even though you were forbidden to do so by the Queen. I prayed it was not true, but I could not ignore the warnings of my own heart."

Angrily, I look away, refusing all memory of our brief time together, when our mourning made a kind of marriage between us. "Curse the Queen. Have not our kind suffered long enough? Did not Gwenth suffer enough? We deserve better."

"And *this* is better?" She stretches a gloved hand to the girl who is rocking in silent weeping. "Gwenth would not have wanted her death celebrated with such . . . cruelty."

"Perhaps, if I had acted sooner, she would not have killed herself. There would be a child of our blood

between us. There would have been a light in our hearts."
I turn to face her. She dims the harsh glare of her golden
eyes.

"Hugh, grief has made you into a monster. You must
stop this. No good can come of it. When the time of the
UnSeelie rises, all must join to help the Queen in holding
back their hunger for death and misery. This time it
promises to be the Battle We Most Fear. The Queen for-
gave you once but she will not a second time and we
need you at the court. We cannot do this without you, old
love. Come with me and leave this dark sorrow behind."

Her words move me; awaken a longing for the joy I
thought destroyed with Gwenth's death. But my jaw sets
against another injury. One she has forgotten to mention.

"I too hear rumors, Aileen. The Queen has whelped a
child."

Aileen purses her lips in annoyance and her eyes flash
like sunlight striking water. "It is mere tale-telling,
spread by boogans with no wit nor wisdom to separate
truth from lies."

"What says the Queen of this charge?"

"Nothing, and why should she? She is above reproach.
There is no child."

I cannot help myself, I reach out and touch her cheek.
Impatience with me spreads a rosy blush across her face
and slender neck. Her skin is warm and she shivers at the
caress of my cold fingertips. I want to go with her, but it
is too late. There is no mercy for me, not even the Queen
could cleanse my honor so stained as it is with mortal
blood. I have no choice but to follow the path I set for
the future of my house and my clan.

"For all that you know, the Queen has birthed and
murdered her offspring like any miller's daughter, hiding
her crime beneath the stones. She has too much power
and no one to temper her wanton desires. Perhaps it is
her lust for power that has—"

"Enough, Hugh," Aileen snaps, and I stop, knowing I
have put my finger into an open wound. As Highborns,

we trust our clans but never the Queen. We serve her, but do not love her.

I turn away so as not to see the tears brimming in those golden eyes. "One day, there will be a child of pure blood born to the House of Inver Chechmaine again. The blood tithe will give us back our future. And were you to ask, you would find many a Highborn lord hopes for just such a resurrection."

I lay a hand on the wretched girl and she uncoils at my command. Her eyes are red with weeping but she is submissive as I dip my needle into the bowl of ink and stab its point under her skin. A bead of blood rises to the surface. I wipe it away to show Aileen. I am in no hurry to collect the blood.

It is only when ordinary noise erupts again that I know she has left. A phone rings, the overhead lights buzz, the door to the shop opens with a chime of artificial bells. I listen for the sibilant hiss of the ink penetrating the girl's skin and force a smile as I hear her moan.

LATER, AFTER EVERYONE HAS GONE, I think about the Queen's bastard child. Aileen's dismissal does not ring true. *How old would such a creature be*? I wonder. *And what sort of mongrel's face does the child have?* For the Queen is a cold bitch, and I cannot imagine her gifting one seed of her own power or beauty, even to an offspring.

But—I think—*how valuable might such a creature be in a game of blood and politics?* I know that answer: for rumor has it that the Dark Lord has sent his servant Red Cap abroad in the world to find the child, to make it his own, and thus taunt the Queen and weaken her more.

I touch the lid of the casket that holds my precious vials of blood and reflect on the girl who challenged me not too long ago. She was difficult to subdue, and her blood rolled away from me, refusing to enter the pipettes. I thought her nothing more than the unexpected descendant of an old throwback; the distant child of a goody wife who once wet-nursed a fairy child with her own and mingled faerie blood and milk into her veins.

I shall find her again, for I laid the trouble knot deep into her skin. And when I do, I will strike a bargain with Red Cap, dupe him into believing she is the child he seeks—for she carries enough of the sap of the Greenwood to feel true. In exchange, I will demand the Un-Seelie court grant me the fertile power of the tithe and I will use her blood and these collected vials to pay the price. There will be no shortage of Highborn women willing to conceive an infant, even if it is under the dark of a withered moon. Light will come from dark, and pure blood will rise again from the polluted springs of mortal veins.

38

Meteora Meets Red Cap

My hands trembled as I lifted and swallowed in one gulp a small glass of the fortifying spirits Baba Yaga kept in the back of her icebox. I let the strong flavor of anise sear my throat, praying it would settle the frantic racing of my heart. Then I poured a second glass. This time I drank more slowly, sipping the fiery brew until my belly was warm and my pulse had slowed. I had not thought to see him out here in the mortal realm. And yet there he was, his cadaverous face reflected in the window of a shop as he strolled down the street. I watched, half hidden in a doorway, as people instinctively avoided him, leaning away as he passed by, as if he were a harsh wind. Or perhaps it was the carrion reek that emanated from his withered skin. Glamour can hide most terrifying things, but not the stench of decay.

I hurried home, frightened and perplexed. For what reason could Red Cap have come here? To this city? To any human city before the turn of the season? I could not help but sense the world unraveling at the borders. The Greenwood was far away, and yet, I could hear the echo of its dissatisfaction even here. My fey bones beneath the mounded flesh felt a tremor in the joints as power shifted from one hand to another. *Red Cap abroad in the streets!* It was the worst of many signs I had been noticing for almost a week now.

The only comfort I had was the grass green envelope in my hand that carried a new letter from my sister. I prayed for her words to bind me to the earth. As I read the letter, my eyes grew wider, my hands more steady. *"We have been dropped into this cesspit for a reason,"* she wrote, and with that sentence, she had given me hope that all the pieces of this unruly game of power were not yet in play. Mayhap a few still waited, hidden and quiet, while the pawns cleared a space for them on a board growing crowded with treacherous foes. I needed her to know just how treacherous they really were.

> *My dearest Serana,*
>
> *As always we are of one mind; even the distance cannot change the concordance of our thoughts. But we tread a muddy path. These wounded birds may have been drawn to us, seeking champions in a game of power. But why us? And where do we seek for truth?*
>
> *As to the girl—since handing me the bag with mandrake roots and seeing my displeasure, she has been reluctant to approach again. When I work in the garden she is a slender shadow leaning against the railing of her balcony. Sometimes I catch the sharp reek of her tobacco and sometimes the animal musk of fear. How can she possibly confront those fears with that mark on her neck? She is searching for an answer without knowing the question. As we surely do, sister, as we surely do.*
>
> *It rained today, and under the shelter of an umbrella I ventured out to the street where the students gather in shops drinking bitter brews. Tucked between the shops are "parlors" where some of the children are changed into walking spells. Their ignorance astounds me. How little*

they realize the spells of undoing and confusion
they allow to be inscribed upon their arms, their
shoulders, their legs, bellies, necks. I saw a boy with
wings etched on his back—did he know that he has
damned himself seven years to be tortured as a
bird lost in a wood? Yes, I saw a few with blessed
spirals, may their lives be always turning toward
the mysteries, but most were dull and stupid, a
heart that will always be broken, a butterfly for a
short and meaningless life, a snake that devours
the will, and barbed wire, proclaiming a life of
pinpricked sorrows.

But now I must reach for the courage to tell you
what near-crossed my path. Hold steady your hand
upon the letter and pray that it will not flame up at
the mere writing of his name. From across the street,
this very afternoon, I saw a monster entering the
door of one of these parlors. The hand that turned
the knob was black and clawed, thorns breaking the
skin at the knuckles. Yes, you know that hand, for
have we not always feared it? While at court, kept
ourselves well clear of its vicious cuff? He sniffed
and I pressed my bulk into another doorway,
terrified of his gnarled face. There was a glamour of
course, a mask that hid the rotted wood of his flesh.
But he wore the glamour badly and I saw him
clearly even though others did not.

Who summons Red Cap to the game before
Solstice? Has the Queen struck a bargain with this
servant of the Dark Lord? Or has he all on his
own crept out of his hole to caper in the light of the
human city? How has he the strength to do it? And
why?

I thought I had some measure of courage and
yet now I tremble to the very marrow of my bones.

What say you, Serana? Are we two strong
enough to push back this darkness? Or is it
beyond our strength? I suspect we should run off

screaming, but now there are children clinging to us so I know your answer already. We will remain.

Have you any sense, dear sister, of what is afoot?

> *More precious to me you are than*
> *ever before,*
> *Meteora*

39

Serana Recoils

Red Cap? She saw Red Cap? Surely not. Not there in her far-city before the Solstice. Not in a place where iron binds the bones. He would not chance it. Not for long at any rate.

Yet how could she mistake him? Why should she lie?

I read the lines on the page again. I smelt the blood, so like iron, slamming through my nostrils. It burnt my nose hairs. I houghed like a goat trying to get the smell out.

Red Cap! I will not say his name aloud lest it become a summons. I hate that Meteora has seen him but it explains so much. The last Red Cap I saw was in a Lowland peel tower, where he waited for unwary travelers, his cap so stained with their blood it was a deep, pulsating, malignant crimson. His teeth were green and he was bent over with the weight of all his sins. No sin eater could have ever cleansed that hide. I left immediately and reported him to the Queen. As I had to, for she must know everything.

The Queen. Does it all come back to her? But what game does she play with the UnSeelie folk? Can they somehow have her in their thrall?

No more. My poor head reels with questions that

have no answers, and soon I will be as useless as my bile-filled boy.

He stayed with me three days, hardly speaking, answering none of my questions, as if I spoke to him in an alien tongue. Then, when the moon became big with herself, as big as a woman in the last stages of birth, I could see he was hungering to leave. And suddenly I did not want him to go. Yes, he was a trouble, a pain under my breastbone, as if I had given him life. Though with the difference in our ages now, I might as well have been his granddam.

He had even—in the depths of one night dream—called me such. "Grandma," he croaked.

In response, I wrapped three more long strands of my white hair around the blue stone. Then I put the stone in his pants pocket. At this rate, I shall go bald.

The three days he stayed with me, he refused to open his eyes for more than a blink. Refused to open his mouth to answer my questions. Allowed me only to lead him into the water room to pee as if he were the old one, not me.

I watched him most of those three days as a mother her newborn, but by the third day, with nothing left in the cupboard for either of us, I left to get more food from the store.

Before going downstairs, I locked the door securely behind me, sprinkling the last bits of all my binding herbs on the jamb. Knowing it was the only thing I could do that might keep the boy safe. Then walking quickly down the street, I went to the bodega.

The Man of Flowers looked at me askance, and I do not blame him. I was a wrecked ship on the shore, red-eyed with sleeplessness, frantic with worry, like a deer before hunters.

"Are you . . . ?" he began. As if by magic, lines like old runes appeared on his forehead, signaling concern.

I cut him off with a wave of my hand. I could not involve him in this. "Grandson," I lied, liking the sound of it.

"Ah," he replied. "The children—they break your heart."

I nodded, but all the while I was thinking about this buying and selling of things to eat. Once I would have searched out the petals of shade-loving trillium or the sweet sap that drips behind the bark of trees. Once I would have beaten out butterflies for the nectar in red flowers. Is that not the burden of my tune these days? Once . . .

Instead, with nearly the last of Jamie Oldcourse's money, I purchased eggs and milk, garlic and peppermint; the tiniest carrots stripped of their earthen coats; a cheese veined with blue like marble; three apples, red on one side and golden on the other, because that betokened summer and winter at the same time; and a package of blueberries so impossibly large I thought they must have been made by magic. After much thought, I also added a crisp hollow cracker that longs to be filled with something sweet. And, remembering the magic brownies, chocolate. I think if there is one thing humans have that the fey do not, it is chocolate. *If the benighted scare-bird wants to eat,* I thought, *then I shall feed him. At least until I winkle out why he is here.*

I also bought a pair of gardener's gloves that were hanging over the potted herbs. They were ugly things, a crass green that never grew in a faerie garden, and far too big for my hands, even with the swollen knuckles I now had, but I desired them.

"Are you here?" the wheat-faced man asked.

And indeed, he was right. I was not there. I was back in that funk of a room with the scare-bird. I was in the Greenwood gathering things to eat. "Where else would I be?" I asked.

He nodded and bagged the groceries without speaking further, but there was another star fruit in the bag when I got home that I had not paid for. My debt to the Man of Flowers was mounting, but I did not have the energy to worry about it. All my worry was turned toward my bile-blood boy.

Outside of the store, I passed some boys as tough-looking as the men of the Wild Hunt, their faces pinched with anger, their eyes dark and compressed like nuts that contained only rotten centers. They were talking about creatures I did not know, *Sticks* they called them. Or perhaps it was *Spicks*. And laughing angrily at a joke about the neighborhood going, though they did not say where. They reminded me of the young Highborns, so full of their own worth they could grant none to any other. I hunched my shoulders and walked on by. They looked through me—old age being better than a Cloak of Invisibility—and did not see me at all.

When I got near home, I stripped a rowan branch of its leaves. Below the tree an odd thistle grew, and I took that, too. One never knows when such things will be found again.

Upstairs, the boy was still sleeping. I made myself a salad of greens and herbs, some to keep me in health, some to keep me safe, especially from the Wild Hunt boys.

And then I lay down by the scare-bird and slept.

ON THE FOURTH DAY, OR rather the night, the scare-bird sat up, smiled, and waved his hand at me, not like a grandson to his granddam, but more a princeling to a servant—and an overbearing princeling at that.

I came over to see what he wanted, and realized that I knew him. Knew him from the green park near the fat river. He was the young man with the pipe who had called the birds. Who played the long-necked lute. Who even played a fiddle, or so said the girl with the spring name. Of a sudden, I remembered that he called himself Robin, and as puffed up as a robin he certainly was.

How could I have not recognized him from the first? What magic had disguised him, besides the magic of a dirty face, wet hair, bile blood, and a cover over his head as he slept? How could I *not* have known before?

And then I remembered the magic brownies, not to think kindly on their chocolate-ness, but to remind myself how they had befuddled my mind—made me laugh and cry and then sleep as though dead. Perhaps he had been even more susceptible to them. Perhaps they had corrupted his very nature and made him unrecognizable—to himself as well as to me.

No wonder, though, that I had taken him in. Not because he had asked for sanctuary, but because of what I owed him. He had given me back my coins, and done it with words that were both Highborn and low. My body knew what my mind did not. *Perhaps now the debt is paid. Even overpaid*, I thought.

But first the princeling beckoned. "Goddess," he said, "but I am starved."

I almost throttled him, but—as if under a summoning— went directly to the kitchen to make him something to eat.

Taking out three of the six eggs I had just purchased, I carefully coddled them in their shells. I did this in case the boy was really a wicked spirit, a changeling who would then be forced to speak out in wonder and disclose himself. But he just gobbled the eggs down and demanded three more. *Three more!* They were to have been my own dinner and breakfast as well. I ground my teeth but said nothing. *Does he not understand how indebted I am becoming to the Man of Flowers, to Jamie Oldcourse? But what princeling ever cares about the woes of others?*

As he ate, I sat down in the big chair by the window, drew a piece of almond-colored paper to me, and leaning on the sill, wrote to my sister of the boy's sleep and wakening and all of my fears.

Sister, I wrote, *if only I had fairy gold, and could spend it prodigally I would, but alas that*

path is closed to me. I would not even care that in
the Greenwood such gold often made my hands
swell and hives to break out on my back and
under my breast. I would dare more damage to
this enfeebled, old body just to have much money
at my command.

But of course I gave the scare-bird the last of
the eggs and went without supper myself, all so I
could question him.

After he finished eating, belching loudly, I put aside
my half-written letter and tried to name him.

"Robin!" I said, but he did not recognize the name, or
else did not want me to know the dart had struck true.
Either way, it was not his True Name. That I would have
known at once for had it been, he would have bowed to
me, groveled, begged to do me service.

However, he gave another name so freely, I know it
was not his True Name either.

"Vanilla Blue," he said. Yet he neither smelled like the
fresh, sharp vanilla nor had any of the longing that the
color blue conjures. I suspected he understood the power
of Names and was playing with me.

Well, two could play such small games. I told him to
call me Auntie Em, borrowing the first initial of my sister's name. For some reason that made him giggle,
though I could not figure out why.

He went to bed soon after, and that was the whole of
our conversation.

As soon as he slept, I finished my letter to Meteora.

So I worry about this boy, your girl, the puzzle
pieces. But mostly I worry about that Red Cap you
saw. Or think you saw, though I do not doubt your
word.

You must tell me if you ever see Red Cap again.
And I will let you know should I see any such
myself. If the UnSeelie folk are truly moving easily
into this world, well—there goes the neighborhood.

(That is a joke I overheard in front of the Man of Flowers store, though it seemed more frightening than funny at the time. Perhaps it was meant to be both.)

Your loving Serana

40

Hawk Casts a Net

I sit outside at a small table that is covered with a thin sheen of dirt and coffee stains. The girl who waits on me takes no notice of the filth, but merely writes my request for tea on a pad and disappears. She has several tattoos, none of them mine. They are crude designs, stamped into her skin with no sense of how the furrows of ink should nestle against the body's curves. She will age and they will age, sagging without grace until her skin resembles the mottled hide of a toad. I turn away, bored and irritated. *Not much longer*, I remind myself. *Not much longer.*

I stare at the humans passing me on the street. They are young, but already their flesh sings of weariness. Better to free them from their anxieties, their uselessness. I do not feel remorse or shame for the bargain I have struck with the Dark Lord's loathsome servant. But I swallow a mouthful of the scalding tea the girl has brought in an effort to wash away the rancid taste of our encounter, for Red Cap poisons the air with his graveyard breath.

Red Cap. I whisper the name without fear, for I know him better now. He tried to impress me with signs of his power; the stink of carnage that flies from his mouth, the claws that scratched and fondled his prick, and the eternal well of pain in his stone eyes. He boasted that his hound was on the trail of the child in a far-off city, that I had nothing to offer him. But I did not purchase his tale for he wears the leather collar of his Dark Lord, and though it is decked with onyx, bloodstones, and rubies, it serves a function other than fashion. He has come to me because he has been ordered by his Lord not to fail or his head will rest on a pike. His own servants will feast on his carcass and another will be enjoined to wear the cap o' blood.

I have no such allegiances to the Queen, nor do I fear her reprisals for she will not venture from the court. And there is no one among the Highborn who would come forth as her champion. She has walled herself away from the bitterness of the clans who have watched their numbers and their world dwindle. They remain at court, mute but filled with anger, clinging to a fading past.

The tea, despite the taste of human pollution, cleanses my palate. I dip my finger into the black brew and begin to trace a wet, circular line on the table. A sending designed to call its brother etched into the neck of the girl who resisted me. I can see her face, a lean oval, the cheekbones rising beneath moss-colored eyes, the kissable truculent mouth, and a small white scar at the corner of her upper lip bearing witness to an old beating. I hesitate, wondering if she might actually be the Queen's lost whelp, for there is in her features and in the defiant blood traces of the fey. I shrug. It doesn't matter whether she is or isn't. I only need Red Cap to believe it and his own hunger makes him an easy dupe.

The pattern forms beneath my finger, and I dip my finger again into the cooling tea to draw more lines across the table's scummy surface. I do not need the girl to come to me to snare her like a hare in a hunter's noose. The knot of trouble on her neck will do as I ask. I do not need to collect her blood, only truss her slowly in the spider's silk of my tattoos: the adder and scorpion to bind her will to mine. When she is weakest, I will claim her, a valuable hostage, in a game of power between the Queen and the Dark Lord.

41

Sparrow at the Crossroads

From her place at the foot of the bed, Lily growled deep within her throat. Sparrow lifted heavy lids and stared at the moon-washed ceiling. She nudged Lily with one foot to quiet her and felt the dog's tensed body. Turning her head toward the bedroom door, Sparrow became aware of the dull thumping and banging from the floor below punctuated by men's raised voices. *Anger?* She closed her eyes again and settled back into the pillow. *Maybe just drunken defiance.* With Alex and Nick it was hard to tell. Mostly they were just bristle and balls.

"Shhh." Sparrow hushed the agitated dog. "It's only the dorks downstairs. Let it go, Lily. They'll pass out soon."

Lily's disapproving growls quieted to a soft rumble, but her head remained lifted, ears erect, snout turned toward the door.

Sparrow scratched her left forearm aimlessly. Lately, it seemed that Alex and Nick had become more outrageous than usual, and their choice in girlfriends had gone from bimbo to beastly. The last pair had been wrong on so many levels, their lips too red, their translucent skin greenish beneath the porch light, eyes too large and wet, peering out beneath a fringe of stringy hair. "Damn tweakers," Sparrow snorted and wondered when the boys had become so desperate.

The itch on her left arm began to burn the longer she

scratched it. Curious, Sparrow raised her arm to the moonlight, wondering if she had unknowingly cut herself, or picked up some sort of allergic reaction to a bug bite. The silvery moonlight fell in a broken pattern on her arm, revealing a curved shadow on her skin that seemed to be the source of her pain. She switched from itching to rubbing, hoping to lessen the fiery irritation on her arm. But she was much too tired to turn on a light and investigate more thoroughly. She'd figure it out in the morning. Reaching down, she stroked Lily's ears, the velvety touch of fur comforting.

Lily stopped growling and licked Sparrow's fingers. *I am here*, the gesture said.

Sparrow smiled, closed her eyes, and curled into a ball, dropping effortlessly back into sleep. And dreams.

In the dream, she lay curled in a fern bed, her back against the warm, rough hide of the deer nestled beside her. She tasted again the wild berries that had stained her lips and felt her hands close around the gathered acorns in her pockets. Surrendering to the sensations, Sparrow instinctively understood this to be a healing dream, a dream of the forest that surfaced whenever she felt threatened. Her arm prickled and she frowned. *Why do I feel threatened?*

Mist angled through the trees, chasing away nesting birds in the branches above. They rose in a clamor of cries and pounding wings. Then the mist reached below the boughs and brushed the shrubs and grasses with icy hands. Delicate ferns bowed, heavy with pearly drops that slowly hardened into frost. Whimpering, Sparrow clenched into a ball, knees to nose. The deer were gone and she shivered as a clammy breeze cupped her face. The scar on her thigh ached. Her lashes were crusted with rime and she could not open her eyes.

Groaning as a wave of tiny stings pierced the skin of her forearm, she was all ice and fire; her face cold as though washed in snow, but her arm throbbing with a scalding burn. Tears brimmed beneath her closed lids as she rubbed her arm, trying to soothe the flaming skin.

Distantly, Sparrow heard Lily's barking and she struggled to rouse herself. Suddenly, she became aware of a second, more demanding voice.

"Wake up! Sparrow, wake up for godsakes! Lily's going fucking crazy!" Marti shouted at her. "Sparrow, wake up!"

The dream dissolved like shredding storm clouds, but the pain continued to blaze on her arm. Sparrow blinked rapidly and opened her eyes wide to the muted gray of early dawn.

"Quiet, Lily," she mumbled. "Quiet, girl. It's all good." She ran a hand down Lily's neck and shoulders, smoothing down the stiffened hackles on the dog's spine.

"No it's not," Marti said, standing at the open door of Sparrow's room. "I thought you were dead and Lily was scaring the hell out of me. She's been barking like that for about an hour and wouldn't let me near you. What's the matter with you? Couldn't you hear it? Are you drunk *again*? Or stoned?"

Sparrow wrenched herself upright on her elbows. "Neither," she answered thickly, her tongue tasting of bile. A wave of nausea rolled up from her stomach to her throat. "Getting sick, I think." She glanced over at Marti hovering at the open door. Her robe was pulled tightly around her body like armor, her arms crossed over her breasts. She was trembling, and Sparrow realized how scared she was, and how angry.

"For fuck's sake, Sparrow," Marti said, and drew a shaky hand across her face. "I can't take this anymore. I don't want to move, but between you howling at the moon, or getting dead drunk, and now that dog turning Cujo on me, I've had it. Some of us get up early to go to work." Turning brusquely from the door, she stormed off down the hallway. Then she slammed her bedroom door. Sparrow could hear the low, pissed-off rumble of a male voice. Mitch. He was here, too, to witness Sparrow's complete humiliation.

"Shit!" Sparrow sat up, dazed and chilled from the fading remnants of her nightmare. Gazing down at her arm, she gave a hoarse cry, for circling her arm—elbow to wrist—was an elaborate tattoo of a snake, its fangs buried in the swollen veins of her wrists. She brushed her fingertips over the black lines. The rows of snake scales shuddered and the muscular coils seemed to tighten their grip on her arm. From its diamond-shaped head, the crimson snake eyes glared up at her. Sparrow gasped as a charge of venom penetrated her veins with fire and then spread a cold numbness across her palm. The skin of her fingers suddenly bleached white.

Sparrow stared, transfixed by the slow undulations of the snake's body, at the fangs digging deeper into her flesh. A splash of new sunlight spilled across the bed, the warming rays falling over her outstretched arm. As it illuminated the tattooed snake, the skin glowed and then faded. Pale scales covered, then concealed the baleful red eyes. Quiet in the dawn's light, the snake settled against her skin and, mercifully, warmed her chilled hand. She wriggled her fingers and the flesh turned pink again.

In the healing sunlight, Sparrow swallowed her fear and studied the lines of the tattoo. *Hawk. It had to be Hawk.* What a fool she'd been to challenge him in his own shop. She had underestimated the extent of his power. And now he was letting her know that he was coming for her.

Exhausted, Sparrow lay back on the bed, drew her knees to her chest, and pulled the sheets tightly over her head, breathing heavily into the musty folds of the fabric, rank with the odor of her sweat. Fear-washed blood churned through her limbs, but when it throbbed against the puckered scar on her thigh, she whispered, "Enough!"

Fear and Hurt. She'd hauled those twin bastards all her life until the one day she fought back. True, she had to flee to save her life. There was no other choice back then. *But the real question is how much longer am I going to keep running?* She uncurled her body and forced her legs over the side of the bed.

"So—what do you want to do about this?" she asked

aloud. She stood abruptly, as though to defy the sudden weakness in her limbs and the terror in her heart. *Fight back*, she wanted to proclaim, but before the words could reach her tongue, she doubled over and vomited into a wastepaper basket by her bed.

Lily scampered out of the room, her ears flat against her head at the sounds of Sparrow's retching.

SPARROW LAY BACK ONCE MORE in bed, waiting. She could hear Marti and Mitch arguing as they got ready to leave for work, banging kitchen cupboards, stomping around the apartment as though to pay Sparrow back for Lily's barking into the wee hours. Then with a jangle of keys, the slam of the front door, they were gone. Sparrow heaved a sigh of relief as the apartment settled into a calm quiet. She was halfway to the bathroom for an aspirin when she heard the keys in the lock and Marti burst into the living room.

"Those little punks have skipped out," Marti announced. "Nick and Alex. They're gone and the place is a disaster."

"Shit!" Sparrow groaned. Rents were due soon, and Baba Yaga wasn't going to like it that they would be short. "How bad?"

"Really bad. Looks they trashed it just to be assholes."

"Crap." Sparrow squeezed her eyes shut against the throbbing pain of a headache. Her throat was scratchy and dry from heaving.

"But I have an idea," Marti said, speaking rapidly. "Mitch and I will clean it up and in return, maybe you could put in a good word to the rental agency so that Mitch and I could move down there."

Sparrow opened her eyes.

"Look," Marti was saying, "I know I was a bitch this morning—and I'm sorry for that—but really, I think it's time Mitch and I found our own place. What do you think?"

"Sure," Sparrow said. "I'll talk to them." It was an

easy lie. There was no rental agency. Just an office where students left phone messages, which Sparrow always answered. How exactly tenants came to the house Sparrow didn't know, but she figured Baba Yaga had her own method for selecting them.

"Thanks a ton," Marti answered, smiling. "We'll take care of it tonight, after work. Look, I'm sorry I can't stay to make you tea, especially if you're getting sick."

"Don't worry about me." Sparrow waved away Marti's concern. She forced herself to smile, even though she felt miserable down to the soles of her feet. "I'm a big girl," she joked. "I can take care of myself. But thanks for the offer. Go now, or you'll be late for work."

"See you later then. Feel better." And then Marti was gone, leaving Sparrow alone, still weak and trembling.

"Okay," Sparrow murmured. "Looks like I'm making a stand right here ... even if it kills me. If not here in Baba Yaga's house, then where else?" She glanced down at Lily who was wagging her tail frantically at the sound of Sparrow's words. "But first an aspirin, then some food for the mighty beast, right, girl?"

Lily barked her approval and danced in a circle.

42

Sparrow's Plan

Sparrow sat in the far back corner of the Central Library, a stack of books at her elbow. The librarian thought she was doing research on fairy tales for a paper and had helped Sparrow use the library's database to search articles and books on fairy lore, tales of fairy possession, and protection from fairies. She had a small spiral notebook and wrote down anything that might be useful to her now. She knew the usual things of course, a cross and holy water, though she shied away from them. She didn't think it right or effective to use the sacred symbols of a religion one didn't know anything about much less believed in.

No, she had been rescued all those years ago in the woods. She was pretty sure it was in nature that she would find her protection, even if she did live in the city.

The last two nights had been difficult, but she'd learned something since Hawk had marked her for a second time: the tattoos had the power to harm her only when she slept at night. With enough coffee, she could stay awake till morning. Then she could sleep, but only restless catnaps to avoid the dreams that still hovered even during waking hours.

In that time, Marti and Mitch had cleaned the downstairs apartment and quietly moved in. Sparrow told them the new lease was coming soon. That gave her a chance to pick up a boilerplate lease at a stationery store and write in the house name and Marti and Mitch's name as well. She decided against a new roommate. Instead, she planned to get a second job like waitressing or something to help pay Marti's share of the rent. She didn't want anyone else in her home while dealing with Hawk.

Leaning back in her chair, she yawned, stretching her arms overhead. The long sleeve of her turtleneck pulled back and revealed the snake's head, its fangs still clamped around her wrist. Sparrow yanked down the sleeve to hide it and returned to the book in front of her. It was a textbook on psychological disorders and Sparrow had thought it an odd choice until the librarian pointed out a section of the book that dealt with patients whose psychoses were clustered around various claims of fairy possession.

"Maybe this could help you find what you need," she'd said, sympathetically.

Their stories unnerved Sparrow, made her wonder and second-guess her own life, for these patients had also grown up in small communities, with histories of child abuse, domestic violence, and tragedy. She tapped her right forefinger against a passage about a girl whose history was a bit too much like hers.

But not one of the patients—not even the girl on the page under Sparrow's finger—had lived what she had lived through, Sparrow reminded herself. Not one had been claimed by the woods, staying two years among the wild, sheltered at night by deer. In those days, when she needed it, she'd found clothing waiting for her beneath a bush or tree; not just stolen jeans and T-shirts, but also woven cloaks of rough wool, felted mittens lined with down feathers, and hats of rabbit skin. For most of the year there was always food growing wild: onions, sorrel, fairy spuds, berries, mushrooms, and nuts. And when there wasn't enough to scrounge in the dead of winter, she would wake to find a small cake in her hand made of seed, dried berries, and coarse-ground flour.

"Match that!" she whispered to the people in the book.

She might never have been found had she not wandered too close to a campground one spring night, attracted by the sounds of human laughter. She'd been spotted by a young couple, who coaxed her closer to their fire. Though she'd tried to resist, it was no use. She'd missed the sound of human voices. They'd fed her cookies, and as she savored the sweet exotic taste, they had asked her a few questions. She tried to remember how to lie, or better, tell the truth without saying too much. But it hadn't worked. While Sparrow waited for the woman to heat up some dried stew from a small clear pouch plunged into boiling water, the man had disappeared. Sparrow thought he had gone to relieve himself, but he returned shortly with a park ranger, who clapped his hand on her shoulder and asked her far more penetrating questions while she shoveled the food into her mouth. Three hours later, she was in custody, the forest far behind her.

Bending over the book again, Sparrow read the case study of a woman who was convinced she'd lived in the fairy world as a child. She described the splendor, the music, and the unbearable longing that filled her heart when she was unable to find the door into Faerie again. Sparrow knew how the woman felt. Twice she'd run away from foster families. Good people but at a loss how to cope with her. Her nightmares unsettled the other children, her shy silence taken for sullenness. But when she'd run back to the woods, something *had* changed. The animals fled from her, the nights were cold, and no food or clothing appeared in the morning. The door to Faerie was truly shut. She was suddenly more alone than she'd ever been in her life.

I stink of the city, she'd thought then. But soon after, she discovered that while the door was closed to her, it was not closed to *them*. She saw and heard what other humans did not: the hooves beneath the long hem of a pretty girl's skirt; a cocky young man's gleaming yellow eyes as he strolled under streetlights whistling; the small voices that chattered in the rosebushes, in the branches overhead. She had followed a man and a woman one winter day because the man's face wavered as he looked at the woman. The woman saw only the handsome face, blond curls over a broad forehead and a white-toothed smile. But when he tilted his head to the side, Sparrow saw the coal-black eyes, hollowed cheeks and fangs. She wanted to warn the woman, but didn't know how without calling attention to herself. So she followed them, but only a little way for the man raised his head and looked behind him. Sparrow ducked into a shop, terrified, for she had seen the horns curled around his temples, and the red snake of his tongue as it tasted the air. That was when she realized *they* hunted here, just as humans hunted in the woods.

As Sparrow scanned the pages of the case studies, she realized the one thing she'd learned on her return to the human world, and that was how to lie. It had saved her from the well-meaning but clueless therapists and the patronizing foster parents, but not from the hunters and creatures who prowled around her in the bars, on the streets, or anywhere she stayed too long. *They* knew she was not difficult but different. And they resented it. She was like the midwife in the story called to assist at a fairy birth who was given the ability to see into the fairy world only to have her eyes gouged out later by a malicious fey.

"Screw that," Sparrow murmured. It was time to even the score somehow. *Not just for me but for all those hunted women*. She would arm herself with whatever was necessary and go after bastards like Hawk. It wasn't actually murder, was it? After all, he wasn't human, of that she was certain. And if others followed . . . ? Sparrow shrugged. She'd worry about that when the time came.

Checking her list of items, she realized that most of the things on it were easy enough to find: Saint-John's-wort, thyme, and comfrey for one's pockets; red verbena, white daisies, primroses, and peonies to shield one from fairy mischief; stakes made from elderberry, ash, and juniper for protection. Iron she could find down by the train tracks, or at any construction site.

And the last thing she needed was silver. A bit of pure silver. The only charm capable of severing the life from that murderous son of a bitch.

43

⸻

Meteora Has More
Questions Than Answers

"Hey, Sophia," Raul called, sauntering between the bins of stacked vegetables toward the little counter, where I was busy refilling the glass jars from newly arrived bags of fresh herbs. I turned to smile at him, thinking wistfully that he reminded me of someone in the Greenwood.

"It's good to see you," I said, meaning it. "How can I assist you?"

"Actually, I'm here to thank you for assisting us," he said with a polite nod of his head. "Sales are up in the herbal shop, Sophia. I gotta hand it to you. You've really turned it around."

"Julia works very hard too," I said, wanting to be loyal to her.

"I know, but everything changed when you came. So the Co-op board wants to offer you a bit more money and a bonus for everything you've done for us. Make it all aboveboard."

"Is this to make sure I stay?"

Raul nodded, sheepishly. "Yeah. But don't say anything about this, okay? I wouldn't want anyone's feelings to get hurt." He was looking toward Julia who was busy stocking boxes of tea in an adjacent aisle.

"Of course, I understand," I murmured, as he handed me an envelope, which I took with a little nod of thanks.

After he left, I peeked inside and saw the bundle of green bills. Green for the color of the forest, green for the color of the fey, green for joy. I was happy as a tick with my newfound wealth and decided that I would share my good fortune, for to be favored by the Goddess is an invitation as well as an obligation to be generous.

I LUMBERED THROUGH THE PARK that afternoon, my hands firmly clasped around the handles of two overflowing cloth sacks. I came to a towering ash tree, set the bags down and groaned as I settled onto the damp grass beneath the tree. It didn't take long before I heard the rustle of wings, the soft chirrups and clicking beaks in the branches above me. I glanced up at the crows, their heads downturned and cocked, the better to view the feast below.

"It's nicer than the rank garbage behind the shops, is it not?" I asked. One flew off the perch and landed on the grass in the shadows. Lifting its wings and shrugging off the feathers, it became a boy in the dappled light.

"Depends," Awxes said, striding toward me. "A crow likes his food riper than a boy. You'd be surprised what a crow will eat when hungry."

"Will this do then for a boy?" I asked, and handed him one of the wrapped sandwiches from my bag.

He held the sandwich to his nose and inhaled its aroma. Between two pieces of dark wheat bread, spread with mayonnaise and mustard, were thin slices of a rare beef, seasoned with garlic and pepper. I would never have eaten such animal flesh, but I was neither a hungry boy, nor a crow—both of whom enjoyed such fare.

Awxes put the sandwich down and gave me a rare smile. His dark eyes glowed beneath the arches of his black brows, and his teeth were white against his nut-brown skin, which was etched with faint white scars. "It's good," he said shyly. "It will do very well for a boy. And his friends," he added, beckoning the pair of crows still waiting in the branches above. They flapped their wings and drove their bodies into the thickest part of a leafy bush, startling a little scream out of a red-faced woman who was running on a nearby path.

A moment later the two girls emerged, scrambling over one another to join Awxes and me at our meal. They touched everything with their fingers, as though it might disappear as treasure does when one wakes from a wishful dream.

"Go on then, eat, for you have earned it," I said.

"How so?" asked Awxes. He used the tail of his black T-shirt to wipe his chin clean of plum juice.

"I know it must be terribly dull following me each day. And regardless of your purpose, it is a thankless job, for I am of no importance really. And yet someone has set you this task." I turned to the younger girl, her wheat-colored hair braided with stray feathers.

"But you ain't *nobody*," she said, licking the crumbs from the corner of her mouth. "You're special . . ."

"Hsssst!" The older girl put a finger to her lips. "Tell nothing."

"I agree," I said with a smile, trying to hide my burning curiosity. "Be quiet. Eat instead." I leaned back against the tree, peeled the paper off of my own sandwich of cheese, tomato, and something called pesto, and began to eat.

And quiet they were, solely intent on the food. Licking their lips, wiping stray mayonnaise and mustard off their cheeks with the back of a dirty hand, they sucked plum pits, crunched the hard flesh of the apples, and gulped down the bottles of fresh water. However, they did not gobble the cookies, but slowly savored their sweetness. Then they lay down on the grass and slept.

Studying the napping children, I wondered whose darlings they had once been? When had they become exiles from their mothers' arms? What names did they carry then? And why had it never occurred to me before that such a taking might be as cruel for them as my own forcible exile? But what had been done to them was permanent now. They had been changed too much to ever be fully human again.

And why, oh why are they tracking me?

Awxes sat up, yawned widely and gave me a little scowl. "What are you thinking? I can hear the scritching of your thoughts from here."

"Do you remember your parents?" I realized with a shock that it was a question I would never have even considered asking in the Greenwood.

A shadow crossed his face. "Not much. Sometimes I think I hear my mother's voice calling me, but it has been so long, I can't be certain. She's dead by now anyway." Awxes shrugged it off. "Don't fret about us. When this is over we'll all be back in our beds again."

"What is *this*?" I asked, hoping for an answer.

"If we speak of it, we'll never get home," he replied, his brow pinched.

"Where *is* home?"

Awxes looked up and silently pointed into the dense, green canopy of trees. *The Greenwood* he meant, but would not speak the word for fear of losing it.

"But you are human," I argued.

"And you are fey," Awxes said. "And yet look how fat and happy you are here. You make money now instead of magic."

Well, up to a point, he was right. I had made a nest here and in my deepest heart I knew that here would I remain for as long as the Queen willed it. And by the time she changed her mind, this mortal body would surely be dead.

But did I really care? The bustle of the Co-op had brought me unexpected friends, a community of sorts to which I could contribute, if not confide. I had learned how to order a decent cup of tea at the coffee shop and now, they never asked me what I wanted, but brought it to me with a smile. At the Farmer's Market I had become friends with Leila, a woman of middle years and dirt under her nails who grew the finest herbs and kept bees that produced a dark, flowery honey as potent as liquor.

"You are right," I said, "perhaps I have changed in these weeks as you have changed. And though I have no power to return you to that home you seek, let me give you a token to remind you of it." I reached my hand into the front of my blouse—one of Baba Yaga's bizarre flowery affairs—and dug around in my bra.

The girls giggled at the sight of me rooting in my blouse until I pulled out the folded wad of white silk. At once the air was filled with the aroma of lavender, hyssop, bay, and the pungent sap that comes only from the budding tips of the needled pines deep in the Greenwood. To me it smelled of my dam; to them, it smelled of Faerie.

I unrolled the fabric and tore it into small pieces, one for each of them. They took the pieces eagerly and held them over their faces, inhaling deeply.

"Thank you," the oldest girl whispered, tucking the scrap beneath her furred cap.

The smaller girl quickly undid a braid and then entwined the fabric as she rewove her hair.

Then in turn, the girls leaned forward to give me a kiss of thanks on each cheek before plunging headfirst into the bushes.

Only Awxes remained, still staring at the small white square of fabric.

"I will tell you this," he said. "You may think yourself hidden among humans, but you are not. Whether fair or dark, they are coming, drawn by the blood that sings in your veins. Be watchful."

"But why me?"

"It may not be you they seek, but you they will find."

Then he stood and followed the others into the shelter of the brush. A moment later three crows burst from the thicket of green leaves and rose quickly above the trees. But not before I noticed that each now wore a white patch of feathers on their wings.

* * *

As I walked home, I pondered over what Awxes had revealed—which was little enough. None of this made sense, unless perhaps Serana and I were meant to serve as the bait for a larger prize. It was not unknown for Seelie and UnSeelie to use worthless fey in their contentious battles for power.

So who might be using us now? *And for what purpose?* I shook my head, unused to such hard thinking. I tallied up the fey encounters I had experienced since my banishment, searching for answers. There were the changelings waiting for me in the forest the night I fled who followed me still. Baba Yaga, whose hands reached down to pull me into the dragon train. *Should I count these in my favor?* I thought I must until I remembered it was not I who mattered if I was bait. Bait is supposed to sit quietly in the snare. Had I not encountered Baba Yaga, I might well have kept running instead of roosting innocent as a hen on her nest.

Had the merchant sold the girl a mandrake, knowing it would come to me? Had Red Cap been looking for me on that street so near to the Co-op?

No, I decided on the last. He would have sent a slave to check the traps, but never come himself. And yet . . . and yet I had seen him, here. *The prize must certainly be worth the trouble,* I thought, growing ever more concerned for my safety and Serana's.

And what about the Jack? The girl? The downstairs trolls?

Of course, that still left the most important question: *Who am I supposed to attract?* Who or what was so important that the Queen should toss Serana and me into the air like lures to the hawk? My bile-faced girl? Serana's wretched boy? Hardly likely. They were nothing more than a pair of lost birds themselves. Yet both were clearly marked by very dark and powerful forces.

Reaching home, I hesitated on the sidewalk, staring up into the tangle of pine boughs that concealed the house. My skin prickled at the thought of sharp eyes following my every movement, waiting for the moment the prey stepped unknowing into the snare with me. Burying my face in my hands, I gave a little moan, for I finally remembered what usually happens to bait.

I was alone with this. Baba Yaga's house was not a fortress but a wayfarers' station for troubled children, and they could not be counted on in a time of trouble. The trolls, the misery-girl and her dog, the young woman who smelled of pressed sheets and expensive soaps— none were a match for what would be coming. How could I defend them, I who could hardly defend myself?

What if I left? A new wave of hope surged through my body. I could pack my few belongings and leave at once, before anyone knew I was gone. The urge to flee goaded me up the stairs, but in my haste, I stumbled on the last step. A hand grabbed my arm, preventing me from crashing headfirst onto the porch.

"Hey, Sophia, you okay?" Jack pulled me upright into his arms and clasped me tightly. My heart pounded and only the steadiness of his body and the strength of his arms caused it to gradually slow its reckless beating. Standing in his embrace, I noticed the fine sprinkle of freckles across his nose, the silver gray hair curling around his temples, the cobalt blue eyes flecked with bronze. I was also keenly aware of his hands warming my back.

"Yes, thanks to you."

"Not at all." His lopsided smile lifted one side of his mouth.

A flush of embarrassment prickled my cheeks as I disengaged from his reassuring arms. With a cold dash of reason, I remembered that I was bait. For all I knew, this Jack too was here precisely to see that I did not slip the snare.

"I was coming to see you. Found a few things for your garden, around back. I was thinking I might be able to set them into the ground if you like."

"That would be nice," I said a little stiffly.

"Do you need any help getting these bags upstairs?" He picked up my two almost empty shopping bags.

My skin still hummed with the warmth of his arms, and his expression seemed just a friendly invitation. I wanted to say no and turn him away. But then, my inability to do so is exactly what made me such useful bait. Silently I cursed my weakness, but it was too late in any case, for I had already given him my hand.

"I have hauled them home a long way," I replied. "I hope you don't mind?" *Was I being coy?* I scolded myself. *How very ridiculous.*

"Be happy to help," he said and started toward the door.

Before I went in, my eyes darted to the mailbox and I saw the green envelope waiting for me. My fingers itched to take it out, but I decided to retrieve it later, when I was alone. No sense in tipping any more of my hand to the Jack. I was risking enough just bringing him into the house.

I had never noticed how small the kitchen was until I found myself standing there with Jack, unpacking the cheese, eggs, butter, salads, packets of tea, the little white bag of brownies that had become my guilty pleasure, two remaining Bosc pears, a handful of red grapes, a package of blackberries, and three emerald-colored squashes. We kept bumping elbows and hips, mumbling "excuse me" and "sorry" though I know that neither of us was in the least bit sorry for the fleeting contact. When it was done, he lingered a moment longer and I realized I owed him something for his act of kindness. *If kindness it was.*

"Would you like a wee dram?"

"Sounds about right." He smiled broadly.

My hands trembled with excitement as I poured a bit of peat-flavored whiskey into two small glasses. Once again, I chided myself for being so silly, but could not slow the cheerful gallop of my heart.

He raised his glass in my direction. "Here's to the bridge that carries us over."

"Indeed," I murmured, wondering what that old

blessing might mean to a Jack. I raised my glass and drank quickly, the whiskey a pleasant fire on my tongue. Jack drank his more slowly, the bright eyes staring at me over the rim of his glass. When he was done, he looked around, boldly taking in the view of my furnishings, the rugs, and Baba Yaga's flowered scarves hanging in a riot of colors on the wall. The bedroom door, alas, was wide open, revealing an impudent tousle of sheets and blankets, and an apricot-colored slip draped over the unmade bed. He turned back to me with that maddening grin.

"Nice place."

"I wasn't expecting visitors." I dodged past him to close the door to the bedroom, my face a cherry red.

He busied himself finishing his drink, and then set the glass down on the table. "Well, thanks for the dram. Like I said, I just stopped by to tell you I picked up some bulbs and perennials I thought you might like for the garden. I'd be happy to help you put them in. Maybe tomorrow?"

"Yes," I said. "I would like that very much." And then I, who have ever been known to burble and warble, became tongue-tied.

Jack gave me a tip of his head and another long glance from those dangerously blue eyes. Then he squeezed past me out of the kitchen, his fingertips lingering on my arm long enough to leave their warmth before heading toward my door.

"G'night, Sophia," he called as he slipped out.

And still I stood gawky and flustered, all thoughts of fleeing from the house banished.

LATER THAT NIGHT I REMEMBERED Serana's green letter waiting for me in the mailbox. I tiptoed down the stairs, listening to the unusual quiet around me. The trolls were gone, which meant there was no booming music, no cacophony of drunken voices. At the mailbox I discovered why. There were new names on the boxes. A couple now lived in the house. I recognized the one name as the

second girl who lived upstairs with the misery-girl—
someone I saw rarely but recognized by the lavish scent
of her perfume on the stairs. How it had happened that
the boys had left was a mystery. But one I was willing to
let lie, being grateful that they were gone.

On the second landing, Serana's letter firmly in my
hand, I heard the dog's snuffling near the door. I waited
until she had my scent, and smiled as I heard the clip of
clawed feet padding away from the edge of the door.

"Good dog," I whispered after her, grateful for her
vigilance. With the other girl moved downstairs, the
misery-girl was alone and in need of companionship. As
I edged away I caught the sound of low moaning. I
turned back, raised my hand to knock on the door, and
then stopped. *Who am I to intrude on her unhappiness?*
If she came to me, I would welcome her. And I sketched
the old sign of consolation on her door. *Let it serve as an
invitation.*

Once in my rooms, I lit the candles beneath a string of
crystals that their light would sparkle across the ceiling.
I put the kettle on, salvaged a few of the cookies from
my shopping bag that the changelings had not eaten, and
finally sat down to read Serana's letter. It was short, but
I was beginning to wonder about her scare-bird boy;
human enough to eat one out of house and home, sly
enough to offer false names, and yet full of the sort of
poison that comes only from meddling with the wrong
sort of folk. I considered, too, her warning about the Jack
while wondering that she had been so quick to bring into
her hidey-hole a creature even more questionable.

The kettle whistled and I got up to make the tea. Pausing, I heard again the faint sounds of moaning. Something
crashed against the floor below me and I tensed, waiting.
Then the house went silent once more. The cat slept at the
bottom of my bed, and even the dog below had not raised
a barking alarm. *So, what am I worried about?*

I finished making the tea, but as I lifted the cup to my
lips I heard scuffled footsteps on the landing, followed by
a soft knock.

"Who's there?" I gripped the teacup fiercely.

"It's me. From downstairs."

I opened the door and was startled to see my misery-girl standing there. But then I *had* invited her. I tried to recall her name but could remember only the slanderous insults of the trolls.

"I know it's late. But can I come in?" Her voice sounded wounded.

"Yes, of course, come in," I answered. "What do you call yourself?" I asked, opening wide the door.

"Sparrow's good," she said, her eyes nervously sweeping the room before settling on the hanging crystals twirling in the heat of candle flame, casting diamonds of light on the walls. And although *I* may do no more magic with them, the pull of their power is irresistible. Sparrow went and stood in their light. She was dressed all in black, but even the baggy long-sleeved shirt could not hide how painfully thin she was, burning like a wick in a candle. Her arms hugged her body, one hand cupped around her elbow, while the other reached across her chest and pressed against the trouble-tattoo on her neck.

"I'll make more tea," I said to fill the silence. Let her decide in her own time what she has to say. How desperate must she be to come here to a stranger's door late at night?

While I waited for the kettle to boil again, I gathered a tea to loosen the tongue: a mixture of heartsease and sage, chamomile and strife-not. It was fragrant and strong enough that even I would have spilled my secrets if prodded. As I poured her a cup, I heard her speaking softly behind me.

"I am having trouble sleeping. I heard your footsteps and thought perhaps . . ."

I turned, mug in hand, shocked to find her already seated at the table as though she belonged there. It was unsettling for at this private table were the few precious things that I had brought hidden beneath my cloak when I was banished. Sparrow absently thumbed the carved acorns and then rattled the amber beads in their dish.

She picked up the silver dove, weighed it in her palm, held it briefly to the light, and then set it down on top of Serana's letter.

I slid the mug over to her.

She looked up, astonished I think to find *me* so close — and that's when I saw above the smeared black liner, her eyes were brilliant green, faint gold sparks illuminating the dark, troubled yolks.

She looked away, ducking her head to sip the tea. Then she grimaced. "Got any sugar?"

I pushed myself to turn away, toward the cupboard, still distracted by those eyes, perplexed by the way they commanded despite the mask of black smudges and her white pallor, despite the cruel tattoo on her neck that was surely the source of her anguish.

"Are you sure you want sugar?" I asked, rattling an empty canister as I searched for where the serving hands had stored it. "I have a good wildflower honey that is much nicer — "

A whuff of air and a hard click caused me to turn back to the table.

Sparrow was gone, her abandoned mug of tea steaming on the table. As I stood there holding the empty canister, I saw, too, that my silver dove was also gone.

How is that possible? I stood like a dolt blinking at the empty chair. Serana's letter was on the floor, the crystals clinked softly, and the cat slept undisturbed on the bed. *How had she managed to slip away so quietly?*

"Mouse not Sparrow," I grumbled angrily.

Picking up Serana's letter, I sat down at the table again, though my head was urging me to go downstairs and confront her. But at the same time, I wondered what desperate need could have caused her to behave in such a fashion? The longer I wavered between outrage and concern, the more I realized that I would do nothing about the theft even though it pained me terribly.

Instead, I reread Serana's letter, irritated that in addition to exile, it seemed we were both to be burdened by difficult children. But try as I might I could not hold my anger against them. Only a mild disappointment and a sharp concern for my sister's well-being filled me as I began my reply.

> *My dearest Serana,*
> *I send you these green bills to aid you in the task of caring for a child clearly used to life in the courts. Who else but a Highborn thinks nothing of being served by a woman, and demanding food as though it is easily conjured from air? Unless of course, he is not a Highborn, but a stolen child petted and played with until returned to this now-foreign world? Remember how the Queen favors such, raising boys like pups at her knee, wrapped in ribbons and kissed until they grew too old as boys will, even in Faerie, and the melody of their voices change.*
> *Sister, can you imagine how we should feel if we had been cast away as children, banished to this dark world having known only the bright? What poisons might we have swallowed, what desperate acts might we have committed if it promised to return us even to the gates of that far-off place?*
> *Press your scare-bird gently. He comes to you following the fading scent of your magic. We are never so old that we do not seek the comfort of our sweetest childhood memories.*

I thought of Awxes' warning to me. I wanted to tell Serana, but I did not want her to worry about me. When I knew more, that would be the time. For now, I would offer only the slightest ware—enough for my farsighted sister to think again about what seems to have followed us out of the Greenwood.

> *If your boy does come from the Queen, perhaps he serves her only seduced by promises we know she will not keep.*

Of course, he may be like my misery-girl, haunted by something, or someone far darker than the Queen. I would say test your Robin, read his dreams that you may discern the source of his unease.

As for my misery-girl, she comes and goes muffled so deeply in her own thoughts it was only my rune of invitation on her door that brought her to my rooms tonight. She has given me the use of a name, "Sparrow," though I think it is a dissembling name, for few here are called by such poetic epithets. She hides much: her small body in large clothing, her flashing eyes beneath a wide smear of kohl, her hair dyed a dirty black, and all too often she withdraws behind a curtain of smoke. If it weren't for the fact that Baba Yaga's dog adores her, and the cat never raises even a whisker at her entrance, I would have believed her to be in thrall to some darkling lord.

But she came seeking comfort and I gave her the kindness of my open face and a place at my table. And how did she reward me? She stole from me the silver dove that was a gift from the Queen herself to our dam. It is in Sparrow's pocket no doubt, being stroked between those hungry fingers. How could I love such a thieving child? And yet, I saw in her eyes that she feels trapped like a sparrow in a fowler's net. If the dove gives her solace then she must have it, though I miss it already.

I took a sip of tea and thought for a moment. I wanted very much to tell Serana about Jack but I shook my head. Another time. Another letter. I would say only what was necessary for her to understand my feelings.

Tomorrow morning I am going to the garden to dig and plant and make of it something beautiful again. That is the only cure for anger when one can no longer give warts, or boils, or curdle milk, or tangle the weft.

But remember, dearest sister; never turn your back on your scare-bird, no matter how prettily he speaks. Whatever they are, these two do not play by the rules of hospitality.

> The one who loves you always,
> M

44

Summoning the Dog Boy

The moon is up. My father calls. Like the best dog whistler, he summons me in a voice so high, only I can hear. The fog in my head has only recently cleared. But I must go. I want to deny him, but how does one resist?

Still, if I cannot stop myself, I can be slow about going there. I have been bathed, put oil in my hair, brushed my teeth. I may be my father's hound, but I will not misrepresent myself. My human part longs to be clean of him, and free. He will hate that I am late, that I am clean, that my heart still beats in its human tempo. But it is the only small rebellion I can make.

I take what I need. What was given me in love: the silver pipe from my mother's hand, the stone from my grandmother's—or as near a grandmother as I shall ever get. She has fed me, cleaned me, kept me through the dark times. I owe her, but can only repay her in silence.

And then I go out the door, down the stairs. I bid no one good-bye, for I dare not intermix their lives with mine. This danger, this horror is all my own. My father waits in the green park.

The green park!

I will not go to him. I cannot. I will not betray my own. Not again. Not as I did my mother. And sitting down on the stoop, I start to weep, not the tears of a dog. Dogs do not cry. But humans do. Even boys, though we try not to let anyone see.

45

Serana Decides

The sound was low, as if someone was trying to hide it, but I heard. It crept into my dreams of the Greenwood and stained the leaves red. I woke to blood, but not my own. A pigeon on the sill bled from its breast. I went to it, and there was nothing there but the gray shadow of its death.

Red Cap! I thought. But when I looked down into the darker shadows of the street, I saw no one awake but the boy on the steps, barely illuminated. It was as if he drew the street light into himself and turned it to ebony.

The sound I had heard was his weeping. Throwing a cloak over my nightgown, I took the key and hung it around my neck where it burned my breast like a brand. Then I hurried down the stairs to the outside door, flung it open so fast, the knob did not harm me, and padded barefooted down the stairs.

His head was buried in his crossed arms and though he did not look up I could tell by the set of his shoulders he knew I was there.

I sat down by him, pulled him into the vastness of my bosom, and whispered, "I have made up my mind. You are going to my sister's house. You will be safe there from whatever troubles you." And I made the sign of the horns and spat through the middle, to make him safe for now.

Safe? He could be in more danger there than here.

Meteora was the one who had seen the Red Cap. She was the one who had invited in the Jack. But if this was a puzzle that needed two pieces together—the boy, the girl—then I had to send him. I did not know how. But as we walked back into the house, he with face averted so I could not see if the tears still glistened in those fey eyes, I was sure I could find a way.

As we passed my eagle mailbox, I saw something in it—a green envelope, the color of the leaves. And I knew, as I always know my sister's heart, that Meteora had sent me money. I would use it to pay the boy's way to where she resided. *She will understand*, I thought, *for she knows my heart as well.*

ONCE UPSTAIRS, I PUT THE boy back to bed and he was asleep within minutes, fear or horror or exhaustion claiming him. Then I went downstairs again to fetch the letter.

Putting the envelope to my nose, I drew in a deep breath. There was a hint of chamomile, a touch of tansy, but nothing more. A good wife would use such in her cleaning. It was a human smell overriding the herbs, not fey.

She wrote: "*Sister, can you imagine how we should feel if we had been cast away as children, banished to this dark world having known only the bright? What poisons might we have swallowed, what desperate acts might we have committed if it promised to return us even to the gates of that far-off place?*"

I sighed. How much the human world had already changed her. Not only could she work for their money, but she understood them so much better than I.

"Thank you," I spoke to the air, knowing my gratitude would find its way to her. Then I counted all the sheets of the green paper money she had included. So many. I could not help but admire her and prayed that it would be enough to get the boy to her house, for I was determined to send him there.

Finally I went back upstairs to finish my letter and warn her of the gift I was throwing her way.

First, however, I cut a few locks of the boy's hair as he slept, though it was tangled with elf knots. I might later be able to do some small conjuration as he slept, for he did not waken. His breath came long and slow, with a little stutter at the end. Quietly, quickly, I stuffed the hair into one of the gardener's gloves I had purchased at the bodega.

Perhaps the hair could tell me why he had come here, or who had sent him. Perhaps it would say if he were the hunter or the hunted. But whatever it finally told me would not matter. I had already decided that he must leave this city for Meteora's. I did not believe—no, I *dared* not believe—that he had come to me for no reason at all. The world does not work that way. Neither the human world nor the fey.

WHEN I HAD FINISHED WRITING my letter, I put it in its envelope and wrote out the address, then stood and placed it on the shelf, next to the batch of her letters, determined to send it in the morning. Only then did I realize that something was not quite right with my sleeping boy after all. The letters from Meteora, tied with a green ribbon, lay an inch to the left of where I had left them, no longer between two of the nails holding the mantel over the fire, but directly on one. I had been most careful about that.

That little thief! He must have taken them down. No one else had been in my rooms. He had read something of what my sister had written. What kind of person would do such a thing, being a spy in the house of a friend? Not Vanilla Blue at all, but definitely Robin O' the Green, the tricksy one. Still, I would not let him know I guessed for that would lose me my one bit of an edge.

Oh, you rapscallion, I thought and determined to sit up all night just to keep an eye on him. To be certain that he actually slept.

And to be certain that I did *not* sleep, I rolled bits of garlic wrapped in peppermint into two tiny balls and shoved one in each of my nostrils. The smell alone kept me up, even without the herbs' wakefulness properties, till the first tendrils of false dawn crept across the windowsill.

In all that time, Robin did not move, but slept deeply, even snoring a bit, probably exhausted by his tears and his mischief combined.

"JOIN ME FOR TEA," I said, as he struggled from the bed— rubbing his eyes and yawning.

I had made a peppermint tisane, strong enough to disguise what else I had put in: the berries, a single blue at the bottom of his cup, twice broken, twice blessed, that he might do my bidding without complaint. I hoped I had that much magic left.

He went to the water room, then came back and took the cup from me, more to soothe any misgivings, I would guess. My own cup, prepared before, had no berries at all. We clinked the cups together, and then he took a huge gulp to please me, to cozen me, or perhaps to remove the sleeping parchment from his mouth. He smiled, then took another sip. And another. Then, without prodding, he said, "I dreamed that I was a crow flying over a landscape that looked like a chessboard."

"A chessboard?"

"Squares of black and red, and . . ." His hand described a draughts board.

"How . . . odd," I remarked, though I thought it all of a piece. Surely it was the Queen's Game he'd dreamt, perhaps the Black Knight's gambit.

He shook his head, till the hair covered one eye. "That's not the odd part. I dreamed I was hunting for something."

"What were you hunting?" I drew in a quiet breath. Waited.

"Some . . . girl," he said, "with purple hair. Or maybe

black. And a tattoo on her neck like a bruise. Isn't that . . . weird?"

The blessed blueberry had done its work. Or else he was guiling me, using the descriptions of the girl in Meteora's letter. How much could he have read while I was downstairs getting my eagle mail? Not enough, I hoped. Though he could have read it at other times, when I was at the shop, perhaps, and I, thinking he slept. I decided to assume that I still had some herbal magicks in me and smiled at him as if fondly. "Definitely . . . weird." But all the while I wondered if he were testing me as I him. And I was beginning to think his dream significant enough for me to act upon it. Farseeing I might be, but he seemed already well ahead of me. I could scarcely wait until he was gone back into dreams so I could do something about my suspicions.

Again the blueberry blessing did not fail me. He yawned. Shrugged. Returned to the bed and fell into sleep. This time I was sure of it.

I shut all the curtains but one that overlooked the trees. The rowan shook silver leaves where the setting moon shone on it. Those spindly trees are nothing like our forests, but they were all I had. "Watch," I whispered to them. "Hold."

Taking his teacup to the window, I stared at the bottom. The leaves were muddied and unclear. I turned the cup from side to side, tried to make sense of the reading. At last I brought the cup back to the cleaning sink and set it down.

Then I took up the glove and shook out Robin's hair onto the low table, making a circle of it with a red candle at the center. I had found that candle in one of the cupboards, pushed way to the back. Found things have great power.

Luckily, there was no wind to disturb the circle of hair and thus destroy my symmetries. Luckily there were no passersby to call out drunkenly and challenge the line of my chant. For once, the streets were still of sirens and motor horns. I judged I had arrived at the moment for my spell.

Pricking my finger with a small pin, I let a drop of blood bead before placing the finger—blood first—onto the flame to put it out.

Yes, blood-castings are dangerous. But the tea leaves were unclear. My scare-bird might have simply been a good boy brought low by dreams. He might have been only a curious lad who looked through my letters as a child reads signs. But I guessed he was something more. The Queen's tool? A spy for the UnSeelie? A minion of Red Cap's? I had to be sure, or at least as sure as my feeble spells might tell me. Because if I was right, I needed to send him to my sister at once, put him next to the black-haired girl, or throw him into the Red Cap's path.

So danger or no, I went the way of blood. The spiral of smoke began to twist upward and I held my breath. Slowly it formed a picture. I was relieved, of course, that such a casting still worked here, in this rough, magic-lorn city.

The twisting smoke made a picture that was as clear as the tea leaves had been muddled. And what the picture showed me made me start. Not with alarm, but with a kind of relief. In the smoke was my trickster and the tattooed girl, their mouths devouring one another, breast to breast, so entwined nothing could part them. And all about them were dancing stars.

As I wrote quickly to Meteora:

> *What have we all unwitting stumbled into?*
> *Blood of my blood, brood of my brood, take care.*
> *This is a deeper, darker, stranger knot than we can*
> *pick apart by ourselves, more mixed and messed.*
> *Come thicket, come thorn, we have already*
> *touched what we should not have. And now we*
> *must continue. The road back is worse than the*
> *road forward so I have chosen the forward path*
> *and drag you along with me as always.*

Then as the scare-bird snored his stuttering snore, I sewed rowan leaf crumbles into his trouser waistband as proof against witches, adding a sprig of the thistle sewn into the lining of his jacket to protect him from the worst. Whatever that worst might turn out to be. Though should he take off jacket or trews, he would be without protection indeed.

MORNING CAME AND ROBIN ROSE half-reluctant from his bed. I gave him another meal, which bound him even further to me by rules of human conduct, if not enchantment. Then I bade him get dressed.

"I have something for you to do," I said. "A letter to deliver."

He smiled the vague smile of one slightly addled, for I'd given him another dose of the blueberry-blessed tea.

The letter I handed him was not the one I'd written to Meteora. I am not such a fool. That other was already safely put into the eagle mailbox as Robin slept his last bit of night away. This note was another I had prepared simply for him, with Meteora's address on the envelope. He could rip it open and read if he liked. All it said was, "A present for you, dear sister."

Then we went to the bus station, a place we were sent to by a man outside of the bodega. I had asked for someone to carry my "grandson" to Wisconsin. We had a momentary kerfuffle with plane (in the air), train (on a rail) and bus. When they were explained to me, and the prices as well, I chose bus. The scare-bird said nothing, still quite bespelled.

We could not walk all the way to the place of buses, but took one of their own to the great corral. The iron surround quite undid me and I swore to walk all the way home. But at the place of buses waited the huge traveling carts, ready to take travelers to far places. The money Meteora had sent just covered the fare, with a bit left over for Robin's food and drink. It would take—so I was told—two days. I asked three people and each said the same. *Three times, the charm's wound up.*

Before he got onto the bus, I handed Robin a cup of

the now-cold blueberry blessed tea and he drank it eagerly enough. I thought it should keep him safely on the bus till time to get off.

Then I spoke to the driver who waited by the door for all his passengers to settle down.

"You will make sure the boy gets off in Milwaukee?" I stuttered over the name of the city since I had spoken it only once before.

"I will be sure he is transferred properly."

"My sister awaits him. He is a bit . . . addled."

The driver smiled. "We say differently abled now."

Oh, I thought, *the boy is differently abled all right.* More than the driver would ever know. The trick had been to get him *inabled* enough for the trip, but I did not say so aloud.

I waved at Robin as the bus pulled out, remembering what I had written at the bottom of my eagle mail.

> *Think carefully before introducing him to your Sparrow. If you do not believe it to be the right thing to do, send him back to me at once. He will have his return in his pocket. But if my smoke vision and his dream are true, they must meet anyway, so why not under our guidance and blessing?*
>
> *With hope, that pale sister of belief,*
> *I am yours always,*
> *Serana*

As soon as the bus had lumbered out of sight, I walked home, a long trip but good enough to clear my mind. And there I made myself a cup of tea untainted by blessings, sorrow, hope, or fear.

46

Meteora Receives a Present

For the better part of a week I worked in the garden with Jack by my side. There was much to be done, and we had little time for it as the cold nights and the sudden downpour of chilly rains proclaimed the advance of autumn. But Jack told me not to worry. There was always one more chance at late summer that would come after the first frost bit the tips of the leaves. It would warm up again for a brief time and flowers would give forth one last burst of blossoms.

As for Sparrow, she avoided me after our encounter in my kitchen, but I was determined not to let it build a wall between us. I waited for her one morning on the porch and caught her as she was about to walk the dog, a charming creature, all mouth and tail. This time Sparrow could not swerve past me because the dog, having decided that I was someone worthy of knowing, sat down and would not budge until I had thoroughly caressed her ears.

"What a lovely dog," I said, looking at Sparrow, who was avoiding my eyes. "What's her name?"

"Lily," she mumbled, tugging at the leash. I caught her eyes and I saw neither shame nor guilt in them, but defiance, which I must admit surprised me.

"Come and see me again," I offered. "Your visit was much too short the other night and I would be pleased to welcome you."

"I might do that. I'm a little busy just now. But soon, maybe I'll stop by for some of that tea." Her face was haggard, bluish circles under her eyes. I guessed that she had chosen not to sleep rather than ride the dark mare that caused her to moan so fitfully in the night. But there was also something else going on for her expression was calm, almost devious, and I noticed with a slight shock that she was appraising me even as I was studying her.

Tugging Lily by the leash, she opened the door to let in a cold blast of morning air, and was gone, leaving me to wonder.

She is planning something, I thought, *she* is *part of the game*. But which part and what side I did not know.

I WENT STRAIGHT INTO THE garden and saw three crows swinging idly on Jack's scarecrow. It wasn't hard to recognize Awxes and the girls by the white patches on their wings. I clambered over the turned-up soil and stood before them as they teetered on the jingling copper arms.

"I'm not the one needs watching," I said. "It's the girl. I saw it in her eyes, which are as fey as any Highborn woman. Fair or foul, it's coming for her and she is preparing to meet it. Follow her if you would find your way home again."

The crows stopped pressing down on the arms and the scarecrow came slowly to a standstill. They gazed at me with black-bead eyes that showed only my own reflection. Awxes sidled along the arm of the scarecrow until he came close to my cheek. Ever so gently—which is rare, for a crow's bill is a fair match for a dagger—he stroked my cheek with the side of his beak. Then he nipped my ear and flew off, the girls close behind him. High in the trees, the other crows, roused by their flight, woke from their arboreal perches with raucous cries, and followed the trio out of the garden.

I watched them wheel in the air. *I am not bait,* I told myself, certain at last of why Baba Yaga had brought me here, *but a guide, a glowworm, as Serana had called us, to push back the dark for this girl. And whose lost child is she? I thought I knew the answer, but would not speak it aloud for fear of making it known. Not even to my sister could I reveal my suspicions.*

SERANA'S SCARE-BIRD ARRIVED WITHOUT WARNING on the second day of a drenching rain that turned the garden into muck and stripped the last roses from their stems. He bounded up the stairs and announced himself with a loud, imperious knock. I opened the door to a young man, sodden as old driftwood, wet elf knots in his dark hair, clothing weighted down by water and mud.

"Auntie Em said I was supposed to stay here," he announced and thrust an envelope into my hand.

"I don't know any Auntie Em," I protested. And then asked, "Wait, are you Vanilla Blue?"

"Yeah, but Auntie Em preferred the name Robin. Thought it suited me better."

He smiled at me, through those tangled curls, his skin pale from the chill, but his eyes dark and gleaming. Without a leave, he came into my house, trailing water, set down two bags and asked, "Do you have anything to eat? I'm pretty hungry. Is that the kitchen?" And pointing out the way for himself, he entered my kitchen and opened the cupboards. I stood there speechless, envelope in hand, as he found my bread, my butter, the two ripe tomatoes, and the cheese. And he talked the whole time about nothing, his mouth working around both words and food simultaneously.

I tore open the envelope and read the note: "A present for you." My first thought was Serana had clearly lost her mind. For what reason could she imagine that I would enjoy her scare-bird, who seemed much more hound than bird to me. And then I had a second thought. Leaving the boy to his food, I trundled down the stairs to the mailbox.

In the box, tucked up like a bird in its nest, waiting for me was a second letter, this one sent so the boy could not read it. Clearly Serana expected it to reach me before he did. But I had forgotten to check the mailbox yesterday, content to remain inside, away from the damp and cold of the storms. I pulled it out—noting the smeared ink on the front and the envelope's seal loosened from what I hoped was the rain—and read it in a single glance.

Then I read it again, growing more concerned as I walked back up the stairs. Once in my sitting room, I glanced at the boy who was now wolfing down a hunk of cheese. Had he guessed there was another letter? Or was he still addled by a berry in a tisane?

Well, I thought, *I still had a way out if I so chose.*

"Show me the return ticket."

He grabbed a pear and took a bite. "I don't have one."

"Yes, you do. My sister bought you one. It says so here in her letter."

"I exchanged it."

"For what?"

He inclined his head toward his bags slumped against my red chair. Next to the duffel bag stood a battered violin case. *A fiddler!* My face grew hot and my hair crackled.

"I wanted a pennywhistle," he said, "but a man on the bus sold me this fiddle instead."

I groaned. Can there be any more unreliable creature in the mortal world than a fiddler? He spells with music and then he is gone. Even the fey have been held captive by a good fiddler.

Chaffed, I refused to prepare food for him but it scarcely mattered for he helped himself to whatever he could lay his hands on. He ate like a boy who had not eaten in days, and perhaps he had not. When he was sated at last, he rose from the table and dragged himself to one of the embroidered chairs, and dropped—wet clothing and all—into its embrace.

I waited. But not a finger did Robin lift to tidy the mess he had made of my kitchen. Dishes, rinds, peelings, and sticky knives all lay on the counters. But from this Queen's pet or Red Cap's hammer not so much as a word of thanks. He took off his shoes, set the wet and filthy socks on Baba Yaga's carved oaken side table. He drew the second chair in front of him, rested his naked feet on the seat, and promptly fell asleep. They were aristocratic feet, the second toe reaching above the big one, the arch high and delicate.

I WENT TO BED, ONLY to be awoken much later in the wee hours of the night by the sound of his fiddle. It was coarse and husky, the wood of poor quality, but he played it well. I knew that it could seduce me, and I had little desire to be enthralled to such a callow, ill-mannered young man.

"Stop that!" I demanded. "I'm trying to sleep."

"Sorry," he muttered, and the house grew quiet again.

But it was impossible to sleep, for denied his fiddle, he rose from the chair, and paced in a circle.

At last I shouted from under my covers, "Play the rude thing then if it brings you peace. But make it soft."

And then I heard the reason Serana sent him to me. Sad indeed was the air he played, a boy lost and grieving in the throat of a tune. No true demon born, no Un-Seelie knows how to keen so quietly into a set of strings. I might dislike his ill manners and voracious appetite, but I could not deny the sorrowful beauty of the music he played.

The rain had stopped; the moon was just peeking out of the tumble of clouds and casting shadows of leaves on the ceiling of my room. For a moment it was like looking back from a great distance at the world I once knew, hearing the undeniable ache in the tune. And even though I was certain he meant me to feel such longing, even though I tried to resist it, I still wept into the pillow for the loss of home.

A FEW HOURS LATER, WHEN he had fallen asleep, I wrote to tell Serana how much I appreciated her present.

Why me? Why in the name of the Goddess, in the name of our beloved Greenwood, have you sent him to me? It is so like you to cast trouble behind your back and I, only because I am but a moment younger, am forced to take the responsibility. It has ever been so.

Remember the miller's baby? How you wanted the little thing while it slept, pretty as a rosebud? And then it woke up, wailed, and shit itself and you were less charmed. Do you remember who returned that mewling creature to its rightful mother? I still carry the scar on my thumb from the silver blade.

And what about that harper? You gave him the power to play a tune to honor you. But he forgot all the other tunes in his head, so drunk on you, and we were forced to dance over and over to that one wretched song. Even you held your hands to your ears by the fourth hour of it but could not bring yourself to unbind his love. It was me they sent to cut the strings and it was me who had to console him when he woke from his dream, his ears still itching with the memory but his hands unable to find the notes.

I am furious because, regardless of the vision that you call your "reason," I know the real reason you sent him to me. You have your little twigs set just so on the branch, and this child disturbs your pretty settings. He is nothing short of an autumn storm. How often when we were little did you forbid me to touch your things: the polished mirror, the ivory combs, the silver hairpins arranged in their perfect patterns. "Paddle Foot," you taunted me, slapping my hand away. "Magpie!" was all I could offer in hurt reply. Though when you weren't looking, I would steal a pin or turn the mirror upside down and then giggle into my palms while you shouted and bullied the little sprites who attended you. Well, you have no sprites to attend you now and so you send this creature on to me, this hound who is all gullet and wet fur.

I stopped writing and shoved the half-written letter between two tins of tea. I needed to cool my head before I sent such harsh words. For as furious as I was at Serana, she was still my beloved sister.

47

~~~

Sparrow Sleeps

Rain battered the windows as Sparrow sat on the side of her bed, surrounded by tattered journals. The ones on the rumpled sheets lay open to reveal certain pages, while the rest remained in a lopsided stack on the floor near her feet. A small bed lamp provided an oval of pale light by which she read the one journal she held in her hands, studying intently the crabbed handwriting, the fading pencil lines all rushing to the edges of the pages.

She'd been on the run when she wrote that entry, fleeing a well-meaning social worker who had spotted her busing tables in a Southwest diner. The woman had probably recognized her from the picture on a missing child report. Sparrow knew the woman had only meant to help. Probably thought she was rescuing a long-lost, abducted child. But when the squad car pulled up, and the woman glanced nervously in Sparrow's direction, she'd snatched the tip jar by the cash register, grabbed her backpack from the shelf under the counter, and split out the back door. She wrote down her escape that night while hiding out in the bus station's restroom. That's what she did when she reached a new town: stuffed her journals and spare clothes in a locker and kept them there for ease of escape.

When Sparrow had been taken from the woods that

first time, she'd refused to cooperate with the authorities after they brought her to the station. The police had called in a child services counselor to get her to talk. Sparrow gave a half smile remembering that earnest young woman with the short brown hair like an acorn cap. She'd smelled of lavender and wet dog and Sparrow had noticed white hairs clinging to her black sweater.

"If you don't feel like talking, honey, why don't you write out your feelings in here." She'd passed Sparrow a speckled composition notebook along with an assortment of colored pens.

Here is the tale of Malia, the deer, Sparrow wrote. And she proceeded to fill the book with every memory of the forest she had, for she could feel the reality of that life already slipping away from her. *I must, to remember it all*, she told herself, and did by writing it down.

Of course, the counselor assumed it was a fairy tale allusion to her abduction. Sparrow was fingerprinted, photographed, and placed in a halfway house until someone could figure out to whom she belonged. All she had with her when she arrived at the halfway house— besides the clothes she had on—was the notebook, a handful of wild berries in her pockets, and a withered lady's slipper that she'd tied into her hair.

Sparrow brought the journal to her nose and sniffed. Each journal had its own scent, its own handwriting, and its own author. Seven books, a dozen tales, and as many different names. She touched each different name, recalling each identity, some of which had lasted a few months, and others for no more than a few days. Like a litany of fairy-tale saints, she could recite her journey in the story of each new name—Malia, Phoebe, Margaret, Katie, Marion, Tina (short for Titania), Vasilisa, Molly, and many more until taking on Sparrow. Sometimes Sparrow thought she had forgotten her own name, the one that lingered on the edge of her memory, no more than a woman's voice whispering it into her ear. What her father had called her didn't bear repeating.

She lifted a mug of coffee and grimaced as she took a

cold swig. She needed it to keep awake. As long as she didn't fall asleep at night, she could just about fend off the nightmares and the new tattoos that had begun to appear on her body. Pushing back her sleeve, she scratched the raw skin on her wrist where the snake still held her in its fanged grip. Two nights ago, another had begun to coil on her shoulder when she made the mistake of dozing off. She'd awoken with a start just before a head appeared over her breast. Later she'd gone to the library and from a snake identifying book discovered it was an adder, the bite not fatal, but painful. It was meant to torture, not kill her.

Sparrow roused herself from the bed and looked at the cache of herbs and roots on her desk. She had almost everything she needed. She'd sharpened the tips of the silver dove's wings into dangerous points. Not much more menacing than the head of a dart. But deadly enough if tipped in what she hoped was the right poison.

Pacing around the room, swinging her arms across her body and slapping her hands across the back of her shoulders, she told herself, "Stay awake, Sparrow." She said it aloud to hear the sound of her own voice. On the bed, Lily lifted her head at the sound.

"You too, you butterball," Sparrow warned the dog.

At Sparrow's voice, Lily yawned, stretching her enormous jaw wide enough to show every tooth, then abruptly scrambled to her feet, leapt off the bed, and headed for the door.

Sparrow snatched up the little dove and followed after her. Someone was stomping up the stairs, and it couldn't be Sophia because Sparrow knew she'd never left into the downpour.

Lily barked at a stranger beyond the door who replied with a single, deep-chested woof. Lily's tail wagged and she dropped her nose down to the gap beneath the front door to sniff.

Well, thought Sparrow, *at least not foe. But who then?* She lifted her head, following the sounds of the footsteps to the top landing.

There were voices, Sophia's stern alto, followed by another, softer, more playful male voice. *Clearly not Jack*, Sparrow decided. The step was heavy, as was the sound of bags and shoes being tossed to the floor. Cupboards were opened and closed; a chair scraped across the kitchen floor. Reluctantly, Sparrow returned to the bedroom, followed by Lily, whose ears perked upright every time she heard the man's voice.

Sitting down on the bed, Sparrow picked up another journal and started to read. Her hands trembled from too much caffeine and not enough sleep. Her body protested, wanting only to sleep, but she wouldn't let it. Tomorrow—if the sun rose, she'd rest briefly before going to work at the bookstore. But that was it. She dared not trust herself to a nap in the late afternoon. The last time she'd done that, she'd slept well past sunset and awoken to the scratching of the new tattoo on her shoulder. Instead she forced herself to read the journals, finding solace in her own peculiar history.

Above her, the sounds of conversation eventually died down, twilight to evening, and Sparrow knew from the creak of Baba Yaga's bed, that Sophia had retired for the night. But where did the other one stay? That apartment was much too small for two.

And then she heard the fiddle, its husky voice unrolling down through the floorboards with a jaunty tune. She grinned, thinking *that* would certainly keep her up! But then she frowned upon hearing the angry muffle of Sophia's voice. Abruptly, the music stopped.

The fiddler started pacing, and in her room below, Sparrow followed his footsteps with her own. She smiled at the spiral pattern of his steps, reminding her of Lily's own dog ritual of turning in slow circles on the bed, her paws ruffling the covers into a nest. Sophia yelled again and the pacing, too, stopped.

Sparrow sighed and sat down on the bed, weary to the bone. *And dangerously bored,* she thought, wondering which journal to reread. She plucked a newer one, one that had crude and mildly pornographic illustrations. She

figured that, at the very least, she could laugh at her
worthless skills.

That's when the fiddle began again in a soft, muted
voice. It hummed through the lathes, sweet notes cascad-
ing down on her like golden dust in sunlight. She put the
journal down, the spine opened to reveal a drawing of an
almost naked man. He had on a coat, but was holding it
open to show his swollen prick. That picture memorial-
ized the first and only time Sparrow had seen a penis.
She'd stared, not with disgust as she presumed he wanted,
but rather curiosity, trying to remember it so that she
could later commit the image of it in her journal. She
had heard enough stories from other runaways and
knew this kind of man wasn't that dangerous. But most
men *were* and she'd managed, despite some close calls, to
keep herself free of any entanglements.

Later, Sparrow couldn't recall the moment the music
had lulled her into sleep. She could only remember the
way the sound had wrapped around her like cloth, swad-
dling her limbs with each draw of the bow. She wasn't
frightened, but soothed. As she closed her eyes, she
caught the familiar scents of the forest, the springy feel
of dried pine needles beneath her palm, and the whoosh
of the wind gusting through the branches. Lily's warm
body lay close to her, the dog's slow, deep snoring as
soporific as the fiddle's music. The memory of the man in
the alley flickered dreamlike on the edges of her mind.
She walked toward him, and he transformed, the dirty
coat giving way to a cowl of pale green leaves and the
ruddy phallus growing into a stalk speckled with heavy
grains of pollen.

SHE WOKE IN THE MORNING, without panic or fear, greeted
by sunlight spilling into her room. Only when she spied
the glint of silver wings on her desk did she remember.
Stumbling toward the bathroom and pulling off her T-
shirt as she went, she stared into the mirror, expecting to
see more of the snake coiling around her right shoulder.

But it had not changed; if anything, the ink had faded from blue black to soft brown. Sparrow rubbed her hand over her skin in amazement.

She walked back to the bedroom, to the sight of the sleeping dog, the books scattered across the bottom of the bed and the outline of her head in the pillows. Clearly, she'd slept the night away.

But how?

She looked up at the ceiling as though it could give her answers. Sophia's mysterious guest? The music? She was grateful for the much-needed respite, but she was cautious too, for many a sweet spell came to a bad end. Nonetheless, she had slept without harm and for that, she offered silent thanks to the unknown fiddler.

.

48

Meteora Insists

In the morning the sun burst forth as though to welcome this errant boy to Jack's promise of a second summer. By midmorning the day was almost hot. I glanced out the window as I cleaned up Robin's mess in the kitchen and saw Jack working in the garden below. Not to plant—no, it was much too wet for that—but to set and build the new paths of the maze.

I shook the boy where he lay sprawled between the two chairs. He woke with a start, saw it was only me, and then stretched and yawned languorously.

"Come on, my lad, you have work to do."

"Work?"

I pulled him by the collar of his grubby shirt to the window and pointed down to the garden. "See that man down there?" And as if he had heard me, Jack looked up from a rock he was hoisting into place and smiled. I opened the window, and leaned out. "I have a new pair of sturdy hands to help you, Jack! He'll be down in a moment."

"Great! There's plenty to do," he called back.

"I am not a gardener. I don't do dirt," the boy said scornfully.

"You are now and you will do dirt if you wish to remain and eat. My sister may have coddled you but I will not."

He started to protest. He needed his hand for playing the fiddle. He was tired after his journey. He was hungry . . .

I paid no attention, and while he was off in the water closet, I rifled through his bag until I found a clean shirt and a pair of socks that while not clean, were at least dry. When he reappeared, I thrust the clothes and his shoes into his arms, and practically pushed him out the door. I shut it hard and turned the lock, keeping his fiddle as hostage.

"Shit," I heard him mutter, and then his feet thudded down the stairs. Lily barked as he passed the landing and he barked back, finishing with an ascending howl. Lily joined him and for a minute or two, the pair did a duet. Then he continued down to the door, clumping like a one-legged farmer.

I returned to my kitchen, grumbling and swearing as I washed dirty dishes, returned them to the shelves, wiped down the counters. Then I cleaned the house, cleaned myself, and dressed for work. Before I left, I chanced a glance out the window to see how Robin was managing in the garden. And there he was, despite his earlier complaints, laughing and joking with Jack as they moved rocks back and forth creating the low wall. After a moment or two of studying him, I softened my heart, thinking he might be a fair-enough lad after all.

LATER THAT NIGHT, ALONE AT my kitchen table, I retrieved my letter to Serana and reread it. It was stinging, true enough—but a fair complaint. Still I did not want this to be the last words on the matter, so finished it with more temperance.

> *He can stay, but he will not eat unless he works. Shutting my ears to his complaints, I sent him to work in the garden with Jack, lifting the mountain of tumbled stones and rebuilding the garden wall. It is dirty labor, but honest. Far more honest than*

the fiddle, which he bought with your return ticket
and tried to charm me with on his first night.

But he has paid me back for this injury—as
only a clever child can. Even as I finish this letter
at my recently cleaned kitchen table, he is standing
in my sitting room, playing his fiddle with aban-
don. He has tracked garden mud and wet leaves
into my house, staining Baba Yaga's red wool
rug—that rug that carried Caliphs across the gold
desert. He finished eating and left the dishes and
now is playing a naughty reel to mock me. The
strings sing like a drunken thrush and I must stifle
again the longing for a time that will never come
again.

Oh, I am angry with you. He will be a handful.
And yet listening to him play, I know it will be
impossible to stay angry—with you my blood
sister or with your scare-bird. I saw Sparrow, a
curious spirit, peeping over the fence to watch him
work. No doubt his fiddle called to her as well. In
the meantime, I will keep him toiling in the garden
with Jack and let the living earth return to him
some sense and humility along with love and
diligence.

Fractious, but still your loving sister,
Meteora

49

The Dog Boy Scratches an Itch

At first I fought the earth, hardly damaging it with the shovel. Then I cursed the earth in the old tongue, the crows screaming back at me. But finally I surrendered to the earth, lying down in the small rutted lanes I had dug and letting the smells overwhelm me.

What smells? Sharp growing things, more white than green. Little mealy-smelling worms and the musty rankness of mole somewhere beneath. The tang of broken rootlets, the freshness of water still unmuddied running deep.

It was as if the earth herself cleansed me. I waited till no one but the crows were looking, knelt there and pissed a long stream. Now I was part of the earth, and it me.

When I stood, shaking myself all over like a dog, bits of old grass and globules of dirt and little stones scattered off me.

"That'll do, boy," the Jack said. "Go off and get your lunch."

I scraped my boot casually over the stream I'd just made, covering it thoroughly, before walking away. I set my shoulders to show how little I cared what he thought, then went back to the house where I grabbed something to eat, first washing because the old woman told me to. Old women seem obsessed with cleanliness. First Auntie Em and now this one.

That was when I heard the girl. Not for the first time. But this time I heard her clearly. The dog had said her name. "Mistress. Take me with you." But she'd left the dog behind. Still she was no mistress of mine, but something more. I didn't know yet what. I could hear her going out of the door.

I put my head under the water tap, letting the water rain down on it. Then I shook like the dog I am, before taking off after her. I didn't mean to catch up, just to follow. She was bent over, her shoulders hunched against a wind that was not blowing, a hood over her head. I still didn't know what she looked like. I hadn't yet seen her face.

The water through my hair had cleansed my ears and had cleaned away the dirt smell. And now I had her scent, a light perfume on the wind. It had heather for solitude, and some other tangle I couldn't quite make out.

I began to whistle the tune, not to make her turn, but to make her remember me. She shrugged deeper into the hooded jacket, and by this I knew she'd heard, but she didn't turn around.

So I stopped whistling and followed silently, from afar. If she looked back, all she would see would be a boy her age, walking along the street, behind but not behind her. *Too far for fear.* I am a tracker, not a killer. It's my father who kills. And I was far from him now. Safe from his whistle. Safe to do what I wanted: my bidding, not his.

I crossed the street to put her off the scent.

She walked now with more determination, as if each step closer to where she was going gave her strength. We were well into the bowels of the city. The smell of buses and cars was overwhelming. I breathed shallowly.

The sun being out, she shrugged off the hood and I was startled to see the color of her hair. It was like an evening sky. I had not expected that from her scent. But still I had it in my nose now. I would know her anywhere.

Watching the back of her night-sky head move, I almost missed what her hands were doing as she stood in front of a storefront, making a strewing motion. She looked left and right but not behind where I was standing, then turned abruptly into an alley on the side of the storefront, disappearing into its depths.

I crossed the street to the storefront and drew a deep breath. On the doorjamb she'd left a scattering of protection herbs. *That* was a tangle I hadn't expected: comfrey, thyme, verbena, Saint-John's-wort. But there was something else, some strong bitter smell. It made my nose itch. And then I had it: peony, a shield against fairy mischief.

Why here?

I looked at the store window, the curtains drawn against the light. The name of the place was scrawled across the window in bloodred letters: HAWK: ORIGINAL TATTOOS. I put a hand on the window and tried to look in, and suddenly I was overwhelmed by a scent that I should have picked up before.

"No!" I said it aloud. And then again to myself. *"No!"* The herbs had overlaid the smell of him, had disguised it enough that I was almost fooled. I couldn't tell how old the scent was, but there was no denying it. Father's smell is the iron of blood and the dry odor of agaric and aminita; it's musk and mallow, root and worm. I gagged at the thought that he was here. Had been here before me. Had sought her but not found her. I grew warm with indignation. So, he was not as good a hunter as me. Perhaps there was still time to warn her of the danger.

I turned away from the window and padded into the alley following after the girl. She was waiting in the dark and I still had so much of the protection herbs up my nose, and my father's odious scent, that I missed her standing there until I bumped into her.

"Who are you and why are you following me?" She stood with her hands on her hips, unafraid. Her face . . . her face was glorious, shining. There was an old scar over her eyebrow. I longed to touch it.

"Me?" I squeaked. "Following you."

"Don't mess with me, or I'll . . ."

"Sounds like fun," I began to regain some measure of control over my voice. "But my old aunt, the one I'm staying with in the upstairs apartment, would probably kill me. She's got me on a tight leash."

"She's your aunt?"

"She and her sister, Auntie Em."

"You're full of shit, you know that?" She stepped away from me, anger flashing in her eyes. Green with threads of gold. Her skin was pale as snow beneath a cap of coal-colored hair. "Just back the fuck up, asshole." She fingered something in her pocket. I could smell the sweetness of fey silver, taste the metal in the air. There was the sharp scent of fear about her but she wouldn't show it. Not she. She braced, ready.

Dogs jump, men coax, I thought. "Hey, *really*, I'm staying with my aunt who lives upstairs from you. I saw you leave and figured I could, maybe, you know meet someone a little bit younger than my aunt who must be a gazillion years old."

"What's her name?"

"Sophia Underhill." Good thing I'd glanced at Auntie Em's letters.

"What's her apartment look like?"

She wasn't going to give up her suspicions easily, this one.

"Red chair, rugs, kitchen table, crystals hanging in the window. Do I need to say more?"

"You're the guy in the garden."

"Yes," I answered, though it pained me to be thought of as a gardener.

"Was that you playing the fiddle the last couple of nights?"

I smiled, just wide enough to charm not to threaten. "It was me." I stopped myself from bowing to her, but only just. "Have I kept you up?" I knew full well that my fiddle brought her much-needed sleep. It was her dreams I'd felt touching the strings like rosin.

She stared a long time, considering me in silence. I let her gaze and didn't turn away.

"You've got your clothes on inside out." I pointed at the tag on her hood. "Who are you hiding from?"

Thin brows arched above the flashing green eyes. "How do you know about that?"

Before I could answer, a door slammed open farther down the alley and the scent of blood and Greenwood sap filled my nostrils. Wrong. The smell was all wrong and I didn't hesitate. I grabbed her and pulled her down behind a pile of stacked trash, its odor rank but at least honest. I put my finger to her lips as she tightened into a ball.

"Who's there?" a voice called and I could hear the spell of command. It was easy enough for my kind to resist. But not the girl. "Show yourself, or I cut you to the quick," came the warning. She'd never make it against one like that.

So I stood and waved my arms, to distract him. I stepped out, away from the trash. A dog learns how to cower. A dog learns how to beg.

"Hey, don't get all twisted, man," I said in a whining voice. "I'm just scrounging for something to eat. I don't have any money, man. Thought I'd check out the trash."

"Come closer, let me look at you." To play the game, I must obey, making my thoughts murk and mud. I shuffled forward, not meeting his eyes, but staring somewhere in the hollow of his white throat.

I knew what he was, Highborn and full of himself, but he would scarce know me in this form. In this gormless shape. Perhaps I should piss myself to make him feel more powerful. But he gave me a measured look, snarled "Bugger off," unlocked the back door and disappeared inside.

I sauntered over to the trash where the girl waited, crouched and hidden. As I approached, I saw the flash of silver in her upraised fist, twin points protruding like fangs between the fingers. The air stank of nightshade and arsenic.

"Poison or not, you'll need far more than that to kill a Highborn," I chided. "It won't do more than wound him. And make him really angry. Come on." I extended my hand. "Let's go back to my aunt's where it's safe."

She bit her lip, but took my hand and stood up. Wariness lay like a harness on her shoulders, washed her skin with a peppery smell. But she was steady. Resolute. I admired that.

"Let me help," I offered, suddenly glad of the chance to betray my father's will.

"Maybe," she answered, pulling up her hood, then shoving her hands into her pockets. "Play your fiddle again tonight, and I'll sleep on it."

It's enough, I thought as I trotted beside her. *A good beginning*. I began to hope, always the wrong thing to do. Hope only ends in disaster.

50

Serana Has Five Days of Peace

You would think that five days of peace, alone and without my scare-bird worries, would have been enough for me to recover my equilibrium, but I worried my way through every hour of the five.

Would the boy remain on the bus? Would he get off at the right place? Would he find his way to Meteora? Did my letter get to her in time? Would she curse me for sending him? Was he the right boy? The wrong boy? Did he have naught to do with this knot?

These and other questions buzzed in my head and when—on the fifth day—a letter came from Meteora, I was forced to write another back at once. At least to share my worries. I wrote my first thoughts quickly and left the unfinished letter on the mantel:

Oh dear Paddle Foot:
I knew you would do the right thing. You always do the right thing. It is annoying, but true. Only you never know when to shut up. There. I have said it at last. And I say it with love and a certain amount of trepidation for I treasure your letters, all I have now of our old life. But really, Meteora, you are so like your name, flashing across any universe you happen to inhabit.
Shut up.

You are best when you are fixing things,
mending broken boxes or heads or hearts. When
you cut the strings that are binders, when you
uncurdle the brownie's milk, when you set aright a
spell that has gone so miserably wrong. Then—oh
then—you are what you are meant to be.

Only for Mab's sake, shut up about it.

The memories you curse me with are so
one-sided. Have you never understood that? The
miller's babe was a mistake, granted. But I recog-
nized it immediately and had not the wherewithal
to take it home. Only you could do it—as you did.
The harper was not there for dancing nor bound
by love, but to twit the Queen and oh! I can still see
her face, a rowanberry red, as he went on his
seventy-dozenth round of the song. And I did not
need to hold my ears, dear sister, having stuck
lamb's wool in them ahead of time. Remember, I
am the farseer, the visioner.

As for touching my things—do you not remem-
ber that as a little one, you burned yourself badly
that way. Look at the puckered skin on your left
ring-man finger. The reminder is still there. You
never seemed to recall that on your own, much as I
iterate. A meddler you were then and still are. A
meddler and a mender.

I sent you the boy so that you can meddle and
mend to your heart's content. I have seen that you
need to fix this broken thing, whatever it is. I can
only clean him up but not make him better.
Something eats at his heart, something coils in his
gut.

I had already cleansed the house of Robin's presence,
burning the lint he left behind, throwing out any food he
had touched, scrubbing the rooms on my hands and
knees with a soap I made of rowan and bleach. Those
first couple of nights my right leg had ached from but-
tock to bone being unused to such a position.

That said, I kept a bit of his hair I found in my good brush and used it for a new casting. The picture that spiraled out of the smoke was as clear as the first. There was something to come out of their coupling, the girl and my scare-bird, if ever they got down to it. Though there was also some strange blurring around the edges of the vision, which was worrisome.

I moved closer to it till the smoke made my eyes water. But all I made out was a single crow feather in the left corner and a bit of gingerroot in the right. And what those two things augured—well, it was anyone's guess. I gave it a good try, though.

Crow feather. I knew the old adage, "One crow for sadness, two for mirth . . ." Could that be what was meant? Or perhaps it was a hunter's sign disguised? I had once seen a hoodie crow bait-fishing, and everyone knows how they use bent twigs and stalks of grass to pull out insects from hills and burrows. And a split-tongue crow can talk in any language. My dam heard one curse an UnSeelie prince in the old tongue, and did she not laugh!

As to the ginger? It could leach poisons. Make a cold man hot. Fix a bilious stomach. Help a woman newly with child. But what it meant here, I might never know. Farseeing is like that. Sometimes meaning emerges long after.

I took up the letter to Meteora and added what I had just seen, saying,

> So now I fear for the gift I sent to you. If they see one, this boy, this girl, they will be swept into each other's arms. But whether that is for sadness or mirth, whether it is only for heat, I do not know. However, I do know this: whatever you give Robin to plant, do not let it be Arum. Never Arum.
>
> This time I am afraid I have been the meddler and you must use all that is left of your magic to mend if you must, or bend if you will, else we might both be broken on this wheel forever.

I was about to crumple the letter, thought better of it, and put it back on the mantel. I would write something fresher in the morning. Then I ran out of the house, needing air and trees and food to sustain me.

I MADE MY WAY DOWN the street to the Man of Flowers store. He saw me and smiled, waved, came over.

"Dona," he said. "The sun has not shined here since you were gone. Is your grandson well?"

For a moment I had to think whom he meant, then remembered I had told him the scare-bird was my kin. And in a way, I suppose he is. "I have sent him off to my sister's."

"You have a sister?" he countered. "Here? That is good. Then you are not, as I feared, all alone in this world." His head nodded. "A grandson, a sister." He paused. I remembered such pauses from the life before, when men found me beautiful and asked me such questions.

"But no husband," I said. I said it softly, so it could be read as he wanted. I do not know why I said such a thing. *Habit? Desire? Loneliness?*

"Ah." He blushed. I liked that. It made him look younger. "May I make you a present of . . ."

I raised a hand between us, surprised at how old my hand was. Always surprised. "No more presents, kind sir, for your generosity shames me. I must repay you."

"Dona, no payment is necessary."

"It is the custom of my people," I said. "I must repay you, or . . ."

He nodded. "Then make me a dinner tonight and let me supply the food and wine. It has been too long since I have had a beautiful woman cook for me."

"Beautiful?" He had never seen me beautiful. Only fat and aching and old.

He took my hand. "There is a life lived in your face, Dona, and a wisdom and laughter in your eyes. There is kindness there, too."

I who had never melted when a lover said such things in my nest, nor lost my heart for more than a night's dalliance, almost wept. "I have never been kind," I whispered to him.

"I cannot believe that."

I let him give me root vegetables, cream, long noodles, three kinds of cheeses, some berries, a sweet basil plant, a bit of thyme, three rosemary stalks, and a round orange fruit as big as his fist.

"I close the store at six."

I told him the number of my house.

"I know."

"Second floor."

"I have seen the plants on the sill."

So I smiled. "I will expect you then, sometime after the store is closed." And I left, my heart thudding so hard, I feared it would burst through the bag of food I had from him as a gift. No—not a gift, but a promise, though I wondered with a shiver if this old body could keep the promise made by my suddenly much younger heart.

51

Sparrow Steals a Letter

All Sparrow had wanted to be was invisible on the street. She'd followed Robin's suggestions as to how to lay her spells on Hawk's shop, because he'd understood her need to exact revenge on the man. She showed him the tattoo on her neck, pulled up her sleeve to reveal the snake's head coiled around her wrist, but stopped short of showing him the half-formed adders on her shoulders. He had said nothing at first, only stared. And then offered advice.

"Go slowly," he'd said, "don't let him feel the noose until it is too late. Circle him. Foul the air but first accustom him to the fragrance."

"Are you sure about that . . . ?"

He'd nodded, his dark curls bouncing. "Very. That one is too powerful to challenge directly. You must use stealth."

Sparrow believed him. He spoke with such certainty. It was as if he knew, knew that her life was nothing short of a fairy tale gone awry.

He'd asked to go with her on her next foray, but Sparrow had refused. The truth was, she didn't entirely trust him. He was handsome—too handsome—and she'd felt the color rise in her cheeks when he gave her that slow, appraising stare. Looking down at his elegant hands had only made it worse. She thought about those hands caressing the neck of the fiddle, or closed around the bow, lifting it over the strings. He had played for her, she knew that. But where the music was taking her, she didn't know. *What if he's more dangerous than Hawk?* She remembered how easily he'd deceived the tattooer, and shivered at the thought. She needed to know about him in the same way that he seemed to know her. That was only fair.

ON THE FOLLOWING DAY, SPARROW waited until Sophia had left the house and Robin was working with Jack in the garden. Then she sprinted upstairs. The door was unlocked so she slipped inside and looked around. The sitting room was a cluttered mess: books, scraps of paper with scribbled music, dirty plates stacked high on the table. In one corner was a pile of men's laundry. Sparrow picked up a sweat-stained shirt, and sniffed its pungent aroma. Just then she heard men's voices in the garden break into loud laughter.

"Don't be stupid," she told herself, and tossed the shirt away.

She peered into the kitchen, searching for the pile of colored envelopes she remembered seeing on the table. A letter had rested beneath the dove and Sparrow had seen the name "Robin," written in a curling script before she knew what it meant. But the kitchen was clean, and there was no sign of the letters on the shelves or in the drawers.

Of course! Sophia had probably hidden them from Robin. She went to the bedroom, and glanced quickly at the neatly made bed and the clothing hanging on wooden pegs. Alongside the bed was a pair of fur-trimmed slippers. The pillows were huge and plump and quite inviting. Intuitively, she slid her hand under the nearest pillow and chuckled. The sheets whispered as she pulled forth the tied stack of letters. There wasn't much time, for she could hear Jack stomping his shoes free of mud on the back steps. They would be putting away the tools and

Robin would soon return. She opened the first letter and read a page. She refolded it and read two more. It was all she needed. She had learned enough.

Enough to know that Sophia and her sister talked about her. "A misery-girl" Sophia had called her. And he a "scare-bird." Sparrow was angry and hurt. Sophia had not extended a hand to her because she was simply a young woman in need of friendship, but rather an oddity in a gossipy game between a pair of weird sisters who thought a good deal of themselves. And she gathered from the veiled, puzzling comments that neither were what they appeared to be either.

No, no, she thought, *trust no one. Except perhaps Robin, for he's one of their "projects." Just like me. Maybe it's time to leave here before it gets more complicated.* She knew she could always run.

But first she had a score to settle.

With Hawk.

FOR TWO DAYS SHE HAD turned her clothes inside out to hide herself from Hawk's notice, strolling past his shop and dropping a small handful of crushed herbs on the doorjambs, front and back.

But this time, when Sparrow turned the corner, she saw a girl dressed in a plaid skirt and white blouse standing in front of Hawk's shop. Every time the girl stepped forward, her foot touched some unseen line and she stepped back. Sparrow bent down to pet Lily, watching the girl struggle between two inducements: one to enter, the other to flee. At last, the girl turned on her heel and left.

"Good!" Sparrow said, rubbing Lily's ears, but staring at the retreating figure of the girl. Clearly the herbs were working, though not exactly the way she had meant them to.

When she arrived home, she paused, seeing the orange envelope in Sophia's box. Deftly, she plucked the envelope out between two fingers, glanced at the writing, and then carried it upstairs hidden in her jacket. Those two biddies had too many secrets and she didn't like being one of them.

Taking off Lily's collar, she went into the kitchen, the dog padding eagerly behind her. After feeding the dog and filling her water bowl, Sparrow turned up the heat under the kettle. She held the letter over the steaming spout and waited for the glue to give. It was easy enough to remove the letter from the envelope, trickier to remove the warning at the end of the page. She folded a tight crease and slid a knife along it, knowing the rough edges would probably give it away. But not until it was too late.

Sparrow folded the scrap in her pocket. Tomorrow was Saturday, and the Farmer's Market would be in full swing. She wouldn't be purchasing that horrible root she had bought last time. This time she would get her hands on the right plant and then let what was to happen, happen. *That should teach those meddling sisters*, she thought.

Refolding the letter, Sparrow placed it in the envelope and held the seal closed until it mostly stuck along the edge. She went downstairs, replaced the envelope in the mailbox, and returned to her own apartment. Tonight she would stay awake as long as she could. She would listen, really listen to the tunes Robin played and make up her mind about him one way or the other before she left for work in the morning.

52

Meteora and the Arum

When I returned from the Co-op, I found Serana's letter waiting for me in the mailbox. The envelope was wrinkled as though it had become damp and then dried. The ink was washed pale and I wondered that it had found its way to me at all. When I turned it over, the back flap sighed open without help from my anxious fingers. And when I pulled out the letter, it was obvious something was amiss.

One page was too short. There was no farewell to me. No matter how angry or hurt Serana might have been at my previous letter, she would never have ended with such an enigmatic phrase: "I do know this." I tucked the letter in the bosom of my shirt and mounted the stairs, lost in troubled thoughts.

The house was deadly quiet. The couple on the first floor worked long days. Of Sparrow I had seen little of late. Sometimes, while in the garden, I would hear her shuffling on the back porch, but when I turned, she would duck inside to avoid me. I had hoped she would come to see me, to make amends of some kind. But once Serana's scare-bird showed up, she had become reluctant to even talk to me in passing.

I entered the apartment and realized that Robin, too, was gone. My eyelids quivered, always a trouble sign. Though I had not seen Robin and Sparrow together, I knew for certain that they had already met. I heard it in the tunes he played each night. The tunes were not meant for these old feet, but for someone much nimbler than I. I only hoped that she was careful, for there were still too many unanswered questions about the boy.

Tapping the envelope against my wrist, I tried to feel the intention of whoever had tampered with the letter. *Could Robin have done this? Maybe.* Yet I had seen the changes in him. Each day spent in the garden with Jack had tempered his callowness, made him more agreeable company.

But *someone* had meddled with the letter. I immediately dismissed the girl Marti and her boyfriend whose name I had never learned. They would have had no interest in my mail, and besides, they were away on holiday. The Hands never went out of my rooms, or so I believed. As for Jack—foolish I may have been for taking up with him, but I trusted him now. Or at least I thought I did.

Then who stood to gain from the letter's knowledge? *Missing* knowledge, I corrected myself. For there was someone who had the better part of Serana's wisdom and that someone was not me. I needed to watch and learn who had stolen my sister's words. I needed to warn Serana that we had been followed from the Greenwood. To whom did we matter so much? Certainly, not the Queen who had sent us away.

I SHOULD HAVE UNDERSTOOD THE moment Robin sauntered into the garden the following morning with the pot of arum in his hands. At first I laughed to see it, thinking it a ribald joke. But by the end of day, I knew it had been a mistake to allow such a potent plant into the Great Witch's garden. Oh, it was trouble all right, the very trouble my sister and I had hoped to avoid.

Two nights later, I walked to the edge of the park, where the trees gave way to the shore of an enormous lake. The full moon cast a glistening path across the restless water. I turned from its light and looked up, searching for a nest I had seen not too long ago, high in the canopy of an ash tree. I tucked my tongue behind my teeth and gave a sharp, short whistle. *"I have need."*

Silently, a goshawk lifted from the dark trees and circled overhead. I held up my arm, wrapped with one of Baba Yaga's shawls and offered her a perch. She alighted amid a flurry of wings and I was shocked by the pain of her talons digging into my arm. I had ridden such hawks as a sprout and never felt fear. But now, I trembled before her golden eyes and sharp beak so close to my face.

I know the rules of calling a hawk to service. Bringing out the remains of a mouse, killed the day before in a trap in the basement of the house, I gave it to her. She swallowed it whole, the whipping tail disappearing last. I tied a rolled letter to her leg and whispered my sister's name and destination. She lunged into the air, her talons raking long scratches in my skin through the cloth. But I did not cry out, only watched as her powerful wings lifted her high above the trees and out across the water's silvery path.

Sometimes a goshawk is more reliable than an eagle. And I only hoped that my letter would reach Serana in time to do some good.

> *Dearest Sister*
>
> *I am troubled. Someone tore away the last lines of your letter before it reached my hands. All that was left was your proclamation "I know this." If I could spell as I once did, I might know the truth of these wayward words. But now I can only stare at the ruffled edge of the paper and wonder who has the advantage of your knowledge. Please write back soon—the hawk will wait for your reply, though not for long.*
>
> *I am edgy. And your Robin even more so since he planted the arum in the middle of the garden. I thought he did it as a joke, an affront to my old age. I went to pull it out stalk and root, but no*

sooner did I touch it than the Jack's own laughter stopped me and I blushed furious, my hands wrapped around it as though to throttle youth and sex. I have left it, but, oh, what misgivings.

I saw Sparrow today, leaning out on her porch, hands clenched on the railing like a fledgling balanced for a first flight. Robin turned his face up to stare hungrily at her. And that damn plant bloomed, spreading pollen everywhere in the sudden gusting of the wind.

Worried as a tree knot,
Meteora

53

The Queen Searches

You travel the edges of the Greenwood, looking for the road that leads to the world. How many roads have disappeared? you wonder. No one sweeps them clean anymore and few carry their old names. Gone are the fairy knolls, the bridge of trees, the fairy's walk that once might have pointed the way to mortals seeking the path between briar and lily. Now it has become difficult for you to even find the roads *out* of the Greenwood. They are covered with iron and rust, with concrete and steel. The grass no longer sings to announce the way, the brush no longer parts to let you through. The old ways are going, soon to be gone for good.

It is love that drives you out of your woods. Love for the clans who mistrust you now, who know too much about you and are consumed with envy. It was the love of your realm that sent you in search of the one thing that might restore vitality, life, and the power of a world both bright and dark. It was love that changed your body from a pure vessel, untouched by age to one ripened by love, torn open by love, altered forever in the act of creation. It was love that kept you in the world too long.

You should have left the child on a stranger's doorstep, even on the steps of a church, though the spires could spear your heart and the crosses burn your flesh. But once you looked into that perfect rosebud face you could not part with her—flesh of your flesh, blood of your blood. You could not stop the tears that flowed any more than you could dam the milk from your breasts. And you knew that only this love could heal your world. So you stayed, wanting more time.

And then it all went so very wrong.

You hid your sorrow; you hid the love that had changed your body. You designed a desperate plan with no certainty of succeeding, hoping for delay. And when the truth was known you did what was necessary, committing murder, holding some hostage to your bidding and forcing others out into an exile you refused to imagine to buy but a little time and confuse them all.

And you knew that He would not rest idle but seek to find. You brought her in the world to strengthen the world through love, but He will use her death to strengthen His world through hate. And if He succeeds, then the balance of your world will tip like a fallen candle whose wick is drowned in the flow of scalding wax.

Oh, for love that aches, that heals, that makes all things possible.

And so you have come alone, treading the paths that no longer announce themselves. But you know it is here, in a city of glass and iron and stone that you must seek first. You must find the hound. You must stop him. Leash him. Or take his heart.

54

Serana Castigates the Arum,
Her Sister, the Boy, the Girl

*Meteora, sister, oh fool, fools both of us. Me to
write the word arum in a letter when I already
knew that someone—even someones—could read
what I wrote. And you for leaving the letter about.*

*Why did you not move forward against the
arum the moment you saw it? Surely you could
have guessed that if there was arum—the Wake
Robin—in the garden, that you should root it out,
burn it, bury it, cut it into a million pieces and
scatter those pieces into dry sea sand. You were
bright enough to know what the mandrake root
meant, but not this? Sister, I weep. It is not only
Robin the plant will awaken. Someone else is
waking, too. Not just your Red Cap. He is dangerous, true. But we both know what the true danger is.*

The crows know it. The stars know it.

*The sleeper wakened is someone more twisty,
more devious, more cunning than we can guess.
And how did I discover this? I read all this in the
tea leaves—spearmint for settling my already
unsettled stomach—upon receiving your latest
letter. The leaves formed a kind of crown, though,
when I turned the cup around, I saw that it was not
a crown but a fence, a hedge, a knot of vines.*

I am so horribly afraid, sister. We have meddled in something larger than we are prepared for. It is a Matter of Kings, of this I am sure. What are such homey tricksters as ourselves doing in this hedge? Surely we will not come out of it whole.

And here I was just thinking we knew what we were about. And I playing with falling in love with an old man. I, who am still young in my heart and giddy.

Fool you, but more fool I not to warn in the letter both top and bottom in code.

Wait! The above was written but an hour ago. An hour. Sixty small minutes. A tick of the human clock. Outside the wind has ceased its moan. The stars are looking coldly down, except for the Red Star. It alone shines like an ember in a long-banked fire.

I have been watching out of my window and feel rather than see something below, coming through the spindly trees. Time is stilled, my sister. The clock that came with this place, stands with its hands clasped at midnight and does not move.

I hear the bells on her horse's bridle. Just the one horse I think, not the entire Fairie Rade. And what is odder than that—the Queen riding alone along a human street? What is she thinking? Who is she seeking? I am so afraid, I am like a mountain shivering through an avalanche.

So I do the only thing I can. I am sending this message stuffed into a wooden locket, tied with twine to a pigeon's neck. The hawk did not stay for an answer. In a moment I shall whisper your name and your city and your street in the bird's ear.

If you do not hear from me again, or if I write and do not say the name of your favorites, consider me dead. She comes now through the trees as if down a straight road. She has already crossed the river of blood, and her coming has stopped all

*the clocks of Christendom. Even the recorded holy
man on the mosque down the block no longer calls
out.*

*It is a moment of reckoning. I shall not give her
your name. I will not tell her where you stay. Not
even if she plucks out my too human eyes and
replaces them with eyes of wood.*

*Sister, speak of me with love. It is something the
Queen will never do. I send a kiss for eternity. I
will not mind the pain as long as you are safe.*

Serana

55

Sparrow Longs

Sparrow plunged her hands into the bathroom sink, the foaming soap clinging to her forearms. She was washing her lingerie—not the cotton panties that were unraveling around the waistband, but the green silk pair, lined with black lace. The bra that matched had a bit of padding to give her too slender body some shape. She almost never wore them, and the few times she had, she'd been too reluctant to go through with any romantic entanglements. Looking up in the steamed mirror, she saw that her normally pale cheeks were pink. The black hair clung to her temples, and her eyes glittered, pale gold grains of pollen still lurking in her eyebrows.

"What are you doing?" she asked the image, still gently squeezing the underwear in the soapy water. The face smiled back, giddy and ridiculously happy, a new emotion for her.

Two days ago, when she'd gone to the Market in search of the arum, there were so many different vendors hawking herbs and wild plants that she'd spent the better half of the morning strolling through the individual stands, chatting with organic gardeners, and rolling leaves between her palms to loose the aromatic oils. A farmer's wife had talked her into buying a bouquet of early fall flowers, yellow black-eyed Susans and purple cone flowers, sprigs of orange bittersweet, and a handful of blue delphiniums. Another had convinced her to purchase a handful of dried lavender. "Sprinkle the buds in your clothes," she said and winked.

Finally, in a small stand nestled beneath a huge spreading oak, Sparrow found the arum. She'd gone online at the bookstore to make sure she knew what it looked like, and she could not imagine why Serana had considered it so dangerous. And yet when she saw its single funnel-shaped blossom, green on the outside and burnt red on the inside, sheltering the tall brown stamen, she felt her pulse race. The closer she got to the plant, the harder it was to breathe properly. And yet the feeling was pleasant, even heady. She'd touched the waxy leaves, and leaned down to sniff the blossom, hoping that—like the herbs—it too would have a lovely aroma. A faint perfume, sweet and dusty, emanated from the yellow pollen packed against the base of the upright stamen. Inhaling deeply, she was suddenly warm all over, smiling.

"Are you interested?" asked the vendor. "Not too many are turned on by this beauty."

Sparrow thought him attractive enough: reddish hair that fell in loose curls to the collar of his shirt, a squared jaw, hazel eyes. His teeth were white and much too even to be entirely natural. *Not the real deal*, she found herself thinking, *a suburban boy slumming on the land. In another year he'll be sick of peddling plants and go back to law school.*

"Yeah. I have a friend who will dig it," she said.

She studied him as he bagged the pot in a paper bag. Next to Robin's angular face, with the narrow gap between his front teeth, and the dark haunted pools of his eyes, this spoon-fed boy in a farmer's dirt-splatter T-shirt was too perfect and therefore uninteresting. She gave him a full smile, conscious that he was staring at her body. For once, that didn't frighten her. In fact she let her hips sway as she walked away carrying the plant.

*   *   *

SPARROW HADN'T BEEN SURE TWO days earlier why the arum was dangerous. It simply felt right. Especially when she'd seen Robin sprawled on the porch taking a break from gardening.

When he saw her, he straightened up. She approached carefully, like a temple acolyte bearing an offering. He'd opened his hands to receive the gift even before he *knew* it was a gift.

"For you," she said in a husky voice. "For the garden."

"Thanks." He opened the bag to glance inside. His head shot up and his eyes gleamed. "*Really*, thanks."

She'd nodded then, afraid to say more and started toward the stairs, feeling the heat from his body on her thighs. At the threshold of the door, even though she tried not to, she'd turned and looked over her shoulder. He'd been staring at her, holding tightly to the bag.

THAT DAY, SPARROW HAD WATCHED Robin from her balcony. Watched him dig in the garden, watched him throw back his head to laugh at something Jack said, watched him tease Sophia. She'd seen Sophia's eyebrows shoot up to the crown of her russet hair and the alarmed expression on her face when Robin showed her the arum.

So, Sparrow thought, *everybody knows it's here to start something.* Even Jack knew, for he'd pulled Sophia aside to whisper in her ear and nod at the plant.

And on the following day, when the afternoon sun had been at its longest point, Robin had looked up and acknowledged her where she stood, leaning into the warm, burnished light. He hadn't said anything, just stared with a smile that was at once hungry and sorrowful. She knew that feeling and as the heat flared in her chest, a ribbon of gold dust lifted from the red throat of the arum flower, swirled around the turgid stamen, and cast its pollen over the garden. She inhaled and caught the familiar scent of its dusty perfume, tasting its sweetness on her lips.

*   *   *

AT THE BATHROOM SINK, SPARROW squeezed the last of the soap and water out of her lace panties and bra and hung them to dry. Standing back to look at them, she rolled her eyes, abashed at the sight, and yet wanting to somehow be ready. She hoped that for once she might feel beautiful. She hoped that making love might be as lovely as she imagined it could be. That for once the invitation to sex would be about sharing not owning, about tenderness and not violence.

Turning off the bathroom light, she returned to the bedroom and shimmied into her old cotton nightgown with the border of white embroidery. Although it was falling apart at the hem and neck, the flimsy fabric around her legs made her feel feminine. And desirable.

As she lay down on the bed, hands resting lightly on her breasts, with Lily dozing the floor, Sparrow waited for Robin's fiddle to play. The melodies were soft that night, and insinuating. As were her dreams.

56

Robin and Sparrow in the Garden

I was asleep and then suddenly awake, all parts of me. Getting up, I played the fiddle softly for a few minutes, then went downstairs past her door.

Listening at the keyhole, I could hear the dog's paws trembling on the floor as she raced through a dream forest chasing a hare. She houghed a little, then settled. I could not hear her mistress, though, and while I longed to tap on the door, to go into the room, which would be hot with Sparrow's breath, I dared not. She needed the healing sleep.

So I tiptoed outside, sat for a bit on the front stoop, all a-tremble. Looking up at the moon, the stars, Mars with its bloody halo, I promised myself not to think on my father, lest it call him to me. But I sniffed the air. It was free of everything except the scent of Sparrow—heather and heat.

I wiped a hand across my brow because I was sweating profusely even though the night air was cool. So I decided to walk swiftly around the garden in the hope that the odors would take me out of my fevered longing.

The ground was still warm beneath my bare feet, the overturned earth comfortable between my toes. In the small, puzzling breeze, the smells of the newly planted flowers and herbs were almost overwhelming. But then the arum, brought hungrily to life under the moon, forced its violent, acrid smell into my nostrils. I could feel it traveling down into my throat. Dragon Root. Wild Turnip. Cuckoopint. Devil's Ear. It was all of that and more. For some reason I began to weep, though the way a dog does, without actual tears.

"Boy, why are you crying?" She whispered it, the sound caressing my ears.

I spun around. Sparrow was standing there, haloed by moonlight, in a long, white, sleeveless, slightly tattered nightgown, the neck scooped low in front. I could see the mounds of her breasts, and below the shadow of her pubic hair. The faded tattoos on her arms took on an unearthly look, as if the snaky forms were beckoning to me.

"What makes you think I'm crying?" I asked.

"Sorry. It's a line from a book I love." She smiled. I could not tell if she was mocking me or simply stating a fact.

"What book?"

"A book called *Peter Pan*. I was given it in one of the twenty or so foster homes I was put in. The only halfway decent one, actually. I took the book with me when I ran away." She smiled. "I *always* ran away."

I stepped a moment closer to her, hoping, praying she would not run away now. "Do you still have the book?"

She didn't step back. "Of course not. That was years ago."

"I thought you were asleep, that the fiddle might have soothed you enough to . . ."

"I needed to think. I was sitting on the dark side of the porch when you came out. I watched you walk out into the garden."

I hadn't smelt her. Or rather, I thought I was carrying the smell from upstairs. I hadn't even heard her. *What kind of a tracker . . . ?* It was that bloody arum that fuddled me.

Well, no more, I thought, taking another step toward her. Now I could truly smell her, the heather, the blood under the fragile shield of skin. The sour/sweet smell between her legs, wet, welcoming. I smiled back thinking that the heat was not just coming from me. She was as aroused as I.

And then she pushed into my opening arms and we kissed, mouths open, tongues thrusting, until we were both so dizzy with the kisses, we sank down into one of the furrows, first she on top of me, then me on top of her.

I waited till she had opened entirely like a flower, pushed her gown above her knees, so tight and taut from my desire and the arum and the moon and the heather smell, I thought I would burst before entering her.

"I am a . . ." she whispered, "I never before . . ."

But I already knew. Virgins simply smell different, new, honest. And then her legs went around my back and we were both ready. I was on my knees and about to . . .

She screamed.

Someone tumbled across my shoulders. There was a startled laugh. A shout.

Sparrow pushed herself away from all of us, her gown once again covering her long, beautiful legs, and she was away, like a deer in the forest pursued by dogs, though none of us—not me or the old lady or the Jack—tried to follow.

57

Meteora Regrets

That damned stalk festered for two nights in the garden. That was all it took for its power to wake the dragons in us all.

Walking out that second night, Jack and I stumbled over Sparrow and Robin in the gardens, twined as in Serana's vision. I laughed in delight and embarrassment, trying to extricate myself. But Sparrow rose from the soil, drew her clothes about her in dark shame and fled before I could stop her. Robin lay there erect, miserable and moaning in the moon.

If only Sparrow could have trusted me. If only she could have believed that such a joyful sight is as old as earth to me. But she did not trust, and ran from us, locking herself away.

In the morning I stood on the landing before her door trying to find the words that might soften her humiliation. I left without knocking, feeling strongly the bolt and lock that shut all of us out.

That night I listened for sounds of her in the room below, as I am sure did Robin, but it was quiet. And after, she would walk the dog, go to work, come home, feed the dog, and then leave again. I caught a glimpse of her on the sidewalk one evening and was shocked to see her looking more like a common tart than the young woman I knew.

I fumed, full of doubt and worry. Was *she* the one who had read my letter? Did she tear away the lines of warning? Was the arum a gift to Robin from her own hands? Or was she being used by another to sow discord?

My anxiety grew even more when Serana's pigeon arrived on my sill bearing the awful news, the missing lines that warned of the arum. As well as telling of the Queen seeking someone in the streets of a mortal city. Like Red Cap, like the glamoured Highborn. Serana's words of warning deepened my resolve to watch over these two nest-starved birds. It was the least I could do for allowing the arum to root in the garden.

58

Sparrow's Anguish

Sparrow reached down and plucked up another shot of Jameson's—one in a long row of them—and tossed it down her throat to the encouraging shouts of the college boys around her. The wire bone of her padded bra dug into her flesh, but she didn't care. It was doing its job to attract buyers, pushing her small breasts up into twin white mounds over the low edge of her T-shirt. Her tattoos and kohl-smeared eyes just made her seem more exotic to the boys goading her into downing the next shot.

Sparrow snorted a laugh and reached for the glass but the bartender leaned over and grabbed her hand.

"That's enough."

"Fuck that," she said, squinting up at him. He was cute enough, hell they were all cute *enough*. She'd take any of them. What did it matter anymore anyway? She should just give it up and be done with it.

"I'm serious," the bartender said, leaning in to take the drink from her fingers. "Folks drop dead, pounding shots like that."

"I can handle it. Really. I never get too drunk. I mean, I just can't 'cause I'm . . ."

"You're what?" asked a soft voice over her shoulder. "What are you?"

She lurched around on the stool, and gasped, the alcohol in her veins like frost.

Hawk smiled at her and inclined his head. His hand began to stroke her neck, the tattooed knot throbbing to life under his fingers. It prickled and then stung like nettles, and she flinched at the pain.

"Leave me alone," Sparrow said, sobriety waking her to his danger.

"Come back with me."

"No," she whispered.

"Hey, dude, who said you could join the party?" a beefy-faced boy snarled at Hawk. "Why don't you fuck off and find someone your own age, asshole." He put a hand on Hawk's shoulder, trying to spin him around.

Effortlessly, Hawk snagged the boy's hand and quickly snapped it back at the wrist. As the boy shrieked in sudden agony, Hawk turned, driving his weight against the wrist bones until the boy stumbled to his knees trying to escape the fierce pain.

"That's it," the bartender shouted. "Get out, you and the girl. You're done here."

Sparrow needed no more prompting but slid off the stool and pushed her way through the crowd of angry college students gathering at the bar behind her. She heard the threatening shouts and turned once to look.

Despite the warnings from the bartender, Hawk continued to hold the boy's bent-back wrist captive, sneering as he writhed in pain. Someone grabbed a book and smashed it across the back of Hawk's head. Hawk relinquished his hold on the boy's wrist but as he lurched forward, he drove his knee into the beefy face under him. Blood gushed on the boy's startled face, his mouth agape with missing teeth.

An angry chorus of shouts rose from around Hawk.

Sparrow tore out of the bar, and began sprinting down the street. Fear pumped through her veins, burning away the last of her drunken haze.

"Stupid girl, stupid girl," she huffed in time to her pounding footsteps.

Ducking beneath the trees, trying to hug the shadows, too afraid to turn around again, too afraid that she would see Hawk loping after her, she kept running. She knew it wouldn't take long for him to extricate himself from the bar. A thrust of a dagger under an arm or the inside of a thigh, and they would all be slipping in blood. All except Hawk.

She swerved quickly off of the sidewalk and staggered into the park, hoping to lose him in its sheltering darkness. Throwing herself onto the grass, she crawled beneath a tall shrub, chest heaving, bits of dirt and decayed leaves speckling her damp lips. She reached into her purse, hand fumbling for the little silver dove. When she found it, she closed her fingers around its smooth body. It wasn't much, but it was all she had.

For long minutes she lay hidden beneath the leaves, listening to the ragged sound of her own breathing. Then everything grew quiet as her breathing slowed, deepened. Now all she heard were the comforting night sounds of small creatures scratching in the dirt, or nesting in the secret shelter of the branches.

Still she waited, unmoving until long after the faint silver of moonlight descended behind the trees. Obviously, Hawk hadn't followed her; or at least, he hadn't found her. She was too good at merging into nothingness.

Finally, as the first stretch of pearly daylight inched above the horizon, Sparrow crept out from beneath the shrubs. Dusting off the dirt and twigs that clung to her clothes, and with a silent curse, she reached up under her T-shirt and unhooked the clasp of her bra. Sliding her arms briefly out of the sleeves, she removed it and stashed it beneath the shrub.

"Never again," she said. She'd been stupid and rash, not once but twice in the last few days. The first time she'd nearly drowned in humiliation while the second had threatened her life and injured an innocent boy. "No more," Sparrow said. She'd go back to the garden and rip the heart out of the fucking arum.

*   *   *

BABA YAGA'S HOUSE, DESPITE ITS usual gloom, was now a welcoming sight. Sparrow bounded up the porch steps two at a time, glancing quickly over her shoulder before she entered the house. The street was empty, the gray smudge of early morning light throwing the tops of the trees in sharp relief.

Satisfied she'd not been followed, Sparrow went in and closed the door firmly behind her.

She didn't see the gleam of neon green eyes peering at her from the tall stand of yews across the street, or the tall figure emerging from the shelter of the trees. Even if she had seen, she might not have known enough to be afraid.

59

Hawk's Discovery

I stand hidden by trees across the street, waiting for the light from a window to betray her room. How could I have not seen what she was before? Were her eyes not warning enough? I inhale again, and my prick thickens as I hold her scent against the roof of my mouth: the saltiness of human cunt and the cloying perfume of the arum. She is fey—more so than human, though she does not know it. I wipe my hand across my mouth, still slick with the blood of those useless boys at the tavern. They tried to stop me, but I have long known how to cut a path through a crowd.

Once on the street I had no trouble finding her, following the trail of scent unfurling behind her. She never saw me as I climbed up into the arms of an outstretched oak and watched over her where she lay squirreled beneath the brush.

She knows what I am. It must be she who left the spells of unbinding on my doorstep. Only chance kept her from knowing me when first she came into the shop.

I did not take her there, not in the grass, not under a tree, though it would have been easy and I ached for it. But for the violation to be complete, I will take her in her own house, the old hag's house. She will not see me coming for I will strew the grounds with my own spells of undoing. And when she is most alone, most vulnerable, I will harvest her blood in a silver bowl and thrust myself deep inside her. Then none will stand against me. I will send word to the Dark Lord that I have found what he seeks because in truth I have, and he will reward me well. In the darkest corners of his courts I will rebuild our clans, until we are strong enough in blood and arms to claim his power for ourselves. Blood to blood, it is the ransom of nations.

I rub a hand against the ache in my groin. I will make it last, I think. Pain and pleasure. One will be hers, the other mine.

60

Meteora Enters the Battle

Two days and nights passed without sight of Sparrow. It was late in the afternoon and each of us still fractious over what had happened. Robin sulked beneath the withered shade of the trees. Jack struggled to balance a new sculpture in the center of the garden, something with a spiral to soothe these brooding, unhappy children.

The third evening, I was kneeling before a dying plant, trying to convince myself to be patient, to wait for Sparrow to appear and make amends.

I plunged my hand into a patch of dried leaves, shuddering as I brought forth a twisted mandrake root. Sitting back on my heels, I surveyed the garden and saw now where the blooms of my new plants were withering. I went to each and found dark tokens of undoing beneath: nightshade blossom, manglewort, even the red spotted caps of kills-quick.

Sparrow. It had to be her, getting back at us, punishing us and the garden for her humiliation. I jerked the odious plants free of the soil, braided the roots to keep them from bleeding malice and rolled them in a bit of my mother's silk I carry in my pocket for protection. The white silk was stained crimson and I could have wept at the profanity were it not for the heat gathering in my breast. I set the evil things down on the new wall and grabbed a handful of stones to pound them into harmless pulp. As I raised my hand I was startled by a crow's screech exploding the stillness.

Awxes appeared out of the darkening sky, leading a multitude of crows, their voices raised in a cry of outrage. Arrowing his body toward the house, he crashed against the glass window of Sparrow's bedroom and the rest of the flock followed by threes and fours, laying siege to the window.

Smoke coiled in a scorched pattern around the window as the crows battered the unyielding glass. Robin staggered to his feet and began to run toward the back stairs. Stuffing stones into my pocket, I followed him from the garden to the house, up the stairway to the second floor, my lungs burning for want of air. Behind me came Jack calling, "Sophia, Sophia!"

On the landing, Lily was lying, stretched out and unmoving, her tongue lolling out of her opened mouth. Blood was speckled over the white fur of her throat. Pounding his fists on the door, Robin was shouting Sparrow's name over and over. But I could see at once no mortal strength could unbind the door from its spells of closing.

"Away," I commanded and pushed him aside. I placed my hands on the door and shuddered at the skin of treachery beneath my palms.

And then, amid the harsh battle cries of the crows, Robin's desperate shouts, even Jack calling out the name that wasn't mine, I descended into a prescient calm. In the willed silence, I heard Sparrow's muffled sob, the soft thump of her body, the harsh rasp of her breath.

I should have thanked the arum then, for the power it awoke in me was not sex, but rage when I needed it most. In my breast a blistering dragon unfurled, and filled my body from feet to hands with fire. The wood smoked and charred beneath my palms, burning away the rune meant to keep us out. I pushed harder with growing strength until the planks cracked free from their hinges and fell away. Steam billowed in turbulent clouds as I—blind with fury—entered the room.

Sparrow lay on the floor, the pale ribbon of her naked body mottled with the shifting shadows of crow wings beating against the window. The air was moist with the rotten stench of wormwood punks burning on the floor. A silver bowl waited by her head. Hovering over her was a man, a quill poised over the soft mound of her belly, ink dripping from the sharpened point. I stepped closer and saw where the white skin of her torso was marked with dark spells. The inside of her thighs were covered with scorpions that she should take no pleasure in either touch or cock; a brindled hound snapped at the curve of her breast as though to tear away the flesh. Black adders slithered into knots over her shoulders holding her in bondage, and between the thin stands of her ribs a stake wreathed in mistletoe stabbed toward her heart.

I should have been afraid when he looked up and snarled. Those high cheekbones, that skin of polished wood, eyes like pulsing garnets. Highborn once, but censured for his taste for blood and treachery. I shuddered at the sight of Sparrow in his grip.

"I know you now, Long Lankin, blood drinker, soul swallower," I cried.

"Go," Lankin ordered, waving his hand to brush me away, thinking me of no consequence to a Highborn such as himself.

But the arum was not done with me and a renewed power surged in my breast. Retrieving stones from my pocket, I hurled them with all my strength, not at Lankin but at the windows. The glass shattered and the crows flooded through the broken panes in a black rush of beating wings, beaks, and talons and headed straight for him.

He threw his arms up, bellowing curses as Awxes attacked his face. The quill skittered across the floor, and the pots toppled over, the black ink burning the floorboards. Lankin's arms windmilled, and he kicked his legs, trying to free himself of the attacking crows.

Leaping up—the murder of crows still mobbing his head and shoulders—Lankin ran for the door, but I was there to block him. I should have stepped aside, but I could not, the rage would not let me. I struck him hard across that cruel face and spun him around. He recoiled and struck me back, howling as the skin of his hand burned the moment it touched my cheek. Pain exploded and my head jerked violently to one side with the blow, but I stayed upright on staggering feet, refusing to move from the doorway. I threw a wild fist at him and felt the skin of his cheek split. He rolled away from the door, shaken by my attack. His blood hissed and steamed where it splashed across my knuckles.

Robin dashed around me, plunged through the flock of crows, and went straight to Sparrow. Pulling her into his arms, he growled and bared his teeth like a mastiff.

Then Jack was there, and he grabbed Lankin by the scruff, threw him against the wall, and pressed his arm across Lankin's throat to hold him prisoner. He could not know the power of the Highborn he treated so rudely.

"Do not touch him," I cried, my hand held out, though useless to offer a spell of protection.

Thick smoke and the crack of lightning sizzled in the room. Jack cried out as the first blast knocked him across the room and into the wall. I, too, was hurled back by the force, but stood again and flung myself forward, over Robin and Sparrow, shielding them from the second blast so that the flying splintered wood would not pierce Sparrow's naked skin.

Crows shrieked and cawed as they were pierced with the flying wooden daggers. They fell to the floor, wings beating frantically, blood mingling with the spilled poisoned ink.

Then a deafening roar and a veil of green smoke filled the room that set us all to coughing. Sheltered between Robin and me, Sparrow never moved.

When the smoke finally cleared through the broken windows, I knew that Lankin was gone. Only then did I raise myself and survey the damage. Two walls blasted open. Four crows dead. Jack rolled into a ball, his shirt covered with splintered wood like the quills of a porcupine, dots of blood where they entered. Two jagged darts of wood had pierced Robin's hand where it lay over Sparrow's face in a protective mask.

"Jack," I called to the slumped figure and he raised his head, then his hand, and answered. "I'm good. And you?"

"I survive."

"Robin? And the girl? Is she all right?"

I sat back on my haunches and Robin gathered Sparrow onto his knees, his terrified eyes searching her face. Her arms were limp, her head rolled back lifeless. But her eyes watched me, moved to follow mine. Sickened, I plucked a tiny arrow from her black hair; elf shot meant to keep her still yet aware of the pain while Lankin marked her. I broke it, and tucked the feathered shaft in my pocket. It would be proof of his cruelty. Released from its paralyzing power, Sparrow groaned and her head fell against Robin's chest.

"She will be. Robin, help me get her to my bed."

We rose, Sparrow in Robin's arms and Jack leading me by the elbow. At the door, I cried at the sight of faithful Lily, lying so still. Jack leaned down and touched the dog, then looked back at me and shook his head. He stroked her, his mouth drawn tight in anger. I sobbed, the arum's power ebbing away and leaving me only tears.

Jack stood back up and held me close while I wept. And I knew then in the deepest part of me, that this was no Trickster Jack. This was a human Jack—a Giantkiller, a humbler of trolls, a Jack who made the princess laugh. He would stand by my side against the dark and he would stay there till we triumphed or died together.

We limped upstairs, in shock and pain.

THE SERVANT HANDS HELPED ME, tearing linen bandages into strips. So dazed and wounded were we all, that no one was surprised by the hands' appearance. Sparrow was placed gently in my bed and afterward I washed

Jack's and Robin's wounds and gave them a special tea brewed strong enough to make them sleep.

I waited quietly until Jack had dozed off, sitting up-right in the embroidered chair, while on my bed Robin had curled like a hound at Sparrow's feet. I sat in the kitchen, meditating, turning the fragments of knowl-edge around and around as the twilight edged into darkness and then night shut us in. Serana's warning had been fair enough—but like all visions it had been ambiguous. The arum had awoken desire in Sparrow and Robin, but it had also provoked Lankin to greater cruelty. It had given me the power needed to fight him, but it had cost the lives of the innocents—Lily and the crows.

The path for all of us led here, to this house and to Sparrow. And I sighed with heavy heart, thinking it right that somehow after all the seasons that had passed, she should come to me. Or perhaps, that I was brought here to find her. My punishment and my chance to set things right.

There could be no denying it now. I had seen the proof in her apartment when she lay nude and prostrate beneath the poisoned quill. I had seen the true color of her hair. In that triangle, the hair blazed like spun gold against her cream-colored belly. I realized then that she had been hiding her hair beneath garish dyes, not want-ing to call attention to herself. But I knew the color of that hair. No one—neither mortal woman nor fairy—had hair of such color. Except the Queen. And there it was, in front of me. The child who had lain on the grass that long-ago summer, who was betrayed by my indiscre-tion, was now the girl in my bed, wounded and in need of my protection. This time, I would not fail.

WHEN THE EVENING WAS FULL, I roused myself from the table, found the last bits of my dam's white silk and bas-ket. Then I slipped into the bedroom and woke Robin.

"Come with me. I need your help."

"Get Jack."

"No. This is your doing and mine. It is our duty now."

Stricken, he looked up at me and rose. We both knew the dead awaited us below. We could not ignore those who had fought for us.

On the landing, the serving hands stroked Lily's body, in a tender farewell. Only then did I realize that the dog—like the hands and the cat and the house—had not belonged to Sparrow at all, but to the Great Witch. She would not be pleased when she learned the news.

The hands wrapped Lily in a brocade cloth and placed her in a leather satchel and carried her away. Robin gathered the corpses of the valiant crows, wrapping each one in a piece of white silk, and I placed them gently in a basket. I wept again when I saw the patches of white feathers on two of the smaller crows. The little changeling girls were dead.

Then Robin and I walked outside carrying our awful burdens. He glanced fearfully back at the house.

I shook my head. "Lankin will not return, at least not for a while. He has wounds, too, you know. In every battle, there is a truce time to bury the dead and bind the wounds. We are wrapped in that truce now. She will be safe until we finish what we must. I promise."

He shivered all over, like a dog new out of the river, but nodded as if he had heard of such a thing before.

And so we walked swiftly into the deepest part of the park where under the trees, we laid down our burdens. There we dug with our hands beneath decaying leaves and laid those small bundles out in a trough of softened earth.

We did not speak nor did we stay long for we were both too exhausted from sorrow, from anger, and from the aches of battle. Besides, we had our injured loved ones to care for at home. We made the last of the trek in a small downpour that seemed to have conjured itself out of a cloudless sky.

*　　*　　*

WE RETURNED TO FIND JACK awake and in my kitchen, starting to cook an extravagant breakfast of eggs folded over herbs, mushrooms, and daubs of cheese. There was soon toast and a mug of tea, hot and steaming, new potatoes frying in a pan, blackened with butter. I felt appetite and life returning. My stomach growled in anticipation.

However, Robin paid scant attention to the food, returning instead to his place at the bottom of Sparrow's bed. She murmured a few words to him, and he stretched out beside her, an arm wrapped around her waist.

Jack had already set the little table, the bone-handled cutlery laid out just so, framing the porcelain plates. A new taper was in the candlestick and it burned with a cheering flame. All my precious things had been carefully placed on the window ledge. I was astonished into speechlessness—would not Serana be amused at that! Wet, cold, my fingers chaffed, and stained with dirt, I sank into the chair and watched Jack take command of the little kitchen.

He moved with grace, long, dexterous fingers cracking eggs, beating them in the blue bowl, turning the pan so that the mixture might cook quickly and evenly. He said nothing, but cast his glance my way, questions lying there between us, but good manners holding them in check. Never speak first when dealing with the fey—that old interdiction. Well, it seemed he learned a thing or two from someone with common sense. Perhaps even his neighbor, Baba Yaga. *How well* does *he know her?*

I let him put the food in front of me. When I took a bite, it was delicious. We ate in silence. After the meal was done, I asked but one thing of him: "Will you help me hide Sparrow and Robin? Others will come."

"Yes. You can stay with me. Just across the garden." He pointed out the window to an old five-story building across from mine. "I have the loft on the top floor."

"Are you sure you want to do this?"

"If you're asking do I know what I'm in for, the answer is yes. Sort of." Then he smiled, brushing back the thick gray hair, those eyes too bright a blue.

"How do you know this?"

"When I was ten years old my mother left us and my father, bitter about it, deposited me into the reluctant arms of my mother's sister, a woman strange and fascinating. She was neither gruff nor kind, but drank small glasses of whiskey, read tarot cards, tea leaves, and told stories."

"Stories?" I asked, sipping my tea.

"Yeah, the kind that make the hair on the back of your neck stand up and send you either running for the shrink's couch or into art."

"And since you are of normal size, I am assuming you went into art," I replied, trying to conceal my ignorance. I have no idea what conjurer he imagined would turn him small. Or why.

He laughed and it was a pleasant sound in my kitchen that drove away the dampness of my joints. I must have guessed correctly.

After we finished eating, he went to wrap the sleeping Sparrow in a blanket. Robin growled at him, a throaty sound I have never heard a human make before.

"Then you'll have to carry her, son," Jack said. "We have to leave here now."

I added, "The truce will end at the moon's height and we still have to make Jack's loft a fortress."

Robin swaddled Sparrow in a blanket while Jack grabbed what extra food remained in my cold storage. I gathered up my treasures and placed them in my pocket and we left, locking the door to Baba Yaga's house behind us. Or what remained of it. It seemed I was being forced into exile again.

Walking close together, we crossed the courtyard, past the garden to Jack's building. An old rickety lift pulled us to the roof and I have not been so frightened of a cage since the time Serana and I tried to trap a Roc and nearly got our fingers nipped off. Besides, being surrounded by so much iron made me wheeze.

But finally we entered Jack's abode and even my cautious sister would have been wild with happiness.

It was a garden of sculptures: wood and leather, twigs and fur, and green plants growing in abundance. There were stones with natural holes, shells with coiled secrets, a tortoise carapace, and dried fronds of bracken. The air was fragrant with the scents of linseed, cedar shavings, and charcoal. Slender stalks of rowan and blackthorn had been woven into the frames around the windows. Safeguards against the UnSeelie court. I wondered if he knew that.

Jack directed Robin toward a large bedroom with a window on the ceiling that looked up at the stars. The wooden bed was covered with a huge quilt of velvet patches stitched together with colored silks. Here the children slept, like chicks storm-fallen from their nest and now returned.

Jack led me to a smaller room at the back of the studio where he stored books and paintings. There was a simple bed covered in a woven cloth of midnight blue and it was as narrow as the cot where once my sister and I shared our youthful secrets. Not with ardor, but with great tenderness he held me in his arms, and in that embrace, I let the terror and grief of our long day recede.

NONE OF US SLEPT PAST the dawn, but it was rest enough. Besides, we had work to do. Jack and Robin had to make the loft safe in case a new battle should break out. I never doubted there would be one soon.

Since the poisonous ink had given Sparrow a fever, my healing skills were sorely tested. I melted beeswax into a paste with some fresh ginger I found in Jack's pantry. I added a bit of my own blood drawn from the crook of my left arm and the sweat of a city mouse caught behind the wall. I added a cobweb from the corner of Jack's bookshelf and the squeezings of rowan berries. It worked albeit slowly. But after a day, most of the frightful tattoos began to disappear—though the one for trouble, no doubt the first, seemed deeply etched.

Jack made a vegetable soup thickened with eggs, but

Robin would suffer no one but himself to feed Sparrow. He raised her head to the spoon, though he managed to get her to take but one sip, or two. She was no more than a ribbon of white flesh now, but I knew how resilient she was—sturdy like her namesake.

AT NIGHT I HEARD ROBIN whispering in the dark, heard Sparrow's feathered answers while Jack and I took turns standing watch. But either we had hurt Lankin more than we knew, or he was plotting with others for a next move. I wondered about that. He did not seem the type to share. On the other hand, he might have been selling information and still looking for the highest bidder. I could guess who the bidder might be. Had I not seen him on the street? Lankin was bad, Red Cap unthinkable. Though I didn't say anything to the others, Jack's loft no longer seemed much of a fortress at all.

IN THE MORNING, I BUMPED into Robin in front of the water room.

"How is she?"

He shrugged.

"I will make another ointment," I said. "And I will be in to rub her down shortly."

"I'll do it," he said abruptly, going back into their room and closing the door.

I suddenly realized that he meant to protect her even from me. They were a pair, the two of them. Touched by fey hands and then abandoned to some awful life between the worlds. It made no sense, even as my own exile made no sense. But I felt reassured knowing that at least they had each other, as I had my sister, though she was far away.

Only then did I realize I had to write to her. I had to try to put words to paper, to tell of our recent encounter. But the story was too new, too raw. I grieved for the crows, those little girls who were lost. I grieved for Lily and her bark. I worried for the two spilling secrets to each other in the bedroom. And worried for my Jack who had unwittingly become a part of it all. So first I made the ointment for Robin to put on Sparrow, and after, came back to the table where paper and pen awaited me.

I got as far as "Dearest Serana," and burst into tears, unable to write another word.

61

Serana and the Crones

I stood still, all atremble with the sounds of the night: the bridle bells, the horses' hooves pacing beneath my window, the uncanny silence of the streets. The Queen had never looked up and seen me, white as bone, as milk in the pail, staring down at her. She did not have to. She certainly knew I was there.

With the first false dawn, she left, going through the curtain of time that separates the Greenwood from the human world. I ran downstairs, to walk widdershins around the block, for all the good that might do me. I passed alleyways where bits of old newspapers and magazines whirled in silent eddies. Where old men slept on the pavement in cardboard boxes. Where feral cats prowled around garbage cans looking for food. And then I came home again just as the city stretched, stirred, came back to life.

I had just sat down, still atwitter, when a knock came at the downstairs door. It was a loud hammering and could have awakened the dead.

One part of me did not want to go down there. But one does not ignore a summons. There are some spriggans and sprites who *can* stand the light. And of course the Highborn can. Someone from the Greenwood could be coming with a message for me from the Queen. It could even have been the Queen herself, turned round again to confront me. I did not dare keep the knocker waiting.

Gathering my skirts about me, I walked slowly down the stairs as if going to my own execution. My unprotected hand turned the iron knob. I did not mind the scorching. What did that small burn matter when surely the Queen could melt me like candle wax whenever she felt like it?

On the doorstep stood a young woman with white-gold curls and a strange, dark center part, and a man the color of crow feathers. Suddenly, I remembered them as if they were part of an old, odd dream. They had been my scare-bird's companions in the park. But how had they found me? And who had sent them?

"What *is* it with you old people?" the girl said, the moment I opened the door. "No landline, no cell? Robin called and told us to get our butts over here. Now."

Surely I looked fuddled, for the crow-colored man said, "Slow down, May. She's just out of bed."

"She *looks* like a rumpled bed, Chim, if that's what you mean," she countered. "And don't forget who else just tumbled out of bed. And just when things were getting . . . interesting."

"He'll wait."

"He'd better."

May. Chim. Now the whole scene in the park tumbled back into my brain. And what had come after.

The girl held out a small, pink object. "Call him," she ordered.

"Call who?" I said. "Call how?" I wasn't just fuddled, I was entirely confused.

"Oh, for God's sake!" she said, and pushed some numbers on the pink object, held it to her ear. Said, "Rob. Yeah. Me. She's here." Then held it out to me again. "Just talk."

I held it as she had, to my ear, and began to talk. "Hello? Hello? Is this a summons? I am ready. I yield."

And then a disembodied voice that sounded like and

not like the scare-bird, said, "Hi, Auntie Em. Had some trouble here."

I dropped the pink thing and then, as if all the strings connecting my body parts had been cut at once, collapsed hard onto the stone steps. Stone, which had never harmed me in the Greenwood, bruised me in unmentionable places.

Chim propped me up against the wall, spoke briefly into the pink thing, saying "Hold on a minute, bro," and then explained that the pink object was called a cell, though all the cells I knew were deep and dark and inescapable. "You can talk to people across the air, all the way to . . ." He stopped talking to me, and said into the cell, "Where the hell you at, Rob?" Then back to me, "Milwaukee."

I remembered the woman shouting to the air, the one almost hit by the yellow car. I had thought her crazed. Perhaps she had been talking to a cell, too.

And then I realized what Chim had said, pronouncing it far differently than I ever had. *Milwaukee. Where Meteora lived.* "May I speak to my sister?"

"Can she speak to her sister?" Chim asked the cell.

I grabbed it before he received an answer. "Meteora. METEORA!" I shouted into the cell, into the air.

The answer, thin, bodiless, came back to me, "Not so loud, sister. And not with that name. It is Sophia, remember?"

And then we wept. Any other time we might have laughed to hear our voices trilling like birds through the cell. Quickly she told me what had happened, and I was relieved to know she was all right.

All right? With the Queen on her solitary Rade, with Red Cap on the loose, with mandrakes screaming in Meteora's garden, the Highborn Lankin breaking into her house, the arum calling all to wake. With the Queen's child, hiding her golden beauty with black dyes, poisoned by Lankin's foul spells.

There was nothing *all right* with any of it.

"I will send aloe cream for your burns," I told Meteora, my words flying through the air, "though it does not smell like aloe, but more like machinery."

She assured me that she had aloe aplenty. "From where I work," she added.

"Had you not set wards?" But even as I asked, I knew that if she had, they would not have done any good. Oh, we could keep out unwitting humans with locks, and pigeons with a scattering of herbs, but not a Highborn like Lankin. Or a Lowborn like Red Cap. Even in the Greenwood we had had no strong magic. Here in the cities, stripped of the little we once had, we were naked to even mediocre spellcasters.

"I will try and find you," I said. "Good-bye. Good-bye. My lovely sister. I will come." Iron rain be damned. If my sister was hurting, I would be there, whatever the cost. I waved my hand toward the west, where I knew she had to be. Then I handed back the pink cell to Chim, thinking: *How can I get there? I have no more money to ride the horseless carts. Or to buy protection from the iron rain.*

Suddenly I had no idea what to do next.

I began to weep again. "I must. I must . . ." The words could not push through the tears or the closing of my throat with sorrow. Finally I managed. "I must go to her. To them. They are in terrible danger. In . . . in Milwaukee." I pronounced it as Chim had. "But how . . ." And then my throat closed down again.

May's hands fluttered. "Okay, no more tears. You'll have me bawling next." She turned to Chim. "Your aunts, the crones. Could they . . . ?"

"Dunno." He shook his head, closed his eyes. Opened them again. "Maybe. They can be fierce."

I managed to stand. Everything in my body ached. I doubted I had enough aloe for these pains. "Fierce is good."

"It's on *your* head then, lady," he said.

I patted my hair. We all laughed at that, but the laughter was heavy and dark. "Let me use the water room first."

"Don't be long," Chim said. "The aunts go to bed around noon. They're night owls."

"Owls are good," I said.

They laughed again, though this time I did not know why.

I WAS NOT LONG AT all. I brought along my dam's shawl for warmth. I also brought an offering of salt and bread in a paper sack for the aunts. In case that mattered.

"Bus or subway?" May said to Chim.

He shook his head. "Neither. If she's anything like my aunts, they'll make her sick." He looked sideways at me. "We hoof it."

And despite May's complaint, we walked.

After a while I stopped counting the blocks. One place looked so like the other. When I asked where we were going, I got a one-word answer.

"Uptown," Chim said.

Walking on the stone walkways is so much harder than striding along any carpeting of pine or grass. I was fairly winded and my feet hurt, but I would not let it show.

The tall buildings became smaller buildings, and many had flat, tan-colored boards blocking both windows and doorways, as if the people who had lived in those places had moved far away. There were fewer of the yellow cars here, more buses, and people all shades of brown chatting on the streets. A friendlier place than where we had come from, perhaps because many of the people here seemed to be Chim's brothers and sisters. *What a huge family he must have*, I thought. And that would mean many aunts. No wonder May had suggested it.

Finally, we got to a place where shadows lay heavy on the ground, even with the early morning light streaming down. We turned into an alleyway. There was nothing that distinguished this alley from any other; it was simply a dark space between brick buildings. The walls were covered with signs, old and weathered, telling of things like milk and cigarettes and beer.

"If the aunts are still up," Chim said, "they'll be here."

"How many aunts have you?" I asked.

"Two," said May.

We went deep into the alley, turned a sharp corner, and there in the semidarkness of the shadows stood two ancient crones hovering over a fire contained in a steel drum. Tall, agonizingly thin, their skin stretched like black paper over fine bones. They each wore a voluminous black ankle-length dress, which only emphasized their height, their thinness. The sleeves of the dresses were rolled all the way up so that their arms were bare. As we neared, they were spreading some sort of ointment along the inside of those scrawny arms.

They must have heard our approach. We weren't quiet. But they took a long time before looking over at us. May they dismissed quickly, Chim they nodded at in recognition, but me they stared at with eyes hard as walnuts.

The taller one signaled me to them with cupped hands.

I was suddenly afraid. There was something royal about them. They may have been Chim's aunts—but were they queens? Well, if a queen beckons, one obeys. I handed them the paper sack with the bread and salt. The shorter crone opened it up, nodded, smiled as I stood warming my hands over the fire, which snapped and snarled at me from behind its grate. Close up, I could see they were not queens, but something else. Something older perhaps.

"It took you long enough to get here, girl," said the taller aunt.

"I had not known I was coming," I said, stuttering between words.

"Lucky we did, then," said the shorter. At which point they both laughed. It was the same as Chim's laughter, a short, staccato cascade.

Then the two put a cape around my shoulders made of some strange yarn, and lucky it was that I was wearing Mother's shawl or the iron strands in the thing would have burned me clear to the bone.

"Sister," said the taller one, "we offer you protection, for we can see that you need it."

I said nothing. Could these two really give me the help I needed? Against the Queen. Against Lankin. Against Red Cap and his Dark Lord. But I nodded. Anytime someone offers protection, whether it works or not, the laws of hospitality take hold.

The two then spoke strange words of binding. Ones I had never heard before.

"Hi-di, hi-di, hi-di ho," they sang. And again: "Hi-di, hi-di, hi-di ho." It went on for some time.

When at last they were through, I said, "Thank you. I am beholden."

"You ain't beholden nuthin'," said the taller one, and to demonstrate that, she gave me her name, Shawnique.

The other added, "Till we earns it." Her name was Blanche.

I nodded again. Somehow the words of their binding, the naming of names—whether True Names or familiar names—and their refusal of payment had stopped my tremors.

"Here I am called Mabel," I said.

"A good name," said Blanche. "Solid as prestressed concrete."

We stood for what seemed like hours more over that fire, the crones humming and chanting—I cannot call it singing exactly as the words were odd and unrhymed. *Syllables of power,* I suppose. I was quiet at first, but by the end I was chanting along with them: "Hi-di, hi-di hi-di ho . . ." And I could feel something more than warmth creep into my fingers. A tingling, a touch of what felt like magic.

Magic—how I had missed it.

When it was full morning, with Chim and May restless behind us, I said to the crones, "Sisters, come to my house. I have butter and jam for that bread, as well as spearmint tea." If they would not take thanks, then I could at least give them hospitality. And what greater than bread and tea.

Shawnique looked at me and laughed. "Tea?"

Blanche said, "Nuthin' stronger?"

"Wine," I whispered, "but it is morning."

They laughed and Chim and May laughed as well. Instead, we went around the corner and upstairs to their own apartment, which was full of dark wooden statues of women with swollen bellies and warriors holding spears. There were fierce masks lining the walls. With such strong guardians, I doubted anyone not invited could get in.

We drank some dark amber liquid that burned my throat and opened it, too, for I found myself spilling out the tale of the Lankin to them. We ate the bread without butter or jam and still it was good. The salt they put in the cupboard.

"We was just about out," Blanche said, "and it was good you brought that. But of course, we knew you would."

Shawnique added, "Now, sister, it's time for us to go to sleep. Past time actually. We gonna dream on your problem. We will find you in the evening. Be ready."

I gave them the number of my house and the street, and then we hustled out of their apartment and into the afternoon sun.

WHEN WE GOT BACK TO my house, stomachs full of bread and warmed by the drink, I told all this to my sister, over the air cell. I said, "Who knew there was such magic in the city, though it is not what we are used to. The crones throb with an odd power I cannot name. They think me strange, laugh at my clothes, but their laughter is not harsh. Not at all. Almost, I think, it is ... *conspiratorial*. Their power is built on something other than leaf and thorn. It has iron at its base, and paving. It has strong bones."

Then May and Chim left, taking the pink air cell with them. And suddenly I felt bereft, who had not even known of such a thing hours before. So quickly have I fallen for this new magic. I will ask the Man of Flowers how to get one. Surely he knows.

Before falling back into bed, I did a last blood casting, this time with my own hair. And the surprise of it was so great, I knew I could never speak it on the air cell or commit it to paper lest the wrong hands touch it, the wrong eyes see it, the wrong ears hear it. Though the Queen had forbidden me to find Meteora, I knew I had to chance it. I dared because of the casting and because of the power of the crones.

In a quick letter to Meteora, sent by eagle mail before I slept, I wrote a short note about Chim's aunts, ending with:

> *Get out a bottle of wine, or even something stronger, the color of old gold. Bake some dark bread—they like it crusty. We will find our way to you. I do not know how soon we will get there. But get there we will.*
>
> *In haste,*
> *Serana*

62

Serana and the Crones
Prepare for Battle

I sent out the eagle mail, first sprinkling some acacia into the envelope, for power, then sealing it on all sides and the flap with candle wax dipped in a drop of my blood and clary. Meteora would know at once if it had been tampered with.

Then I lay down to sleep, exhausted by the night's activities and the morning's walk to the sisters' place and back.

I slept through until nearly dark, then woke to a scritch-scratch at the front window, followed by the same sound at the back. A black eddy of crows was whirling in the alleyway, and two of them were squatting uncomfortably on the sill. I tapped on the glass to shoo them away and the larger bird stared at me with walnut-colored eyes.

I *knew* those eyes. Opening the window, I said in the old tongue first and then in a clumsy translation, "My house is yours, my sisters. My heart is yours, my sisters. My way is yours, my sisters." I hoped it was the right thing to say.

The crones flew in, changing to human form as they touched the floor.

"Whooo-ee!" said Blanche. "You are some slow girl. I told you to be ready. Gotta listen. Listen and learn." She shook herself all over, as if to shake off the last of the birdness. But some of it remained, in the way she cocked her head, to see out of the corner of her eye, the way her arms fluttered. I wondered that I had not noticed it before.

"Will you take tea with me?" I said. "Bread and jam?"

"We'll go for that wine you talked of this morning," said Shawnique.

"Should be late enough for you now," added Blanche.

They laughed together, though whether it was *at* me or some small joke of their own I did not know.

"Wine, then." I quickly poured three glasses, theirs to the brim and mine but a quarter full. I put out bread, too, for I did not dare drink on an empty stomach. The wine was a full-bodied red, to bring blood to the cheek and heat to the loins. The Man of Flowers had brought it to our dinner, but neither of us had taken much then. Both—I think—had wanted to be careful our first time together. How far away that seemed now. How fruitless in all senses of the word.

The crones drank their wine in large, noisy sips, talking about its flavor, about the vines from which it had been taken, the side of the vineyard slopes. I could not tell if they were having fun with me, or being serious. Either way, the wine got drunk in record time. I even offered to pour my small glass into theirs.

"You're gonna need the heat, girl. Up there," said Blanche, pointing to the ceiling.

I had no idea what she meant. But I drank the quarter glass quickly, and suddenly suspected I knew. *"Flying?"*

They looked at me as if I were a slightly stupid and very much younger sibling.

"Hold out your arms, girl. Pull the sleeves back," Shawnique said.

As I followed her orders, she took out a small porcelain jar from a hidden pocket in her dress. When she opened it, the smell was sharp as wind, clear as air, light as clouds. I drew in a deep breath, smelling toad essence, almond oil, sweet flag, and water plantain. Maybe even—I thought—a touch of belladonna.

She put two fingers in the green ointment and then rubbed it along the undersides of her arms. "Take the *unguenta* like this," she said. "Under the arms, on the hands, wrists, forearms. Don't use too much, but don't spread it too thinly either."

"Don't want you fallin', darlin'," added Blanche with a smile, her teeth white against her dark face, reminding me of Chim. "Chasing you down and catching you up gonna slow us a pocketful."

"Not to mention SPLAT!" said Shawnique and they both began to cackle again.

I did as they did, two fingers into the ointment, then rubbing it on my arms. Everywhere the *unguenta* touched me, my skin began to tingle. Then the tingle went deeper, until I could feel it in my bones as if they were unknitting and then knotting up in a new way.

We went to the back window, climbed out, sat on the sill, squeezed tightly together. I could feel the sisters on either side of me so thin yet so strong. They might as well have been as hollow-boned as the birds they mimicked. I worried I was too heavy for what they had planned.

"She sure is a plump one," Blanche said, cackling, as if she could read my mind. "A pigeon?"

"She gonna surprise you, sister," Shawnique replied. "There's something fierce in Mabel. She gonna surprise us both."

Then she pulled out a jay's feather from a different pocket, dipped it into the pot of ointment, closed the pot, disappeared it into the folds of her dress, and anointed us each on the forehead.

This time there was no tingle, only a sharp sudden opening of what felt like a third eye. Somehow I could see more clearly, feel more clearly than I had a moment before.

"We gonna be lifted above the gravity of this situation," Blanche said, nudging me with her sharp elbow.

"What is . . ." I began, but before I could finish what I was asking, we began to rise from the sill . . . and fly.

And yet, the sisters still looked like themselves, and I could see my own hands were still hands, not wings. I feared we would be revealed, three old women lifting above the ground, flying into the sky. I squinted my eyes to follow them as they flew ahead of me, and even as I watched, they morphed into crows, black against the black sky.

And then I understood. I would be both woman and bird until the *unguenta* wore off. Ordinary folk would see birds, but not anyone with fey blood. How long that transformation would hold, the sisters surely knew. Turning my head carefully, I looked at my broad shoulders, my wings, my talons that lay like a shadow over my real body. Shawnique was right. I *was* a surprise.

I thought: *Oh, sister, to be able to fly again, across this vast city so spectacularly hung with lights like imprisoned stars. To dip, to soar. To lift my sagging body above the gravity of the situation.* And with that we flew into the darkening skies.

OF COURSE WE TOUCHED DOWN often. The crones, like many old women, had small bladders. And our arms frequently went numb. Our eyes watered. Backs ached. Also we had to avoid phone lines and the telescopes of bird-watchers who would know what we were not. And city folk up checking out their neighbors.

"We calls them *jeeper-peepers*," Blanche told me.

I learned quickly. I had to. It was either that or die. And I was not ready to die. I had a sister to save, a boy and girl to bring together, Long Lankin to confront, a Red Cap to vanquish, a puzzle to solve. I had not felt so well in days. *In weeks.*

I was ready for everything ahead of me.

Everything. Except. Perhaps. The Queen.

63

Sparrow and the Bananachs

Wrapped in a blanket and sitting at Jack's huge kitchen table, Sparrow wrote a letter on a piece of blue onionskin paper. It felt weird writing a letter. She had never actually done that—put words on paper to someone else: a salutation, followed by "How are you?" "Doing fine," and all the other glib things people sent each other. She'd never even had the chance to write home for money. *And let's face it*, Sparrow fumed, *it was these damn letters that got Sophia—it's hard to call her by her right name—injured in the first place.*

She glanced over to where Sophia lay resting on a small day bed. Her arm was bandaged and secured in a homemade sling. *Jack's a good medic*, she thought. *At least he seems to know what he's doing.* But Sophia was pale, and Sparrow noticed her breathing was labored.

On the other side of the room, Robin was watching out the window, scanning the backyards and the garden for further signs of attack. Jack was in the kitchen, rattling the pots and then opening and slamming drawers in preparation for cooking. *Or maybe just sharpening the knives*, Sparrow thought, hearing the soft scree of blade against a hone.

Sparrow read over what she had written so far:

Dear Auntie Em,
*   You and your sister Sophia sure have a wacked*
sense of humor. I know your true names now but
I'm not so stupid as to use them here. You can't
believe how many weirdos are out there looking
for these letters. Honestly, you guys have no idea
about secrecy. Good thing you know nothing
about e-mail or Facebook, otherwise the whole
mess of my life and Robin's would be all over
cyberspace right now and that skull's head
wouldn't have needed to attack Sophia. And then
I'd be dead. Or worse—bound by blood.

Sparrow bit the end of her pen cap, thinking she should probably explain those last few sentences.

*   Don't panic. I guess I should have said that first.*
*   Sophia's all right. Jack and Robin made it to her in*
*   time. But that's why I am writing—to warn you*
*   about what's coming.*

What is *coming*? Thinking about the last few days, all she could understand was that for the first time in her life, all the insanity, the danger, the oddness of her identity were coming together. And the crazier and more dangerous it had become, the more true.

Hawk—or Lankin, as Robin explained—had nearly succeeded in killing her. She shuddered, remembering opening the door, the sting of the elf shot, and then falling. She remembered too the way he'd undressed her, caressed her, and then slapped her hard across the face. She had wanted to scream, to writhe in pain, even fight back when he'd taken the needle to her flesh. But there was nothing she could do, not even weep. The crows had swarmed through the broken glass and flooded into her room. Sophia had broken the spell of binding. But even then the trouble had not ended.

"*Be careful,*" Sparrow continued . . .

. . . the shit is hitting the fan here and it's really dangerous. Last night a couple who live in the apartment below mine, just back from their holidays, got attacked by someone right in their apartment. The cops have been and gone. We're pretty sure they saw the mess upstairs. Probably have it figured for something drug related. Sophia thinks the bad guys were looking for her and maybe me, too. You know already about Lankin. And how we pretty much scooted out of there with just our skins. After the cops went, Sophia realized that she'd left your letters behind. Like I said, you guys don't know much about keeping secrets. She hustled back there and two seconds after we saw the lights go on in her apartment window, Jack started cursing.

From our window we saw these walking dead guys heading up the back stairs after her. Jack grabbed a rusty pole and Robin took a kitchen knife—I wanted to come but they yelled at me to stay put. I don't know what happened exactly. I saw Sophia in the window turn and then it went dark as the lamp was knocked over. Jack and Robin must have got there pretty quick because a second later I see those thugs crashing out the window trying to make a quick getaway. One had Jack's pole in its belly. Only they don't fall—they fly with huge raggedy wings, snake-necked like vultures. They didn't have bird heads, though—just human skulls.

Sophia wasn't hurt too badly. A nasty gash across her left arm. Jack cleaned and stitched it up and has been taking care of her. You're wrong about him by the way. He's a handy guy to have around. He won't let her get up until he's sure there's no infection.

So here's the thing. Get here as quick as you can. Tell the crones Jack's got a bottle under the

*bed reserved just for them. It seems he knows their
type only too well.*

> *See you soon,
> Sparrow*

"Sophia, do you want to add anything to the letter?"
Sparrow asked, putting down the pen.

"That would be good, thank you." Groaning, Meteora
lifted herself off the couch and shuffled over to the table.
Beneath the untidy swath of hair, her face was pale,
beads of sweat dotting her upper lip. But she smiled gra-
ciously at Sparrow. "Just a few words."

She leaned over the paper and wrote in slanted, curling letters that drifted like vines across the page.

> *P.S. Forgive me, dearest Sister. I have let
> Sparrow write my letter. I am in too much pain
> right now to sit and give it the thought it needs. Oh,
> how I wish I could speak to you in Robin's toy. I
> dare not let the others know how much the
> bananachs hurt me. I have so precious little magic
> in me and they too much. Jack's cures are
> working—but they will not work for long. I need
> you. I will fold this letter until it is small enough to
> tuck beneath the wren's left wing. I can only hope
> she finds you. There is much to tell you, but too
> dangerous to commit to this page.*

> > *Blessed is the mother that bore us and
> > the sister who dwells in my heart.
> > M*

"Will she come in time?" Sparrow asked, watching
Meteora's fingers delicately fold the tissue of onionskin
paper until it appeared no thicker than a thin dime.

"Of course she will come," Meteora answered. "She's
my sister." She went to the window, gently pushing a

vigilant Robin to one side. Opening the window, she gave a low whistle. A small wren, no bigger than a child's fist, appeared at the ledge and allowed Meteora to tuck the letter beneath his striped wing. She fed him some bread crumbs from her palm and then he was gone, smaller and smaller until he was hardly a pebble in the sky.

"That's it then," Meteora said, turning.

Sparrow smiled, envious for a moment of the old woman's unshakable faith in her sister. She was completely confident that Auntie Em would simply show up at Jack's house, in a town she'd never seen before. *But then*, Sparrow thought, *she's traveling by "air" with a couple of crones. And that I can't wait to see!*

64

Robin Binds the Wounds

Once spilled blood would have excited me. Once I was my father's son. Now I am the grandson of a healer, a friend of a gardener, and I bind the wounds.

Sophia's cut was nasty, but not deep into the bone. Jack showed me where to look for infection. I did not tell him I would smell it. But I watched his competent hands stitch and mend, and when, at last, he trusted me with the changing of the cloths, I washed my hands carefully, before doing the binding.

Precious fluids. The smell of my beloved's sweat and lust. The way I marked my territory in the garden. And now my great-aunt's blood. These three have helped me walk away from my father's world, from his whistles and commands. I will not go back.

65

Meteora Moves to Vinnie's House

We needed too many things: food, bandages, and most importantly news. As Jack was the only one of us who might have safely ventured outside without drawing the attention of the UnSeelie hordes watching the house, I anointed his left eye with a bit of my spit that he might have partial sight into Faerie. Perhaps it was a rash act, but I had only the right intent that he should protect himself from the UnSeelie in the streets below and at the same time gather news of their whereabouts. But then I forgot the old tales, and the dangers to mortals who can see into our world.

He returned a shade lighter than he had left. Even sick as I was with the bananachs' poison, I noticed immediately the somber expression on his blanched face, noted the way his hands trembled slightly when he placed the bags on the table.

"What happened?"

He turned to me, the skin across his jaw rippling with agitation. "As I was walking out of the grocery store, a man in a red baseball cap nearly slammed into me. I thought it was just a guy so I sidestepped to avoid him. He hissed and when I looked at him a second time, he whipped off the red cap and I saw him more clearly. Pointed teeth, long ears, green cast to his pale skin. I didn't look away quick enough. My face showed that I recognized what he really was."

"We gotta run," Robin said bluntly.

Jack disagreed. "Sophia's too sick."

"They've marked you," Robin argued. "Look out the window. See for yourself."

Jack peeked around the edge of the curtain and we all heard the sharp intake of his breath. "Damn!"

"If we do not get out of here *now*, there will only be more of them. And not much we will be able to do to stop them on our own." Robin moved toward Sparrow, his instinct to protect her making him agitated.

"I know a place," Jack said, stepping away from the window. "It's not too far from here, but just the sort of place to throw them off the scent. Lots of iron."

"But my sister is already on her way."

"Can you get word to her?" Jack had started gathering up things and tossing them into a huge cloth bag. I noticed that he slipped in his carving tools, but whether for defense or because he was sentimental about them I could not tell.

"I will leave her a message. One the UnSeelie will not find."

"Then make it quick." Robin's eyes were trained out the window. "There are two more monsters sniffing around the garden. And if *they* are here, then Red Cap won't be far behind."

Jack told me where we were going, and I whispered the words to a mourning dove who was napping on the sill of his kitchen window. She was a simple creature, incapable of anything but one or two thoughts at a time. However, it was all I needed. I pulled a hair from my head, and tied it around her leg—for though we were different, my hair, like the feather, would serve to identify her as my nest mate. The dove would not speak to anyone but my sister—indeed she *could* not, for none but my sister would be able to jog the message from her memory. I bid her fly through Sparrow's shattered windows, then up to my door that I knew still stood ajar, and wait inside until my sister should arrive.

My legs were shaking, my head light from the fever. It was becoming harder to breathe. "How will we get there?" I asked, unable to imagine running or even walking a short distance to safety.

"We'll take the Charger. It's in the garage. We can avoid being seen by anyone hanging around the alley or the garden." Jack stuffed extra bandages and a sweater into his big bag.

"Charger?" I envisioned one of those great warhorses.

He laughed. "You really are out of this world, sweet Sophia. It's my car, a Dodge."

"A muscle car," added Sparrow.

Now I was thoroughly confused. His words dodge and muscle and charger all had different meanings for me, so I focused on the one word I understood. "I cannot travel in one of those machines of iron and noise. That will kill me faster than the poison. Please," I begged, my mouth dry with panic, "there must be some other way!"

"She's right," Robin said, coming to put his arm around my shoulder. I leaned against him, weak and frightened. "Sparrow and I are human enough that we can stand it for a short while. But Sophia won't be able to manage."

And that's when I saw the shocked look on Jack's face. I knew he thought me unusual, and even possessed of some magical skills, at least by the standards of this world. But I saw now that he had never considered that I might not be fully human. Or that Robin and Sparrow might be only partially so. Shadow chased the light from his eyes as he absorbed the news.

"So if not human, what *are* you?" he asked at last.

"Fey," I answered, hoping that was enough.

The light returned and he smiled his lopsided grin. "I always thought you were supposed to be—"

"Young?" I interrupted, irritably. "Well, consider it a first," I wheezed. "I'm old and fat, and even though I've no more power than a thimbleful of sand, I am still proud of what I am." It was stupid really. We had other far more important things to consider and there I was muckle-mad about my wounded pride.

Jack put his arms around me and kissed the top of my head. "I was going to say I thought the fey were shades of green. Silly joke. I think you are quite perfect, Sophia. Wouldn't change a thing about you." He looked out, over my head at Robin and Sparrow, standing by the door. "What if we cover her? Will that be enough to protect her from the iron in the car?"

"Possibly." Robin grabbed a sheepskin rug off the floor and draped it around my shoulders. Jack added two quilts, and before I knew it, I was swaddled from head to toe.

We took the back stairs that led directly to the garage, Jack in the lead, followed by Sparrow clutching rowan branches pulled from the chairs for protection. I came lumbering after them like a bear just out of her den, and last was Robin cradling his fiddle.

They bundled me into the front seat next to Jack, while Sparrow sat behind me and patted my shoulder. Jack revved the engine and I thought my heart would burst from the whirring iron all around me, every turning cog and piston casting poisonous dust into the air. Robin opened the garage door, jumped into the backseat with Sparrow and we sped away leaving behind a shocked and outraged Boggle and Bloody Bones that had been left to watch. But Jack was right, for even they could not follow the iron trail of the machine.

The journey was worse than I had imagined. Once Jack pulled over that I might hang my head out of the window to vomit. What a sight I made. I could not hold my mind together, raddled between my misery and fear of the machine, the thought of Red Cap's host desecrating the garden, my grief at mayhap never seeing my sister's face again, anguish at looking so ravaged in front of the children and Jack. Although I had managed till now to find some small measure of dignity in this disgraceful middle age, the dodging, charging muscle car had turned me into nothing more than a wretched and retching hag.

WE DROVE FOR WHAT FELT like days, weeks, an eternity, though they assured me it was less than an hour's tick on the clock till we arrived at a small, shabby house in a desolate neighborhood of the city. Not far away were the massive girders of a huge bridge spanning a river, separating this ill-tide collection of houses from the brighter lights of the city on the other side.

As Jack carried me from the car to a redbrick house, I noticed wild shapes and lines painted in riotous colors on the home's walls and fences. Swirls and whirls, whorls and wobbles. Even the street signs were marked with black and red letters. Most were meaningless, but here and there amid the outsized letters and curled symbols I saw the wriggles of warding spells that might protect this house and others from malicious influences.

Good, I thought, hope rising. *Fighting without hope*, as my dam used to say, *is the road to ruin*.

Once inside the house—its walls covered in fox grape vines, which offered even more protection—Jack set me down and led me into a small sitting room. There he had me sit down like an invalid—which I nearly was. I perched on a huge lumpy couch along whose spine rested four very large sleeping cats. Each opened one eye in my direction and then closed it again, unperturbed by my presence. The house smelled of dried lavender, sweet incense, and the faint whiff of cat pee. It also smelled of power. Not a lot but—another hope—perhaps enough.

Jack had gone off somewhere though I could still hear him, speaking quickly to someone. And then I heard a woman's voice, low, tremulous, breathy, urging Sparrow and Robin to hurry in with their bundles.

"I need to close the door from the prying eyes of my neighbors," she said. "Snoopy, gossipy . . ." I did not catch the last of it because of the sound of their running footsteps.

Then I heard the key in the lock and a scratching sound, which I took to be her sketching another warding sign on the door's wood.

I closed my eyes and sighed. *Safe at last.*

"Sophia, this is my Aunt Vinnie."

Had I dozed off? Certainly I had not heard them come close. I opened my eyes. "Hello, Aunt Vinnie," I began, then goggled.

Time away from the Greenwood had changed her, though I could not say for certain how long ago it had been since our court had seen her. She was old now, humpbacked and with a mouth full of buckteeth through which her speech whistled. But still I recognized those gray-blue eyes, the long silver braid wrapped around the crown of her head, and the soft gentleness of her hands as she laid them on my forehead. I knew her smell.

"Lavinia," I whispered. "Milk-mother to all." I remembered her when she was young and buxom, milk flowing in her breasts but no child of her own to nurse for death had taken that babe early. A servant sent into the world to find a wet nurse for a Highborn lady had found a distraught Lavinia, standing on a bridge overlooking a rushing river. The servant had coaxed her with music and Lavinia had followed, through the veil and into the Greenwood. For seven years she served as wet nurse to those few precious children that had been born to Highborn mothers whose own milk was too thin to nourish. Lavinia had remained young in the Greenwood, and beautiful, glamoured by her grateful lords. And then, when there were no more births, she was returned—I had heard—to the very bridge where she had been found.

She chuckled in a low voice. "It's Vinnie now," she said, "but I don't remember you," she added, squinting at my face.

In spite of my illness, I blushed. "I am not as I was then."

"Like me," she replied. "Glad to know I am not forgotten Under the Hill. I hope to return one day." Her blue eyes sparkled.

"So do I," I croaked, throat tight with emotion. "So do I."

WE HUNKERED DOWN AT VINNIE'S for the next two days as Vinnie brought me teas and tinctures of the very herbs I would have selected for myself, including a few I might have overlooked. She was the only healer I could have imagined with the skills in this world to rid me of the bananachs' poison. For the first time I wondered: was it only chance that had brought Jack into my life, and his Vinnie, or had someone else had a hand in my destiny?

Jack hovered and I saw similar questions dancing like fireflies in his eyes but I was not ready to share answers with him. And neither, it seemed, was Vinnie.

But not all of my questions were about me. As Vinnie bustled around me, checking my bandages, brewing tea, occasionally throwing back her head to laugh at one of Jack's teasing remarks, I wondered how she felt about her exile in the Greenwood? About her return home to this world? I could not answer those questions for myself, let alone an almost stranger. I was only aware that I had been changed—outside and in—and I was like a stone in the middle of the stream that longs for the solid feel of the shore but can no longer decide which one.

ON THE NEXT EVENING WHEN I felt the poison ebb and leave my body for good, I rose from the couch, gave the cats a brisk rub behind the ears, and went in search of the others. I paused at the kitchen door to delight in my returning health and the sight of my friends there.

Jack was cooking, swooping back and forth between table and a collection of bubbling pots like an alchemist intent on the transformation of lead into gold. At the table, chin resting on her palms, Vinnie listened to Sparrow sing a song penned by that fairy-touched poet Yeats, while Robin played his fiddle. And I saw clearly in Sparrow's face the reflection of the Queen—beauty like a flame — something that she could no longer hide beneath the black hair and smudged eyes.

I entered the room, found my own chair, gently pushed a calico cat off the seat, and joined them, glad to be in their company. And gladder still that we seemed so safe and unharmed in this warded house made of sturdy bricks. *Ah — seeming.* You would think a fairy — even an aged fairy — would beware of such a transitory state.

The song ended, and supper was served. We grabbed our forks and plates and amid noisy conversation, tucked into the platters filled with the Jack's offerings: brown bread and butter, savory vegetables with dried apricots and prunes, rice for me, and lamb stew flavored with mint for the others.

Midway through the meal, the calico cat settled into my lap and gently kneaded my thighs. Whistling between her teeth, Vinnie poured neat glasses of Scotch, that very human drink. We held up our glasses, the Scotch bright as amber, and drank to our health.

Is this how it should be? I thought. *Halfling and Highborn, young and old, man and maid, fairy and mortal sitting together thus at a single table in friendship and in peace?*

It must be so, for I felt a great warming rush of happiness that had nothing to do with the drink. Yes, I longed in my heart to see my sister's face and know her safe. Yes, I longed to touch the sweet fields of the Greenwood again. And yes, I feared what was coming. But for the first time since my banishment, I did not feel alone.

66

Serana in Flight

The sisters flew wingtips apart. They understood how to catch the coasting parts of the air, the eddies of wind. They knew from long experience how to rest upon a breeze. While I, new come to flying in my cumbersome body, pumped my wings more than I needed to. My arms grew tired. My thighs, stretched out behind me, grew tired. My eyes straining against the blowing winds grew tired as well.

And still we flew, until I began to spiral down and the crones came on either side of me, to help with a soft landing.

What might a watcher have seen? Crows mobbing a hawk, I expect. But that was not what was going on. They guided me to a meadow, leaving me to catch my breath, there beneath the safety of a towering pine. Then they flew off, coming back with food and water, entering the meadow in their human shapes. And I, with barely enough energy to eat, though they made me, sitting on either side and putting the food in my hands.

"You ain't aerio-dynamite yet," said Blanche.

"Aerodynamic," corrected Shawnique.

"That, too."

They both laughed while I sipped at the water, munched the berries, and ate the small, hard apples they gave me.

Then Shawnique drew a flask from her skirts. My, that dress had pockets!

"Just a small sip, Mabel," she said. "We got a long road ahead."

"A sky road," added Blanche, who seemed to have a talent for the obvious.

"We can't count on your sister or her Jack having a bottle of the good stuff." Shawnique licked her lips.

"She means a single malt," explained Blanche, though that explained nothing. "An Islay. Peatier the better."

"I like my whiskey neat and my men the same way."

I nodded as if I understood a word of what they were saying, then took the proffered sip. The drink was body temperature and mellow-tasting, until it hit my throat and then it burned down to my belly where it sat, like a little furnace, warming me up.

"Look at the color in this girl's cheeks," said Blanche. "She's on fire! She's a hot one! Mabel—*are you able*?"

Shawnique took the flask from me. "She's about as able as she's gonna get. Now you take a sip, sister, and so will I, and then it's liftoff time."

"How much farther?" I asked. "Are we almost there?"

"Not for a while yet," said Shawnique.

"Plenty more miles to go," added Blanche.

"So we gotta keep movin'. We gotta get there before the shit really hits the fan," Shawnique said. She began crooning the *Hi-de-ho* again.

Blanche chimed in.

And then me.

They stood, Shawnique depositing the flask back in her pocket with nary an extra movement, and then before I quite understood it, they were in the air.

Suddenly, my arms and legs felt renewed. Though I wondered silently about that shit and that fan. Sounded awkward at best, messy at worst. Would I ever understand humans?

I leaped into the air, arms windmilling till I was caught by a gust and lifted farther up.

"Coming, sisters!" I cried. Even to my own ears, it sounded like the hawk's scream, "Kreee-aaah."

"Listen to her now!" cawed Blanche. "She's got it!" And she raced ahead of me into the dark.

IT TOOK US ANOTHER DAY, with frequent stops, plus sips of the energizing brew, to get within one state and two counties away. I did not even ask what a state or county was. They sounded vast.

But my flying had improved until I was almost as good as the crones. They even took to complimenting me, though in an offhanded way.

Shawnique said, "We're making you an honorary crone, Mabel."

And Blanche said, "Pretty good for a white chick."

"Peep! Peep! Peep!" I made the sounds of a chick at her.

That made them howl with laughter, and they called me "chicken hawk," which was the first really funny thing either of them had said. Or at least that I understood.

Flying would have been fun if we could have done most of it by day. If we were not in a hurry to get to Milwaukee. But Shawnique warned we had to do most of our flying by night or in the times between dusk and the true dawn.

"Hard to disguise us completely in the light of day, Mabel," she said. "There are some human folk with farsight."

"And scopes," added Blanche darkly.

I already understood about the scopes. Humans with farsight—now *that* surprised me.

WE GOT TO METEORA'S HOUSE just as the sun was rising, settled down as birds in the garden furrows and then slowly stood up in human form. To this day, I am not sure how the sisters knew which street was which. And when

I fly by myself, I have to come down often just to walk the streets in my human form till I find where I am going. I have learned to read maps.

But once in the furrows, I began to shiver. There was something dirty—something horribly evil—polluting the ground. As my human form overtook my feathered body, I let out a huge sigh.

Is it the arum? I wondered. But there was too much of the smell and it was everywhere.

"Whoooo-eee," said Blanche. "That is some odorama. Something stinks to high heaven, sister."

"I was thinking the other direction myself," Shawnique said. She flicked away some of the dirt from her skirts.

"Arum," I said, sniffing.

Shawnique added thoughtfully, "And nightshade, manglewort ..."

"And mandrake," said Blanche, wrinkling her nose dramatically.

Now the sun was full on us.

"But something else." I didn't want to say what I feared the most.

"Blood spilled in anger, in terror," said Shawnique. How could she say it so dispassionately? But then, she did not know Meteora and the others.

"And some spilled in shame." Blanche looked down at her hands, which were wrangling together.

"So it's begun." Shawnique reached over and untangled her sister's fingers.

"Then we better find them and get them out of here." I kept my voice steady.

Shawnique came over and put her arms around me. Her skin was cool, from the flying, but so was mine. I inhaled her essence—pear blossom, rose petals, driftwood, musk, partly to be comforted, but also to help dissipate the smells of the befouled garden.

"Now, Mabel," she said, holding her hand up. "You gotta be wary. They may be dead people in there. Even your sweet sister. So be prepared. This ..." She gestured to the garden. "This is a *bad* sign." Shaking her head, she added, "Blanche and I better go in first."

"Not me!" Blanche backed away, holding up both her hands. "You *know* I don't like dead folks. Fight and run, that's my motto. Fight and *run*!"

I kissed Shawnique on her cheek, and it was surprisingly soft. "She is *my* sister, Shawnique. If she is gone, I want to make sure she looks all right before anyone else sees her. Tidy her. Hold her. I want . . ." My voice began to break up.

"You're right, honey," she said. "I'd do the same for mine."

"I'm not dead over here," Blanche said, waving her right hand.

"Not yet," snapped Shawnique. "But you'd better shape up or you *will* be!"

I left them to squabble and was already walking toward the house, but I thought how much they sounded like Meteora and me. Sisters!

The door was closed, but not locked, so I went in. Remembering the description from Meteora's letters, I took the stairs two at a time. My heart was hammering in fear and anticipation.

Meteora's door stood wide open, which was a surprise. And when I went in, even more surprising was what was inside. On the table were the remains of a meal for two people, as if they had—a day or two ago—suddenly run off and left everything to molder. Two mugs, still half full of cold tea, porcelain plates on which the remains of eggs had congealed, a candlestick with the burned-down candle wax dried and hard.

A dove was sleeping on the table, leaning against an empty bottle of wine.

Where had the dove come from? And then I saw the open window. On the sill were a variety of small items, some of Meteora's "precious things." She was such a jackdaw.

But of my sister and the boy and the girl and the Jack there was no sign.

I sighed heavily and turned, just as the dove shook itself and woke. It flew to my shoulder and plucked a single hair from my head.

"Stop that," I yelled.

"Listen," the dove said in its cooing voice. "I have one message and one message only."

"Tell me. Is it good news or bad?"

"Listen," the dove said again. "I have one message and one message only."

"For green's sake . . ."

"Listen," the dove said again. "I have one message and one message only."

I knew then that all I *could* do was listen. The dove would deliver its message and go. And lucky it was that I was the one for whom the message was meant.

"Sister, we have fled the bananachs," the dove said. "We have gone to stay with Jack's Aunt Vinnie, an Old One, at Sixth Street and Elm, by the Bridge of Trees. The dove will show you the way." The dove finished and shivered three times, then sat still on my shoulder. I lifted it down with gentle hands, cradling it carefully before getting us both downstairs on shaking legs.

The sisters were gone.

I looked around the garden, circled the house three times widdershins, and was about to try again when a well-dressed young woman stuck her head out of a window on the first floor.

"Who are you and what do you want?" Her voice was sharp and frightened at the same time.

Of a sudden, I remembered there were other tenants in the house. "My sister . . . Sophia . . ." I stumbled on the name. "Old woman. Upstairs room?"

"Ah, haven't seen her in a couple of days," she said. "Haven't seen any of them. Now get outta here before I call the cops."

Then she truly did withdraw, slamming the window down hard.

"Thank you," I called out, but she did not answer.

So I walked over to the garden, wondering where the

sisters had gone, but afraid to call out. The pink and gray paving stones were set out in a mazed pattern. Perhaps there would be more clues here. Just as I was about to walk the maze, the crones came out of another house, looking flustered.

Shawnique raised her right hand to stop me. "Don't go in there," she said. "Trouble. Trou-ble. I smelled it, and it's nasty stuff."

"Something's been marking its place," added Blanche. "Pee everywhere. And black turds big as oranges."

"They are not here," I said, holding the dove in both hands to show them. "My sister nor her friends. The dove had a message. We are to follow and . . ."

"Well, girl, why didn't you say that right off," Shawnique scolded. "Time wasted is time gone. Let's get into those furrows and turn back into birds."

"But there are folks in the house. On the bottom floor. Looking out of windows."

"Can't be helped. We shouldn't be changing into feathers in the day either."

"We calls this Needs Must," added Blanche.

"How many folk in that house?" Shawnique asked, talking right over her sister.

"One. Maybe two."

"Hell's bunions." Shawnique laughed. "Even if they see us, they'll never believe their eyes. Not enough of them to confab. Let's go."

Quickly, we went to the farthest part of the garden, as far from the rank musk of the wicked plants as we could manage, then lay down. Shawnique was at the very end of the furrow. Blanche lay head to foot with her. And I put myself beneath Blanche's feet.

"Hi-de-hi-de-ho . . ." Shawnique began and Blanche and I joined in.

On the fifth or sixth iteration, I began to change. I could feel my bones reshaping, my hair turning to feathers, my nose elongating into a beak. At the last moment, I remembered to let the dove go or it would have been held in the talons of a hawk and probably die of fear.

The dove flew straight out of the furrow and in seconds, two crows flew after it. And I, wings reaching out to feather the air, came last out of the dirt. But it did not take me long to catch up, and we remarked the dove's flight, following it closely into the blue and lightening air.

67

~~~~~~~

Dark Passage

We remained at the table, late and later still into the night. The bottle of Scotch made a slow journey around the table. Glasses were filled, tunes played, songs sung. We should have been more afraid, but at least for the moment we refused such thoughts.

And haven't the bravest of our Seelie warriors spent the night before a battle doing just this? Celebrating their lives together, holding it precious before the threat of losing everything, even life itself? That is what it says in all our ballads and great songs. "So drink to the life I would love to have lived . . ." goes one. And "Brother, I stand, with my sword ready, my staff at my side . . ." If I could have remembered more than two verses of any of the old war ballads I would have sung it to rouse us. But such things had not been the leaf and stem of my life back then. I usually fell asleep beneath the Queen's table and never heard the songs all the way through. Perhaps, that was just as well, for though we five were brave, we were hardly warriors. And when had bravery alone stood against dark magic and won? It had to be magic against magic for us to have a chance. So I took another sip of the amber liquid and let it burn down into my stomach for comfort and warmth.

In the lapse between one fiddle tune and the next— and just as Vinnie was lifting the bottle for another round—we were startled by a gust of wind that rapped against the windowpanes. Four cats leaped to the ledge, tails twitching, fur lifting along their spines.

"What is it, boys?" Vinnie set the bottle down on the table. "Are the rats playing beneath the sill again?"

The cats' ears flicked, agitated, but they refused to turn away from the glass. An old marmalade tom with a chewed ear arrowed his head low and, nose against the pane, growled softly.

From where I sat, I could see only the pale reflection of our candle's flame and Sparrow's face leaning over it.

The wind gusted again, this time hammering the panes loose in their wooden frames. The startled cats hissed, backs arched high, as little windlings, normally the shyest of creatures, wriggled spindly fingers and filmy bodies through the narrow cracks. Once inside, trailing torn wings, they flung themselves wildly around the room with the frenzy of mayflies. They hid, darning themselves into Vinnie's braid, ducking down behind Sparrow's ear, nestling in Robin's fiddle, their voices trilling out from its wooden belly. One, folding its wings, wriggled into the breast pocket of Jack's shirt. I held my hands up to them, beckoned them not to fear and four of the poor wee things landed on my palm, their silken touch a cold puff of air.

In soft, whispery voices, they cried, "They come, they come. The Seelie and the Unseelie, the shriven and the cursed, the newly made and soon-to-be-dead."

One of them even fluttered up to my face and puffed, "Flee, flee for here will they meet and here will be blood."

Another joined her, crying, "Their war destroys us as easily as summer lightning sweeps grass into flames."

I spoke a swift prayer that Serana be protected as she rode high in the night sky with the crones. She was flying toward a storm she did not know was so soon gathered. *No*, I castigated myself. *It was I who drew her into this. I alone. My speaking to the boggans of the Queen's child; my calling Serana to Milwaukee; my leaving the dove to lead her here. My fault. Mine.* I did not say it aloud. I did not have to.

But of those at the table only Vinnie had wits enough to act.

"We're outta here," she barked, clapping a black hat on her head. She picked up a heavy walking stick, its handle stout and club-shaped, its point wrapped in metal. Iron by the smell of it.

"Where to?" Sparrow asked, threading her fingers through her hair, dislodging the windlings.

"The Bridge of Trees. Here, you'll need this." From a closet she pulled out three more rounded sticks, the length of my arm. White ash, they were, with animal spells inscribed in black, "Baltimore Orioles, Chicago Cubs, Detroit Tigers."

With a strange smile, Jack grabbed one and, gripping the wooden handle with both hands, swung it with obvious pleasure. "You kept my bats," he said. "I thought Mom sold them along with my cards."

Vinnie grimaced. "She was crazy, not stupid. Those are ash—you never give away ash. And they come in handy when the rats prove too much for the cats. Like now."

"I'll take my fiddle," Robin said, refusing a bat and instead tucking his fiddle under his arm, the bow hanging from the crook of his forefinger and thumb.

"Bit risky, isn't it?" Vinnie asked.

"It can do things." Robin lifted the fiddle to his chin and scraped the bow against the strings. The fiddle howled and the windlings wailed, ducking into cups and bowls. All the cats scattered out of the room as though their tails had caught fire. The planked floorboards rumbled, lifting from their frame, nails screeching and popping from ancient grooves. Puffs of malignant brown spores chuffed up from the twisting floorboards, and I caught the scent of burial dirt, spiced with bone and blood. I choked on it, and the others coughed hard, gasping in the thickened air.

"Stop! Stop!" I shouted.

And he did, placing the fiddle back underneath his

arm. His skin was white, the hooded eyelids a bruised lavender. His mouth turned cruel, and his eyes made a chill throb through my recent wound. Those eyes were suddenly black mirrors, smooth as polished stone. And when he tossed his head, the coils of hair parted, revealing the long shape of his ears. Then he shuddered and the pale skin flamed rose once more.

"What *are* you?" I whispered.

"Don't fear me, Sophia," he answered softly. He held out a hand toward Jack, who had been gripping his bat more tightly, ready to swing. "Or you, good Jack."

Vinnie clucked her tongue softly against the roof of her mouth. Only Sparrow waited, hands in her pockets, an understanding sadness like a shadow on her face.

Robin spoke softly. "I am like Sparrow. A mistake. Something that shouldn't have happened. I am the darkness to her light, the UnSeelie bound to the Seelie. Born too low and sent away to the world of man in the guise of a hound. To seek and to find." He shuddered and I saw the hound beneath his skin, a dark hound, with long floppy ears and bloodred eyes. Then he shuddered again and was only Robin, the scare-bird, the fiddler, the one who followed Sparrow faithfully and would come wherever and whenever she whistled. As he spoke, his mouth was a bruise in his face.

"And do you serve them still?" I asked. "Or are you free?"

"Free. Like Sparrow. Like you and your sister. I could not stomach the taste of blood, nor the lash my Master was certain to give me as reward for doing his bidding. I refused to answer when he called me to his side. Your sister found me in that state of refusal, Sophia. I was poisoned, left to die slowly over days, tortured by nightmares. I wandered in my grotesque form, following the lingering scent of green that I knew was your sister. She found me on the doorstep. She was right, you know. You *are* glowworms pushing back the darkness."

"*You read her letters!*" I was appalled, but not surprised. Had not Sparrow read mine?

"All of them. I knew I had to come here, for after your sister, it was Sparrow I was to seek and find. I had to warn her. Explain it to her."

"Explain *what*?" Was this at last to be the true reason for my exile?

"The Queen exiled you and Serana not as a punishment, but to provide protection to her child. She counted on Sparrow finding one of you, light drawn to light. I was sent to hunt Serana, and thereby the girl, should she come. My Master found another, here in your city, Meteora, to do his bidding."

"Lankin," I said, bitterly.

"Yes. I didn't know that until I came here. Your sister was right to send me here. But I was so blinded by the arum, I could not guard Sparrow. Lankin found her and nearly . . ." He shuddered like a dog, his skin wrinkling with fear.

"But if we are meant to protect her, why are we here now?" I asked, confused, wanting all the little threads to braid together in a single strand. "Should not someone inform the Queen? Is this not her affair?"

"My mother, if that's who the Queen is, left me on my own a long time ago. I've been running ever since. But not anymore," Sparrow said. "Robin and I are here to make a stand for ourselves." She reached out to twine her fingers in his, sounding both brave and magical. It was then I noticed in the bright light of the kitchen that the trouble tattoo on her neck was almost gone. Clearly there was power in their union, healing power.

"We'll be making a stand in the boneyard if we don't hightail it outta here," Vinnie snapped. "Run now. Talk later." She nudged Sparrow toward a low door in the kitchen and behind her Robin followed close, then Jack, still gripping the bat uncertainly.

I hesitated until I saw the gray slag-heap faces of the Boggles pressed against the windowpanes. Too big to creep in as the windlings had done. Kept out by the wards for now, they waited. Waited—but not for long.

Darting after the others, I found myself descending

into a musty, dark cellar. In the dim light of a single bulb the floor appeared like an ocean of shifting fur. Cats—dozens of them—swirled in agitated circles around our ankles, hissing and spitting. Kittens mewled from baskets stacked around the edges of the room.

From above, we could hear the sounds of the front door being splintered and a window shattering. The cats flowed up the stairs behind us in a wave of caterwauls and flashing teeth, their claws scrabbling on the wooden stairs.

"Come, quick. There's a tunnel here that leads out to the bridge. The cats will hold them for a while." Vinnie bent low and scurried into a small narrow passage.

"Is that our escape route?" asked Jack for all of us.

"No, it's where we will make our stand," Vinnie told him. "Better than this small, closed-in place."

"How come I never knew about this tunnel?" asked Jack.

Vinnie laughed deep in her throat. "And why would I tell an angry, active boy about something like this?" she said. "Do you think I was crazy?"

"Well," Jack said, hesitating a moment longer than necessary, "yes, actually I did."

That made her put her head back and laugh full out. The laugh, like a calming spell, settled us all.

There was no light in the tunnel; we felt our way by running our hands against the smooth walls. I could smell the river and it carried the fresh tang of the Greenwood. Vinnie had chosen well.

The smell grew stronger and, abruptly, the way led upward again, rising to a gentle slope. Ahead, Vinnie called to us to stop. Moonlight slivered into the tunnel, as she shoved a shoulder against a matted wall of twigs and branches, forcing an opening.

We pushed out of the tunnel and were on the banks of a narrow river directly below the bridge. A cluster of ancient oaks surrounded us, and I could imagine in centuries past how they must have filled the banks on either side of the river. Now all that was left of them was a meager stand of twisted trunks.

A rustle in the tangled branches made me glance up and I heard the *krawk* of a crow hiding in the leaves. And then another.

"Awxes!"

He cawed again, exhorting us to move along. He and the rest of his murder were here, watching.

"Have you not lost too much already, old friend? I bid you go and be safe." But he stayed, and with him the others of his black brood.

Then I looked up at the bridge, where we were to make our stand. The stench of iron grabbed me by the throat and I stumbled, doubled over by the rank taste of it. Vinnie grabbed me and hustled me toward a narrow set of concrete stairs.

"It won't be so bad on top," she said. "And they won't follow us so easily this way."

"Where are we going?" I asked.

"Not the briared path of righteousness, nor the lily path of wickedness, but the green path to—"

"Elfland! The road to Elfland, atop this monstrosity?" I was heaving with the stench of iron.

Just then I heard Red Cap's horns blaring in the distance, a call that curdled the mist and drove the stink of sweating hounds and farting Bogglemen on the winds. There was no more time to resist. Red Cap and his minions would be as incapacitated as I by the iron. Vinnie was right. We had to go up there onto the bridge.

68

The Bridge

Vinnie cackled as she bullied me up the stairs. "Gotta find a way wherever you can. The old paths don't disappear so easily, even when the mortal realm changes. They lurk behind the factory, ghetto, suburban mall. *You* may choose not to use them. But some do. That's why I'm here. To watch what comes over the bridge."

We were standing suddenly on the bridge, a wide-open expanse that stretched like a road between the banks. Though I could feel the threaded bones of iron buried in the concrete flesh, I *could* stand. Suddenly the worst of the pain and illness subsided. On the far banks hung a sheer curtain of golden lights reflected in the shimmering surface of the river below. Along the edges of the concrete and metal bridge I could see the faint outline of trees, smell the pungent pine.

It *was* the way to the Greenwood, to Under the Hill and Elfland. For a moment, I thought of abandoning my friends and throwing myself at the lights of home just to be living again in my woods. For just a moment.

Behind me, I heard Sparrow sob and I turned, realizing that I was not the only one entranced by the sight. Robin had his arm around her, consoling, pulling her toward the middle of the bridge. On his face was a mixture of pain and hope. Faerie had always meant the dark halls of the UnSeelie to him. Now—for the first time in his life—he craved the light of the summer courts.

Awxes and the crows traced slow circles in the air above us. Even Jack had lowered his cudgel to stare in wonder at the undulating lights.

Standing beside me, Vinnie's ancient face softened until I saw the remainder of the young woman I had once known. *Is that true of my face*, I wondered, *here in the glimmering reflection of the Greenwood*? I laid a hand to my cheek as if I might find it young and firm again.

"Every time I come up here I can almost touch it," Vinnie said. "I can't cross anymore, only get close enough to remember those years ago, the infants put to my breast. But alas . . ." She laughed sharply. "No insurance or job security with the fey." She seized my shoulder, her grip strong. "Will you open it for us?"

"Open it?"

"Yeah. Only *you* can open the way. You're one of them."

And then I tasted bitter gall. I was here, but by my banishment the way would not open to me. Vinnie had miscalculated. She had thought I could save us all and so brought us here, to this bridge before a door that would never open to me.

"I cannot," I stammered, spinning away from her grip. I turned my back to the door.

Vinnie glared at me. "Or maybe you're as hard-hearted as the rest of the fey. Haven't I done enough? Don't I deserve this? Don't they?" Her chin jutted toward Robin and Sparrow.

Miserable, I looked down at my feet and whispered, "I have been banished, too. By the Queen's own decree I can never return. There is nothing I can do here. Nothing."

"You can try," Jack whispered in my ear.

I turned, looked at him. *Really* looked. His honest face stared back at me. *For him*, I thought, *I could try and fail. But I could try.*

Just then Vinnie spoke again. "Trying won't cut it now." She spun me around and there on the streets leading to the far side of the bridge was the Dark Lord's Hunt riding toward us. The Highborn ranks were marked by the silver tines of horns rising above the carved death masks. The Hunt flowed across the paving, the silver shoes of their mounts leaving trails of sparks. By their sides, the hellhounds bayed, running hard. And behind them loped boogans, ogres, even snarling knucklebones, their rock-hard knuckles striking sparks on the surface of the road.

Overhead bananachs flew, their great tattered wings blocking all sight of the stars.

And we—a small band of misfits, two humans, two halflings, one banished fairy, and a murder of ragged crows—were alone on the bridge to face them.

And it was my fault. My fault for meddling. The guilt of it began to eat at me again till I suddenly remembered that I had been sent here to meddle. Sent here to protect Sparrow.

Protect Sparrow.

"Get behind me," I cried and thrust myself in front of them. "I may be banished but the law of the courts still applies. They dare not harm me, lest I have done them harm."

"But you *have* offered offense," Robin said quickly, "for there rides Lankin and you struck him."

"The offense was his when he entered the Great Witch's house," I said with more confidence than I felt.

"You still need us at your side," Jack argued and stood to the left of my shoulder, his ash cudgel held high. Vinnie flanked me on the right. Behind me, I felt the children, imagining them still holding hands and making one another strong. Awxes and the crows drifted back and forth above us, wings brushing against the wall of light and making it ripple with the sound of chimes.

The Hunt approached, and the huntsman blew his horn, calling the slavering pack to heel. The Dark Lord turned to the rider beside him and silently commanded him to go forth. As he approached, I saw him clearly in the glowing lamplight, his silver mask shaped like a half skull, the human side beautiful, the other twisted in pain. Around his shoulders he wore a cloak of burgundy wool, dyed with the blood of innocents: Red Cap, soul drinker, blood eater, bone cruncher, hater of life.

"Stay," I said. "I must meet him alone."

"No," Jack argued.

"It is the only way."

And I walked away from them toward the center of the bridge, toward Red Cap and the UnSeelie horde.

Oh, sister, I thought—glad she, at least, was not here—*Sister, remember me*. For well I knew that Red Cap's swords and arrows could do what mortal weapons could not. Knew that only the eternal law that binds us both held in check his murdering hand.

"You have no right to hunt those under my protection."

The Highborns and Red Cap broke into raucous laughter, slapping their thighs, rattling their spears and quivers of arrows. An ogre lumbered to the front, turned, displayed his huge, bare arse, and farted, loud as a trumpet.

Removing his mask, Red Cap handed it to a rat-faced page that had scurried up on clawed feet to take it from his master's hands. Red Cap shifted his weight on the back of his horse. Clearly he was more used to skulking than riding.

"You! You have no power to fight me, Meteora. There be nothing you can do to stop me. Capuchon be my name. Use it if you dare!"

That he knew my true name and spoke it aloud was frightening enough. But I did not dare show my fear. Nor did I speak his name aloud, for I knew there would be a trick in it, else he would never have given it to me so readily.

"No power, you say?" I called back. "Ask your servant, and see where I marked him when he violated the treaty and came uninvited to the home of the Great

Witch." I pointed to the Highborn in a wraith's hollow-eyed mask in the line of horsemen behind him.

Red Cap turned in the saddle to look at them.

"Hah! Show your face," he commanded and then cursed loudly when Long Lankin ripped the mask from his face with a jerk, revealing an angry gash marring the plane of his cheek. It had festered into a ragged furrow as all ill-gotten wounds must. Obviously he had not told anyone, shamed to have been bested by an old woman. So far it was the only glimmer of hope we had. Could I bluff my way a little longer?

Red Cap stood up in his stirrups, his eyes slitted into twin daggers. "And who, little bag of pus, gave you such power?"

"The same goddess who awarded it to you." The words came to me suddenly, like a gift. "Before we existed, power flowed in the heart of earth, shaping rock and soil, water and air. I have learned that even trapped in this mortal body I can find that power without the leave of Elfland. It is mine by the right of She-Who-Birthed-All." I knew as I spoke these brave words that they were true. In part. Though aged and weakened, I was not wholly without magic. I held it in my mouth like a wintered berry, withered, but still sweet and nourishing. And I had seen that the mortals here had power, too, though we of the Greenwood scarce acknowledge it. Lavinia's milk had had the power to suckle and sustain our infants. Clearly the gifts flowed both ways. Faerie to mortals, mortals to the fey. So when would we honor that truth?

"What gives you the right to claim these mortals as your own?" Red Cap asked.

"The law."

And then he laughed again, the Hunt following suit. The sound echoed over the water of the river.

Red Cap broke through that laughter. "The law was broken when we were denied a tithe in blood. I have come to claim it."

I whirled about and stared behind me, at Sparrow, at

Robin, looking small and lost in the bridge's wide-open arms. Jack and Vinnie held their feeble weapons before them, ready to fight. For a moment, doubt troubled me, and then no more. The Highborn could kill us but they could not defeat us. Slowly I turned back.

"Those are mine now," I said.

"There is no one with the power to grant such rights to you."

"The Queen—"

"*Especially* the Queen!" Red Cap shouted. "She played her game and lost. She has no cause to tread these roads, no claim to the blood marked by my servant to be my sacrifice. That tithe be mine and I be seeing you threshed as barley beneath my heel lest you vow to serve me."

There was a sudden hush. The bridge seemed to ring out with the silence. Even the crows had stopped cawing. The hellhounds lay down at the feet of the horses. Everything was still.

Once again Doubt, my old familiar, sat on my shoulder, whispering in my ear: *"What have you accomplished with your meddling? Had you not always left politics to the Highborn? Did your sister not warn you to leave these children alone?"* Wise words to sing in the ear of a small, insignificant fey who liked only her pleasures. But I was not that creature now. I had changed, my sister had changed, as our world had changed. All of us had changed.

Except the Queen.

And then it occurred to me. *The Queen.* Searching the streets of that iron city where Serana lived. Mandrake roots twisted like strangled lovers. A girl marked with the sign of trouble. And us, sisters of the Greenwood sent forth to meddle. Why had it taken me so long to understand what it all was for?

"What mark?" I shouted back defiantly. I searched the skies for Serana, praying now that Serana *would* appear. Surely the two of us changed creatures could stand against Red Cap. But even without her, I had to try.

Squaring my shoulders, I shook old Doubt off. "What mark proves your claim, you old bogie?"

"Ho! Bring me the girl!" Red Cap demanded.

Two of his ogre pets lumbered toward us, but before they could reach us Sparrow shoved past Jack and Vinnie and came to stand beside me.

"Fuck you," she shouted. "You don't own me, asshole." She tore off her shirt, and in the stark light of the streetlamps her pale torso gleamed, revealing the bare and flawless skin of her shoulders. She turned and showed her neck, curved like the white arch of the swan. Even the twisted knot of trouble was gone.

Only then did Red Cap frown. The mount beneath him stumbled, quivering with the heat of its rider's rage. "How is this possible?" he asked, turning in the saddle to glare at Lankin.

Even I wondered. I knew the spells of unbinding. I had worked them a little. Goodywife spells. And I knew that all but this last one, the one on her neck, had faded. But how had this one been so completely removed that the Red Cap's glare, like yeast to dough, had not raised it up again? Surely not just the fiddle, not just the stay at Vinnie's. Surely there was something I was missing.

"I come to claim what is mine," Sparrow called. "I woke Robin and his blood is bound to me as mine is to him."

Robin came quietly to stand beside Sparrow. He was changed too. His eyes gleamed green and gold. There was no longer a hound's shadow beneath his skin. Horns budded on his high forehead and along his neck scrolled a tattoo of briar and rose together.

"Cast-off whelp, spittle of a mudwife's lips," Red Cap hissed in frustration.

"But yours nonetheless," Robin cried out, "and so I have made a pact already. The tithe is paid, Father. You cannot amend it."

Father! And then I saw what I had not before, how like they were around the jawline, around the eyes, though there was no cruelty in Robin's face.

"Then you own her," Red Cap roared, "what good it be to you." His mouth was a thin line, a frown that could bring down bridges. Then he suddenly smiled, which was infinitely worse than his frown, opening his arms, though even I could read those arms as the bars of a jail. "Come and be welcomed back into our house again. All will be forgiven. Rule with me." Almost carelessly, he put his fingers to his lips, and suddenly he whistled, though it was so high, only the dogs actually heard it and they stood by the feet of the horses, threw back their awful heads and howled. One even shat down a black steed's leg, and was kicked in the head for his misdeed, dying in a puddle of blood, which only excited the other dogs.

Robin shook his head. "You mistake my meaning, Father. For there is human blood in me, no matter how hard you have tried to erase it with your iron rod. I have surrendered unto Sparrow the gift of that blood." He held up his hand, palm toward Red Cap. "See here where the line of our bloodletting still heals. And on her the same."

Sparrow held her hand up, too, palm forward, but with her middle finger raised in defiance.

"No! No!" Red Cap's voice was a shriek now, like the wind in a storm, as high as his whistle had been, but no longer cruel. "It be not happening thus. This bitch, this knot of grass does not command you in my place. I have no fear of her or you. For there be no law without the Faerie courts, and here on this bridge, I alone decide the outcome. There be blood yet spilled and my hat will be red with it. Ho!"

His sword left its scabbard, and swift as lightning it flashed toward Sparrow. I gave no thought but flung myself between her and its point. Sparrow fell beneath me, screaming as I screamed and the sword exploded in my flesh. The blade bit deep below my heart, scraping against the bones of my ribs. Hot blood cascaded across my chest. Dazed, I wanted to rise, but could not find the strength. Deafened by the sound of my heart's slow beating, I could only watch what happened around me.

Robin, Jack, and Vinnie stood over Sparrow and me

as we lay huddled within the protective cage of their legs. Jack swung his bat and the crack of the ash caved in an ogre's skull. Then he lifted the bat once again, its light tip stained with the ogre's green blood and took aim at the next UnSeelie creature.

Meanwhile, Vinnie struck her iron club against the hounds that leapt at us. One and two fell, and a third raked her arm with its teeth before she shoved the club down its throat and it died a shuddering death.

Elf darts flew like swift birds through the air and were stopped by the wailing of Robin's fiddle. Rosin puffed in the air and the crash of the bow buckled the concrete, hurling chunks of broken road and exposing the staves of iron beneath.

Yet I despaired, for no matter how valiant my mates were, I knew it would not be enough. Not nearly enough.

Then through the howling and wailing, I heard a booming pair of voices calling across the river. The booming was really a strange low keening sound, almost like a banshee's voice, though I realized that it came from two black crones afloat in the sky. They were holding hands and singing down lightning from the heavens. "Hi-de-ho," they chanted, a sound that struck me as deeply as the sword. The lightning struck the bridge, making the hanging wires spark and those sparks hit the buckled paving and jumped to the bridles of the horses who screamed and tried to throw their riders.

"Hi-de-ho!" the two sang until all but Red Cap and Lankin were unmounted.

Near them, but now falling slowly from the sky, her wings scattering in a cloud of feathers, was a bulky woman, pale as a milkweed. She touched down softly onto the bridge, then came racing toward me, faster than such a woman had any right to run.

"Paddle Foot!" It was Serana, in the ugliest dress I have ever seen. But ugly dress, fleshy body, she was my sister and I felt her pulse as though it were my own.

"Sister," I cried. And then I fainted.

When I came to, I thought it was Serana's hands

pressing against my chest, trying to stop the flow of blood. But it was Sparrow who stanched the wound, weeping and calling to me to have courage, to stay with her as the fight roared over our heads. Parts of the bridge, bits of iron, were falling all about us, as thick as summer rains. Though surprisingly, none struck us, for Sparrow held me in the protection of her arms. And it was then I knew for certain why Red Cap had sought to claim the girl and why the Queen had banished us here to be her hope for return.

I could feel in her touch the royal richness of her fey blood, blood that thickened with the summer sun, blood like the green healing sap of the trees bringing resurrection from their winter's death. But she was also something new. Not just the Queen's child. She had a magic made greater by her human side and all the sorrows she had borne.

Sparrow poured her light into me and had I not stopped her, she would have emptied herself of the gift to see me healed. This I could not let her do. Weak, but alive, I roused myself and held her face between my hands. "Enough, child," I said. "You have done enough."

"Will you look at that," shouted Vinnie, swinging her cudgel against a kucklebones' legs, knocking it flat against the ground. A second strike pummeled its ugly face.

Sparrow and I turned and there was Serana, my brave sister, crouched like a tiger on Red Cap's back, a fat, aging tiger but one whose claws still could make a mark. She raked at his face and he flailed on the back of his horse, both astonished and furious to be caught so short, and by an aged dam. And while she fought him, the iron parts of the bridge rained down so hard I feared for her life.

Meanwhile, the black crones slid and leapt beneath the bellies of the horses, calling back and forth to each other. And the faerie horses, their eyes rolling with terror, once again bucked their riders to the ground.

Almost, I thought. *Perhaps,* I prayed. Hope beat in my

breast like a caged bird. And then I wailed, holding out a hand useless to help, as I watched Red Cap reach his long arms behind him, grasp Serana, and fling her to the ground. She hit the concrete, and bounced, hard. Curling in agony, she tried desperately to stay clear of the trampling hooves.

I could not stop screaming her name, trying to rise and the blood erupting anew from my wounds when I saw him sword in hand, searching for her amid the agitated horses.

That was the moment of my greatest despair. I could think of no greater loss, no greater horror, than to lose Serana, twin beat to my heart. There on the bridge, that span between the mortal world and that of our realm, I thought to die with her, the crones, Vinnie, the children of our blood, and my Jack, still fighting to protect me. I struggled to my feet to meet this death with honor. And wavering as I stood, I heard a sound I thought never to hear again.

The bright thrilling cry of the Seelie horns.

I turned and saw the wall of golden light flare, for a moment blinding all on the bridge. The flock of crows scattered, their wild caws heralding the arrival of the Queen's court, riding through the shower of light to join us on the bridge. They came swiftly, the bells of their bridles ringing madly, the arrows of our archers nocked in the great ash bows. As they came, the UnSeelie withdrew from us in haste to the far side of the bridge, scrambling up onto their twice-addled mounts and dragging with them their wounded. Their dead they left unceremoniously behind.

And just as suddenly Serana was there, her arms wrapped around me. Blood calls to blood and so did ours, mingling from the wounds we carried along with the tears. We touched one another's faces with wonder and then we laughed, for I think we had not really understood how aged we were until we saw our reflection in the other's eyes.

When the Queen arrived at the midway point of the

bridge, there was another stillness in the air, though no menace in this one. She sat straight-backed on the snowy mare, holding a torch high, the gold corona of her hair like the sun. In its light, her eyes blazed with fury. She called out to Red Cap, "You are forbidden to hunt a child of the royal blood."

"Hah! Old Queen, the girl stinks of human meat. No glamour can hide that. Ho!" He snarled, but defeat was written on his face.

"And yet she is both. Blood of my blood and blood of the mortal that sired her. There is no shame there."

"Ho! No shame? Then why hide her so long? This mongrel whelp—"

"This Highborn Queen has the right to command you who are nothing more than a servant." She smiled at him, and I felt my bowels curdle at that smile. "I hid her so you could not do what you have tried."

"Monstrous!"

"But true," cackled a voice from behind the horses. A path was made and Baba Yaga as I remembered her— naked and coarse—a satchel slung over one shoulder, strolled to Red Cap, who was still seething in pent-up rage. "I have not forgotten you," she said, wagging a bony finger in his direction. "You offered no sacrifice to me, no gesture of respect which I am owed. Your creatures desecrated my house and gardens. And the house of my friend, the Jack. Very bad manners. By right of law, I could eat you, but I doubt I would like the taste."

Red Cap looked down, like a boy chastised.

Lankin kicked his mount, forcing it through the throng of boogans and nightstalkers until he was close enough to look down from atop his horse at Baba Yaga. "We owe no allegiance to you, old hag. The Dark rises and you are history." His lips pulled into a sneer. "Red Cap, forget that bastard child, we have no need of her blood, for I have found another way." He held up a crystal flask and when he opened it, the ripe scent of mortal blood filled the air, thick and cloying as almond paste. The still-living hounds bayed and their jaws snapped hungrily.

Without warning, Baba Yaga reached out a clawed hand and with a powerful swipe tore open the neck of Lankin's mount. The terrified horse reared up, and wild with pain, splattered hot blood over the concrete.

Bellowing commands, Lankin struggled to control his panicked horse but he was thrown to the ground as the horse collapsed on its side, and the flask of human blood shattered next to him.

The boogans, ignoring the thrashing legs of the dying horse, threw themselves down on all fours and lapped at the slick puddles of the mingled blood. Lankin was left to grovel beside his slain horse, desperately trying to gather up the broken shards of glass and save some of the contents.

Ignoring the frenzied bodies feeding at her feet, Baba Yaga tore handfuls of flesh from the dying horse and consumed it in huge mouthfuls, her jaws cracking with pleasure. We all watched silently as she ate her fill. Even Red Cap withdrew, reminded I am sure that the Great Witch could never be claimed by either side. She was her own universe.

Finally, having finished her meal, and licking her fingers, Baba Yaga looked down at Lankin, and sniffed. "That's for killing my dog. You should have kept the fuck out of my house."

She walked over to where Sparrow and I waited, still clinging to one another. She removed a cloth bag from her satchel and handed it to Sparrow.

"Your journals. You left them behind."

Sparrow took the bag in both hands and the tears formed in her eyes. "Lily," she said. "I couldn't save Lily. I'm sorry. I loved that little dog."

Baba Yaga smiled, a not entirely pleasing sight as bits of Lankin's horse were still visible in her iron-capped teeth. She patted the satchel. "Her bones are here. The Hands saved them for me. I will make another Lily. That little shit Red Cap has no power over those under my protection. Including you." She leaned down and gave Sparrow an unexpected kiss on the forehead. "See," she whispered to Sparrow, though I was close enough to hear, "now both sides will think very hard before giving trouble for you."

Then she turned and tapped me lightly on the cheek. "You've done well, little one. My garden looked good and will look good again. As for those very bad boys of the first floor, they are now keeping the rusalki company in the lake. It's time for me to go home again for a while." The burning embers of her eyes flared to life. "The fall semester is about to begin. And the little chicks will be looking for a place to live."

She strolled to the Queen who slid from her horse to greet the Witch. How odd it was to see them standing there, youth and beauty bowing her head before Baba Yaga's aged body. Baba Yaga spoke to her softly, and the Queen's gaze followed to where Sparrow and I still huddled together on the ground. I saw her smile weakly, and then nod. Baba Yaga stepped away and the Seelie court parted to let her pass. She walked away down the bridge with her vigorous stride, and then she was gone, swallowed up by the darkness long before she reached the veil of lights that hid the Greenwood and Faerie.

~~~~~

69

Sparrow Begins a New Tale

Sparrow sat at the small table fashioned from a root that protruded from the cavernous wall of her room in the Queen's chambers Under the Hill. She had not quite gotten used to the oddness of being beneath the ground, like a mole. While she no longer found the dark, earthy smell difficult, nor even the lack of light a problem—the glowworm lanterns shed a lovely light—sometimes she dreamed of rivers and high-rise buildings and wished for a double latte or a BLT on wheat toast.

But for now, the Queen's chambers were deemed a better place for her than up in the Greenwood, where disgruntled Highborns from both courts might still take offense at her presence. They would do her no harm, the Great Witch had seen to that, but they could be cruel and petty, and the insults cut as easily as a knife.

"They need time to get used to the idea," Robin had told her after the meeting of the Council. "But they will. Because we are here, there will be new life in the old clans. The women will come first to thank you when their bellies swell, and as sons are born, so too will their lords."

"Is that all we are? Fertility idols?" Sparrow joked.

He'd placed his hand on her belly and smiled. "What's wrong with that? Perhaps we should give them a lesson in how to procreate? There is a newly plowed field not too far from here. And the moon is full."

"Not another public performance for me," she'd answered tartly. "Once was enough."

"In the furrows, you mean," he'd answered, but smiled, to show he understood. Her private performances with him were proof enough that once was not exactly enough. For either one of them.

Sparrow pulled out a new journal, this one bound in leather. She opened it, and held it to her nose, inhaling the perfume of the rosemary leaves that had been pressed into the margins of the cream-colored paper.

"Almost hate to write on it," she said aloud. At her feet a puppy stirred and whimpered. Sparrow glanced down at the fat-bellied creature, a gift from the Great Witch. The puppy's white fur was spotted with the occasional liver-colored blotch. Sparrow reached down and tickled the pup behind her ears until she settled down again, yawned a wide pink-mouth yawn, and promptly fell back to sleep.

Returning to the pages of the journal, Sparrow wondered where to start this story of her life. Should it begin with Baba Yaga in the park? With Sophia's arrival at the house? Or the tattoo? None of those appealed to her. What about Robin? Sparrow flushed red at the table remembering Sophia and Jack tripping over them in the garden. It sure wasn't how she'd imagined her first time. Her face softened, thinking about sharing a bed with Robin at Jack's house. He'd held her, nothing more, offering comfort and explanations.

"Do you know who you are?" he'd asked.

"Is that a trick question?"

"It's an important one."

"Then tell me. Who am I?"

He'd whispered a name into her ear. *Passerinia*. A name he'd found etched on the spine of a green leaf near a spring. It belonged to her, given her by the Queen herself. It meant Sparrow.

Sparrow had wept when she heard it, for she remembered, long ago, on a sunny day, being rocked to sleep in the arms of a woman with shining hair singing her name softly in a lullaby. Only once and yet it had lain in her memory like a seed.

Two nights later, at Vinnie's and in bed once more together, Robin had given her his true name. *Articus*.

"Does it mean Robin?"

"No—it means something cold. But he who named me wanted me to be ice."

"You're not ice at all." She'd snuggled closer.

He told her his story then, and it was even uglier than hers. The mother raped and destroyed by Red Cap, the life of servitude, the beatings, and the blood. He too had wept, grateful tears when she put her arms around him. And that time when he'd kissed her, she responded. There was no feverish rush, but something more thoughtful, more confident. He was gentle and she opened up as before, but without fear, without the arum's heady charge.

Later, as Sparrow lay on his chest amid the tangled sheets, Robin had said, "We can change everything, right here and right now, if we choose."

"How?"

"A pledge of blood. The fey need mortal blood and in the past blood was taken as a sacrifice in the tithe. The Queen put a stop to it, perhaps when she was thinking of you. But what if we pledge our blood to each other— mortal and fey together?"

"Can we do that?"

"We can try. It would certainly shake up the Council."

Robin had retrieved a small knife from his pants pocket and returned to the bed. He cut a line in the center of his hand and closed his palm around the flowing blood. He had handed Sparrow the knife.

"Too bad we couldn't just spit on it," she said, eyeing the knife. But she took it and biting down on her lower lip, cut a gash into her palm, then quickly pressed it against his.

"Do we say anything?"

"Ouch!" And then his face grew serious. "I give you, daughter of the Seelie Queen, the pledge of my blood, the tithe which you require."

"And I give you, Robin, the pledge of my blood, the tithe which you require," she'd answered.

"Then it is done and none may take offense," he'd finished.

Robin had bandaged their hands, less to stanch the wounds than to protect Vinnie's sheets from stains. In the morning when they'd risen, the wounds were healed and there were only pale scars on their palms.

Sparrow sighed, recalling how she'd felt Robin's power flowing through her, as he must have felt hers. It was like being a little drunk and very happy. That last night at Vinnie's, she suddenly discovered she knew the words to all of the songs Robin played on his fiddle. She also knew that the tattoo of trouble was fading, for she could feel the lines of ink crumble on the surface of her skin like a scab over a healed wound.

And what of the Queen? So long parted, they met again on a bridge in the midst of battle. Not the best place for a reunion. But later, when Sparrow felt the shivering thrill of passing through the veil into Elfland, the Queen had called a halt to her procession. Slipping down from her horse, she had come to Sparrow, who was mounted up behind Robin on a black horse.

"Walk with me," she had said.

And while the rest of the court waited on the path, Sparrow and the Queen faced each other in the twilight shadows beneath the oaks. The Queen who had seemed so powerful on the bridge now trembled. She reached out a hand and touched Sparrow on the cheek.

"Forgive me."

Sparrow closed her eyes, the years of anguish falling from her shoulders. "You abandoned me."

"Not entirely. I sent the deer to wait on you. I prayed to keep you safe until you were grown. But it did not happen thus. Those sisters," and she sighed, with a mixture of annoyance and respect.

Sparrow had laughed at that. "Still, they made good. I wouldn't be here if it weren't for Meteora. And her sister isn't half bad either."

The Queen chuckled softly. "Even the powerful must never forget the power of the smallest of our clans."

"My father . . ." Sparrow began, almost afraid to ask.

"Is no more," the Queen answered. She looked away and Sparrow saw the smooth expression crumple for a moment before returning, serene and regal. "For a mortal to lie with a Highborn fey is to invite madness. Death has freed him of that affliction."

Sparrow and the Queen stood awkwardly, until Sparrow offered the only gesture possible to free them from the past. She put her arms around the Queen's neck and held her, until the stiffness left the Queen's body and she responded at last, leaning in to receive the embrace of her lost child.

DIPPING HER PEN INTO AN inkwell, Sparrow began to write on the first page: "This is the tale of Sparrow who fell from the nest, was lost, and then found again by Cock Robin." Then she leaned back and laughed at her own joke until the little dog at her feet woke and started barking.

70

Meteora Writes a Letter

Dearest Sister,
 *You have just left with the crones, and though I
long to see your face every day, I was not surprised
you decided to travel in the world with them—for
it seems that in such a short time, the world we
knew has changed, perhaps for the better. I was
amazed as were we all when the crones entered the
Greenwood. Who among us would have guessed at
their true shapes? I marveled at their beautiful
black skin, smooth as polished obsidian, and their
regal bearing, dressed in robes of woven feathers,
glass beads, and gold. Their power was undeniable
and they are as old as the country from which they
first came.*
 *Sparrow and Robin are joined now, and the
Council has decreed a new house, a new clan that
signals the union between fey and mortal with
rights afforded unto it in the world of Faerie. The
Queen was eloquent about that—as were the
crones of course, it being a lesson their kind
learned long ago while we were hiding behind our
closed borders. Alone each world will destroy itself,
but twined together we can rebuild the strands that
once wove our histories. Can you imagine, dear
sister, a return at last of the goblin markets?*

It gives me an odd sense of accomplishment, of strength. Power shared is power restored. Even the Dark Lord has agreed to a limited truce and keeps Red Cap on a very short leash. His bloody hat is barely pink now. I think he is not long for our worlds. As for Lankin, I have not seen him, though a sprite whispered in my ear that he has been imprisoned in a box of bloodstone that is kept in the Queen's treasury. However, a boogan told me flatly that was wrong and that Lankin had been chopped into a million pieces and fed to the fishes off the coast of Manx. So who knows?

I am happy enough here. I am still recovering from my wounds and Jack, my beloved Jack, tends me. The courts have allowed him to stay as my consort, though there is nothing of that unequal nature in our friendship. I watch him at his work, the sprites hovering around him, singing their surprised joy as he creates his sculptures. He whistles those stolen tunes as he works, for he refuses to change. I suspect he may have a bit of fey blood somewhere in that strange past, but I will never say that to him.

Like you, when offered the chance to return to my youthful self I chose not to. I rather like who I am now, though I admit to having made a few improvements. However, I am no sylph for there is nothing as beautiful to me now as a face that wears its history well. Even the Queen now slips off the mask of youth and in quiet moments sits with me, two older women, our hair graying, watching the children as they come at last into their own between this world and the other.

Vinnie comes and goes as she pleases for the doors of Faerie are open again to those who can see them. She never stays here long. She says her cats need her. Though cats do not seem to need anything except the occasional tin of food. She promises to remain the carrier of all our letters.

But you, Serana, my beloved sister, how fare you in the world? I sorely miss you. You must tell me all.

And so our letters begin again.

Your loving sister,
Meteora

P.S. Robin says to please remember him to Chim and the rest. He and Sparrow hope to come in the spring to play music in the park.

71

Three Crones

My Dearest Sister, Meteora:
I have but a small time to write before we three take to the skies again. You would not believe what I am learning. Flying is not just wings up and soar. There are loop-de-loops, dives, stoops, back wings, soft landings and hard.

And it turns out that three really is a magic number. Shawnique and Blanche have been waiting for me for quite some time, even before you and I were thrown out of Faerie. You see, they have farsight much greater than mine, but I am getting there. I know, for example, that my scare-bird will soon be a father. I believe even you had not guessed that. I wonder if he and Sparrow even know yet. Best not tell them. Let them reveal it to you. Act surprised. I know you can do that.

And tomorrow, since the crones and I will be grounded by bad weather, the Man of Flowers will stay the night. But I don't need foresight for that. We have been growing closer for some time. I even work in his store now and then. Oh, not for money, but to help out. And to pay him back that I not be beholden. Oh—I now know what a "spick" is, and the boys who said it all came down with bloat tongue one week, and prick rot the next. Some-

thing else crones taught me, and helpful it certainly was. I think those boys will stay out of the neighborhood for a while. It is quieter with them gone.

Jamie Oldcourse stops by now and then. She thinks she is my one friend, besides my "boss," Mr. Flores. I let her keep thinking that. She might not approve of the loop-de-loops. Or Shawnique and Blanche.

I hear them scratching at the window, so must close with love. Next week I am going to learn a tame-iron spell. Shawnique promises that it will change my mind about living in the city. But I am already changed, you see. If I need a touch of the Greenwood, I can simply go across several streets and avenues to the park by the sluggish river and visit with the made-woman. She says little, but sometimes after many days with the crones, I find such silence comforting. She's a good listener, though. Even better than you.

> Your sister for always—for that will never change,
> Mabel Serana Farmers

About the Authors

World Fantasy Award winner **Jane Yolen** is an author of children's books, fantasy, and science fiction, including *Owl Moon*, *The Devil's Arithmetic*, and *How Do Dinosaurs Say Goodnight?*

Mythopoeic Award winner **Midori Snyder** is the author of eight books, including *The Innamorati*, *The Flight of Michael McBride*, *Soulstring*, and the Oran Trilogy. She lives in Arizona with her husband.

Want to connect with fellow science fiction and fantasy fans?

For news on all your favorite Ace and Roc authors, sneak peeks into the newest releases, book giveaways, and much more—

"Like" Ace and Roc Books on Facebook!

facebook.com/AceRocBooks